# Animal Dreams

"Kingsolver is giving a new voice to our literature. *Animal Dreams* solidly establishes Kingsolver as someone who will give her public more than one great book."

—*Los Angeles Times Book Review*

"An emotional masterpiece. . . . A novel in which humor, passion, and superb prose conspire to seize a reader by the heart and by the soul."

—*New York Daily News*

"A well-nigh perfect novel, masterfully written, brimming with insight, humor, and compassion. Kingsolver's clear, purposeful prose spins the narrative like a spider's web, its interconnected strands gossamer-thin but tensile, strong. This richly satisfying novel should firmly establish Kingsolver among the pantheon of talented writers."

—*Publishers Weekly*

"One of the year's best works of fiction."

—*Detroit News and Free Press*

"A glorious tapestry. . . . *Animal Dreams* is rich fodder for our own sweet, satisfying dreams."

—*Denver Post*

"A fascinating world of myth, memory, and dreams. Following Codi Noline home is definitely a worthwhile journey."

—*Dallas Morning News*

"Barbara Kingsolver gives us the gift of a trip to forgiveness and love through lovingly sensual detail, characters we all know and yet wish we knew better, through evocations of an Arizona landscape both nurturing and mysterious."

—*Minneapolis Star Tribune*

"Kingsolver achieves a fully realized and profoundly moral vision, one that is rooted in the land and our relationship to it."

—*San Francisco Chronicle*

"You'll treasure *Animal Dreams*. A beautiful, memorable novel full of scenes and images that linger in the mind."

—Tony Hillerman, author of
*Talking God* and *Thief of Time*

"Barbara Kingsolver demonstrates a special gift for the vivid evocation of landscape and of her characters' state of mind."

—*New York Times Book Review*

"A novel full of aching sadness—as well as joy, humor, insight, and wonderful writing."

—*Arizona Daily Star*

"*Animal Dreams* literally bursts with life. Its description of how one woman finds her way back from the edge of despair seems absolutely perfect. . . . *Animal Dreams* leaves the reader filled with wonder and hope."

—*Houston Post*

# About the Author

BARBARA KINGSOLVER'S ten published books include novels, collections of short stories, poetry, essays, and an oral history. Her work has been translated into more than a dozen languages and has earned literary awards and a devoted readership at home and abroad. In 2000, she was awarded the National Humanities Medal, our country's highest honor for service through the arts.

Ms. Kingsolver grew up in Kentucky and earned a graduate degree in biology before becoming a full-time writer. With her husband, Steven Hopp, she co-writes articles on natural history, plays jazz, gardens, and raises two daughters. Their family divides its time between Tucson, Arizona, and a farm in southern Appalachia.

# ALSO BY BARBARA KINGSOLVER

### FICTION

*Flight Behavior*

*The Lacuna*

*Prodigal Summer*

*The Poisonwood Bible*

*Pigs in Heaven*

*Animal Dreams*

*Homeland and Other Stories*

*The Bean Trees*

### ESSAYS

*Small Wonder*

*High Tide in Tucson: Essays from Now or Never*

### POETRY

*Another America*

### NONFICTION

*Animal, Vegetable, Miracle: A Year of Food Life*
(with Steven L. Hopp and Camille Kingsolver)

*Last Stand: America's Virgin Lands*
(with photographs by Annie Griffiths Belt)

*Holding the Line:*
*Women in the Great Arizona Mine Strike of 1983*

# Animal Dreams

## A NOVEL

### BARBARA KINGSOLVER

HARPER PERENNIAL

NEW YORK • LONDON • TORONTO • SYDNEY • NEW DELHI • AUCKLAND

HARPER ● PERENNIAL

A hardcover edition of this book was published in 1990 by HarperCollins Publishers.

HarperCollins books may be purchased for educational, business, or sales promotional use. For information, please email the Special Markets Department at SPsales@ harpercollins.com.

First Harper Perennial edition published 1991.
Reissued in Perennial 2003 and 2005.
Reissued in Harper Perennial 2013.

The Library of Congress has catalogued the hardcover edition as follows:

Kingsolver, Barbara.
    Animal dreams : a novel / by Barbara Kingsolver.—1st ed.
        p.   cm
    ISBN 0-06-016350-X
        I. Title.
    PS3561.I496A86        1990        813'54—dc20        86-46571

ISBN 978-0-06-227850-0 (pbk.)

20  LSC  20  19  18  17  16  15  14  13

*in memory of Ben Linder*

# AUTHOR'S NOTE

Grace, Arizona, and its railroad depot are imaginary, as is Santa Rosalia Pueblo, although it resembles the Keresan pueblos of northern New Mexico. Other places, and crises, in the book are actual.

I'm grateful for the example provided by many nonfictional volunteers from the United States who went to live and work for a new social order in Nicaragua during the decade following the 1979 revolution. Alongside the Nicaraguan people, they have made indelible contributions to that country, and to history.

For their support and contributions to this book I also owe a warm debt of thanks to my editor at Harper & Row, Janet Goldstein, my literary agent, Frances Goldin, and my remarkable family, especially Jessica Sampson (locomotive engineer extraordinaire), Wendell and Ginny Kingsolver, Joe Hoffman, and Camille Hoffman Kingsolver, who has attached me securely to this world.

# CONTENTS

# Animal
# Dreams

# HOMERO

# 1

# The Night
# of All Souls

**H**is two girls are curled together like animals whose habit is to sleep underground, in the smallest space possible. Cosima knows she's the older, even when she's unconscious: one of her arms lies over Halimeda's shoulder as if she intends to protect them both from their bad dreams. Dr. Homer Noline holds his breath, trying to see movement there in the darkness, the way he's watched pregnant women close their eyes and listen inside themselves trying to feel life.

A slice of white moon from the window divides their bodies deeply into light and shadow, but not one from the other. No light could show where one body ends and the other begins when they're sleeping like this. Maybe a mother's eye could tell, but that is the one possibility that can't be tried.

Halimeda's bed is still made. In the morning she'll rumple it so he'll believe she slept by herself, and then the girls will make it again. Their labors at deceiving him are as careful as surgery. But morning is worlds away now, it's still early night on the Day of All Souls. The two of them spent the whole day playing in the cemetery with neighbor children, Pocha and Juan Teobaldo and Cristobal and the twin babies, helping Viola Domingos build a bower of marigolds over the grave of a great-grandmother who is no part of this family.

For a long time he stands gripping the door frame, which is exactly the width of a newborn's skull and curves similarly against his palm. He watches his daughters, though there's nothing to watch, and thinks these words: "A great-grandmother who isn't their business." He decides this will be their last year for the cemetery and the Day of All Souls. There are too many skeletons down there. People count too long on the oblivion of children.

They're deep in the corpselike collapse that takes hold of children when they are exhausted, but still he won't risk going in to stand over the bed the way he once would have. He would see the usual things: unraveled braids and the scraped shins hidden from his punishing antiseptics. Tonight he would also see cheeks and eyelids stained bright yellow from marigold pollen. He's spent a lifetime noticing small details from a distance. From the doorway he smells the bitterness of crushed marigold petals on their skin.

There is a deeper draft of breath and they both move a little. Their long hair falls together across the sheet, the colors blending, the curled strands curving gently around the straight. He feels a constriction around his heart that isn't disease but pure simple pain, and he knows he would weep if he could. Not for the river he can't cross to reach his children, not for distance, but the opposite. For how close together these two are, and how much they have to lose. How much they've already lost in their lives to come.

# COSIMA

# 2

# Hallie's Bones

I am the sister who didn't go to war. I can only tell you my side of the story. Hallie is the one who went south, with her pickup truck and her crop-disease books and her heart dead set on a new world.

Who knows why people do what they do? I stood on a battle-ground once too, but it was forty years after the fighting was all over: northern France, in 1982, in a field where the farmers' plow blades kept turning up the skeletons of cows. They were the first casualties of the German occupation. In the sudden quiet after the evacuation the cows had died by the thousands in those pastures, slowly, low-ing with pain from unmilked udders. But now the farmers who grew sugar beets in those fields were blessed, they said, by the bones. The soil was rich in calcium.

Three years later when my sister talked about leaving Tucson to work in the cotton fields around Chinandega, where farmers were getting ambushed while they walked home with their minds on din-ner, all I could think of was France. Those long, flat fields of bone-fed green. Somehow we protect ourselves; it's the nearest I could come to imagining Nicaragua. Even though I know the bones in that ground aren't animal bones.

**She left in August** after the last rain of the season. Summer storms in the desert are violent things, and clean, they leave you feeling like you have cried. Hallie had never left me before. It was always the other way around, since I'm three years older and have had to do things first. She would just be catching up when I'd go again, swimming farther out into life because I still hadn't found a rock to stand on. Never because I wanted to leave. Hallie and I were so attached, like keenly mismatched Siamese twins conjoined at the back of the mind. We parted again and again and still each time it felt like a medical risk, as if we were being liberated at some terrible cost: the price of a shared organ. We never stopped feeling that knife.

But she went. And true to the laws of family physics, the equal and opposite reaction, I was soon packed up too and headed northeast on a Greyhound bus. In our divergent ways, I believe we were both headed home. I was bound for Grace, Arizona, where Hallie and I were born and raised, and where our father still lived and was said to be losing his mind. It was a Sunday. I had a window seat, and in a Greyhound you're up high. You pass through the land like some rajah on an elephant looking down on your kingdom, which in this case was a scorched bristling landscape and the tops of a lot of cars. It wasn't all that different from my usual view of life, because I'm tall, like my father and Hallie. I don't look like who I am. They do, but I don't.

It was midmorning when I stepped down off the bus in Grace, and I didn't recognize it. Even in fourteen years it couldn't have changed much, though, so I knew it was just me. Grace is made of things that erode too slowly to be noticed: red granite canyon walls, orchards of sturdy old fruit trees past their prime, a shamelessly unpolluted sky. The houses were built in no big hurry back when labor was taken for granted, and now were in no big hurry to decay.

Arthritic mesquite trees grew out of impossible crevices in the cliffs, looking as if they could adapt to life on Mars if need be.

I was the only passenger getting off. The short, imperious bus driver opened the baggage door and made a show of dragging out luggage to get to mine, as if I were being difficult. A more accommodating woman, he implied, would be content with whatever bags happened to be right in front. Finally he slapped my two huge suitcases flat out in the dust. He slammed the doors and reclaimed his throne, causing the bus to bark like a dog, leaving a cloud of exhaust in the air, getting the last word, I suppose.

The view from here was orchards: pecan, plum, apple. The highway ran along the river, dividing the orchards like a long, crooked part in a leafy scalp. The trees filled the whole valley floor to the sides of the canyon. Confetti-colored houses perched on the slopes at its edges with their backs to the canyon wall. And up at the head of the canyon was the old Black Mountain copper mine. On the cliff overlooking the valley, the smelter's one brick smokestack pointed obscenely at heaven.

I dragged my bags to the edge of the street. Carlo, my lover of ten years, whom I seemed to have just left, would be sending a trunk from Tucson when he got around to it. I didn't own very much I cared about. I felt emptied-out and singing with echoes, unrecognizable to myself: that particular feeling like your own house on the day you move out. I missed Hallie. Carlo, too—for the lost possibilities. At the point I left, he and I were still sleeping together but that was all, just sleeping, with our backs touching. Sometimes Hallie would cough in the next room and I'd wake up to find my arm over his shoulder, my fingers touching his chest, but that's only because it takes your sleeping self years to catch up to where you really are. Pay attention to your dreams: when you go on a trip, in your dreams you will still be home. Then after you've come home you'll dream of where you were. It's a kind of jet lag of the consciousness.

Carlo loved Hallie. When he and I moved back to Tucson the three of us contrived a little household in a bad neighborhood, with jade plants on our front steps that kept getting stolen till Hallie thought to bolt down the pots. We played house to beat the band. Hallie and I made prickly-pear jelly, boiled and strained and poured blood-red into clean glass jars. We'd harvested the fruits from the physical therapy garden of the hospital where Carlo worked. A nun saw us out there with our grocery sack while she was walking an old man around the little race track, and Hallie and I just waved. We said we were living off the land.

Our home fell apart when she left. She was our center of gravity, the only one of us who saw life as a controllable project. Carlo was an orphan like me. We forgot about the jade plants, they went crisp as potato chips out on the porch, and Carlo withered as if he needed water also. Every man I'd ever loved had loved Hallie best and settled for me. It didn't bother me as much as you might think; I could understand it. I loved her too.

And now his life with the Noline women had run its course. He could go where he pleased. Carlo was a rolling stone: an emergency-room doctor, which gave him a kind of freedom almost unknown to the profession. You can always find work if you're willing to take up with a human body as soon as possible after one of life's traumas has left off with it. Carlo and I met in medical school, and in our years together he and I probably had more addresses than the Grace, Arizona, phone book. Along the way I'd landed a few presentable jobs, but in between I tended to drift, like a well-meaning visitor to this planet awaiting instructions. My career track had run straight down into the weedy lots on the rough side of town. It's the truth. For the last six months in Tucson I'd worked night shift at a 7-Eleven, selling beer and Alka-Seltzer to people who would have been better off home in bed. There wasn't a whole lot farther I could go. Now I was here.

A high-school friend, Emelina Domingos, had offered to meet my bus but I'd told her, No, don't bother, I'll make my own way. The plan was for me to live in the Domingos' guesthouse. Not with my father. My relationship with Doc Homer had always improved with distance, which is to say that mail was okay and short, badly connected phone calls were best. I thought I should still keep some miles between us, even though he was ill and conceivably dying. It was going to be touchy. He would be an unwilling candidate for rescue, and I was disaster in that department myself. But he had only two living relatives and the other one was behind the wheel of a Toyota pickup headed for Nicaragua. I stood my suitcases side by side and sat on them for a minute to get my bearings. I think I was hoping Emelina might still show up.

There was no evidence of human life, or life that was *ongoing* in any obvious way. The one vehicle parked in front of the courthouse, a blue station wagon, had four flats and a bumper sticker stating "ONE DAY AT A TIME." I suspected it had been there in 1972, the year I finished high school, when I last climbed on a Greyhound and turned my back on Grace. There wasn't a soul on the street today and I thought of those movies in which a town is wiped clean of its inhabitants, for one reason or another—a nuclear holocaust, say, or a deadly mutant virus—leaving only a shell of consumer goods. The point, I think, is to make some statement about how we get carried away with all our trappings, but this wasn't the place to shoot a movie like that. Grace hadn't yet entered the era of parking meters, for example. There were iron rings mortared into the block wall of the courthouse where a person could tie a horse.

I tried to imagine Doc Homer coming downtown on horseback, looking silly, his tall, stiff spine bouncing up and down against his will. I erased the fantasy from my mind, feeling guilty. It was too late to be taking imaginary revenge on my father.

There wasn't much to Grace's commercial district. The window of the Hollywood Dress Shop leered from across the street, framing a ferocious display of polyester. The headless mannequins were dressed to the nines, with silver vinyl loafers and red nail polish. If I moved a little I could put my reflection there in the window with them: me in my Levi's and Billy Idol haircut. (I was the one with a head.) A friend of mine used to make bizarre collages like that— Nancy Reagan in mink among the slaves on an Egyptian mural; Malibu Barbie driving sled dogs in the Iditarod. She sold those things for good money.

The Hollywood Shop was flanked by Jonny's Breakfast (open all day) and the movie theater. Back behind these buildings ran the railroad tracks. On the other side of Jonny's were the State Line Bar and the Baptist Grocery. I tried to place myself inside these stores; I knew I'd been there. Directing Hallie through the grocery aisles on a Saturday, ticking off items from Doc Homer's list. Sitting in Jonny's afterward, hunched in a booth drinking forbidden Cokes, reverently eying the distant easy grace of the girls who had friends and mothers. But I couldn't see it. Those things didn't seem so much like actual memories as like things I might remember from a book I'd read more than once.

I had lied on the bus. I'd told the woman sitting next to me that I was a Canadian tourist and had never been to Grace. Sometimes I used to do that, tell tales on buses and airplanes—it passes the time. And people love you for it. They'll believe anything if you throw in enough detail. Once I spent a transatlantic flight telling a somber, attentive man about a medical procedure I'd helped develop in Paris, in which human cadavers could be injected with hormones to preserve their organs for transplant. I would be accepting a prestigious medical prize, the name of which I devised on the spot. The man seemed so impressed. He looked like my father.

I didn't do it anymore, I was more or less reformed. What I'd said that morning was the truest kind of lie, I guess, containing fear at its heart: I *was* a stranger to Grace. I'd stayed away fourteen years and in my gut I believe I was hoping that had changed: I would step off the bus and land smack in the middle of a sense of belonging. Ticker tape, apologies, the luxury of forgiveness, home at last. Grace would turn out to be the yardstick I'd been using to measure all other places, like the mysterious wornout photo that storybook orphans carry from place to place, never realizing till the end that it's really their home.

None of this happened. Grace looked like a language I didn't speak. And Emelina wasn't coming. I hefted up my suitcases and started to walk.

Oh Lord, the terror of beginnings. I dreaded having to see all the people who were going to say, "How long are you home for, honey?" Possibly they would know I'd come for the school year. We would all carry on as if this were the issue: the job. Not Doc Homer, who'd lately begun addressing his patients by the names of dead people. Since I really did need to come, I'd gotten myself hired to replace the high-school biology teacher who'd recently married and defected without warning. I had practically no teaching qualifications, I should add, and things like that get around. It's tough to break yourself as news to a town that already knows you. Grace formed its opinions of Hallie and me before we had permanent teeth. People here would remember our unreasonable height in seventh grade, and our unfortunate given names; our father actually named my sister Halimeda, which means "thinking of the sea," however reasonable a thing that might be to do in a desert. And my own name, Cosima, means something to the effect of "order in the cosmos" which is truly droll, given my employment history. I must have sensed the lack of cosmic order in my future, early on. Maneuvering for approval, I'd shortened it to Codi in the third grade, when Buffalo Bill and the Pony Express held favor with my would-be crowd.

Hallie was a more natural abbreviation, from the time she could walk people never called her anything but that, although *Halimeda* actually had some truth in it; she made you look for things beyond what you could see. I could imagine Doc Homer dreaming up these names, confident we'd both take noble courses. Suddenly I felt dragged down by emotions as I walked along, as if I'd swum out into a calm sea and encountered a bad undertow. I carried my suitcases toward the edge of town.

An old, densely planted pecan orchard stretched out from the edge of the courthouse square, and somewhere behind it lay Emelina's place. The reflected sky ran like a vein of silver in the irrigation ditch, but when I left the street and stepped under the canopy of trees it was dark. If you've never walked through an old orchard, you have to imagine this: it presents you with an optical illusion. You move through what looks like a hodgepodge thicket of trees, but then at intervals you find yourself at the center of long, maddeningly straight rows of trees, standing like soldiers at attention. There's a graveyard in northern France where all the dead boys from D-Day are buried. The white crosses reach from one horizon to the other. I remember looking it over and thinking it was a forest of graves. But the rows were like this, dizzying, diagonal, perfectly straight, so after all it wasn't a forest but an orchard of graves. Nothing to do with nature, unless you count human nature.

A bird scream rang out from the leaves and echoed up my spine with a shiver that ended in my scalp. I believe it was the first sound I'd heard since the gear grinding of the bus. I stopped to listen. Quiet. Then another bird answered from behind me, close by. It sounded like the throaty, exotic laughter of a foreigner—like a jungle bird. The peacocks. These orchards were full of peacocks, living more or less wild and at the mercy of coyotes but miraculously surviving in droves. There was a local legend, supposedly true, about how they got here a hundred years ago: the nine blue-eyed Gracela sisters came over from Spain to marry nine lucky miners in the gold camp, sight unseen. Back then these hills were run through with gold veins and drew a crowd of men who had too much money and too little love. The sisters were just children, and only agreed to come if they could bring their birds with them in the hold of the ship. Their legacy in Gracela Canyon was a population of blue-eyed, dark-haired descendants and a thousand wild peacocks. Their father stayed behind and got rich by proxy, for he'd literally sold his girls for a gold mine.

The branches were ringing with bird calls now. And I could hear kids laughing. A whole chorus of them screamed at once. Toward the far end of the orchard I could make out children's silhouettes jumping and dancing under the trees. It was dark in there for midday but I definitely saw kids: little girls in billowy dresses and boys in white shirts. I couldn't make out their game. The tallest boy had a stick and they were chasing something and flailing at it. I walked down the row toward them, towing my bigger suitcase like an anchor. I was traveling light in theory, but I'd dragged with me into

Grace a substantial reference library. It had taken me a lot of nervous weeks to narrow down what books to bring. At the very last minute I'd thrown out Gray's *Anatomy* because Doc Homer would have it.

I stepped over the irrigation trenches, mindful of my Italian leather uppers. I'm picky about shoes, and there was no replacing these now. I smiled, thinking of the awful silver loafers in the Hollywood Shop. I envisioned my predecessor at the high school dressed like that, standing in front of a classroom of fifteen-year-olds, twisting her white chiffon scarf as she explained cell division. What would these kids make of me? My shoes were pointed and my, as the magazines say, personal style leaned toward apologetic punk. I'd never had a teacher who looked like me; probably there was a reason.

I stopped to massage my aching shoulder. There was something up there at the edge of the orchard all right, a bunch of kids, and something in the trees over their heads. I thought about skirting around the little gang to avoid spoiling their fun, or maybe, actually, because I was afraid. I tried to move quietly. Whatever it was they were chasing, they were going to get it.

I could see plainly then that it was a heavy-bodied peacock shuffling from side to side on a low branch. Apparently the creature was too dull-witted or terrorized to escape, or possibly already injured. The children pursued it ferociously, jumping up and pulling at its long tail feathers, ready to tear it to pieces. The boy with the stick hit hard against the belly and they all shrieked. He hit it again. I couldn't see the stick but I heard the sickening whack when it made contact.

I looked away. I'd arrived in Grace, arrived at that moment in my life, without knowing how to make the kind of choice that was called for here. I'm not the moral guardian in my family. Nobody, not my father, *no one* had jumped in to help when I was a child getting whacked by life, and on the meanest level of instinct I felt I had no favors to return. Especially to a bird. It was Hallie's end of my conscience that kept pinching me as I walked. I dropped my bags and walked a little faster, trying to think of some commanding thing to say. If they didn't stop soon the thing would be maimed or dead.

"Stop it!" I yelled. My heart was thumping. "You're killing that bird!"

The boy froze like a rabbit in headlights. The other kids, down on their knees, stared too. I'd arrested them in the act of grabbing fistfuls of bright paper and candy that sparkled on the ground. The mute peacock swung over their heads on a wire. Its fractured body hung in clay shards the size of plate, held together by a crepe-paper skin.

When I was ten I'd demolished a piñata exactly like this one, with blue paper wings and a long glossy tail of real feathers. At a birthday party. At some time or other every child in Grace had done the same.

After an impossible few seconds they went back to scrambling for their prize. Two older girls helped the smallest kids scoop candy into piles in their laps. A cluster of boys elbowed and slapped each other behind the girls' backs.

I felt disoriented and disgraced, a trespasser on family rites. I walked away from the little group of kids back toward the place in the center of the orchard where I must have left my suitcases. I wondered in what dim part of Grace I'd left my childhood.

# HOMERO

# 3

# The Flood

The leaves shine like knife blades in the beam of his flashlight. The rain has slowed, but the arroyo is still a fierce river of mud and uprooted trees that won't crest until dawn. He is wet and chilled to his spine. The girls are lost. The sound of the flood makes his blood cold.

They wanted to gather prickly-pear fruits for jelly. They knew a storm was coming and they went anyway, while he was in his workroom. He follows the narrow animal path between thickets of thorn scrub along the bank, shining his light along the edge of the rising water. Acacias lean into the river with their branches waving wildly in the current, like mothers reaching in for lost babies. The girls ignore his cautions because they are willful children who believe nothing can harm them. Hallie is bad but Cosima is worse, pretty and stubborn as a wild horse but without an animal's instincts for self-preservation—and she's the older. She should have some sense.

He forces his body through the bank of oleanders near the house and turns back toward the riverbed to search the arroyo to the south. He has no idea which way they would have gone; they roam this desert like pocket mice. And everything in a desert is poisonous or thorned. Good Lord, he has already lost a wife, and did not think his heart would live beyond her. *Wished* it wouldn't. He slashes at the oleanders with the metal flashlight. He'd meant to cut these down when Cosima was born. One well-chewed leaf could bring on cardiac arrest in a child. He'd seen a case years ago, or was it later, after the girls left home? That blue girl?

Doc Homer sits up in his bed and stares at the orange pill bottles on the windowsill. There is light at the window. It's a Sunday morning in August. It is only a month ago he lost that blue girl. His own daughters are grown and living somewhere else, looking after themselves, but his heart is still pumping hard. His circulatory system believes they are still lost.

He turns his pillow and rests his head on it carefully because his brain gets jostled and things move around inside his head like olives in a jar of brine. Think about the flood. He is going south on the near side of the arroyo. He stops to look back upstream and his light finds them, by pure luck, on the opposite bank. Cosima's thin, waving arms shine like the crisscrossing blades of scissors. They are screaming but he only sees their mouths stretched open like the mouths of fledgling birds. Absolute expectation, Papa will save us. The road is washed out, and he has to think how else he will get to them. He realizes, stunned, that they have been huddled there for half a day. The road has been washed out that long.

How does he reach them? A boat? No, that wouldn't have been possible. He sits up again. He has no clear image of reaching them, no memory of their arms on his neck, he only hears them crying over the telephone. And then he understands painfully that he wasn't able to go to them. There is no memory because he wasn't there. He had to call Uda Dell on the other side of the arroyo. Her husband was alive then, and went down the bank on his mule to find them in a washed-open coyote burrow with seven pups the girls wanted to save.

"There were seven," she'd wailed over the telephone. "I could carry four but Hallie could only get one in each hand and we didn't want to leave the other one. He would have gotten drowned." Cosima is sobbing because in the end, after crouching for half a day in the small shelter of that gravel bank, waiting for the mother coyote to come back and save her children, they had to leave them. He hears Hallie shrieking in the background. They're both crying as if they are drowning themselves. Drowning pups.

When he gets them home they sit hugging each other on the davenport, wrapped in the black-and-red crocheted afghan. They won't stop shaking. They want to know if the baby coyotes died. If animals go to heaven. He has no answers. "We tried to put them in the paper bag we used for the prickle pears, but it fell all apart." The tears stream out until the afghan is wet and he thinks there will be no more fluid in them to run the blood cells through their veins. He makes them drink orange juice. God, why does a mortal man have children? It is senseless to love anything this much.

# Cosima

# 4

# Killing Chickens

Emelina's was a pleasant, ramshackle place with animals, an old plum orchard and five boys. When I walked up the drive with my suitcases they were preparing to kill roosters. Emelina's eyes and mouth drew wide and she looked briefly like a surprised fish. "Codi, this is *Sunday*, I thought you said *tomorrow*."

"No, it was today, I'm here," I said apologetically. I was glad I hadn't waited any longer at the courthouse.

"Shoot, you look like a fifty-dollar bill. Where'd you get that haircut, Paris, France?" She gave me a hug and waved her hand at the driveway. "I'm sorry about this mess. We've just got the water boiled for the birds. Shoot."

I'd just witnessed what I'd thought was going to be the slaughter of a peacock, so I laughed, but this time it was real murder and mayhem. The drive was lined with pails, paper bags, and a tragically stained wooden block that had been used before. Emelina's twins, who were about ten, each held a fat white rooster by the feet. A younger brother was riding a tricycle precariously over the rocky ground. I put down my suitcases.

"Curty and Glen, look at you," I said. "And Mason. You guys are getting too big."

"Aunt Codi, look. If you hold them upside down they go to sleep," Glen said.

Curty said, "No, they get hypnotized."

"Well, either way it's a handy trick," I said. "You don't want them to see what's coming."

Emelina looked dismayed. "Codi, we don't have to do this now. What a god-awful thing to do in front of company."

"I'm not company. You're all set up, so do it. You can't go out of your way for me if I'm going to live here."

She rolled her eyes. "Go on back to the granny house then. John Tucker was supposed to sweep it out this morning before he went to his baseball practice but I'll fall over dead if he did it right now, instead of feeding the baby. I'll bet you fifteen dollars he's laying in the house watching the MTV."

John Tucker was Emelina's oldest, but I couldn't picture him old enough to feed the baby. I hadn't yet seen the baby, since he'd only arrived six months ago. But over the years Emelina and I had kept up. I'd taped her kids' school pictures to the woodwork of Carlo's and my many ill-furnished apartments. Sometimes repairmen would ask if they were my boys.

I went around to the side yard and pushed open a wire gate that wouldn't have kept out a determined hen. The guesthouse in the back faced the big ranch house across a huge brick courtyard that was wild and overrun with flowering vines. Every inch of space was taken up with fruit trees, painted flowerpots, and lawn chairs that looked like they'd been there since the last war. I could hear chickens clucking softly somewhere out of sight, and at the back of the courtyard a goat stretched its neck to get at a fig tree.

The guesthouse had a pink door flanked by pots of geraniums, whose crimson flowers stood out against the white walls like wine stains blooming on a tablecloth. Inside, the little house was whitewashed and immaculate. There were two brick-floored rooms: a living room and bedroom. The light pouring in the windows was stirred up by the motion of fig branches outside. The bed had a carved headboard, painted with red enamel, and a soft-looking woven spread. It was a fairytale bed. I wished I could fall down and sleep a hundred years in this little house with pale crisscrossing shadows on the walls.

I heard the goat moving around outside, munching loudly and bumping against the wall. I opened cupboards. Everything was spotless. The east window in the living room looked straight out onto the granite wall of the canyon a few yards away, a startling lack of view. Emelina's place was the last and highest on her street, backed up against the canyon. The floorboards of her front porch were on a level with her neighbors' roofs.

I took my time exploring. I savored the first minutes in a new home. Carlo would always go straight to unpacking boxes, looking for the sheets and coffeepot and swearing that we were going to get better organized, while I stepped stealthily over the bare floors, peeking around corners and into alluring doors, which generally turned out to be the broom closet. But there was that thrilling sense that, like a new lover, the place held attributes I had yet to discover. My favorite book as a child was *The Secret Garden.* It's embarrassing to think I'd merrily relocated again and again, accompanying Carlo to the ends of the earth, because of the lure of a possible garret or secret closet. But it might be true.

I tried out the two very old chairs in the living room. They had rose slipcovers and were comfortable. In a corner near the window was a beehive fireplace, and next to it, a clay vase of peacock feathers. Every home in Grace had one of those; it was a local feature. You could pick up half a dozen peacock feathers on any given day, in the orchards, as you went about your business. When the vase was full, you took them to one of the old women who made real-feather pinãtas, and then you started your collection over. The practice had not been allowed in our house because Doc Homer said the feathers were crawling with bird mites; he dreaded to think what those old women's houses were harboring in the way of microorganisms. It became Hallie's and my joke. Whenever he unreasonably forbade us to do something, we'd look at each other and mouth the words "bird mites."

The bathroom and kitchen must have been added on about mid-century. The refrigerator looked prehistoric, but worked. It contained a loaf of fresh bread in a paper bag, some tomatoes and figs, a block of goat cheese, and a six-pack of Miller Lite. Emelina's estimation of the bare essentials. I popped open a beer and went back around the house in time to witness the demise of the second rooster.

"Is it okay that there's a goat loose in the courtyard?" I asked Emelina.

"Shit! I'm going to tan John Tucker's hide. *John Tucker!*" she yelled. "Get your damn goat out of the garden, please, or we'll have him for dinner!"

There was a noise from inside and the back door slammed.

"You don't really want to watch this, Codi," she said. "But I guess you see a lot worse in your line of work."

I sat on the porch rail. I was no longer in the doctoring line of work. It's true I'd been educated to within an inch of my life, and had done well in medical school. My mistake was assuming medicine was a science like any other. If it's carburetors you know, you can fix cars, I reasoned; if it's arteries and tendons you fix people. For reasons that were unclear to me, I'd learned the science but couldn't work the miracle: I'd had a crisis while trying to deliver a baby. My problem turned out to be irreversible. Emelina knew all this. I was *here,* after all, with no more mission in life than I'd been born with years ago. The only real difference between then and now was wardrobe.

"Tell me if I can help," I said.

She ignored me. "Okay, watch your hands, Curty. Keep them way back." Emelina was small, but didn't give that impression. Her jeans had "Little Cowboy" stitched on the label, and undoubtedly belonged to one of her sons. Emelina and I graduated from high school the same year, 1972. Under my picture in the yearbook it said, "Will Go Far," and under Emelina's it said, "Lucky in Love." You could accept this as either prophecy or a bad joke. I'd gone halfway around the world, and now lived three-quarters of a mile from the high school. Emelina had married Juan Teobaldo Domingos the same June we graduated. Now J.T. worked for the railroad and, as I understood it, was out of town most of the time. She said it didn't bother her. Maybe that's as lucky as love gets.

Curty laid his hypnotized rooster on the block and held its feet, keeping the rest of his body as far away as possible. It never regained consciousness. Emelina swung the axe over her shoulder and brought it down on the mark. The pink, muscular neck slipped out of the collar of feathers as if the two parts had been separately made. The boys hooted and chased after the body as it thrashed across the dirt. But I was fascinated by the head: the mouth opened and closed, silently, because the vocal cords were in the part that had been disconnected.

"That's the way, Curty," Emelina directed. "Don't get blood on your brother. Dip him all the way in. Now pluck him quick or he'll go stiff on you. Start with the wings, see how Glen's doing?" She wiped perspiration out of her eyes.

I was amazed by the muscle definition in her upper arms and her easy command of the axe. Her hands stayed surprisingly clean through the whole operation. She reminded me of Hallie, the way she could do things. Though of course Hallie would never decapitate anything.

"I can't believe you're watching this," she said when both boys were settled down to plucking feathers. She went inside and came out with a beer. She sat down next to me on the wide wooden rail, knocking the heels of her sneakers against the crossbar like a child. I was very conscious of my height. Sometimes I had an acute feeling that small women were better put together somehow, more in control of their bodies.

"You used to have a hissy fit when we'd go over to *Abuelita's* and she'd be killing chickens," Emelina said. "Remember? Even when we were big, twelve or thirteen."

"No, that was Hallie. She's the one that had such a soft heart. We've always been real different that way. She'd cry if she stepped on a bug." I drained my beer. "She's still like that, except now she cries about bag ladies. I swear. She gives them quarters and then she wishes she'd given them a dollar."

I stared out at the treetops and the leaf-green gables of the roof on a house below us. The shingles were an odd, elaborate shape like the spade in a deck of cards. I wondered in what decade they'd stopped making shingles like that, and how this neighbor might repair the roof after a bad storm.

"You really do look great," Emelina said. "That's a terrific haircut, I mean it. You'll stand out in a crowd here till you get your first cut down at Beth's Butcher Shop."

I ran my fingers over my weedy scalp, feeling despair. I'd spent my whole childhood as an outsider to Grace. I was willing to march downtown and submit myself to butchery this minute if that would admit me to the club. I'd led such an adventurous life, geographically speaking, that people mistook me for an adventurer. They had no idea. I'd sell my soul and all my traveling shoes to *belong* some place.

"I always forget you have so much auburn. Doc Homer had the same coloring, didn't he? Sort of reddish before he went gray?" She fingered her own shoulder-length hair. "Speaking of him . . ."

"Speaking of him," I said.

"Have you talked to him?" She looked apprehensive. Emelina was my informant. When he started getting lost on his way home from the drugstore, she was the one person in Grace who thought to call me, rather than just draw him a map.

"I'll go up and see him tomorrow."

"And where's Hallie gone? You told me, but I forgot."

"Nicaragua," I said. "To save the crops. Cross between Johnny Appleseed and a freedom fighter."

Emelina laughed and I felt disloyal. I hadn't meant to sound glib. It was just hard to put Hallie into the context of regular life. "I guess it's really dangerous," I said. "But she's excited about it. She'll be happy." I was sure of this. Hallie didn't have my problem. She belonged wherever she was.

Emelina nodded. She watched the boys, who sat cross-legged on the driveway, transfixed by the importance of their task. They were dappled with blood and looked like they'd been through a strange war themselves—a children's war.

A scarlet bougainvillaea covered the front porch. In fact, it was so overgrown that the wood of the vine seemed to be supporting the structure over our heads. The breeze coming up the valley felt like a warm liquid against my arms and face. I held the sweaty beer can against my temple and watched the bougainvillaea arms swaying around us like seaweed under the ocean.

"No," Emelina said after a while. "I'm sure it was you that had a fit over the chickens. You'd start, and then Hallie would do it too. She always followed whatever you did."

"No. Hallie? We're chalk and cheese. Somebody ought to do a study on us, if they want to know how kids in the same family can turn out totally different. She was born with her own mind."

"Maybe she was, but she copied you like a picture," Emelina said. "She used to get so pissed off at me because I wouldn't go along with your boycott of *Abuelita*'s chicken and rice."

I didn't remember organizing boycotts. "Well, you're the witness here. Blood all over the driveway and I didn't faint."

"People change," she said. "Not everything stays with you all your life."

**I sat watching** my suitcases for a good fifteen minutes, as if they might become inspired to unpack themselves, and then I went into the bedroom and lay down for just a minute, letting my shoes drop one at a time onto the brick floor. I tried to think how far Hallie might have gotten by now. Guatemala. Maybe farther. It was frightening to speculate on specifics; I'd been rationing my thoughts about her, but now I was exhausted and my mind ran its own course. I thought of Hallie at border crossings. Men in uniforms decorated with the macho jewelry of ammunition. No, not that far. I pulled her back to Tucson, where I'd seen her last and she was still safe.

She'd come by the 7-Eleven, all packed up, at the end of my graveyard shift. She knocked her knuckles on the plate glass to get my attention. I locked the cash drawer and took off. Sparrows were ruffling themselves in the sheets of fresh rain on the asphalt. As I walked her across the parking lot to her truck I could see just how we'd look to somebody, hanging on to each other by the elbows: like two swimmers in trouble, both of us equally likely to drown.

Or maybe only one of us was holding on for dear life. It was hard to believe I'd once been the one to strike out bravely for college, leaving Hallie crying in front of the Baptist Grocery. Now it seemed like I was the baby of the family, the one with no firm plans who's allowed to fiddle around forever keeping everyone young.

Hallie was headed for a war zone. She walked straight through the puddles, dragging me along, and I had to stretch out my legs and drench my shoes to keep up with her. When Hallie was intensely excited she had a wild-animal look to her that could stop people in their tracks. A vibration came from her skin, like a bell that has just been struck. Her hair was long and reckless, curling wildly in the humidity. Every part of my sister could stir rebellion. I was thinking that if anything happened to her I wouldn't survive. I couldn't see that there would be any method, or any point.

As long as I held Hallie's arm she would still be here, she wouldn't be climbing into the truck, turning the key, driving south through Arizona and Mexico and the perilous places farther on, wouldn't be stopped at a roadblock by men who might blandly shoot her in the head for being twenty-nine years old and alone and female, wearing blue jeans, carrying antihistamine pills in her glove compartment. It seemed like a chain of events I could hold back, there in the parking lot, with the bones of her elbow securely gripped in my hand.

Her little beat-up pickup looked impossibly loaded, like the tiny burros you see in postcards carrying elephant-sized burdens without complaint. I wasn't worried about the truck. I asked where she'd put her antihistamines. We knew of a photographer who'd been shot, ostensibly for running drugs, because he had a baby-food jar of aspirin and vitamin tablets in his camera bag.

Hallie said her pills were no place easy to find.

I put my head on her shoulder. "What if our houseplants die?"

"They won't," she said. Hallie knew I wanted easy answers.

I lifted my head again and she stared at me, thoughtfully. The sky had cleared. The early-morning light behind her head was orange, making her hair glow, and she looked like an angel. She never had any idea how she looked to other people; she thought she was plain.

"If the flea beetles start getting at the ones on the porch," she said slowly, "dust them with Celite." Hallie worked for the Extension Service and answered the Garden Hotline, 626-BUGS. For a period of years ending on that day, garden pests were her life.

I hugged her with all the strength in my arms. "Hallie," I said, "could you please just change your mind now and not go?"

"You really love me, so you want me to stay here and keep the suburbs safe for geraniums."

"I know how I ought to feel," I said. "I just don't."

Her breath expanded her chest against my arms, and I thought of the way a tree will keep on growing after a fence is wired around its trunk. The unbelievable force of that expansion. And I let her go.

She started up her truck and waved from the corner, not a mournful gone-forever wave but a chin-up wave like you see in the World War II movies, where everybody is brave because they all believe in the same thing. I told myself because I had no other choice that Hallie would do all right. That we were both going to live.

I walked the six blocks home under dripping trees and a sun that was already too hot. Across the street I heard a woman say to her companion in an odd accent, "It's the *Desert* Museum. I had understood him to say the 'dessert museum,' and obviously I was expecting something quite different." I thought: this is how life is, ridiculous beyond comprehension. What I felt wasn't pain but a hollowness, like a drum with the skin stretched tight. It took me five minutes to get our front door open, because everything in Tucson with moving parts gets cantankerous in the rainy season. Hallie had meant to put graphite in the lock before she left.

A white balloon left over from her going-away party followed me from the living room into the kitchen. It was the size of a head, and had lost some helium so it hung at eye level, trailing its string along the floor like a tired old ghost. Static electricity drew it along behind me. I swatted it away from my head while I plundered the refrigerator. I found some red bell peppers that had been absurdly expensive at the health-food market, and washed one and ate it standing up in the kitchen. After that I found a paring knife and went to work on a cucumber. I didn't feel like cooking breakfast just for myself. Carlo was at the hospital and I had no idea when he was due back.

The phone rang and I jumped, I suppose because I felt guilty for standing in the kitchen eating costly vegetables. I was afraid it was going to be somebody with garden pests, but they'd already turned off the Garden Hotline. It was Hallie calling from a pay phone this side of the border to tell me she'd forgotten to graphite the lock.

"I knew you'd call about that." I was filled with a strange joy because she felt the same way I did: that we couldn't survive apart. I just stood still for a minute, giving Hallie's and my thoughts their last chance to run quietly over the wires, touching each other in secret signal as they passed, like a column of ants. You couldn't do that kind of thing at international rates.

"There's a library book, too," she said. "Those Baron Münchhausen stories. I found it in with my books when I was cleaning out my room."

"I know. I saw it. I'll take it back today."

"That book's got to be overdue, Codi. You were reading it in the car a month ago when we drove to Bisbee."

I took a bite out of the cucumber and chewed before answering. I wanted this phone call to last forever. I wanted to recall every book we'd ever read aloud together while driving. "You're right. It's overdue."

"Take it back and pay the fine, okay? Libraries are the one American institution you shouldn't rip off."

"Yes, ma'am," I said. "Miss Patty Hearst the Second." I heard her trying not to laugh. Hallie was intellectually subversive and actually owned a copy of Abbie Hoffman's *Steal This Book,* but by nature she was perversely honest. I'd seen her tape dimes to a broken parking meter.

"Apart from moral reasons, they'll cancel your card."

"I don't know why you think I'm such a library outlaw. I'm all paid up over there." I munched on the cucumber. It wasn't that different from eating an outsize apple, say, or a peeled peach, and yet anyone looking in the window would judge me insane. "Don't worry about me, Hallie," I said finally. "Just worry about yourself."

"I'm not worried about myself. I'm the luckiest person alive."

It was an old joke, or an old truth, grown out of all the close shaves she'd walked away from. Bike wrecks, car wrecks, that kind of thing. I'd always been more or less a tragedy magnet, but Hallie was the opposite. One time she started out the door of the old science library at the university, and then turned around and went back in because she'd left her sunglasses by the microfiche machine, and two seconds later the marble façade fell off the front of the building. Just slid straight down and smashed, it looked like Beirut.

Hallie didn't believe she was invulnerable. She was never one of those daredevil types; she knew she could get hurt. What I think she meant was that she was lucky to be on her way to Nicaragua. It was the slowest thing to sink into my head, how happy she was. Happy to be leaving.

We'd had one time of perfect togetherness in our adult lives, the year when we were both in college in Tucson—her first year, my last—and living together for the first time away from Doc Homer. That winter I'd wanted to fail a subject just so I could hang back, stay there with her, the two of us walking around the drafty house in sweatshirts and wool socks and understanding each other precisely. Bringing each other cups of tea without having to ask. So I stayed on in Tucson for medical school, instead of going to Boston as I'd planned, and met Carlo in Parasitology. Hallie, around the same time, befriended some people who ran a safehouse for Central

American refugees. After that we'd have strangers in our kitchen every time of night, kids scared senseless, people with all kinds of damage. Our life was never again idyllic.

I should have seen it coming. Once she and I had gone to see a documentary on the Abraham Lincoln Brigade, which was these Americans who volunteered without our government's blessing to fight against Franco and Hitler in the Spanish Civil War. At that point in U.S. history fascism was only *maybe* wrong, whereas communism was *definitely*. When we came home from the movie Hallie cried. Not because of the people who gave up life and limb only to lose Spain to Franco, and not for the ones who came back and were harassed for the rest of their lives for being Reds. The tragedy for Hallie was that there might never be a cause worth risking everything for in our lifetime. She was nineteen years old then, and as she lay blowing her nose and sobbing on my bed she told me this. That there were no real causes left.

Now she had one—she was off to Nicaragua, a revolution of co-op farms and literacy crusades—and so I guess she *was* lucky. Few people know so clearly what they want. Most people can't even think what to hope for when they throw a penny in a fountain. Almost no one really gets the chance to alter the course of human events on purpose, in the exact way they wish for it to be altered.

I loved her for feeling so strongly about things. But I'd watched Doc Homer spend a lifetime ministering his solemn charity to the people of Grace and I'm not sure whose course was altered by that, other than Hallie's and mine, in a direction we grew to resent. It's true that I tried myself to go into medicine, which is considered a helping profession, but I did it for the lowest of motives. I did it to win love, and to prove myself capable. Not to move mountains. In my opinion, mountains don't move. They only look changed when you look down on them from a great height.

# 5

# The *Semilla Besada*

I'd agreed to move into the guesthouse on the
condition that I wasn't going to impose on Emelina's family life, but
apparently her life was beyond imposition. She sent John Tucker
over in the morning to fetch me for breakfast.

He stood tentatively outside my screen door, unsure of what to
do with all his limbs. "Mom says she'll break your face if you don't
come over for breakfast."

"Okay, sure," I said, following him back to the house. John
Tucker was the most appealing kind of adolescent. I couldn't begin
to picture the man he would soon become—armpits and arrogance,
scratching the back of his neck, throwing a baseball. Out of the
question. He was wearing a cap to cover what looked like an overly
enthusiastic summer haircut.

"I know you don't have anything to eat over there yet," Emelina
said. "Everything was closed, yesterday was Sunday. Today you can
get on your feet. J.T. called from El Paso and said to be sure and give
you a kiss." Emelina buttered a piece of toast and handed it to
Mason, who was four going on five. "Glen, don't put jam on your

brother. If you want to wear plum preserves today that's your nickel, but not Curtis's. Curty, honey, don't hit. John Tucker, help him with that, will you?"

"He called from El Paso?" I prompted. Conversations with a mother of five are an education in patience.

"Yeah, he's in Texas. He's got to stay for an investigation. So are you going to be able to stand living in that shack?"

"It's not a shack, Em. It's nice out there. I like it."

"Codi, honey, there was goats living in there at one time. And Grammy lived there too, before the goats. But she said she got the ague in her bones and she decided she had to move in upstairs." Grammy was J.T.'s mother, Viola Domingos.

"Mom, make Glen stop," Curtis said.

"Glen, for heaven's sakes, just eat that toast and put it out of its misery. The bus is going to be here in a minute and you don't even have your shoes on."

"No, but I know where they are," Glen declared.

"Well, go get them."

"School doesn't start till next week," I said, alarmed that I might be wrong. I was always having dreams like that.

"No, but they've got this summer thing for kids. They go up there to the river park and shoot each other with bows and arrows or something. Tomorrow's the last day. So you think you'll like it out there? We make enough noise over here to raise up the quick and the dead."

"It's fine. I used to live three blocks from a hospital ambulance entrance." I didn't add: with a man who reattached severed body parts for a living. I buttered my toast, holding my elbows in close and keeping an eye out for wayward jam knives. "So what kind of an investigation?"

"Oh, J.T.? He put sixteen cars on the ground outside El Paso. A derailment. Nobody got hurt. Oh shoot—John Tucker, honey, will you take the baby in the living room and watch him a minute? I can't hear myself think."

John Tucker took the baby from Emelina's lap and carried him under one arm into the next room. The baby waggled his arms and legs like a swimmer in green stretch pajamas.

"Okay. Mason, sweetie, put your feet up here on my lap and I'll tie your sneakers for you." Emelina took a gulp of coffee. "So they all had to give a urine sample—J.T., the fireman, the brakeman, and some other person, I can't remember who. Maybe another engineer. It all had to happen within a half hour of the accident; the company made a very big deal out of that. J.T. says, here they were out in some cow pasture with sixteen boxcars of frozen mixed vegetables scattered from hell to breakfast, and all the damn supervisor cared about was making sure which person pissed in what jar."

The boys seemed unmoved by this off-color narrative. Having Emelina for a mother would neutralize the thrill of swear words.

"You know what, though," she said, looking startled. "Damn. We were just joking about drug tests, the day before yesterday. Grammy made a poppyseed cake for Curty's and Glen's birthday and J.T. said . . ."

"Mo-om."

"I'm sorry, Curtis, I forgot. He doesn't want us to call him Curty. Their actual birthday was yesterday."

I wanted to hear the rest of the derailment story, but this conversational flow was akin to freeway driving in L.A.; you don't back up. "Well, happy birthday," I said. "You boys get handsomer every time I see you, you know that?"

Curtis's ears turned red.

"You can say 'Thank you, ma'am,' can't you? Codi, they've all been asking me when you were going to get here till I thought they'd turn blue in the face, and now they're acting like they were raised outside in a pen with the dogs."

"That's okay." I felt a little intimidated myself. Even though I'd kept up with the family, it was inconceivable that in my absence from Grace Emelina could have produced this whole blue-eyed tribe of human beings.

"Mom, can I sleep out in the pen with Buster tonight?" Mason asked.

"No sir, you can't. So when we were eating that cake, J.T. was saying how he'd better not have an accident on the railroad, because poppyseeds show up some way on the drug test."

"That's true, they would." I reconsidered this. "He'd register positive for opiates. Poppyseeds are related to heroin. Is he going to be in trouble?"

"No, they know it wasn't his fault. It was a sun-kink or some darn thing with the rails. The drug test is just to cover their ass. You know who else was on the train? The other engineer and the brakeman were both guys we went to school with, you might remember them. Roger Bristol and Loyd Peregrina. Loyd lived up at Whiteriver for a while but he's moved back."

I paid attention to my heart rate, to see if it would react in any way to this information. It didn't seem to.

"Aunt Codi, say something in Greece," Glen said.

"In Greek," Emelina corrected, giving me an apologetic look. "I already told them you looked like a fashion model and had lived overseas. They think you know David Bowie."

"Your mother exaggerates," I said.

Glen didn't seem too disappointed.

"So, Em, if I'm going to live here do I have to buy a pair of those silver loafers from the Hollywood Shop?"

She nodded seriously. "I'm pretty sure they won't let you teach down at the high school without them."

The school bus honked outside. "Okay, scoot," Emelina said. "Mason, give me a kiss."

The boys stampeded out the kitchen door, all legs, leaving the baby beached on Emelina's lap. His eyes roamed anxiously around the quiet kitchen, taking in the emptiness.

Emelina and I took each other in. All morning I'd felt the strange disjuncture that comes from reconnecting with your past. There's such a gulf between yourself and who you were then, but people speak to that other person and it answers; it's like having a stranger as a house guest in your skin.

"So what's new?" she asked.

"I don't know, everything. I don't think Grace has changed, but it feels different. There's a lot I don't remember."

Emelina smiled. "I know what you mean. Senility strikes." It was an odd thing to say; Doc Homer's exact problem was that his mind had begun to roam in alarming new pastures.

"I guess so," I said.

"Well, some things never change." She leaned forward and said in a low voice, "Grammy still collects figurines of Elvis."

I had to laugh. We'd known J.T.'s mother as children, of course—people here spent their childhoods tearing through the homes of their future in-laws—and I remembered her living room, which we used to call the Elvis Museum. She denied that the ones that were whiskey bottles were whiskey bottles. She'd always told us aftershave.

"So it's all over with Carlo? Or just a vacation?"

"I don't know. Over, I think. It's taken me all this time to figure out he's not going to tell me the secret to a meaningful life." I was serious. I'd loved Carlo best when he provided me with guidance.

"I used to think the ideal husband would be Doctor Kildare."

"Carlo's an emergency-room surgeon. A man that decides which way to sew a thumb back on would have a good hold on life, wouldn't you think? I just assumed it would rub off."

"Gross," Emelina remarked.

"I think it was his eyebrows. You know how he has those kind of arched, Italian eyebrows?"

"No, I never got to meet him. He was always at the hospital."

That was true. He was shy. He could face new flesh wounds each day at work, but he avoided actual people. "Well, he had this look," I said. "He always seemed right on the verge of saying something that would change your life. Even when he was asleep he looked like that."

"But he never did?"

"Nope. It was just his eyebrows."

I did miss him, or at least I missed being attached to someone in theory. Carlo had beautiful hands and a legendary sense of direction.

Even when we were in Venice, where the tourist books advise you that "part of the Venice experience is wandering the narrow *strade* until you find yourself lost," we wandered but never got lost. The man had a compass needle in his cerebral cortex. And for all that, he'd still in the long run declined to be the guiding star I needed. Just as my father did. My father was dying on me.

Emelina collected the plates and cups. She stood up and tied on an apron over her bathrobe, miraculously keeping the baby situated on her hip throughout the operation.

"Well, you're no worse for the wear of five children in fourteen years," I said, and she laughed, probably not believing it. Emelina was noticeably pretty. That combination particular to Grace, the pale blue eyes and black hair, never failed to be arresting, no matter how many versions of it you saw. The eyes were a genetic anomaly—in the first hours after birth, the really pure specimens of Grace's gene pool were supposed to have whitish, marblelike irises. I'd seen pictures. Doc Homer had written it up for the *American Journal of Genetics*, years ago.

"And John Tucker's a teenager," I said. "Are we that old?"

"I am. You're not." She started to clear the table with one hand. "Every minute in the presence of a child takes seven minutes off your life." I took the baby from her and she said, "Don't say I didn't warn you."

"They're your treasures, Em. You've got something to show for yourself."

"Oh, yeah. I know," she said.

The baby's name was Nicholas, but nobody called him anything but "the baby." I'd read somewhere that the brain organizes information in sets no larger than four—that's why Social Security and phone numbers are subdivided; possibly four children's names were the limit on parental memory. I sat in the rocker and settled nameless Nicholas on my lap, his head at my knees. My long thigh bones exactly accommodated his length.

Emelina scraped toast corners into a blue enamel pail and ran a sinkful of hot water. "I don't think I could stand to let Mason go off to kindergarten next year if it wasn't for the baby. It kills you to see them grow up. But I guess it would kill you quicker if they didn't."

"I remember you saying you were calling it quits after four."

"Famous last words."

While I watched her move around the kitchen, my fingers tingled with the pleasure of stroking the baby's fine black hair. It was longer by several inches than his big brother John Tucker's; someone had taken shears to that boy with a vengeance. Probably Emelina. A woman who beheaded her own chickens would cut her kids' hair herself.

Emelina washed and rinsed the plates and set them into the wire rack to drain. I sat feeling useless, though Nicholas seemed comfortable and was falling asleep on my lap. When that happens you feel them grow heavier, as if relaxation allowed them to be flooded with extra substance. A constriction ran across my lungs. I'd come close to having a baby of my own once, but I thought of it now so rarely that the notion of myself as a mother always caught me off guard.

In spite of the heat outside, Emelina's dishwater was fogging the window. A little collection of potted plants stood in a row on the windowsill. Prayer plants. I was struck with a sudden, forceful memory of Emelina's grandmother's house. Hallie and I called her *Abuelita* too, though of course she was no relation, and the old woman called us "the orphan girls," *huérfanas*. Nobody ever thought we could understand Spanish. The house had a stale, old-lady smell, but we loved her boxes of "pretties": cast-metal carts with broken wheels, lead soldiers, huge washers and carriage bolts, every species of unidentifiable metal part. Her dead husband was a blacksmith. There were also boxes of ancient dress-up clothes in satiny fabrics as brittle as paper. Our best playroom was the sunny alcove crammed with plants where we stalked lions through the parlor palms, dressed in our finery, more glamorous than Beryl Markham and the Baroness von Blixen could have managed to be in their dreams. We confronted real dangers in the form of rickety iron stands holding heavy, breakable pots and fragile plants. The

African violets were furred like pets, and the prayer plants had leaves like an old woman's hands, red-veined on the back, that opened wide in the sun and folded primly together in the shade. *Abuelita* instructed us to sit and watch them, to try and catch them in the act of closing their leaves. Hallie always waited the longest, patient for enlightenment long after Emelina and I had returned to our rowdy diversions.

"You know, I'm so used to J.T. being gone," Emelina said, bringing me back. "I think he'd be underfoot if he were here. I'd give us about ten days, then I'd probably shoot him. Husband murder in Grace, oh boy." She seemed to be answering a question, however circumspectly, that I wasn't sure I'd asked.

"How long has he been on the railroad?"

"Just since the mine shut down, which was . . ." She frowned at the glass she was drying, decorated with white pigs in red bow ties. "Ten years, about."

"They used to always say they'd hire again up there when the price of copper went up."

"Well, you know, that's talk. Nobody's waiting around anymore. Now it's pecans and plums. And the railroad, thank God for that. I think we could live off the orchards if the boys didn't eat like horses and outgrow their shoes every ten days. Get this, now they're too fashion conscious to wear each other's hand-me-downs. Remember when boys didn't give a shit what they wore? We never should have got satellite TV." She turned around, drying her hands on her apron. "Is that rascal gone to sleep? Thanks, Codi. I'll take him upstairs and put him down for his nap." She lifted the baby onto her shoulder like a sack of valuable flour. "You got big plans for today?"

"I thought I'd make an excursion into the city," I said. "Check out the dry goods at the Baptist Grocery."

She laughed. "If you can wait awhile I'll go with you. Grammy can listen for the baby. She ought to be home pretty soon from her meeting." Emelina rolled her eyes as she left the kitchen. "Stitch and Bitch Club on Mondays, bright and early."

I stood at the window looking out at the grove of trees that ran the length of the canyon. Plum, pear, apple. And quince, I believe, though I couldn't identify a quince tree to save my life. I only remembered the word because of the way people here pronounced it—"queens"—with their Spanish-influenced vowels. In the distance I could make out white satellite dishes perched among the cacti on the red cliff—one to each house, like dogs. Well, that was something new. The sky was overcast. In the orchards on the other side of the river I could see men working among the trees. I remembered them beating the branches with long poles, bringing down scattered showers of pecans. Frailing, that was called. In the older orchards sometimes they had to climb up into the tallest trees to reach the upper branches with their poles. But it was too early in the year for that. Pecans didn't ripen till late fall.

Hallie and I had played in this house once or twice as children, when a pair of pigeon-toed girl cousins of J.T.'s had lived here. Now it belonged so securely to Emelina. It was hard to realize how fully life had gone on. Of course, it would. I could have stayed here, or gone away as I did, it made no difference to Grace.

I washed the baby's cup, running my finger around the inside rim. While the sun left the windowsill and moved on to other things, I noticed, the prayer plants had closed up when I wasn't watching. They stood in a self-satisfied row, keeping their thoughts to themselves.


**"You keep some** of the dirt on them, and you just stuff them down in paper bags and keep them somewhere dark," said Lydia Galvez. "Do you have a root cellar?"

"No, uh-uh. We did, but the boys got into it and figured out how to cave it in some way," Emelina said.

"Well, you could put them anyplace dark. The bottom of a closet would do."

Lydia Galvez was the wife of John Tucker's little league coach. I'd been introduced. We'd discussed John Tucker, baseball, and Emelina's talent for producing boys. The whole town had been betting this last one would be a girl, Lydia Galvez told me. Now they were talking about dividing gladiolus bulbs.

"I've got some black," Lydia was saying. "Do you have any black? I could spare you some. They're not a *true* black, I'd really call it purple, but they're supposed to be important."

Emelina gave me a glance, so I knew she was trying to wind things up. Our whole afternoon had gone pretty much this way. Lydia, like everyone else, had no earthly notion of what to say to me, or I to them; I rarely even remembered who they were. But we were all polite, as if I were Emelina's lunatic maiden aunt.

I sat down on the wall in front of the courthouse and watched myself in the plate-glass window of Jonny's Breakfast, which was empty at this hour. My reflection stared back, looking more alone than anything I'd seen in my life. It occurred to me that I'd never drawn a breath here without Hallie. Not one I could be sure of. I was three when she was born. Before that I wasn't conscious of my place in the world, so it didn't matter.

Later, it mattered more than anything. Doc Homer drilled us relentlessly on how we differed from our peers: in ambition, native ability, even physical constitution. The nearest thing to praise, from him, was "No one else in Grace knows *that*!" Or, "You are *Nolines*." We stood out like a pair of silos on a mid-western prairie. As far as I could see, being *Nolines* meant that we were impossibly long-limbed like our father and all the Noline relatives we never got to meet. He and mother came from a part of Illinois (this is a quote) where people were reasonable and tall.

The height, at least, wasn't lost on Hallie and me. We turned out to be six feet on average—Hallie one inch over, and I, one under. In high school they used to call us forty percent of a basketball team. We didn't play sports, but they still said that. Height isn't something you can have and just let be, like nice teeth or naturally curly hair. People have this idea you have to put it to use, playing basketball, for example, or observing the weather up there. If you are a girl, they feel a particular need to point your height out to you, as if you might not have noticed.

In fact, Hallie and I weren't forty percent of anything—we were all there was. The image in the mirror that proves you are still here. We had exactly one sister apiece. We grew up knowing the simple arithmetic of scarcity: A sister is more precious than an eye.

"You tell that daddy of yours I need a pill to get rid of my wrinkles," Lydia said loudly.

I made an effort to collect myself. "Okay."

I should have said, "You don't need any such thing," or something like that, but I didn't think fast enough. I wasn't managing this first day all that well. I had a lump in my throat and longed to get back to my cottage and draw the blinds. Grace was a memory minefield; just going into the Baptist Grocery with Emelina had charged me with emotions and a hopelessness I couldn't name. I'd finished my shopping in a few minutes, and while I waited for Emelina to provision her troops for the week I stood looking helplessly at the cans of vegetables and soup that all carried some secret mission. The grocery shelves seemed to have been stocked for the people of Grace with the care of a family fallout shelter. I was an outsider to this nurturing. When the cashier asked, "Do you need anything else?" I almost cried. I wanted to say, "I need everything you have."

**It was past midnight** but a cold moon blazed in the window and I couldn't sleep. I lay on my back in the little painted bed in Emelina's cottage. I hated sleeping alone. As little as there was between Carlo and me, I'd adjusted to his breathing. All my life I'd shared a bed with somebody: first Hallie. Then in my first years at college I discovered an army of lovers who offered degrees of temporary insanity and short-term salvation. Then Carlo, who'd turned out to be more of the same. But companionable, still. Sleeping alone seemed unnatural to me, and pitiful, something done in hospitals or when you're contagious.

I'd finally reached that point of electric sleeplessness where I had to get up. I tucked my nightgown into my jeans and found my shoes out in the kitchen. I closed the door quietly and took a path that led away from the house, not down past other houses but straight out to the north, through Emelina's plum orchard and a grove of twisted, dead-looking apples. Every so often, peacocks called to each other across the valley. They had different cries: the shrill laugh, a guttural clucking—a whole animal language. Like roosters and children, on a full-moon night they would never settle down completely.

I wanted to find the road that led up the canyon to Doc Homer's. I wasn't ready to go there yet, but I had to make sure I knew the way. I couldn't ask Emelina for directions to my own child-hood home; I didn't want her to know how badly dislocated I was. I'd always had trouble recalling certain specifics of childhood, but didn't realize until now that I couldn't even recognize them at point-blank range. The things I'd done with Hallie were clear, because we remembered so much for each other, I suppose, but why did I not know Mrs. Campbell in the grocery? Or Lydia Galvez, who rode our school bus and claimed to have loaned me her handkerchief after Simon Bolivar Jones chucked me on the head with his Etch-a-Sketch, on a dare. In fact, I felt like the victim of a head injury. I hoped that if I struck out now on faith I would feel my way to Doc Homer's, the way a water witcher closes her eyes and follows her dowsing rod to find a spring. But I didn't know. I could have lost the homing instinct completely.

I was on a road that looked promising, anyway. I could hear the river. (Why does sound travel farther at night?) I had my mother's death on my mind. One of my few plain childhood memories was of that day. I was not quite three, Hallie was newborn, and I'm told I couldn't possibly remember it because I wasn't there. The picture I have in my mind is nonetheless clear: two men in white pants han-dling the stretcher like a fragile, important package. The helicopter blade beating, sending out currents of air across the alfalfa field behind the hospital. This was up above the canyon, in the days when they grew crops up there. The flattened-down alfalfa plants showed their silvery undersides in patterns that looked like waves.

The field became the ocean I'd seen in storybooks, here in the middle of the desert, like some miracle.

Then the rotor slowed and stopped, setting the people in the crowd to murmuring: What? Why? And then the door opened and the long white bundle of my mother came out again, carried differently now, no longer an urgent matter.

According to generally agreed-upon history, Hallie and I were home with a babysitter. This is my problem—I clearly remember things I haven't seen, sometimes things that never happened. And draw a blank on the things I've lived through. I told Doc Homer many times that I'd seen the helicopter, and I also once insisted, to the point of tears, that I remembered being on the ship with the nine Gracela sisters and their peacocks. For that one he forced me to sit in my room and read the *Encyclopædia Britannica*. Novels were banned for a month; he said I needed to clear my mind of fictions. I made it to Volume 19, driven mostly by spite, but I still remembered that trip with the Gracelas. They were worried about whether the peacocks were getting enough air down in the hold of the ship.

I would concede now that all these things were fabrications based on stories I'd heard. Memory is a complicated thing, a relative to truth but not its twin. It was a fact that our mother had been terrified of flying. This part of our family history was well known in Grace. In her entire life she never left the ground. When her health deteriorated because of a failed kidney and a National Guard helicopter bore down from the sky to take her to Tucson, she'd explained to the men that she wasn't going to fly. When they ignored her, she just died before the helicopter could lift itself up out of the alfalfa. The big bird hovered for a minute, and went away hungry.

It wasn't her aversion to flight that was impressive; people in Grace didn't travel much by car, let alone by air. I think the moral of the tale, based on the way people told it, was the unsuspected force of my mother's will. "Who else would have married Doc Homer?" they seemed to be saying. And also, I suppose, "Who could have borne those unconforming girls?" People never said this directly, but when we were willful they would tell us, without fail: "You didn't suck that out of your thumb."

It made sense to me. I had no visual memory of a mother, and could not recall any events that included her, outside of the helicopter trip she declined to take. But I could remember a *sense* of her that was strong and ferociously loving. Almost a violence of love. It was the one thing I'd had, I suppose, that Hallie never knew. As the two of us grew up quietly in the dispassionate shadow of Doc Homer's care and feeding, I tried to preserve that motherly love as best I could, and pass it on. But I couldn't get it right. I was so young.

And somehow Hallie thrived anyway—the blossom of our family, like one of those miraculous fruit trees that tap into an invisible vein of nurture and bear radiant bushels of plums while the trees around it merely go on living. In Grace, in the old days, when people found one of those in their orchard they called it the *semilla besada*—the seed that got kissed. Sometimes you'd run across one that people had come to, and returned to, in hopes of a blessing. The branches would be festooned like a Christmas tree of family tokens: a baby sock, a pair of broken reading glasses, the window envelope of a pension check.

Hallie and I had a favorite *besada* in the old Domingos orchard, and one cold day on the way home from school we tucked wisps of our hair into its bark. Secretly. We'd hidden in the schoolyard to snip the ends off our braids and tie them up together with a pink thread unraveled from my coat button. If Doc Homer found out, he would construct some punishment to cure us of superstition. We agreed with him in principle—we were little scientists, born and bred. But children robbed of love will dwell on magic.

I stopped suddenly in the center of the road, in the moon's bright light, with shadow trickling downhill from my heels like the water witcher's wellspring finally struck open. I'd found the right path. The road angled up out of the orchards toward the top of the canyon. The steepness of the climb felt right. I would come back in daylight and go the rest of the way to Doc Homer's, past the old helicopter landing pad up in the alfalfa field. Those fields would surely be abandoned now, like half the cropland in Arizona, salted to death by years of bad irrigation. I didn't want to go up there now and see it all under moonlight, the white soil gleaming like a boneyard. It was too much.

I turned back down the road feeling the familiar, blunt pressure of old grief. Even the people who knew me well didn't know my years in Grace were peculiarly bracketed by death: I'd lost a mother and I'd lost a child.

# 6

# The Miracle

I was fifteen years old, two years younger than my own child would be now. I didn't think of it in those terms: losing a baby. At first it was nothing like a baby I held inside me, only a small impossible secret. Slowly it grew to a force as strong and untouchable as thunder. I would be loved absolutely. But even in the last months I never quite pictured the whole infant I might have someday held in my arms; that picture came later. The human fact of it was gone before I knew it. But evidently that word "lost" was somewhere in my mind because I've had thousands of dreams of losing—of literally misplacing—a baby.

In one of the dreams I run along the creek bank looking among the boulders. They are large and white, and the creek is flooded, just roaring, and I know I've left a baby out there. I thrash my way through mesquite thickets, stopping often to listen, hearing nothing but the roar of the water. I feel frantic until finally I see her in the middle of the water bobbing like a Cortland apple, little and red and bright. I wade in and pull her out and she lies naked there on the bank without so much as a surname, her umbilicus tied with a man's black shoelace such as my father might wear. I see her and think, "It's a miracle she's survived."

That thought is the truest part of the dream. Really there would be nothing new or surprising about a baby being born in secret and put into a creek. But to pull one out, that would be a surprise. A newborn has no fat yet; it wouldn't float. It would sink like a stone.

Loyd Peregrina was an Apache. He took me out four times. Our football team was called the Apaches, but Loyd was also a *real* Apache, and the kind of handsome you could see coming down the road like bad news. When he first asked me, I thought he'd made a mistake, or a joke, and I looked to see who was watching. Nobody was. Four Saturdays in a row, for exactly one lunar month: the odds of getting pregnant out of that were predictable, but I was unfathomably naïve. I was a motherless girl. I'd learned the words *puberty* and *menarche* from the *Encyclopædia Britannica*. The rest I learned from girls in the schoolyard who weren't even talking to me when they said what they did.

Loyd wouldn't remember. For me it was the isolated remarkable event of a tenuous life but for Loyd—with his misspelled name and devil eyes—it was one in a hundred, he was a senior and ran around with everybody. Also he was such a drinker in those days that I was frankly surprised to hear he was still alive. He never knew what he'd spawned, much less when it died. Even Hallie didn't. It's the first time I understood that even with a sister I could be alone. At night I lay feeling my limbs, seeing what Hallie still saw, which was nothing near the truth, and I felt myself growing distant and stolid. I was the woman downtown buttoning her child's jacket, her teeth like a third hand clamped on a folded grocery list, as preoccupied as God. Someone important and similar to others. I was lured and terrified. I couldn't help but think sometimes of escape: the thing inside me turning to blood of its own accord, its bones liquefying, leaking out. And then one evening my savage wish was granted.

I never did tell Hallie. I kept quiet, first to protect her from the knowledge of terrible things, and later to protect myself from that rock-solid element she came to own. That moral advantage.

It divided me from the people I knew, then and later, but in broader human terms I don't pretend that it sets me apart in any great way. A miscarriage is a natural and common event. All told, probably more women have lost a child from this world than haven't. Most don't mention it, and they go on from day to day as if it hadn't happened, and so people imagine that a woman in this situation never really knew or loved what she had.

But ask her sometime: how old would your child be now? And she'll know.

# 7

# Poison Ground

Emelina was up with the chickens. I heard her out in the courtyard pulling honeysuckle vines away from the old brick barbecue pit. They came out with a peculiar zipping sound, like threads from a seam in rotten cloth. "You can see we haven't been festive for a while," she said. She was organizing what she called a "little fiesta" for the Saturday of Labor Day weekend. It was a family tradition; they roasted a whole goat. (Not John Tucker's.)

I found a broom and pitched in, sweeping up the pieces of a broken flowerpot I'd come to think of as part of the décor. Emelina asked, in the carefully offhand way a good mother would ask, if I'd been up to the school yet. I'd received numerous calls about a teachers' meeting.

"I know about the meeting, but I haven't gone up there yet," I confessed. School would begin the following Tuesday. I needed to get organized and see what kind of shape the labs were in, but I kept putting it off, on grounds of terror. I hadn't actually taught school before. When Emelina wrote me about the opening at Grace High School it had seemed sensible to apply. While Carlo slept I'd sat up

in bed with my legal pad and a small reading light, feigning compe-
tence, attempting to organize the problem areas of my life into man-
ageable categories: I had no real attachment to selling lottery tickets
at 7-Eleven; Doc Homer was going off the deep end; Carlo was
Carlo; Hallie would be leaving at summer's end, and without a destination for myself I'd be marooned. Grace was something. If I got
this job I could spend ten months in Grace seeing about Doc
Homer, possibly without his noticing. I reasoned that I wasn't qualified and didn't have a chance of being hired, and so I felt bold
enough to apply.

They hired me. The state had some kind of emergency clause
that in a pinch allowed people to teach without certification. And of
course I did have a world of education in the life sciences. Also, I
believe my last name had something to do with it. Nothing else I put
down in my wobbly writing on that application could have
impressed anyone too much.

I dumped the shards of the flowerpot into a plastic trash bag,
making the satisfactory sound of demolition. I started in with
Emelina on the honeysuckle vines. As we dragged them out she
looped the long strands around her arm like strings of Christmas
tree lights. "You excited about starting?" she asked.

"Nervous."

"Well hell, Codi, you're bound to be better than the last one.
John Tucker says she was scared of her shadow. Some senior boys
chased her into the teachers' lounge with a fetal pig."

Emelina's faith in me was heartening.

"Did I tell you J.T. called this morning?" she asked. "They're
going to make it home for the fiesta. Him and Loyd. Do you remember Loyd?"

I yanked at a vine that was rooted right into the crumbling
adobe. "Sure," I said.

"I didn't know if you would. I think you were the only girl in the
whole high school that never fell for him."

It was humid and hot. I'd tied a bandana around my forehead
and already it was soaking wet. The salt stung my eyes.

"I went out with Loyd a few times," I said.

"Did you? Him and J.T. are real good buddies. He's straightened out a lot. He's real sweet." She unburdened herself of the loops of vines, laying them in a pile, and stood up with her hands on her waist, arching her back. "Loyd, I mean." She laughed. "Not J.T. He's just the same as he always was."

I took off my bandana and wrung it out. The dark drops on the hot brick dried up instantly, leaving behind a white lace of salt. Just like the irrigation water on the alfalfa. In just this way the fields get ruined, I thought to myself.

Emelina kicked tentatively at the brick barbecue pit. "You think this thing will stand up after we get the vines out of it?"

"I think they're what's holding it together," I said.

She cocked her head and looked at it thoughtfully. "Well, if it falls down we'll just have us a roasted-goat disaster. We'll just have to get extra beer."

On the morning of the fiesta she sent John Tucker and me to town for last-minute supplies, including extra beer, although the barbecue pit showed every sign of standing through another Labor Day fiesta. I followed John Tucker down a path I didn't know, a short cut through a different orchard. "What kind of trees are those?" I asked John Tucker. The branches were heavy with what looked like small yellow-green pomegranates.

"Quince," he said, with a perfect short "i," not "queens." The Spanish-flavored accent of Old Grace was dying out, thanks to satellite TV, I suppose. I watched the back of his shorn head; the path was narrow and we walked single file. At thirteen he was my height, a head taller than Emelina. It must shift your liaison with a child when you have to look up to him.

I caught a glimpse of bright car windshield through the trees, and knew where we were. You could picture Grace as a house, with orchards for rooms. To map it of course you'd have to be a botanist. We left quince and entered pecan, where the ground was covered with tiny, immature nuts. "So what's happening with these orchards?" I asked, kicking at a slew of green pecans the size of peach pits. "I've been seeing this all over."

"Fruit drop."

John Tucker was already a man of few words.

The Baptist Grocery was nondenominational, but harked back to a time when everything in Grace, including grocery stores, was still segregated. This wasn't recent, but maybe a century ago. Here the Hispanic and Anglo bloodlines got very mixed up early on, starting with the arrival of the Gracela sisters. By the time people elsewhere were waking up to such ideas as busing, everyone in Grace had pretty much given up on claiming a superior pedigree. Nowadays the Baptist Grocery peddled frozen fish sticks to Protestant and Catholic alike.

John Tucker shopped like an automaton, counting out bags of chips and jars of salsa. Since he seemed interested in efficiency, not congeniality, I suggested we split up. I would go to the liquor store and meet him in front of the courthouse.

Drinking establishments had proliferated in Grace since my day. The mine had closed in the interim, of course; bars and economic duress are common fellow travelers. I passed the Horny Toad Saloon and the Little Dipper plus the one I remembered, the State Line, which was no more situated on the state line than the grocery was Baptist. New Mexico lay thirty miles to the east. I think the name referred to the days when Gracela County was dry and people had to drive to the border for beer.

Emelina had advised that I'd find the best price on beer at the Watering Hole, a package store. I located it on the corner of Main Street and the depot alley, which led down past the old movie theater to the railroad station. The theater had been remodeled into an exercise salon and video rental store called the Video Rodeo, with a huge hand-lettered sign in the window announcing "NINTENDOS NOWHERE." I stared for a good half minute before I made out that it meant "NOW HERE," not "NOWHERE." The calligrapher got cramped.

The Watering Hole was closed, with a sign on the door saying

"BACK IN TEN," so I waited. The placard was lettered in the same hand as the "NINTENDOS" sign. Maybe one person actually ran all the stores in Grace from behind the scenes, like the Wizard of Oz, powerfully manipulating people through hand-lettered signs. It was hot and my mind was fraying at the edges. I wiped the sweat out of my eyes and massaged my prickly scalp, thinking I must look like a drowned hen, but maybe nobody would recognize me today. Living without a lover was beginning to produce in me the odd sense that I was invisible.

A pretty, old carob tree stood near the door of the liquor store, throwing dappled shade on the sidewalk. I knew that its twisted, woody-looking pods could be crunched between the teeth and tasted like cocoa. I sat on a concrete block and leaned my back against the trunk. Apparently this was a frequent waiting spot. Fallen carob pods lay all around my feet. I picked one up, polished it on my T-shirt and bit down: the first sensation was sawdust, but then the splinters turned strongly bittersweet on my tongue, a nostalgic tang. I looked up into the leathery leaves. Hallie had told me carobs were dioecious, which means that male and female parts are possessed by separate individuals. In plain English, they're like us; it takes two to tango. This one was loaded with fruit, but there wasn't another carob tree in sight. I looked all the way down the main street and down toward the depot. No male carobs. I patted the trunk sympathetically.

The door of the Watering Hole was opened by a proprietor who looked as if she might not be legal drinking age herself. In fact this must have been the case because after she bagged and rang up my purchase she asked if I'd mind waiting while she went next door to the Video Rodeo and got her dad. He arrived shortly to accept my money and put it in the register. I suppose they switched off, since she probably wasn't old enough to rent out porno movies either. I recognized neither father nor daughter, and they didn't make a point of knowing or not knowing me: a relief. The daily work of remeeting people was overwhelming, and Emelina's party was going to be a whole lot more of the same.

I took my paper bags and headed across the street. A red pickup truck beeped its horn and startled me—I'd charged right across without looking. I froze up, like one of those ridiculous squirrels that dart one way and then the other and are doomed to end up a road kill. Except my life was in no danger here; he'd stopped. It was Loyd Peregrina, looking exactly like himself. If anything he looked younger than fifteen years ago. His arm was out the window and I hurried out of his way thinking it was a turn signal, that he was trying to turn right. It didn't occur to me till he'd gone on down the street that he was waving at me.

I stayed in the shower forever trying to rinse the salt out of my scalp and skin. I had fantasies of not going to this thing, but Emelina would be hurt, and also my house sat in the middle of the party like a floral centerpiece. It would be hard to pretend not to be home. I put on the most minimal thing I owned, a white cotton dress, and sneaked out my front door.

It was like a high-school reunion. Everyone was boisterously friendly and dying to be filled in on the last decade and a half, which in my case was not that pretty a picture, and of course they asked about Hallie. Children ran underfoot like rebel cockroaches. Emelina, my guardian angel, kept setting me up in conversations before running off to clean up some mess the kids had gotten into or check on the goat.

J.T. came over and gave me a hug that lifted me off the ground—but that's J.T., plus a few beers. It really was nice to see him. "I hear you wrecked a train," I said.

"Wrecked her good," he said. J.T. was broad-shouldered and dark, with the kind of face that's made more handsome, not less, by the scars of teenage acne. We'd known each other since we were babies. His older sister Pocha was at the party, and his brothers Cristobal, Gus, and Arturo, all of whom had been our neighbors when Hallie and I were small. I remembered playing Dutchman's tag with them at the graveyard on All Souls' Days—it was always a huge family picnic up there—until Doc Homer decided the grave-yard was off limits. (Bird mites no doubt.)

People were jammed into the courtyard belly to elbow and it soon got too noisy to talk. I stood near the edge of things, in the shade of an olive that was probably planted when the house was built, middle-aged as olives go. A band called the Sting Rays, featuring one of J.T.'s formerly pigeon-toed cousins, was belting out "Rosa Lee." I spotted Loyd across the way, but would have had to step on a hundred toes to get to him. He was leaning against the wall with his arms crossed, paying attention to a small woman in a strapless dress. Loyd looked like someone in a cigarette ad, except he wasn't smoking: white T-shirt, white smile, those models are always the picture of health. His hair was mink black, in a ponytail. And he had terrific arms. I hate to admit things like this, but in a certain frame of mind I am a sucker for good muscle definition.

A woman approached me suddenly from behind and shouted, "Codi Noline! God, honey, you look like a rock 'n' roll star."

In my sundress and dimestore thongs I looked no more like a rock 'n' roll star than Mother Teresa. "I'll take that as a compliment," I said. "I take them where I can get them nowadays."

"Lord, I know what you mean," she said. It was Trish Garcia, who was a cheerleader and clandestine smoker when I'd last known her. Now she smoked openly, had a raspy cough, and looked like a cartwheel was out of the question. "I heard Hallie's in South Africa."

I laughed. "Nicaragua."

"Well, what in the world's she doing there?"

In high school, Hallie and I were beneath Trish's stratum of normal conversation. I remembered every day of those years, no lapses there. Once in the bathroom I'd heard her call us the bean-pole sisters, and speculate that we wore hand-me-down underwear. I wondered how the rules had changed. Had I come up in the world, or Trish down? Or perhaps growing up meant we put our knives away and feigned ignorance of the damage. "She's teaching people how to grow crops without wrecking the soil," I said. "She has her master's in integrated pest management."

Trish looked indifferent, but she was working hard at being

unimpressed, whereas before it came naturally. I took this as a good sign. "Well, I guess it pays good," she said.

"No, they're not really paying her, just living expenses is about all, I think. She's doing it just to do it. She wants to be part of a new society."

Trish stared. I pretended Hallie was there at the party somewhere, about to walk up behind me. "Six or seven years ago they threw out the dictator and gave all his land to the poor people," I said. "But they need a lot of help in the farming department now, because these soldiers keep attacking the poor farmers from across the border and burning up their crops."

Hallie would laugh at "farming department." She'd laugh at the whole scene, the education of Trish the Cheerleader. She would love me.

"The Communists," Trish said knowingly. "I heard about that. I heard they're thinking about sending the Marines down there to stop them from doing that."

"No, it's the other way around," I said patiently. "The Marines aren't rooting for the new society. The U.S. is paying the contras, the guys that attack the farmers." Hallie would not laugh now, she would be inflamed. She said we were a nation in love with forgetting the facts. She saved clippings that proved it. When Castro released those prisoners from Mariel: One day the headlines said we'd gotten him to free all these wonderful political prisoners. A month later when they were burning down halfway houses in Miami the papers castigated Fidel for exporting his hooligans and junkies.

Trish fiddled with her bra strap. "Hallie always would just up and do anything under the blue sky," she said.

"You're right," I told Trish. "I wish I were that brave. I'd be scared to death to be where she is."

"Well, you know, we can't all be the hero," she said, jutting her lower jaw to blow smoke up toward the olive branches. If I could have drawn blood, if I'd known how to do that with words instead of a needle, I would have. I wasn't sure what Hallie craved but I knew it wasn't glory.

"How's Doc Homer?" she asked.

I hadn't yet found the valor to go see him. I feared seeing him in failing condition. And still disapproving of me, on top of it. "Hard to say," I said.

I felt a tap on my shoulder and turned to see Loyd, grinning broadly. "Too good to speak to an Indian boy on Main Street?"

The tingle of a blush started behind my ears, and I ignored it. I'd learned since high school that in an emergency shyness can be disguised with a completely fake bravado. "You tried to run me down, Loyd! I ought to turn you in for reckless driving." I ran my fingers through my hair. "Actually, I didn't think you'd know who I was."

"Are you kidding? How many beautiful six-foot-tall women you think we've got in this town?"

"Five eleven," I corrected. "I'm the shorter of the bean-pole sisters." I felt suddenly drunk, though I wasn't, chemically speaking. Trish drifted off toward the barbecue pit.

He looked at me for a long time, just looked. Grinning. His left hand was fingering the tip of an olive branch and I expected him to snap it off but he didn't, he only took in its texture as someone might eat chocolate or inhale a cigarette.

"You want another beer?" he asked.

So that was going to be it, no filling in the last fifteen years. No constructing ourselves for each other—otherwise known as falling in love. "Think you can get over to that ice chest and back before this party is over?" I knew he wouldn't.

"In case I don't, I've got your phone number." He winked.

"Don't you worry. You'll be hearing from my lawyer."

I felt adrift and disappointed, though I hadn't held any conscious expectations of Loyd. I looked around at other faces, wondering if they all held secret disappointments for me. Doña Althea, the ancient woman we used to call the "Peacock Lady," was holding court in a lawn chair under the fig tree. She was the one who used to collect the feathers for piñatas. She looked today like she always had, dressed in black, fierce and miniature like a frightening breed of small dog. Even with her braided crown of silver hair she wasn't five feet tall. J.T.'s mother, Viola Domingos, and several other women sat in a group with her, fanning themselves in time to the music and drinking beer. J.T. and Loyd had apparently been commandeered into serving them food; the goat had been pronounced done. People were beginning to move toward the makeshift table, which I'd helped Emelina improvise from the doors to Mason's and the twins' rooms, covered with embroidered tablecloths compliments of the Stitch and Bitch Club. There was enough food to save an African nation. Potato salad, deviled eggs, *menudo,* tortillas and refried beans and a thousand kinds of dessert. I heard somebody say in a high-pitched voice, "*Tomato soup* in that cake? I wouldn't have guessed that for love nor money."

I wasn't in any hurry. I moved out of the way of the principal rush and stood near the gate to the side yard, near my little house. I noticed a dog lying very still and alert, just on the other side of the gate. It looked like an oversized coyote but it was definitely a domestic creature. It had a green bandana tied around its neck. This dog didn't belong to Emelina's household—I was pretty sure I knew all the family animals. It sat with its mouth slightly open and its ears cocked, staring steadily through the wire gate at the people inside.

"You thinking about crashing this party?" I asked the dog.

It glanced up at me for a second, with a patient look, then fixed its gaze back on the crowd. Or maybe on the roast goat.

"I'll bring you some of that, if you're willing to wait awhile," I said. "Nobody's going to miss one little bite."

The dog didn't respond to this promise.

All the old men had served themselves first and were settling down into a huddle of folding chairs near the front door of my cottage, holding their plates carefully horizontal above their knees. I started to move away, out of deference, but I noticed they were talking about fruit drop. I plainly heard one of them say the words, "poison ground." I stood four feet away and invisible, I suppose because they were men, and women talked to women. They asked questions of each other, to which they apparently already knew the answers.

"Do you know how much sulfuric they put in the river? He said the EPA give Black Mountain thirty days to shut down that leaching operation."

"Damn, man, that's *veneno*. How long you think we been putting that on our trees?"

"When did anybody ever tell the Mountain what to do?" The man who said this had a remarkably wrinkled brown face, like an Indian mummy I'd once seen in a roadside museum. "They'll pull some kind of strings," he said.

A man who sat with his back to me spoke up. "They won't fight the EPA. It's not worth it. They been saying for ten years that mine is dead. They're not hardly getting anything from that leaching operation."

Another man nodded at this, pointing his fork toward the head of the canyon. "Just enough to pay the taxes. That's all. They'll shut her down."

"You think so?" asked the one who reminded me of a mummy. "They're getting gold and moly out of them tailing piles. If they wasn't, they wouldn't keep running the acid through them. You boys know that damn company. They're not going to stop no leaching operation on account of our pecan trees." His voice trailed off and he was quiet for a minute, his callused fingers fooling with an unlit cigarette. I heard women's voices rising randomly over the din of the party, calling out instructions, reining in their kids. The party seemed like something underwater, a lost continent, and I felt profoundly sad though it wasn't my continent. I would go get a bite to eat, say something grateful to Emelina, and slip back into my house.

The man with his back to me said, "It's in Ray Pilar's apples and quince." He pronounced it "queens."

Another man, younger than the others, said, "It's going to kill every damn tree in this canyon. If I'm wrong, my friend, you can shoot me."

The man with the wrinkled face said, "If you're right, my friend, you might as well shoot yourself."

# 8

# Pictures

The dead mountain range of tailings on the lip of the mine had sat for decades, washed by rain, and still was barren as the Sahara. From a distance you might guess these piles of dirt to be fragile, like a sandcastle, but up close you'd see the pinkish soil corrugated with vertical ridges and eroded to a sheen, like rock. It would take a pickaxe to dent it.

It was high noon and I knew where I was. I bypassed the old mine road at the top of the canyon and stayed on the unmarked lane that people called, for reasons unknown to me, the Old Pony Road. All Grace's streets went by odd names that had mostly to do with picturesque forms of transportation: the Old and New Pony roads, the Goatleg, Dog-Cart Road, and the inexplicable Tortoise Road. Amazingly, most or all of these also had official, normal-sounding names like West Street and San Francisco Lane, which were plainly marked on painted aluminum street signs and totally ignored. Maybe somebody had just recently dreamed up these normal names and hammered up signs to improve the town's image.

From the canyon's crest I could see down into the isolated settlements at the north end of the valley, some abandoned, some buried in deep graves of mine tailings, through which, presumably, Black Mountain now ran quantities of sulfuric acid. Far to the south lay open desert. The road I was on would pass through one more flock of little houses, all settled like hens into their gardens, before reaching Doc Homer's drafty two-story gray edifice.

I bypassed the main entrance of the hospital, the only one of the ghost town of Black Mountain buildings that was still in use. The hospital itself had finally closed—people had to leave Grace for a more equipped town if their problems were major—but Doc Homer's office in the basement could handle anything up to and including broken limbs. He wasn't working there today. I'd called him at home; I was expected.

"Cosima? *Cosima Noline!* I want you to look." A heavyset woman in a housedress and running shoes was standing at her mailbox, shouting at me. "Child, will you look. If you aren't the picture of your mother."

My mother was dead at my age. The woman put her arms around me. She was nobody I recognized.

"We've been so anxious to see you!" she said at a convincing decibel level. "Viola told us at sewing club you'd got in, and was staying down with her and J.T. and Emelina till you can help Doc get his place straightened out and move in up here with him. Oh, I know Doc's glad to have you back. He's been poorly, I don't expect he'd tell you but he is. They said when you was overseas you learned the cure they used on that actress in Paris, France. Bless your heart, you're a dear child." She paused, finally, taking in my face. "You don't remember me, do you?"

I waited, expecting help. It had been fourteen years, after all. But she offered no hints. "No, I'm sorry," I said. "I don't."

"Uda!" The woman said.

"Oh, Uda. I'm sorry." I still didn't have the foggiest idea who she was.

"I won't keep you, hon, but I want you to come for dinner soon as you can. I've baked Doc a squash pie I've been aiming to take up there. Hang on, I'll just run get it."

I waited while she hurried on her small feet up the path to the house and disappeared into the cave of honeysuckle that had swallowed her front porch. Uda returned directly with a covered pie tin that I accepted along with a bewildering kiss on both cheeks. I wondered how many people in Grace believed I'd flown in fresh from Paris with a cure for Alzheimer's.

**He'd told me** two years ago. I had no idea if it was the confirmed truth or just his opinion, since Doc Homer made no distinction between the two. And if it was true, I still didn't know what to think. What we are talking about, basically, is self-diagnosed insanity and that gets complicated.

Carlo and I in fact weren't living in Paris (we never had), but in Minnesota; we'd already come back from Crete. Hallie had kept decently in touch with Doc Homer but I hadn't, and felt guilty, so I engineered a visit in Las Cruces. God knows how long he would have waited to tell me, otherwise. This meeting was not a plan he'd cooked up to give me the news, but my idea, sprung at the last minute. An accident of science, actually. Someone had recently spliced the glow gene from a glowworm into a tobacco plant, and the scientific world was buzzing over this useless but remarkable fact. All the top geneticists were meeting in New Mexico and my boss wanted me down there to take notes. I was working at a high-powered research lab; this was prior to my moving back to Tucson and falling into convenience-mart clerking. If I ever wrote down on paper my full employment history, I assure you it would look like the résumé of a schizophrenic.

And in my professional upswings I had more of what passes for confidence; it dawned on me that it's an easy bus ride over the state line from Grace to Las Cruces. I'd phone Doc Homer.

I was astonished when he agreed to come. "Barring unforeseen difficulties at the hospital," he'd said over the phone. I didn't know yet that the hospital had closed; that he sometimes forgot.

"You always say that." It was true, that was his standard disclaimer on every promise to Hallie or me, but it was uncharacteristic for me to tease him. Truthfully, after such an ice age, there was no such thing as characteristic. I tried out joking, more or less to see if it would work. "You'll say that at your own funeral, Pop," I'd said boldly into the receiver. Later, after he told me, I could have bitten my tongue off for that.

We met in the lobby of the Holiday Inn, just for a couple of drinks since he said he had to get back to Grace that night. The bar was done up in this madly cheerful south-of-the-border décor, with a blue tile fountain and silk bougainvillaeas climbing out of clay pots shaped like pigs. It was somebody's idea of what Old Mexico would look like if you didn't have to take poverty into account. The waitresses wore swishy miniskirts with ruffles in contrasting primary colors. In this setting my father told me he had a terminal disorder of the brain.

All I kept thinking was that he must be wrong. I doubted he'd had a CAT scan. The thing to do would be to check into the University Hospital in Tucson and get a neurological workup, to rule out other things, but I didn't try to talk him into it. The nature of my relationship with Doc Homer, which had eluded me over the phone, came back instantly when I saw him. There are all the small things you love and despise about a parent: the disappointed eyes, the mannerisms, the sound of the voice as much as the meaning of the words, that add up to that singular thing—the way you are both going to respond, whether you like it or not. It had settled heavily over our table and I could hardly breathe. I knew this man. He wouldn't seek out a second opinion to stack up against his own. He'd suffer his own doubts but never anyone else's. The waitress swished over and brought us fresh margaritas. The trickle of the fountain put me on edge, the way a running toilet will, or any sound of water going to waste. "What are you going to do?" I asked Doc Homer.

"I don't see a need to do anything special, for the time being. I'll make arrangements when the time comes."

My stomach was tight. I felt perversely annoyed with the smiling clay pigs. I touched my lips to the coarse salt on the rim of the margarita glass, and the crystals felt like sand in my mouth, or broken glass. I thought of walls I'd seen in Mexico—high brick *hacienda* walls topped with a crest of broken bottles imbedded in cement, to keep people on their correct sides of the fence. If they want to provide an authentic Mexican flavor they should have something like that in here, I thought.

"Nobody else knows," he said. "And I'd like for you not to mention it to your sister."

I stared at him. I knew it wouldn't matter what came next, whether I said "Okay," or "Why?" or "That's not fair," which is what I mainly felt. Dr. Homer Noline had stopped talking, there being nothing more to say, in his opinion. I imagined him going back to Grace on the bus and lying that night in his bed, tired but wide awake, recalling the events of his day and wondering what pathways of thought in his brain might be slipping off track. Trying to remember what vegetable he'd cooked for dinner or what tie he'd worn. He might be confronting these thoughts with fear, or only clinical interest. I really didn't know.

For the first time in my life then, and just for a few seconds, I was able to see Doc Homer as someone I felt sorry for. It was a turning point for me, one of those instants of freakishly clear sight when you understand that your parent might have taken entirely the wrong road in life, even if that road includes your own existence. I pitied Doc Homer for his slavish self-sufficiency. For standing Hallie and me in the kitchen and inspecting us like a general, not for crooked hems so much as for signs of the weakness of our age: the lipstick hidden in a book satchel, the smoldering wish to be like everyone else. Being like no one else, being alone, was the central ethic of his life. Mine too, to some extent, not by choice but by default. My father, the only real candidate for center of my universe, was content to sail his private sea and leave me on my own. I still held that against him. I hadn't thought before about how self-sufficiency could turn on you in old age or sickness. The captain was going down with his ship. He was just a man, becoming a child. It became possible for me to go back to Grace.

**I arrived at the house,** nervous, ludicrously armed with Uda's squash pie. But he was in his darkroom. Not waiting. He called it his workroom, I think to try to legitimize his hobby to himself. Doc Homer made pictures. Specifically, he made photographs of things that didn't look like what they actually were. He had hundreds: clouds that looked like animals, landscapes that looked like clouds. They were pressed between slabs of cardboard, in closets. Only one was framed. The matting and framing were my present to him one Christmas when I was in high school, after I'd started making my own money. It had cost me a lot, and was a mistake. His hobby was a private thing, too frivolous in his opinion to be put on public display. I should have foreseen this, but didn't.

Nevertheless, he'd hung it in the kitchen, God only knows why because the man was far from sentimental, and there it still hung. It was the first thing I noticed when I knocked on the screen door and walked in. The photo was my favorite, a hand on a white table. And of course it wasn't a hand, but a clump of five saguaro cacti, oddly curved and bumpy, shot against a clear sky. All turned sideways. Odd as it seemed, this thing he did, there was a great deal of art to it.

I put the pie in the refrigerator and nosed around a little, telling myself it's what a good daughter would do. I pictured these good daughters—wifely and practical, wearing perms and loafers and Peter Pan collars. I didn't remotely look the part. As I crept around the house it felt to me like a great, sad, recently disclosed secret. The kitchen seemed smaller than when I was a girl, standing on a bucket to reach the sink, but that's natural. It was also crowded with odds and ends you wouldn't expect in a kitchen: a pair of Piper forceps, for example, washed with the day's dishes and sitting amongst them on the drainboard. This didn't signify any new eccentricity on his part. He'd always had a bizarre sense of utility. I could picture him using the forceps to deliver a head of cabbage from a pot of boiling water. Holding it up. Not in a show-off way, but proud he'd thought of it, as if he were part of a very small club of people who had the brains to put obstetrical instruments to use in the kitchen.

The rooms were cool and stale although it was hot outside. I stepped through the living room, over the old Turkish carpet, which looked malnourished, its bare white threads exposed like ribs. Doc Homer could afford better, I heard somebody say in my mind, a voice I couldn't identify. "All the money he's got up there." Which of course wasn't true, we never had much, that was just what people thought because we were standoffish. Beyond the living room was the parlor where he used to see patients who'd come to the house, embarrassed, it seems to me now, at night when the office was closed. At present the parlor was shockingly cramped. The door to the outside porch was blocked by furniture I didn't remember: two sofas and something that looked like a cobbler's bench. Folded on a sofa was one thing I remembered well, a black crocheted afghan with red flowers. Hallie and I used to drag that thing around everywhere, our totem against disaster. It looked cleaner now than I'd ever seen it.

Magazines and journals were everywhere. His *American Journal of Genetics* was still organized chronologically on the shelf. That was his pet interest; they'd once published his article on the greatly inbred gene pool of Grace, with its marble-eyed babies. (He'd even rigged up a system for photographing the newborns' eyes, for documentation.) The trait first began showing up in the fifties, when third-cousin descendants of the Gracela sisters started marrying each other. Emelina would have been one of his subjects. You needed to get the gene from both sides; it was recessive. That's about what I knew. For me it was enough to understand that everyone in Grace was somehow related except us Nolines, the fish out of water. Our gene pool was back in Illinois.

Other magazines, many in number, were piled on the floor. I picked up a *Lancet*: 1977, my first year of med school. There was an important article on diabetes I remembered. Underneath, a recent *National Geographic*. There was no order at all. Though if I mentioned it he'd come up with some elaborate rationale before he'd admit to disorganization. South Sea Islands and Islets of Langerhans, I could see him saying, and not meaning it as a joke. The smell of mold was making my eyes water. I was inclined toward the stairs, to go up and see what kind of shape the bedrooms were in, but I didn't have the heart. It wasn't my house. I forced my hand to knock on the darkroom door.

"Open. I'm about to start printing."

I closed the door behind me. There was only a dim red light bulb. "Hi, Pop," I said.

He looked at me, unsurprised and not very much changed, I could see as my eyes adjusted. I was prepared for frailty and incoherence but he was lucid and familiar. The same substantial hands and wrist bones, the straight nose and low, broad mouth—things I also have, without noticing much. He motioned for me to sit.

"So how are you these days?" I asked.

He ignored the question. We hadn't been together since the Holiday Inn lounge, two years ago, but from Doc Homer you didn't expect hugs and kisses. He was legendary in this regard. Hallie and I used to play a game we called "orphans" when we were with him in a crowd: "Who in this room is our true father or mother? Which is the one grownup here that loves us?" We'd watch for a sign—a solicitous glance, a compliment, someone who might even kneel down and straighten Hallie's hair ribbon, which we'd tugged out of alignment as bait. That person would never be Doc Homer. Proving to us, of course, that he wasn't the one grownup there who loved us.

I sat carefully on a cool file cabinet. He was adjusting black knobs on the enlarger, preparing to make a print. When he switched on the bulb an image appeared against the wall, in reverse: white trees, black sky, mottled foreground. I'd learned how to look at negatives many years before I read my first X-ray. He shrank the frame into focus, shut it off while he slid a rectangle of paper into place and set the timer, and then projected the picture again, burning it into the paper. In the center were two old men hunched on a stone wall, backs to the camera.

"They look like rocks," I said. "It's hard to see where the wall ends and the men start."

"Men who look like stones," said Doc Homer. His speech was more formal than most people's writing. Who else would really say "stones"?

"Except for the hat," I said. "That hat's a giveaway."

"I'm taking it out." He held a small steel spatula into the beam of light and waved little circles over the area of the man's hat, as if he were rubbing it out, which is exactly what he was doing. Photographers call this "dodging," and the spatula was a "dodging tool," though in all probability this one was something used in gall-bladder surgery. When I was little I called it the Magic Wand.

The timer rang and he shut the projector off. I looked at his face in profile in the faint red light. Deep lines ran from his nose to the corners of his mouth. He didn't look well, but maybe he never had. He picked up the print by its edges.

"You haven't heard anything from Hallie, have you?"

He shook his head.

"You're sure you don't want me to tell her you've got, that you're sick? I'm sorry to bring this up, but it's hard to be the only one. I think she'd want to know."

He appeared not to have heard me. I knew he had. Doc Homer never argued, he just didn't participate in conversation that didn't please him.

"So did the man's hat go away?" I asked.

He slipped the paper into a dishpan of clear liquid. "We'll see." He seemed suddenly happy now, almost friendly, as he often did in here. The darkroom was the nearest I'd ever come to feeling like I had a dad. We stood without talking and watched a gray image grow on the paper like some fungus with a mind of its own. I thought about the complex chemistry of vision, remembering from medical school the textbook diagrams of an image projected through the eyeball, temporarily inscribed on the retina.

"I never thought about how printing a photograph duplicates eyesight," I said. "It's the same exact process in slow motion."

He nodded appreciatively and my heart warmed. I'd pleased him. "Probably there is no real invention in the modern world," he said. "Just a good deal of elaboration on nature." He lifted out the slick print and slipped it into a second tray, the fixer.

"The stone has no head," he pronounced, correctly; it looked like a rock wall with two extra rocks balanced on top. You'd think it was just a simple snapshot of what it looked like. His finest art defeated itself. God only knows what was the point, but it made him smile. When the timer rang again he took the photograph out and slid it into its final bath. He fished out several other prints and attached them with small clothespins to a wire. Then he dried his hands on a towel, one finger at a time. These gestures made me think of all the years he'd spent alone, doing his own dishes, his laundry.

I felt our visit drawing to a close, like a scientifically predicted death. We would go out into the light, find a little more to say, and then I'd go.

"There's a pie for you in the kitchen," I said. "From Uda. Who is she?"

"Uda Ruth Dell," he said, as though that explained it.

"I mean, what is she to me? Did I use to know her?"

"Not especially," said Doc Homer, still studying the photographs. "No better than you knew anyone else."

"She knows all about me, and then some," I said. "She probably knows what I had for lunch."

"You're in Grace," he said.

"Well, I was embarrassed because I couldn't remember her. She wasn't very helpful. She just stood there waiting for me to rack my brain and come up with her name. She sure knew me right off the bat."

Doc Homer didn't care for expressions like "right off the bat." He switched off the red light before opening the darkroom door, passing us through a moment of absolute darkness. He knew, but refused to accept, that I was afraid of the dark. The click and blackness plunged me into panic and I grabbed his upper arm. Surprisingly, he touched my knuckles lightly with his fingertips.

"You're in Grace," he said again, as if nothing had happened. "There is only one of you for all these people to be watching for. And so many of them for you."

I'd lived all my life with a recurring nightmare. It would come to me in that drowsy twilight where sleep pulls on your mind with tempting music but is still preventable. When I let down my guard the dream would spring again, sending me back into weeks of insomnia. It had to do with losing my eyesight. It wasn't a complicated dream, like a movie, but a single, paralyzing freeze frame: there's a shattering pop, like glass breaking, and then I am blind.

Once, years ago on Crete, Carlo and I were driving on a badly rutted gravel road to get to a beach on the south of the island. A truck loaded with blood oranges kicked up a rock that broke the windshield in front of my face. I wasn't hurt, the rock only pocked the glass and spun out a spiderweb of cracks, but I spent the rest of the day in mute hysteria. Carlo never did know what was wrong. Any explanation I could think of sounded like superstition. My dream was very much more than a dream. It had so much living weight to it, such prescience, it felt like something that was someday bound to happen.

The insomnia, on the other hand, wasn't such a big problem as you might imagine. I worked around it. I read a lot. In med school I did my best studying while my classmates were in the throes of rapid eye movement. I still considered my night-prowling habits to be a kind of secret advantage I had over other people. I had the extra hours in my day that they were always wishing for.

Emelina would not understand this. The night before school started, she brought me warm milk.

"Don't worry about it," I said. She'd also brought out a blue embroidered tablecloth, which she shook out like a little sail and spread efficiently over my table. She felt the place needed more homey touches.

"You've got to have your sleep. They had a special on *Nova* about it. This man in Italy died from not sleeping for around eight months. Before he died he went crazy. He'd salute the doctors like he was in the army."

"Em, I'll live. That's too pretty, that tablecloth. Don't you need that?"

"Are you kidding? Since Grammy joined Stitch and Bitch she's been embroidering borders on the dish rags. What happens if you just lie in bed and count backward from ninety-nine? That's what I tell the boys to do when they can't settle down."

"Insomnia's different," I said. It was hard to explain this to people. "You know the light that comes on when you open the refrigerator door? Just imagine it stays on all the time, even after you close the door. That's what it's like in my head. The light stays on."

Emelina made herself comfortable in my other living-room chair. "You're like that Thoreau guy that lived at Walden Pond. Remember when we read that in Senior English? He only had two chairs. We need to get you some more stuff in here."

I was surprised that Henry Thoreau entered into Emelina's world view. "If I want company I can always go over to your house," I pointed out.

"That's the God's truth. I'm about ready to move out. Tonight Glen and Grammy got into it, oh boy, she says he's *impudent*. That's her all-time favorite word. Whenever Mason gets mad at somebody he yells 'You're impotent!' And people laugh, so we'll never get him to stop now."

I drank the milk. I could stand some mothering. I wondered if I'd had this in the back of my mind when I moved in here.

Emelina scrutinized my clean, white walls. "Codi, I hope you'll take this the right way, but I don't see how you can live in a place and have it feel like nobody lives there."

"I have things in here. My clothes, look in the closet. And

books. Some of those books are very personal." This was true. Besides my *Field Guide to the Invertebrates* there were things Hallie had sent me over the years, and an old volume of American poetry—incomprehensibly, a graduation gift from Doc Homer.

"Your room was like this when we were in high school. I had posters of Paul Revere and the Raiders and dead corsages stuck in the mirror, every kind of junk. And when we'd go over to your house it was like a room somebody'd just moved out of."

"I'm neat," I said.

"It's not neat. It's *hyper* neat."

"Can you imagine what Doc Homer would have said if Paul Revere and the Raiders turned up in his home? Without an appointment?"

She laughed.

"Emelina, who's Uda Ruth Dell?"

"Well, you know her, she lives up by Doc Homer. She used to take care of you sometimes, I think. Her and that other woman that's dead now, I think her name was Naomi."

"She used to take care of us?" I'd been trying all day to place her. I couldn't believe I'd draw a complete blank on someone who'd been a fixture of my childhood.

"Sure. Uda's husband Eddie saved you and Hallie's life that time when you got stranded in a storm down by the crick."

"I don't have any idea what you're talking about."

"Yes you do. When you and Hallie almost drowned in that flood. You were just little."

"Well, how do you remember it, then? I don't."

"Everybody knew about that. It was a famous incident. You hid down in a coyote burrow and wouldn't come out and Eddie Dell found you and drug you out. You all stayed at Uda's. Doc Homer must have been working at the hospital or something."

"I don't remember anything about that."

Emelina looked at me peculiarly, as if she thought I might be pulling her leg. "It was a real big deal. There was a picture in the paper of you two and Eddie the big hero, and his mule."

"I guess I do remember," I said, but I didn't, and it bothered me that my childhood was everyone's property but my own.

"You know what you are, Codi? I don't know if there's a word for it, but it's the opposite of 'homemaker.'"

I laughed. She was still distressed by my blank walls. "There's a word. Home wrecker. But I'm not one."

"No I don't mean in the sense of home wrecker. I mean in the sense of home ignorer."

"Oh, that way," I said. I was playing dumb. I knew what she meant. My first boyfriend in college was a Buddhist, and even he had had more pictures on his wall than I did. It wasn't anything noble; I couldn't claim a disdain for worldly things. Hallie had once pointed out that I had more shoes than you'd find in a Central American schoolroom with class in session. What I failed at was the activity people call "nesting." For me, it never seemed like nesting season had arrived yet. Or I wasn't that kind of bird.

After Emelina left for the night, I wrote Hallie. I had a general-delivery address for her in Managua and I asked, the way we did when we were kids leaving notes for each other in secret hiding places, "Are you there yet? Are you reading this now?" I told her about the dead alfalfa fields around Gracela Canyon, which I thought would interest her professionally, and I told her Doc Homer seemed pretty much the same as ever, which was the truth. And I asked if she remembered the time we almost drowned in a coyote den.

# 9

# The Bones in
# God's Backyard

Grace High School, backdrop of the worst four
years of my life, was as familiar as one of my bad dreams. Walking
toward it up Prosper Street filled me with dread. The building itself
had a lot of charm, though, which surprised me. As a child I'd paid
no mind to the façade. It was a WPA-era building made of Gracela
Canyon's red granite, with ornate egg-and-dart moldings on the
white-painted eaves and woodwork over the doors. The school was
actually built by the mining company, in its boom years, and with
minerly instincts (or possibly just the proper tools) it was built right
into the steep side of the canyon, sunk into rock. It was in an old
part of town where the cobbled streets wrapped up and around
behind the buildings, occasionally breaking into flights of steps and
elsewhere so steep as to make motor vehicles pointless. The principal form of exercise in Grace was just getting from your house to
wherever you needed to go.

The school had four floors, and each one had a street-level

entrance. I'm pretty sure the building was in some record book on account of this. The main entrance was on the side, halfway up the hill: floor three. Carved into its granite arch was a grammatically suspect motto in Latin, CAUSAM MEAM COGNOSCO, which boys used to quote like pig latin or the inane "Indian" talk we heard in movies.

I checked into the principal's office, where his secretary, Anita, gave me a set of keys and an armload of official-looking papers and cheered me on. "There's a million forms there: grade forms, class roster, some new thing from the DES, and your CTA. It all has to be filled out."

"What, you mean I have to work for a living here? Somebody told me teaching high school was easy money." I looked through the stack of forms. "What about DOA? I may need one of those."

Anita looked at me oddly for half a second, then laughed. "We'll just call the coroner when they bring you in."

I smiled. Doc Homer was the coroner of Grace, and had been for the entirety of my life and then some. Obviously Anita didn't know who I was; she looked like a recent graduate herself. Anyone in high school now would have been a toddler when I left Grace. This filled me with hope. Walking those wainscoted halls, still painted the exact same shade of toothpaste green, made me shrink into my skin, and I had to keep reminding myself: None of them knows you as Doc Homer's misfit child. No one here has seen you in orthopedic shoes.

"The kids'll just love you," Anita said, surprising me. "They're not used to anybody so . . ." she paused, tapping a complete set of maroon fingernails on her metal desk and presumably fishing for a tactful adjective . . . "so *contemporary.*"

I was wearing a dark green blazer, tight jeans, and purple cowboy boots. I ran a hand through my hair and wondered if I should have paid a call to the Hollywood Shop, after all. "Do you think I'm not enough of an authority figure? Will they revolt?" The teachers' meeting, two days prior, had been devoted primarily to theories of discipline.

Anita laughed. "No way. They know who turns in the grades."

I found the room where I would be teaching General Biology I and II, and made it through the homeroom period by taking attendance and appearing preoccupied. I'd finally paid my preparatory visit to the school a few days earlier, so I knew what to expect in the way of equipment: desks and chairs; some stonetopped lab benches with sinks and arched chrome faucets; an emergency shower; a long glass case containing butterflies and many other insects in ill repair; and a closet full of dissecting pans and arcane audiovisual aids. The quaint provisions led me to expect I'd be working in something like a museum, or a British movie. When the kids filled the room for first period, though, they gave it a different slant. So far in Grace I hadn't seen a lot of full-blown teenagers. I wasn't expecting skateboard haircuts.

The girls seemed to feel a little sorry for me as I stood up there brushing chalk dust off my blazer and explaining what I intended for us to do in the coming year. But the boys sat with their enormous high-top sneakers splayed out into the aisles, their arms crossed, and their bangs in their eyes, looking at me like exactly what I was—one of the last annoying things standing between them and certified adulthood.

"You can call me Codi," I said, though I'd been warned against this. "Ms. Noline sounds too weird. I went to this high school and had biology in this room, and I don't really feel that old. I guess to you that sounds like a joke. To you I'm the wicked old witch of Life Science."

This got a very slight rise out of the boys, not exactly a laugh. The girls looked embarrassed. A tall boy wearing a Motley Crüe T-shirt and what looked like a five-o'clock shadow on his scalp pulled a cigarette out of his pocket and thumped it against his knuckles.

"I was told we'd need an authority figure in the classroom, so I dug one up." I went to the closet and wheeled out a human skeleton. "This is Mrs. Josephine Nash."

I'd found her downstairs in a storage room filled with damaged field-hockey equipment and gym uniforms from the fifties. The skeleton was in pretty good shape; I'd only had to reattach one elbow with piano wire and duct tape (provided by the janitor). The name—along with an address in Franklin, Illinois—was written in fine, antique-looking letters on the flange of her pelvis. When I discovered her in the storage room I felt moved to dust her off and hang her up on the heavy cast-iron stand and wheel her up to my lab. I guess I was somewhat desperate for companionship.

"Miss," one of the boys said. "Miss Codi."

I tried not to smile. "Yes."

"That's Mr. Bad Bones." He enunciated the name in a way that made everybody laugh. "The seniors use him for the Halloween Dance."

"Well, not anymore," I said. Mrs. Nash was my compatriot from the Midwest; a possible relative, even. I could see her as somebody's mother, out pruning roses. "This isn't a toy," I said, my voice shaking slightly. "It's the articulated skeleton of a human being who was at one time, fairly recently, walking around alive. Her name was Josephine Nash and she lived in Illinois. And it's time she got some respect in her retirement."

I glared at them; teenagers are so attached to their immortality. "You never know where you're going to end up in this world, do you?" I asked.

Nineteen pairs of blank, mostly pale-blue eyes looked back at me. You could have heard a cigarette drop.

"Okay," I said. "Chapter one: Matter, Energy, Organization and Life."


**"I don't know** if I'm going to live through this," I told Emelina, collapsing in her kitchen. Her kitchen chairs were *equipales* that took you in like a hug, which I needed. My first day had gone as smoothly as anybody could reasonably hope—no revolts, no crises major or minor. Still, I couldn't put a finger on what it was, but standing in front of a roomful of high-school students seemed to use up a ferocious amount of energy. It made me think of those dancers in white boots and miniskirts who used to work bars in the sixties, trying desperately to entertain, flailing around like there was no tomorrow.

Emelina, Mason, the baby, and I were all exiled to the kitchen; Viola had taken over the living room with her friends for a special afternoon meeting of the Stitch and Bitch Club. They were preparing for their annual fundraising bazaar, and as a backdrop to our own conversation we could overhear the exchange of presumably vital information:

"Last year the Hospital Equipment Committee didn't make fifteen cents on them sachet cushions."

"Well, it's no wonder. They stunk."

"Lalo saw in a magazine where you can make airplanes out of cut beer cans. The propellers go around."

Emelina set a cup of tea in front of me. I picked it up and let the steam touch my eyelids, realizing that what I needed most at that moment was to lie in bed with someone who was fond of every inch of my skin.

"It must be weird, going back to that school," she said.

"Oh, sure. It is. I didn't let myself think too much about that part of the job. Till today."

Mason was on the floor, coloring, and Emelina was moving around the kitchen in an effortless frenzy, closing drawers with her hip, cooking dinner, and feeding the baby at the same time.

"Let me do that," I said, scooting myself over to the high chair and taking the cereal bowl from Emelina.

"Here, he makes a pretty fair mess, let me give you Grammy's apron," she said, tying around me a splendid example of Stitch and Bitch enterprise. The baby snapped up cereal as fast as I could spoon it in, wasting little on mess as far as I could see.

"You're having dinner with us tonight, right?"

"No, thanks," I said.

"Honestly, Codi, if you think one more mouth to feed is any trouble you're out of your mind. If I woke up one day and had six more kids I don't think I'd notice."

"No, Em, thanks, but I feel like resting in peace."

"You're not dead yet, hon."

From the living room we heard Viola raising her voice now in Spanish, saying something about peacocks: *pavones.* The other women answered in Spanish, and I could follow just enough to know that they'd moved rapidly onto the subject of fruit trees. Doña Althea sounded agitated. Her high-pitched voice was easy to recognize, exactly what you'd expect from a very small, strong-willed woman. Emelina raised her eyebrows as she looked under a pot lid. "Do you know the boys won't even speak Spanish to their Grammy?" she asked in a subdued voice.

I glanced at Mason, who was absorbed in his coloring book, though probably listening. "Is that a problem?"

"Oh, yeah. Viola's big on all the traditional stuff. She's real tight with Doña Althea. She wants us to raise the boys *puro,* speaking Spanish and knowing all the stories. Seems like it might be easier with girls, but these guys . . ." She shrugged her shoulders. "My parents were always so modern, you remember how Mom is, electric can openers all the way. I always felt like she wanted me to grow up *blonde,* you know? My dad told me she actually wanted to name me *Gidget!*"

I laughed. "No. He was pulling your leg."

"No, he wasn't. And poor Tucker was named after a car."

Tucker was a younger brother who'd died in infancy, before I ever knew the family. To tell the truth, I'd forgotten him, in spite of his name passed on to Emelina's first son.

The baby was sitting with his mouth opened unbelievably wide, waiting for my attention to return to his dinner. I poked in the next bite. A scattering of loud laughter like a rainstorm came from the other room, and all of us in the kitchen were quiet. This gang of old women staked out such a presence, we felt almost crowded out of the house. Mason actually gathered up his papers and started to go outside.

Emelina called him back. "Wait a minute, Mason, before you run off, come show Codi your hand. Codi, could you take a look at his hand? There's some kind of bump on it. Do you mind?"

"Why would I mind? Let's have a look." I felt uncomfortable, not because she'd asked, but with myself, playing doctor. I *was* a doctor, technically, which is to say I had the training, but it unnerved me to think people saw me in that role. Both Emelina and Mason were quiet while I examined his hand. I bent the wrist back and forth and felt the lump on the tendon. "It's a ganglion."

"Is that bad?" Emelina asked.

"No, it's not serious at all. Just a little bump. Usually they go away on their own. Does it hurt, Mason?"

He shook his head. "Only when he has chores to do," Emelina offered.

I put a kiss on my fingertips and rubbed it into his wrist. "There you go, Dr. Codi's special cure." As he ran off it occurred to me, with a certain self-punitive malice, that this was the extent of special curing I was licensed to dispense.

"So what's it like up there at the high school?" Emelina asked. "Don't you keep feeling like Miss Lester's going to catch you smoking in the bathroom?"

"*I* never smoked in the bathroom," I said, scraping the bottom of the cereal bowl and wiping the baby's mouth with his bib. I'd never seen such efficient eating in my life.

"Oh that's right, Miss Goody Two-Shoes, I forgot. You didn't do things like that." Emelina smiled. She'd been at least as virtuous as I was in high school; the difference was she was popular. Virtue in a cheerleader is admirable, while in a wallflower it's gratuitous.

"Miss Goody Orthopedic-Shoes," I said.

She hooted. "*Why* on God's green earth did you and Hallie wear those shoes? I never did ask. I figured the polite thing was to just ignore them. Like when somebody has something hanging out of their nose."

"Thank you. We wore them because Doc Homer was obsessed with the bones of the foot."

"Kinky old Doc," she said, stabbing a wooden spoon into a pot of boiled potatoes.

"You have no idea. He used to sit us down and give us lectures on how women destroy their bodies through impractical footwear." I delivered his lecture, which Hallie and I used to ape behind his back: "Of the two hundred bones in the human body, more than a quarter are in the foot. It is a more complicated instrument than an automobile transmission, and it is treated with far less consideration."

Emelina was laughing. "Really, you have to give him credit. All my mom ever told me was 'Sit up straight! Don't get pregnant! And wear a slip!' "

"Doc Homer wasn't that great on pregnancy and underwear, but Lord knows the Noline girls were not going to have fallen arches."

"Where'd you get those god-awful things from? Not the Hollywood Shop, I know that."

"Mail order."

"No."

"Swear to God. Hallie and I used to burn the catalogues in the fireplace when they came but he'd still get those damn shoes. For the sizing he'd draw around our feet on a piece of paper and then take all these different measurements. I expect I spent more time with Doc Homer getting my foot measured than any other thing."

Emelina found this hilarious. I know she thought I was exaggerating, but I wasn't. In a way we were grateful for the attention, but the shoes were so appalling. They affected our lives, the two of us differently. Hallie just gave up trying for image, while I went the route of caring too much. It was harder for me, being the first to break into junior high, then high school, in these shoes. I suffered first and therefore more.

"I'm positive that was the whole reason I hardly ever had any dates in high school," I told Emelina.

"That's ridiculous," she said. "The only reason boys didn't ask you out was because they thought you were too good for them. You were so smart, why would you want to run with a Grace boy? That's what they thought."

The meeting in the living room was beginning to break up. We lowered our voices automatically.

"No," I said solemnly. "It was the shoes. It's a known fact. The day I left Grace I bought a pair of gladiator sandals and my sex life picked right up."

**Emelina eventually remembered** a letter for me she'd been carrying around a while. She'd stuck it in the diaper bag when she picked up the mail, and then forgotten it, so it suffered more in its last hundred yards of delivery than it had in its previous fifteen hundred miles. Of course, it was from Hallie.

I went home to read it, like a rat scurrying back to its hole with some edible prize. I settled into the living-room chair, polished my glasses, and scowled at the postmark: Chiapas, near Mexico's southern border, only days after she left. That was a disappointment, anything could have happened since then. I slit it open.

*Codi dear,*

*I've been driving the way you're supposed to here, like a bat out of hell, the wrong way out of hell whenever that's possible. I'm getting the hang of outlawry. You'd be proud. I burned up the road till around La Cruz and then slowed down enough to enjoy the banana trees going by in a blur. The tropics are such a gaudy joke: people have to live with every other kind of poverty, but a fortune in flowers, growing out of every nook and cranny of anything. If you could just build an economy on flowers. I stayed in a house that had vanilla orchids growing out of the glutters and a banana tree coming up under the kitchen sink. I swear. There were some kind of little animals too, like mongooses. You would know what they are. I'm happy to be in a jungle again. You know me, I'm always cheered by the sight of houseplants growing wild and fifty feet tall. I keep thinking about 626-BUGS and all those sad ladies trying to grow zebrinas in an arid climate.*

*I wanted to take the coast highway as far as Nayarit,*

where it gets rugged, but I paid the price for that little adventure. (Doc Homer would say: I paid a dollar for my shiny dime.) I broke, not bent but flat out busted an axle in Tuxpan and spent two days waiting around while a man with a Fanta delivery truck and time on his hands brought in a new one from Guadalajara. The only hotel was a two-story pension with live band (euphemism) on weekends. I spent the time mostly sitting on my balcony watching pelicans dive-bomb the sea, and remembering our trip to San Blas. Remember those pelicans? If you'd been there, in Tuxpan, it would have been fun. I couldn't bring myself to do anything productive—there were people I could have talked to about crops and the refugee scene, but instead I spent one whole morning watching a man walk up the beach selling shrimp door to door. He had a pole over his shoulders, with the bucket of shrimp hung on one side and on the other side a plastic jug of water. Every time he sold a kilo of shrimp he'd pour out that much water and drink it, to balance the load. I watched him all the way down the bay and thought, *I want to be like that.* Not like the man selling shrimp. Like his *machine.* To give myself over to utility, with no waste.

But I was useless, lying around those two days. Saving my strength for what's ahead, I guess. I get more jumpy as I move south, like a compass needle or something. Saw an awful lot of dead cropland in the interior, and I know it will be worse in Nicaragua. War brings out the worst in production agriculture.

Tomorrow I cross the border, but it's hard to say where the border is, because this whole part of Chiapas where I am now is camps of Guatemalans. This whole livelong day I drove horrible mountain roads in the rain and saw refugee camps, one after another like a dream. They say the Guatemalan army is on a new scorched-earth campaign, so people come running across the border with the clothes on their backs and their hearts in their throats and on a good day the Mexican cops don't bother them. On a bad day, they make them wake up the kids, take down their hammocks, and move into somebody else's district. It's a collective death. A whole land-based culture is being relocated out of its land—like a body trying to move out of its skin. Only the portable things survive. The women have their backstrap looms and woven clothes, like you see sometimes in import stores. All those brilliant colors in this hopeless place, it kills you.

Right this minute I'm sitting in the rain, waiting for the mail truck/water delivery (I keep expecting that same guy with his Fanta truck) and watching four barefoot kids around a cook fire. The one in charge is maybe six. She's sharpening cooking sticks while these damp black chickens strut around shaking themselves and the toddlers pull logs out and roll them to make sparks. I'm just on edge. You live your life in the States and you can't even picture something like this. It's easy to get used to the privilege of a safe life.

I know you're worrying but you don't have to, since we've established that I'm the luckiest person alive. Even though I don't feel like it. I'll write from Nica next. I'm sure I'll be happier once I'm put to some use. I miss you, Codi, write and make me feel better.

Love from your faithful adoring slave-for-life,

Hallie

The ending was an old joke: in our letters we used to try to outdo each other with ingratiating closures. The rest of the letter was pure Hallie. Even in a lethargic mood she noticed every vanilla orchid, every agony and ecstasy. Especially agony. She might as well not have had skin, where emotions were concerned. Other people's hurt ran right over into her flesh. For example: I'll flip through a newspaper and take note of the various disasters, and then Hallie will read the same paper and cry her eyes out. She'll feel like she has to *do* something about it. And me, if I want to do anything, it's to run hell for leather in the other direction. Maybe it's true what they say, that as long as you're nursing your own pain, whatever it is, you'll turn your back on others in the same boat. You'll want to believe the fix they're in is their own damn fault.

The strangest thing is that where pain seemed to have anesthetized me, it gave Hallie extra nerve endings. This haunts me. What we suffered in our lives we went through together, but somehow we came out different doors, on different ground levels.

**Friday night after** the first week of school, the dog with the green bandana showed up again at the gate. I saw it when I came outside after my solitary supper to water the morning glories and potted geraniums on my front step. The heat seemed to wilt them right down to death's door, but water always brought them back. I could only wish for such resilience.

"Hi, buddy," I said to the dog. "No barbecues today. You're out of luck."

Thirty seconds later Loyd was standing at the door with a bottle of beer. "I told you I'd get back to you with this," he said, grinning. "I'm a man of my word."

"Well, okay," I said. "I guess you are." I wasn't sure how I felt about seeing him in my doorway, other than surprised. I pulled a couple of folding chairs onto the patio, where we could see the sunset. The sky was a bright, artificial-looking orange, a color you might expect to see in the Hollywood Shop. "Are you going to have one too, or do I drink this alone?" I asked him.

Loyd said he'd just take a soda because he was marked up and five times out. I was mystified by this information.

"I'm marked up on the call board at the depot," he explained. "To take a train out. Five times out means I'm fifth in line. I'll probably get called late tonight or early tomorrow morning."

"Oh," I said. "It sounded like baseball scores. The count is three and two and it's the bottom of the seventh."

Loyd laughed. "I guess it would sound like that. You get used to talking railroad talk like it was plain English. Around here that's about all everybody does, is railroad."

"That, and watch the fruit fall off their trees."

Loyd looked at me, surprised. "You know about that, do you?"

"Not very much," I said. I went into my house to get him a soda, picking my way over the rough bricks of the patio because I was barefoot. I will say this much for Doc Homer's career as a father: my arches are faultless.

When I came back out I sat down and handed over a Coke, letting Loyd fight with the easy-off twist cap himself. I had to use pliers on those things. It didn't give Loyd two seconds of trouble. He palmed it, then tipped his head back and drank about half the bottle. The things that aggravate me most in the world are the things men do without even knowing it.

"So is that your dog?" I asked.

"That's Jack. You met? Jack, this lady here is Codi Noline."

"We've met," I said. "I sneaked him some goat spare ribs the other day at the fiesta. I hope he's not on a special diet or anything."

"He's in love, is what he is, if you gave him a piece of that goat. That was one of Angel Pilar's yearling billy goats. Jack's had his eye on those spare ribs ever since last summer."

Jack looked at me, panting seriously. His tongue was purplish, and his eyes were very dark brown and lively. Sometimes when you look into an animal's eyes you see nothing, no sign of connection, just the flat stare of a wild creature. But Jack's eyes spoke worlds. I liked him.

"He looks like a coyote," I said.

"He is. Half. I'll tell you the story of his life sometime."

"I can't wait," I said, really meaning it, though it came out sounding a little sarcastic. Our chairs were close enough together so that I could have reached over and squeezed Loyd's hand, but I didn't do that.

"It was nice of you to come by," I said.

"So this was your first week of school, right? How's life with the juvenile delinquents of Grace?"

I was a little bit flattered that he knew about my job. But then everybody would. "I don't know," I said. "Pretty scary, I think. I'll keep you posted."

The sky had faded from orange to pale pink, and the courtyard was dusky under the fig trees. Every night as it got dark the vegetation around the house seemed to draw itself in closer, hugging the whitewashed walls, growing dense as a jungle.

Loyd touched my forearm lightly and pointed. On the cliff above the courtyard wall, a pair of coyotes trotted along a narrow animal path. Jack's ears stood up and rotated like tracking dishes as we watched them pass.

"You know what the Navajos call coyotes? God's dogs," Loyd said. His fingers were still resting on my forearm.

"Why's that?" I asked.

He took his hand back and cracked his knuckles behind his head. He leaned back in his chair, stretching out his legs. "I don't know. I guess because they run around burying bones in God's backyard."

Jack got up and went to the courtyard wall. He stood as still as a rock fence except for one back leg, which trembled, betraying all the contained force of whatever it was he wanted to do just then, but couldn't. After a minute he came back to Loyd's feet, turned his body in a tight circle two or three times, and lay down with a soft moan.

"Why do they do that? Turn in circles like that?" I asked. I'd never lived with a dog and was slightly infatuated with Jack.

"Beating down the tall grass to make a nice little nest," Loyd said. "Even if there's no tall grass."

"Well, I guess that make sense, from a dog's point of view."

"Sure it does." He bent forward to scratch Jack between the ears.

"We take these good, smart animals and put them in a house and then wonder why they keep on doing the stuff that made them happy for a million years. A dog can't think that much about what he's doing, he just does what feels right."

We were both quiet for a while. "How do you know what the Navajos call coyotes? I thought you were Apache." I felt vaguely that it might be racist to discuss Loyd's breeding, but he didn't seem offended.

"I'm a lot of stuff," he said. "I'm a mongrel, like Jack. I was born up in Santa Rosalia Pueblo. My mama still lives up there. You ever been up there to Pueblo country?"

"No," I said.

"It's pretty country. You ought to go sometime. I lived up there when I was a little kid, me and my brother Leander. God, we ran wild all over that place."

"You have a brother? I never knew that."

"Twin," Loyd said. "He's dead."

Everybody's got a secret, I thought, and for the first time that evening I remembered the child of Loyd's that was unknown to him. It felt furtive and strange to hold it in mind in his presence, as if I were truly holding it, and he might see it.

A dust-colored peafowl hopped onto the courtyard wall and then into the fig, rustling the leaves and warning us off with a throaty, chirruping sound. She was awkward and heavy-bodied, no more flight-worthy than a helicopter.

"So you're Pueblo, and Apache, and Navajo," I said.

"My dad's Apache. We boys left Mama and came down to White Mountain to live with him, but it didn't work out. I ended up in Grace with my mama's sister. You knew my *tía* Sonia, right?"

"I don't think so. Is she still around?"

"No. She's gone back to Santa Rosalia. I need to go up there and see her and Mama one of these days."

It sounded like a strangely scattered family. I still wasn't clear on the Navajo connection.

"Can I use your phone?" he asked suddenly.

"Sure. It might be in use, it's Emelina's and J.T.'s phone. They just ran an extension out for me."

He looked toward the main house as he ducked into my front door. Emelina and J.T. were both home tonight, and Loyd seemed a little guilty about not going over to say hello. It would have been easy for him to come by on the pretense of visiting them, but he hadn't. I wondered if Loyd still had a reputation as a ladies' man. Though it was nothing to me, one way or the other. Jack raised his head and peered at me through the darkness, then got up and moved slightly closer to me. I stretched my leg and rubbed his back with my bare foot. His coat was a strange blend of textures: wiry on top and soft, almost downy underneath.

Hallie and I almost had a dog once, back when our Tucson house was on the underground railroad. Hallie had come home one night with a refugee woman and child and a little cinnamon dog. The mother had been tortured and her eyes offered out that flatness, like a zoo animal. But I remember the girl, in a short pink dress and corduroy pants, following that puppy under the bathroom sink and all over the house. I had no reason to believe, now, that any of the three was still living. The woman and her daughter were eventually arrested and sent back to tropical, lethal San Salvador. And we'd decided realistically that we didn't have room for a dog, so it went to the Humane Society. Terms like that, "Humane Society," are devised with people like me in mind, who don't care to dwell on what happens to the innocent.

Loyd came back out, being careful not to slam the decrepit screen door. "I'm next in line," he said. "Three guys ahead of me laid off to watch the Padres game. I better get home." Jack got up instantly and went to his side.

"Well, thanks," I said, still thinking of the cinnamon dog. I held up my bottle. "It's nice to see you again, Loyd."

He stood there grinning, the fingers of his right hand playing with Jack's nape. I didn't know quite how to finish off the evening. Loyd hesitated and then said, "I've got to drive up to Whiteriver, a week from Saturday. To see about something."

"Well, that sounds mysterious," I said.

"To see about some game birds. Anyway I thought you might like to get out of here for some fresh air. You want to go?"

I took a deep breath. "Sure," I said. I wasn't sure at all, but my mind had apparently made itself up. "Okay. I could use some fresh air."

Loyd gave a funny little nod, and went out through the gate. Jack disappeared behind him into the cactus jungle.

# HOMERO

# 10

# The Mask

He is lying on his own examining table, resting his eyes. The telephone buzzes quietly but Mrs. Quintana, his receptionist, has given up the battle with insurance forms and gone home.

He places his long hands over his face, the fingertips lightly touching his forehead, thumbs resting on the maxillary bones beneath his eyes. His office in the hospital basement is cool even in this late-September heat, and pleasant in winter as well. As practical and comforting as a cave. The lack of windows has never been a problem; artificial lighting is adequate. He has just examined his last patient of the day, a sixteen-year-old with six small gold rings piercing the cartilage of her left ear. She is expecting twins. They will be born small, and in trouble. There was no reason to tell her everything.

He imagines the procedure by which the tiny gold wires were inserted through flesh and spongy bone. It would have to be painful. He is mystified. Children devote slavish attention to these things, but can't be bothered with prophylactics.

He drifts between wakefulness and sleep, thinking of Codi. Her eyes are downturned and secretive, her heart clearly hardened against him already, to have done this. Her hair is in her eyes. She flips it sideways, chewing the inside of her lip and looking out the window when he talks to her. She'd wanted pierced ears at thirteen; he'd explained that self-mutilation was preposterous and archaic. Now they discuss shoes. He wants to ask, "Do you know what you have inside you? Does your sister know?" Hallie is young to understand reproductive matters but it's impossible that she wouldn't know, they're so much of a single mind, and he is outside of it completely. He has no idea what he can say.

She's in the fifth or sixth month, from the look of her, although Codi was always too thin and now is dangerously thin, and so skillful at disguising it with her clothes he can only tell by other signs. The deepened pigmentation under her eyes and across the bridge of her nose, for one thing, is identical to the mask of pregnancy Alice wore both times, first with Codi, then with Hallie. It stuns him. He feels a sharp pain in his spleen when he looks across the breakfast table each morning and sees this: his wife's face. The ghost of their happiest time returned to inhabit the miserable body of their child. He can't help feeling he has damaged them all, just by linking them together. His family is a web of women dead and alive, with himself at the center like a spider, driven by different instincts. He lies mute, hearing only in the tactile way that a spider hears, touching the threads of the web with long extended fingertips and listening. Listening for trapped life.

# COSIMA

# 11

# A River on
# the Moon

Loyd and I didn't go to Whiteriver. He was called
out on Friday for a seven-day stand on a switch engine in Lordsburg.
He seemed disappointed and promised we'd go another time. Loyd
didn't have much seniority on the railroad; he'd only moved back to
Grace a few years earlier, and at Southern Pacific he was still getting
what he called "bumped" a lot. It was hard to plan his time off.

I was somewhat relieved. I'd been unsure of what I was getting
into, and had my doubts. Once I found out, I had more.

I'd asked J.T. what "game birds" were. He and I were out working in the old plum orchard one evening, pruning dead branches out
of the trees. My job was mainly to stay out of the way of falling timber. It was a fair distance from the house, and Emelina had asked if
I could go along to keep an eye on him. She wasn't the type to worry,
but a man hanging from the treetops wielding a chainsaw is a nerve-
racking sight, believe me. Even if he isn't your husband.

J.T. informed me that game birds were fighting cocks. He was taking a break just then, leaning on one hand against a tree trunk and drinking what seemed like gallons of water.

I was stunned. "You mean like cockfights."

J.T. smiled. "You been talking to Loyd?"

"He invited me to go with him up to Whiteriver. He said something about game birds, and . . ." I laughed at myself. "I don't know, I was thinking of something you'd eat. Cornish hens."

He laughed too. He offered me the jar of water and I drank from it before handing it back. I was surprised at the easy intimacy I felt with J.T. We hadn't been friends in high school—he was, after all, captain of the football team. Through no meanness on his part, but simply because of the natural laws of adolescent segregation, we might as well have gone to high school on different planets. Being neighbors again now brought back what we'd forgotten then: we had a relationship that dated back even before Emelina. We were next-door neighbors in toddlerhood. We'd played together before male and female had meaning.

He turned up the glass jar and drank it to the bottom, tensing the muscles in his jaw when he swallowed. J.T.'s whole body shone with sweat. I briefly imagined him naked, which disturbed me. I'd slept with someone's husband before—an Asian history professor in college—mistaking his marital status for something comforting and fatherly. But I was devoted to Emelina. No, that wouldn't happen.

It was early October, and still hot. Grace was supposed to have the perfect climate, like Camelot or Hawaii, and it's true that growing up here I could hardly remember an uncomfortable day, temperature-wise. Most of the homes had neither air-conditioning nor central heating, and didn't need them, but this fall had turned into hell warmed over. Down in the desert, in Tucson, every day was in the hundred-and-teens and the TV weathermen were reporting the string of broken records almost proudly, like scores in a new sport. In Grace no one kept track especially, but we suffered just the same.

J.T. knelt down to start the chainsaw again, but I spoke up before he could yank the cord. "I thought cockfighting was illegal."

"Most everywhere it is, but not in the state of Arizona. And up on the reservation they've got their own laws. Loyd's not a criminal, if that's what you're asking."

"I guess I don't know what I'm asking. I just can't see Loyd and cockfighting."

"His daddy was real big in the sport. He was kind of a legend up there in Apache country."

"So Loyd's got to keep up the tradition," I said, without sympathy. I knew Loyd's father was also a renowned drunk.

J.T. asked, "You an animal lover?"

"Not to extremes," I said. "I eat them." I thought of how unmoved I'd been watching Emelina chop off heads for our Sunday dinner, that first day in Grace. "But watching animals kill each other for sport," I said tentatively, "that's kind of an unsavory business, isn't it?" I looked toward the edge of the orchard. It was getting dark fast. Already I could see moonlight reflected in the irrigation ditches.

J.T. sat on his heels and looked straight up into the branches over our heads. "I don't know why I mess with these trees," he said. "They're sixty years old. They don't produce worth a damn anymore. I could cut them down and get a lot better out of this ground, not to mention the firewood. But my daddy gave me this orchard." He picked up the stone of a plum, weathered shiny white like a tooth, and rubbed it with his thumb. After a minute he raised his arm with a quick overhand snap and threw it toward the river. "Loyd's old man didn't have one damn thing to give him but cockfighting." J.T. looked at me. "I'm not crazy about it either, Codi. But you've got to know Loyd before you decide."

**I dropped the subject** of cockfighting. Loyd had begun to come by fairly regularly in the evenings, which is to say regular for a railroad man: I'd see him three days in a row, and then not at all for a week. It reinforced the feeling that we were only casual acquaintances, meeting nearly by accident, and I tried to limit my expectations to the point where I paid no attention to how I looked in the evenings. Sometimes as I walked around the brick floors of my living room and bedroom I'd realize I was listening for the jingle of Jack's tags, and then I'd click on the radio.

When Loyd did show up we would drag our lawn chairs out for a view of the sun's parting shot at the canyon wall, and we'd talk about nothing in particular. For instance, he told me the story of Jack's life. Jack's mother was a coyote that Loyd took in when he was living up on the Apache reservation. She'd been crippled with buckshot in her shoulder, and had gone into heat. Loyd saw her one night skirting the arroyo behind his house, trying to get away from a pack of males. He got her attention with a low whistle, and then he left his front door open and went to bed; next morning, she was curled up under his cot.

I didn't question this. For one thing, he seemed to hold a power over females of all types. But truly Loyd had the most unselfconscious way of telling a story I'd ever heard, as if it didn't matter whether I was impressed or not, he was just going to give me the facts. It seemed as if he didn't care enough, one way or the other, to lie.

"I kept her shut up in the house for a week with my dad's old dog, Gunner. Gunner lost one of his back legs when he was a pup and he could get around real good, but he'd never in his life mounted a female. I thought she'd be safe with him."

This matter-of-fact talk about heat and mounting made me slightly edgy, or rather, edgy once-removed. I felt like I *ought* to be uneasy with Loyd, but I wasn't. To him it was life and death and dogs. Sometimes Loyd seemed about twelve.

"Well, Jack is here to tell the tale," I said. "So I guess she wasn't safe."

Loyd smiled. "Nope. Old Gunner had his one chance at love. He got into some poisoned coyote bait right after that. He died before the pups were born."

"How do you know they were his? She could have been pregnant already."

Loyd asked Jack, as politely as you'd ask a favor from a friend, to roll over. "See that?" Over Jack's heart was a white patch with a black crescent moon in its center. "That's Gunner's. There were seven pups, two black and five brown, and every one of them had that badge."

"How did you know which one to keep?"

He hesitated. "Dad decided," he said finally. "And Jack. Really I guess Jack's the one that decided."

They were nothing electrifying, these chats with Loyd in the dark, but they were a relief from my days at the high school, which were spent in a standoff just shy of open war. Occasionally Loyd took the tips of my fingers and rubbed them absentmindedly between his own, the way he would surely stroke Jack, if Jack had fingers. The night of the story of Jack, he also kissed me before he left, and I was surprised by how I responded. Kissing Loyd was delicious, like some drug I wanted more of in spite of the Surgeon General's warning. Later on, when I slept, I had dreams of coyotes in heat.

I also saw Hallie. Her hair moved around her like something alive. "I've kissed a man who kills birds," I confessed, but she looked past me as if she didn't have a sister. Her eyes were pale as marbles. I woke up confused, too shaken to get up and turn on a light.

I'd dreamt of Carlo, too, on several occasions, for no good reason I could see. He'd written me a letter that was fairly medical and devoid of passion. He did miss me, though, and that sentiment brought comfort as I lay in my empty bed. It meant I was lonely by choice, or by difficult circumstances such as an ailing father; these things are supposed to feel better than being lonely because nobody wants you. Lately I'd started thinking about Carlo with a kind of romantic wistfulness, which I knew was bogus. The truth is, we'd essentially promised each other from the beginning that we wouldn't stay together. "No strings," we said, proving that we were mature medical students without spare time. The odd thing is that we did stay together, physically, and so I suppose falling out of love was our hearts' way of keeping the bargain. The end was always curled up there between us, like a sleeping cat, present even in our lovemaking.

Especially there. Carlo and I had gone to bed together for the
first time one early dawn during our rotation in pediatric intensive
care, after we'd worked all night trying to save a Papago baby
brought in too late from the reservation. We'd gone straight from the
dead baby to my apartment, my bed. There was hardly any talk that
I remembered, we just held on to each other, joined, for as long as
our bodies could stand it. I wanted anything that would stop that
pain, and Carlo was strong medicine. Not happiness, nothing joyful,
only medicine.

There was one other time of desperate, feverish connection that
I particularly remembered. This was much later, when Carlo and I
were living abroad. Carlo had been granted the opportunity to spend
a year in an unbelievably remote clinic, halfway up the tallest mountain in central Crete.

The work was rugged, but in December we took a trip away from
the village, to Venice. The clinic closed for some combination of
clan ritual and Greek Orthodox holiday that practically evacuated
the village. We set off for Italy feeling like truant school kids, drinking wine in tin cups on the train and reeling with the heady sense of
getting away with something. Before that he'd scarcely managed an
afternoon off, much less a week. Then Carlo came down with a cold
on the overnight ferry to Brindisi, and by the time we reached
Venice we were both burning up, our skin hot to the touch, like fur-
naces. Our bodies' internal combustion gave rise to an unquench-
able craving for carbohydrates, and for each other, so we checked
into the *Penzione Meraviglioso* and for a week ate plates of pasta and
made a kind of sweaty, delirious love previously unknown to either
of us, in a bed that was memorably soft and huge.

The *Penzione* looked out onto the cold, damp Grand Canal and
a dim little plaza ominously named the Piazza of the Distraught
Widows. (Distraught or Inconvenienced, it could translate either
way.) The origin of this name was unknown to the elderly matron,
who was born and raised in the building. She brought food up to us
and was alternately scandalized by our appetites and worried for our
well-being. She was of the opinion that in damp weather any illness

at all would find its way to the lungs. She ventured to tell us we ought to see a doctor.

Carlo spoke Italian. His father had come to America on a steamer carrying cured leather and Chianti. He explained in grammatically imperfect but polite terms that we were both doctors. We could not be in better hands, he said. For my benefit, later, he'd translated the double entendre. By the end of the week, Carlo and the matron were bosom friends. In spite of his notorious shyness, whenever she brought us hot tea he would sit up in bed with a shirt on and give opinions on the infertility of her eldest daughter and the lung ailment of her son-in-law who worked in the glassblowing trade. I lay beside him, meanwhile, with the sheets pulled around my neck, feeling sinful and out of place, like a whore taken home to meet Mother. The matron didn't ask for my opinions, probably because she didn't believe I was actually a doctor. Which I wasn't, technically. I did some work at the clinic—rural Crete was not overly concerned about licensure—but to be completely honest, I was Carlo's paramour. I did the shopping. I learned the Greek words for oil and soap and bread.

I know that a woman's ambitions aren't supposed to fall and rise and veer off course this way, like some poor bird caught in a storm. All I can say is, at one of the many junctures in my life when I had to sink or swim, Crete was an island, a place to head for, new and far away. I had just dropped out of medicine in my first year of residency, a few months shy of becoming a licensed M.D. I'd discovered there was something serious, mainly a matter of nerve and perhaps empathy, that stood in my way. I learned all this while a baby was trying to be born feet first. I couldn't think how I was going to tell Doc Homer, and I'll admit I was attracted just then to the idea of putting an ocean between myself and that obelisk of disapproval. It also helped that Carlo really wanted me to go with him. But I had no mission beyond personal survival; it was nothing like Hallie's going to Nicaragua. Our village had its own kind of bleakness, the bones and stones of poverty, but the landscape was breathtaking. Our classmates were treating intestinal parasites in Niger and Haiti, black lung in Appalachia, while Carlo and I set broken legs on the steep slope of Mount Ida, mythical birthplace of Zeus. Poverty in a beautiful place seemed not so much oppressive as sublime. Basically it's the stuff of the world's great religions, I told myself, although I knew better.

**It was 100 degrees** in the shade, and the burgeoning minds of Biology I and II took a field trip to the river; our putative goal was to get some samples of water to examine under the microscope. We were learning about the plant and animal kingdoms, starting right down at the bottom of the ladder with the protozoans and the blue-green algae. I could easily have collected a gallon of river water myself and brought it in, but the school had no airconditioning and I'm not completely without a heart. I'd played it tough with the kids long enough to prove my point, if there was one, and I was tired of it. We all were.

I knew the trip to the river would turn into a party. I didn't try too hard to go against nature. The tall kid with the skinhead haircut, whose name was Raymo, was the first one to get wet up to his T-shirt. It took about ninety seconds. I only drew the line when boys started throwing in girls against their will.

"Okay, knock it off, scientists, Marta says she doesn't want to get wet," I said. Marta shot me a lipstick-red pout when they put her down, but she'd shrieked "No" and I felt there was a lesson to be learned here, all the way around.

"I've got a ton of sample bottles here, so let's get going." I sat a safe distance up the riverbank under an ash tree, labeling full bottles as they were brought to me. I'd suggested that they collect shallow and deep water, moving and stagnant, but they went far beyond this, collecting anything that moved. It was enough to make you believe in the hunting instinct. There was a low, grassy island in the middle of the riffle, and several kids were out there on their knees catching bugs and frogs. Raymo actually caught a six-inch perch with a net fashioned from his T-shirt. "Sooner or later I figure we'll get around to fish," he said. "A fish is an animal, right?"

"Right," I said, and let him dump it, along with the frogs, into a mop bucket we'd cajoled from the janitor. I don't know what teaching in a big-city school is like, but at Grace High we were flexible about interdepartmental appropriations.

Back in the lab, we rounded up all the creatures visible to the naked eye and made a home for them in an aquarium that had once held blue and orange Ping-Pong balls used for some mystical experiment in physics. Marta and two other cheerleaders disposed of the Ping-Pong balls and took over the terrarium project. They made a pond on one side for the fish, and an admirable mossy island on the other side, complete with a beach, and a cave they called the Motel Frog. They refused to deal directly with the clients, though. Raymo transferred the fish and frogs (with his bare hands) from the mop bucket.

The next day we got out the microscopes. The kids groaned, preferring to do experiments on the frogs. It's hard to get people interested in animals that have no discernible heads, tails, fins, or the like—and plants, forget it. There's no drama. You just don't have the skulking and stalking and gobbling up of innocent prey in the plant world. They don't even eat, except in the most passive sense. In college I knew a botany professor who always went around saying, "It takes a superior mind to appreciate a plant." Hallie and I were a case in point, I guess. We divided the world in half, right from childhood. I was the one who went in for the instant gratification, catching bright, quick butterflies, chloroforming them in a Mason jar and pinning them onto typewritten tags with their Latin names. Hallie's tastes were quieter; she had time to watch things grow. She transplanted wildflowers and showed an aptitude for gardening. At age ten she took over the responsibility of the Burpee's catalogue.

But now I was on my own in the Garden of Eden. I was expected to teach the entire living world to these kids. I would write Hallie and ask her advice on how to turn adolescents on to organisms that have no appreciable sex life. In the meantime we were doing protozoans, which I could handle. I drew huge, fantastic pictures in colored chalk of what we could expect to see in this river water: strands of Nostoc like strings of blue pearls; multi-tentacled hydras; rotifers barreling into each other like hyperactive kids. I demonstrated the correct way to put a drop of water on a glass slide, coverslip it, and focus the scope. The lab grew quiet with concentration.

They couldn't see anything. At first I was irritated but bit my tongue and focused a scope myself, prepared to see the teeming microscopic world of a dirty river. I found they were right, there was nothing. It gave me a strange panic to see that stillness under powerful magnification. Our water was dead. It might as well have come from a river on the moon.

**For homework I assigned** my classes the task of being spies. They were to find out from their parents what the hell was going on with this river. The pH, which we tested, from some areas came in just a hair higher than battery acid. I couldn't believe the poisoning from the mine had gone this far. Protozoans are the early-warning system in the life of a river, like a canary in a mine. And this canary was dead. We took a closer look at Raymo's perch (named Mr. Bad Fish) and the frogs in the terrarium, which seemed in reasonably good health. But then, they'd been awfully easy to catch.

"It can't be legal," I lamented to Viola as we sat on the front porch with three of the boys and four grocery bags of snap beans. Emelina and John Tucker were in the kitchen canning as fast as we could snap. When it came to childbearing and gardening, Emelina seemed unable to walk the path of moderation.

"It's not legal," Viola said grumpily. "What difference does it make?"

We worked in silence for a while. The aluminum bowl between us rang like a bell when we threw our hard green beans against its sides. Mason hadn't managed to master the art of snap beans and had fallen asleep in the glider. The twins elbowed each other like irritable birds on a wire. Viola had been overseeing the boys in the garden most of the morning, and for once seemed tired. She was wearing lavender stretch pants, an embroidered blouse, and a base-ball cap with the insignia of the Steelworkers' Union. J.T.'s father had worked in the smelter for forty years, from age eighteen until he died of lung cancer. The cap sat forward on Viola's head because her long hair was pinned in a thick circle at the back. According to Emelina, Viola felt the boys were losing touch with their past, but looking at her now I couldn't get a fix on what that past might be. I thought of the Elvis whiskey bottle collection up in her room. I didn't really know Viola the way I knew Emelina and J.T. and the kids. She was always skirting around the edges of rooms with her hands full, just ready to go somewhere, too busy to sit down and talk.

"They'll have to pay a fine if they don't stop polluting the river," I said cheerfully. "The EPA will shut them down if they don't clean it up." At Emelina's urging, I'd gone down to the courthouse and filed an affidavit with local authorities on the pH and biotic death of the river. I used the most scientific language I could muster, such as "biotic death" and "oxygen load." I'd written Hallie about it.

Viola said without looking up, "They're just going to divert the river."

"What?"

She bent over with a soft groan and took another double handful of beans out of the grocery bag between her legs, and set them into her apron. Curtis and Glen had stopped hitting each other for the moment and were having a race. It took them forever to snap any beans because they had to stop every two minutes to count who had done the most.

"Dam up the river," Viola said. "That's all they have to do to meet with the EPA laws. Dam it up and send it out Tortoise Canyon instead of down through here. The EPA just says they can't put it down here where people live."

"But then there would be *no* water for the orchards. That would be worse than the way it is now."

"That's right. But it's okey-dokey with the EPA. The men all had a town meeting about it yesterday, with this hot-shot guy from

Phoenix. They sat and talked for about nine or ten hours and finally what he told them is if Black Mountain dams up the river, it's out of the jurisdiction of the Environmental Protection Agency." Viola reeled out the long words scornfully, as if she were glad to get them out of her mouth.

"That's impossible," I said. "There are water rights."

"Nobody around here's got water rights. All these families sold the water rights to the company in 1939, for twenty-five cents an acre. We all thought we were getting money for nothing. We had us a *fiesta*."

I stared at her. "So do you know for sure that's what they're going to do? Divert the river?"

She shrugged. "Who knows what anybody is going to do for sure? We could all die tomorrow. Only the Lord knows."

I wanted to shake her. I wished she would look me in the eye. "But this is what you've *heard* is going to happen?"

She nodded once, never taking her eyes off the snap beans that flew through her hands and rang freshly broken into the aluminum bowl.

I still couldn't believe it. "How could they do that?"

"With bulldozers," Viola said.

**Loyd and I made** another date for Whiteriver, this time on a Sunday in October. The evening before, I went with Emelina to hear Chicken Scratch music at the outdoor restaurant run by Doña Althea's four daughters. The same traveling Waila bands had been coming over from the Papago reservation for decades, substituting sons for fathers so gradually that the music never changed. Emelina's normal taste ran to Country—Merle Haggard and Dolly Parton; but Waila was something special, she said, she was crazy about it. Her boys, enlightened by MTV, rolled their eyes. She took Mason and the baby with us because, as Emelina put it, they were too little to have a choice.

The restaurant was outdoors, in a walled courtyard that was a larger, more baroque version of Emelina's. Flowers bloomed every-where out of pots shaped like pigs and squatty roosters, some of which had lost body parts, and two enormous old olive trees sparkled with tiny Christmas lights that evidently knew no season. Carved out here and there in the thick adobe wall were rounded niches that were home to weather-worn saints the size of a G.I. Joe; some, in fact, looked suspiciously like dolls in saints' clothing. In a corner, near where the band was setting up, stood a four-foot-tall, almost comically thin St. Francis of Assisi. He looked venerable and tired (also hungry), and was surrounded by a postmodern assortment of glazed ceramic and plastic birds.

The tables and chairs were of every imaginable type, following the same theme, and the flatware too—like snowflakes, no two alike. The effect was completely festive, in spite of Doña Althea's daughters. All four of them (who each had *Althea* lodged somewhere in her name) were over sixty, as thin as St. Francis but without his animal magnetism. They moved through the crowd with efficient scowls, taking orders and bringing out heavenly food from the little kitchen, all the while acting as though they couldn't quite under-stand why they'd agreed to go to all this trouble. You would think they'd have figured it out by now. It had been the most popular restaurant in town for half a century.

With tender, paternal attention the Alvaro Brothers unwrapped their musical instruments, which traveled in comfort, nestled in bright-blocked quilts. The men appeared to be three generations, rather than actual brothers. The elder Alvaro, dressed in cowboy boots and a formal Western shirt, cradled a gunmetal saxophone that reminded me of World War II planes. A middle-aged Alvaro with shoulder-length hair played accordion, and two boys in T-shirts played bass guitar and drums. The old sax player stepped up to the microphone. "We are the Alvaro Brothers," he said. "If we make too much noise, let us know."

It was the last time any of them smiled. From the instant they began to play, they stood motionless with their mouths turned down in concentration. Everybody else was dancing in their seats. Chicken

Scratch music is Mexican-spiced Native American polka. It sounds like a wild, very happy, and slightly drunken wedding party, and it moves you up and down; you can't keep still. A line of older women in dark skirts and blouses, possibly Alvaro Sisters or Alvaro Wives, stood near the kitchen, swaying a little and tapping their feet. Several couples began to dance, and I could tell Emelina was itching to join them, but she held herself back. Mason showed no such restraint. He was out of his seat in no time, front and center, jumping in circles and running into people's legs. The younger people moved aside when the Papago women moved out from the wall and began to do the traditional six-step dance. They moved in a loose line, slightly bent over, shuffling over the gravel and sounding—if not looking—exactly like the scratching hens that give the music its name.

The place was packed. It took forever to get served and there were some mixed-up orders, and nobody cared. The music was so buoyant. One of the Althea sisters actually cracked a smile. After forty-five minutes the bass player plucked his lit cigarette from the bridge of his guitar and the Alvaros took a break.

Emelina told me she and J.T. had come here on their first date. They were fourteen. Viola had come too, but fortunately she spent the whole time in the kitchen advising Doña Althea on the *menudo,* Viola's specialty. J.T. was thus able to eat his whole meal with one hand on Emelina's knee, under the table.

"Just think," I said. "If you'd come on another night, the soup of the day would have been something else and you and J.T. might never have gotten married."

She smiled an odd little smile. "I don't think there's anybody else in this town I could have married but J.T. It was like we had each other's names printed on us when we were born."

"Seems like there's a lot of that in this town."

"Oh, yeah. And people do what their parents did. The father's a hoghead, the son's a hoghead."

I smiled. "What's a hoghead?"

"Locomotive engineer. I don't know why they call them that."

She pecked her fingertips on the tabletop, watching the Papago women talking to the musicians.

For a while I'd believed that Emelina and J.T., with their congenial partnership and all those miles between them, were like Carlo and me, parallel lines that never quite touched. I was wrong. Two nights before when J.T. came home at 3 A.M. they made love in the moonlit courtyard, urgently, with some of their clothes on. My house was dark but I was awake, invisible in my kitchen. I felt abandoned. Emelina was nothing like me.

"It's dangerous," she said suddenly. "Shit, you can't think about it but it's hell, the railroad. Did you know Fenton Lee, in high school?"

"Sure."

"He was in a head-on wreck two years ago. Bringing his train out of the yard in El Paso, at night, and somebody else was coming in, lined for the same track. Nobody knows why. Maybe a signal failed. Southern Pacific says no. But J.T. says it happens."

"So Fenton was killed?" I remembered him plainly, in horn-rim glasses. He had blond bangs and a loud laugh.

"Yeah, it was real bad. They heard the crash all over the yard. The one engine climbed up the other one and sheared off the top. There wasn't a whole lot left."

I felt numb. A train wreck and Fenton dead in it were beyond what I was willing to imagine.

"You can jump off, when you see that coming," Emelina told me. "Fenton's brakeman and conductor jumped off, and the other crew did, but Fenton stayed on. I guess he didn't really believe it. I told J.T., 'If you ever see a headlight coming at you, don't you dare save the train. You get your butt out of there.' "

The band started up again and Emelina's mood quickly lifted. Our food arrived and Mason snapped back to the table. Emelina resettled the baby in the rickety high chair. "So you're going up to the rez with Loyd tomorrow," she said, her eyes twinkling. "This is getting serious. If I was your mother I'd tell you to wear garlic around your neck." She dipped the tip of her spoon into her refried beans and fed it to the baby. He took the spicy brown mush like manna from heaven. "But since I'm not your mother," she said soberly, "I'd advise you to wear nice-looking underwear."

She embarrassed me. "It's nothing serious," I said. "We're not exactly couple material, are we? Me and Loyd-with-one-L."

She looked up, surprised. "He can't help how his name's spelled." She paused a minute, studying me. "What, you think Loyd's dumb?"

Now I had embarrassed myself. "No, I don't think that. I just can't see myself with a guy that's into cockfighting."

I'm sure Emelina suspected this was nowhere near the whole truth. She was thinking I did hold Loyd's misspelled name against him, and a lot of other things. That I couldn't see myself with a roughneck Apache hoghead who was her husband's best friend. I felt myself blush. I was just like Doc Homer, raising himself and Hallie and me up to be untouched by Grace.

"I'll tell you something, honey," Emelina said, pausing her spoon midway enroute to the baby's open mouth. "Half the women in this town, and not just the single ones, would give up Sunday breakfast to go to Whiteriver in that little red truck."

"I know that," I said, paying attention to my enchiladas. I didn't know how to apologize to Emelina without owning up to something I wasn't sure I felt. Strictly speaking, I didn't think I was better than Loyd and half the women in Grace. I was amazed, in fact, by Loyd's interest in me. I also didn't think it would last very long.

Emelina directed her energies back to mothering. "Mason, honey, don't pull all that stuff out with your fingers," she shouted affectionately above the music, which had risen in pitch. "I know it's stringy. I'll cut it up for you." She reached across the table, expertly dissecting Mason's chicken burro.

For some reason I glanced up at the baby, whose eyes and mouth were wide. Something was severely wrong. He wasn't breathing. I knocked over my chair getting to him. I reached my finger into his throat and felt something, but couldn't dislodge it. He made a voiceless gag. I stood behind his chair and pulled him up by the armpits, folded him over my left arm, and gave him four quick whacks between the shoulder blades. Then I rolled him over so he was face up and wide-eyed but still head down; supporting his head with my right hand, I tucked two fingertips under his breastbone and poked hard. A small, hard, whole pinto bean shot out of his mouth like a bullet.

The whole operation took maybe thirty seconds. Emelina picked the bean up off the table and looked at me. Her face was ashen as the baby's.

"He was choking," I said dumbly, laying him carefully on the table. "That's the only way you can get something out of the windpipe when it's in that far."

He lay still for about half a minute, breathing but still looking gray, and then he coughed twice and began to scream. His face turned rosy purple. Several women from nearby tables had whipped the napkins off their laps and were crowding in close around us. The music stopped. Emelina stared at her son like he was something she hadn't ordered, set down on the table.

"It's okay to pick him up," I said. "He'll be sore in the ribs, but he's okay."

She held him against her shoulder. He was still shrieking, and I don't think there was a person in the restaurant now who wasn't staring at us. At me, actually. Emelina looked up with enormous eyes, as if I were one of the saints in the wall: Our Lady of Blocked Windpipes. She wiped tears off her chin with the back of her hand.

"It's no big deal," I said.

It really wasn't. I'd just done what I knew how to do.

**Emelina begged me** to sleep in the house with them that night, in case he stopped breathing again. There was no reason in the world for that to happen, and I told her so. But she was quietly beside herself. J.T. had left for El Paso that morning, for two weeks this time because of some mess about the derailment. Viola was out late at another so-called "emergency meeting" of her women's club. I think Emelina felt lonely, or vulnerable—afraid of the simple fact that life held possibilities she couldn't handle alone. It must have been a rare experience for Emelina, and I felt for her. While we were making up a bed for me in the baby's room, I stopped and hugged her. She held on to me like a child.

I knew better than to expect sleep. I lay curled on my side, listening in spite of myself to the baby's soft exhaled breaths, and I kept turning my mind away from the one thought that kept coming back to me, persistent as an unwanted lover's hand, that I'd saved a life.

I thought about Loyd instead. I knew nothing about where we were going tomorrow; I hadn't seen that country. My mind turned over various expectations, none of which I recognized as my own. Who did I think I was, and what did I want from an Apache cockfighter with a misspelled name? His body, yes. But I couldn't take that risk, and end up needing more.

At some time in my life I'd honestly hoped love would rescue me from the cold, drafty castle I lived in. But at another point, much earlier I think, I'd quietly begun to hope for nothing at all in the way of love, so as not to be disappointed. It works. It gets to be a habit.

A pack of coyotes set up a sudden racket near the house, yipping and howling, so close by they sounded like they had us surrounded. When a hunting pack corners a rabbit they go into a blood frenzy, making human-sounding screams. The baby sighed and stirred in his crib. At seven months, he was just the size of a big jackrabbit—the same amount of meat. The back of my scalp and neck prickled. It's an involuntary muscle contraction that causes that, setting the hair follicles on edge; if we had manes they would bristle exactly like a growling dog's. We're animals. We're born like every other mammal and we live our whole lives around disguised animal thoughts. There's no sense pretending. Tomorrow, I thought, or the next day, or the day after that, I would have sex with Loyd Peregrina.

# 12

# Animal Dreams

On Sunday morning I put on jeans, changed into a denim dress, then back into jeans again, feeling stupid. I can get into a mood where I annoy myself no end. At the moment when I got completely fed up and stopped caring, I had on jeans and a white cotton shirt and silver earrings, so that's what I wore. And yes, I'll admit it, nice underwear.

I waited on the porch and was relieved when Loyd pulled up before Emelina's household had roused. It was a little odd, living with a family that paid attention to my social life.

Jack stood up to greet me from the back of the pickup and I rubbed his ears. "I brought lunch," I told Loyd, sliding into the cab with a basket Emelina had helped pack the night before.

He smiled wonderfully. "That's mighty white of you."

I didn't know what to make of that. It was something people said, but usually when they said it both people were white.

I asked him to detour past the Post Office so I could check for mail. There was no regular mail delivery in Grace, probably on humanitarian grounds. A daily route up these stairstep streets would have put some postal employee into a cardiac high-risk category. Every family had a box at the P.O., which they could check daily or annually, as they pleased. Emelina leaned toward annual. I persuaded her to turn over the key to me; I was the only member of the household expecting mail.

The mailboxes were built right into the outside wall of the Post Office. I peeked through the little window of the Domingos family drawer and saw the striped margin of an airmail envelope.

"Hallie!" I called to Loyd, waving the envelope as I bounced back to the truck. He didn't seem to register. "My sister Hallie. In Nicaragua." I checked the postmark to make sure this was true, and it was. Mailed nearly three weeks ago. The stamps, two alike, were bright and beautiful, carrying across oceans and continents a child-like revolutionary hopefulness: a painting of a woman picking red coffee beans, and her baby strapped on her back. Hallie was in the fields of her dreams.

I ripped it open and read quickly. She'd arrived mid-September, was fine, got my letters, she spent a few days in Managua and then backtracked straight to the rural area near Chinandega. She'd expected (or feared) a little formality but they put her to work the day she arrived, wearing her one and only dress. "I'm in seventh heaven," she wrote, and I could see her hiking up that dress and striding across the plowed rows, leading a battery of stunned men. "This cotton's been getting sprayed to death and still eaten up with weevils. Cultivation practices are pitiful. I know exactly what to do. I think we'll get productivity up about 100 percent from last year. Can you imagine? You'd think it was Christmas, everybody's already talking about how the collective could use this prosperity: they could get a secondary-school teacher in here full time, or a good adult-ed program."

I got a vivid picture of Hallie's face and could hear her voice as I read. Her hair would be restrained in a red bandana, her face tense with concentration and her eyebrows knit at angles like accent marks. I could also recall her exact expression as she lay on our living-room sofa in Tucson with her long legs propped up, one hand pushing the hair up from her high forehead, while she calmly dis-

pensed information over the Garden Hotline. I understood the full
extent to which she'd been wasting her life on house plants.

The letter was short. She was living in a two-room house with a
widowed mother of four young children, who insisted that Hallie
have one of the rooms to herself—a luxury that made Hallie uncomfortable. There was nothing to spare. The day she moved in, a
request went out to the neighbors and somebody brought over a
plate and a tin cup for her, and somebody else brought a fork. Both
women had recently lost sons.

The territory she would have to cover, giving crop advice, was
huge. She was issued a horse. There were problems with the roads,
she said, that made Jeeps a less desirable mode of transport for short
trips: horses usually weren't heavy enough to trigger the land mines
the contras buried in the roads. The horse's name was *Sopa del Dia;*
she was white with gray spots.

She signed it, "Your insane-with-love sister Hallie," with a P.S.:

*Re your question about botany: tell your students plants do
everything animals do—give birth, grow, travel around (how
do you think palm trees got to Hawaii?), have sex, etc. They
just do it a lot slower. Bear this in mind: flowers are the sex
organs of plants. Tell the boys to consider that when they're
buying their dates corsages for the prom.*

And a P.P.S.:

*Sure I remember when we almost drowned in a flood. Plain
as day. God, Codi, don't you? We found those abandoned
coyote pups, and the river was flooding, and you wanted to
save them. You said we had to. I was chicken because Doc
Homer would spank the shit out of us and I wanted to run
for it, but you wouldn't let me.*

"My sister's saving people's lives in Nicaragua," I told Loyd.
"She's a doctor? I thought she was a farmer."

"People can't live without crops. There's more than one way to skin a revolution."

He nodded.

I wanted him to know more than this about Hallie. That she was also a human being who did normal things. That she'd tried once, just as an example, to teach Carlo and me to break-dance. She'd thrown her hair around like a prissy rock star and we died laughing. In wool socks on the hardwood floor she could moonwalk like Michael Jackson.

I kept folding and unfolding the letter. "She has to ride a horse, because there's land mines in the roads."

The cab of the truck shuddered every time we hit a pothole, but Loyd drove calmly, his mind far away, the way I imagined *he* might look riding a horse. I'd never seen him so relaxed. I looked back a few times to check on Jack, who seemed equally content. I presumed he'd walked around in circles a few times back there before curling up in his nest of imaginary tall grass.

"Is there anything you know of that you'd die for?" I asked Loyd.

He nodded without hesitation.

"What?"

He didn't answer right away. Then he said, "The land."

"What land?"

"Never mind. I can't explain it."

"The reservation? Like, defending your country?"

"No." He sounded disgusted. "Not property. I didn't say property."

"Oh."

We passed by another of Black Mountain's mines, abandoned for years, the buildings standing quiet as a shipwreck. The huge windows of the smelter were made of chicken-wire glass, but a lot of them were broken out anyway; inside loomed the dinosaur skeletons of old machinery. Next to the smelter were the concentrator and a hovel of shacks under rusting tin roofs. Beyond them lay more fallow alfalfa fields, their soil crusted white from all the years of slightly salty irrigation water. Hallie could have stayed right in Grace and done some good, but of course there was the question of relative desperation of need. Nobody was dying for lack of this alfalfa.

The edge of these fields was the southern border of the Apache reservation, just fifteen minutes north of Grace. I hadn't been there before, and was surprised it was that close.

"Are you kidding?" he asked. "Gracela Canyon used to be *in* the reservation. The whites took that little section back after some guys hit gold down there."

"Is that true?"

"Look it up, Einstein. It's in the town records. They only gave the Apache this land in the first place because it looked like a piece of shit."

To some extent that must have been true: it was dead-looking country, though not as dead as the used-up cropland. It didn't look *murdered*. Here the gentle hills were pale brown grading to pink, sparsely covered with sage and fall-blooming wildflowers. Along the creekbeds were tall stands of cottonwoods. Their yellow leaves rained down. Every now and then we'd pass through clusters of homes that you couldn't exactly call towns, with long horse corrals strung between the houses. Red horses raised their heads and galloped along beside us for the short distance they'd been allotted, expertly turning aside just before they reached the ends of their corrals. Loyd waved at the people we passed, and they waved back.

"Do all those people know you?" I asked, incredulous.

"Nah. Just my truck."

Eventually we stopped in one of the settlements that was distinguished from the others by its size and the presence of a store. Rusting soft-drink signs nailed across the front porch marked it as a commercial establishment. Through the screen door I could see shadows of men in cowboy hats. Loyd pulled his parking brake, squeezed my hand, and held on to it for a second. "You want to come in?" he asked doubtfully. "It's only going to take me ten minutes."

"I know what this is about," I said. "J.T. told me you're into fighting cocks."

He nodded slightly.

"Well, is it okay for me to go in with you? Are women allowed?"

He laughed, then dropped my hand and flipped his index finger against my cheek. "Big old roosterfighting Indian boogeyman might get you."

"I'm a big girl," I said. I got out and followed him up the wooden steps, but regretted it once we were inside. A short man leaning on the counter looked at Loyd and resettled his hat on his head, ignoring me completely. This wasn't going to be any of my business. I bought a lukewarm soft drink from the old guy behind the counter. He grasped it through his apron and screwed off the cap, leaving a broad asterisk of dust on the white cloth. The other men watched this gesture in silence.

"I'll be outside," I told Loyd.

I sat in a wooden rocker on the porch. Jack had lifted his head and cocked his ears but hadn't moved from the truckbed.

Almost immediately I could hear Loyd raising his voice. "I told you I want Apodaca's line and not any of the others. I want gaffers. I'm not interested in knife birds."

The short man said, "Loyd, I'm telling you, you got to go up to Phoenix. They're getting goddamn tourists at those knife tourneys. It's a circus. You can get two hundred birds through there in a day."

"Don't tell me what I want. Do you have gaffers out there, or did I just waste a tank of gas?"

Their voices dropped lower again. I felt uncomfortable listening in, though I was fascinated and slightly appalled by the notion of "knife birds." It was encouraging that Loyd didn't want them, whatever they were. The words the men used were as mysterious as Loyd's railroad talk. He evidently spoke a lot of languages, not even counting Apache and Pueblo and Navajo.

Across the street from the store stood a substantial-looking whitewashed church—the only white building in an adobe town. It was shaped like the Alamo with a bell tower. The ground in front was planted with petunias, phlox, and marigolds: pink, purple, orange, in that order. One thing Hallie always said she loved about Indian reservations and Mexico was that there were no rules about color. She was right. It was really a splendid combination, now that I looked at it, but in some orderly country like Germany they'd probably arrest you for planting this in front of your house; in suburban Tucson they'd just avoid you. Keep their kids inside when you went out to weed.

People trailed out of the church in twos and threes, mostly women, carrying out the same color scheme in their blouses and skirts. They all looked at me as they passed, not with hostility, but with the kind of curiosity you'd have if you noticed an odd plant had popped up in your garden: you wouldn't yank it out right away. You'd give it a few days to see what developed.

I could hear roosters cock-a-doodling somewhere, and I was curious. As I went down the steps an adobe-colored dog scooted out of my way and ran under the porch. The store, I discovered, had a deep backyard. The chain-link fence was overgrown with weedy vines, but I could still see in: it was a rooster garden in there. Roosters in small cubicles laid out in neat rows, one bird per cage. They strutted and turned in circles, eying each other as if each moment were new, as if they hadn't for all their natural lives been surrounded by these other birds. They had red faces and glossy black feathers that threw off iridescent flashes of color, like a hummingbird's throat. Beautiful. But the claustrophobic energy was tiring to watch.

I heard a door slam and I quickly went back around front. Loyd was ready to go, but not in the bad mood I expected. By the time we got to the edge of town he was smiling.

I offered him the last of my soda. "So, did you waste a tank of gas?"

He put his arm across the back of the seat, his thumb touching the nape of my neck, and shot me a sideways look. "No way."

We weren't headed back toward Grace. We drove north. There were no more towns, just reddish hills and a badly rutted road. "Was that Whiteriver?" I asked.

"No. This is what you'd call the Whiteriver metropolitan area."

"You used to live here? After you left your mother's pueblo?"

"Around here. We lived up at Ghost River. It's a little higher ground up there. It's nice, there's trees."

"You and your dad and . . . " I wanted to ask about his dead twin brother, but then again I didn't. Not today.

"And Jack," he said.

"Whatever happened to Jack's coyote mother?"

"After she had her litter, she left us. She went back to live in God's backyard."

I was quiet for a minute, taking in the hills. "And where are we headed now?"

He smiled. "Who wants to know?"

"A hometown girl, looking for some adventure."

"Well, then, we're headed for some adventure."

Loyd kept both hands on the wheel in the washed-out stretches, driving like a race-car driver—I don't mean fast, but skillfully, with that generous kind of concentration that seems easy as a reflex. We were gaining ground, getting higher, passing through intermittent stands of evergreens. In between were meadows, solidly carpeted in yellow flowers, punctuated by tall white poppies with silver leaves and tissue-paper petals. In the distance, the southern slopes of the mountainsides were dappled with yellow. We passed through another tiny enclave of houses and horse corrals. The people there would have been born into that life; I couldn't imagine it. For some reason I thought of Hallie's first letter—the babies playing around the cook fire, in the refugee camps. But this wasn't like that; it didn't look desperate, just lonely. It was hard to understand why a person would stay. Loyd hadn't. But then again, he wasn't born here. And yet he seemed drawn back, for reasons beyond fighting cocks.

The road smoothed out a bit and Loyd took his right hand off the wheel and laid it on my leg. For a little while he and I both pretended it wasn't there. Then I asked him, "What would these people around here say if they knew you had your hand on a white girl's thigh?"

He smiled. "They'd say I was a lucky son of a bitch."

He lifted the hand and ran his palm up the length of my arm, from my wrist to my shoulder, lightly, just stroking the hairs and not the skin. My nipples stood up and my scalp tingled and my whole body wanted that hand on it, everywhere at once. But he took it back and put it on the steering wheel, and I pitied myself for envying a steering wheel.

"You still haven't told me where we're going," I said.

He nodded at the road. "That's where we're going. We're almost there." After a minute he geared down into four-wheel drive and turned off the dirt road onto a side path, not really a road but a pair of tracks in the gravelly ground. If you hadn't known it was there, you'd never have seen it.

If we are going to see some more people about gaffers and knife birds, I thought, I'm going to have to sit and be still, be a white girl. No matter what, I'm going to have to stop thinking about kissing Loyd. I looked away from his face, out the window. There was nothing out there now but fields of yellow flowers, rocky red hills in the near distance, and off to the east very high mountains softly blackened around their tops by a pelt of pine forests. It would be cool up there now, even today. I pictured myself lying under the pines on a floor of brown needles. It was hard to keep Loyd out of the picture.

**"What is this?"** I was out of the truck, entranced, before he'd even set the brake.

"Kinishba," Loyd said. "Prehistoric condos."

That's just about what it looked like. Out there in the middle of God's backyard, without a fence in sight, sat a long rectangular building made entirely of carefully set stone, no mortar. Dozens of small doors opened into it across the front.

"Can we go inside? Is it allowed?"

He hooked his elbow around my neck, like a friendly wrestler, as we walked toward the site. "It's allowed. I allow it."

"What, are you the landlord here?"

"Till somebody tells me I'm not."

He let me go and turned toward the truck, whistling once. Jack leaped in a high arc over the tailgate and streaked through the field of foot-tall grass, looking like the soul of happiness. He headed downhill toward what must have been a river; I could see cotton-woods. We were in higher country here, with more vegetation.

"That's a good dog," I said.

"Yep. That's a good dog."

The doors were no more than four feet high. I ducked through one into a small, rectangular room with a dust floor. It was cool as a cave, and quiet. The door was a square of bright light with the silhouette of Loyd coming through. Even inside the room, the ceiling was low, just inches above my head. I touched it. "People were short back then. Didn't eat their Wonder bread."

"They would've had to build a special room for you. You would have been their queen."

I laughed, though it struck me I'd been complimented. Was that how Loyd saw me? Not as a grain elevator on the prairie, but a queen? At the back of the room a door led into another room, which was darker, having no openings to the outside. Two more doors led out of that room—one to the side, and one up through the ceiling, which was made of thick, curved trunks of small trees. There was another whole set of rooms on top of this one.

"Can we go upstairs?"

He shook his head. "I wouldn't trust those beams. They're kind of old."

"How old?"

"Eight hundred years."

I looked at him. "Are you kidding?"

"Nope."

We went from room to room, changing directions in the dark until the compass points were entirely lost to me. It was a maze. Loyd said there were more than two hundred rooms—a village under one roof. The air smelled cold. I tried to imagine the place populated: stepping from room to room over sleeping couples, listening through all the noises of cooking and scolding and washing up for the sound of your own kids, who would know secret short cuts to their friends' apartments.

"The walls are thick," I observed.

"The walls are graveyards. When a baby died, they'd mortar its bones right into the wall. Or under the floor."

I shuddered. "Why?"

"So it would still be near the family," he said, seeming surprised I hadn't thought of this myself.

Without warning we came out into a bright courtyard in the center, surrounded by walls and doorways on all four sides. It was completely hidden from the outside—a little haven with a carpet of fine grass and an ancient ash tree. A treasure island. I was drawn to the shade. "We should've brought the picnic basket," I said, settling under the ash. The ground was cool. My brief vision of a living city was gone; it seemed ghostly again. For eight hundred years, those bones in the walls had been listening to nothing more than the dry skittering of lizards.

"We've got all day," Loyd said. He sat about two feet away from me, clasping his hands around his knees and looking at the toes of his boots.

"So who built this place, eight hundred years ago?"

"My mama's folks. The Pueblo. They had their act together back then, didn't they?"

They did. I couldn't stop running my eyes over the walls and the low, even roofline. The stones were mostly the same shape, rectangular, but all different sizes; there would be a row of large stones, and then two or three thinner rows, then a couple of middle-sized rows. There was something familiar about the way they fit together. In a minute it came to me. They looked just like cells under a microscope.

"It doesn't even look like it was built," I said. "It's too beautiful. It looks like something alive that just *grew* here."

"That's the idea." Loyd seemed as pleased as if he'd built it himself.

"Of what? The idea of Pueblo architecture?"

"Yep. Don't be some kind of a big hero. No Washington Monuments. Just build something nice that Mother Earth will want to hold in her arms."

It was a pleasant thought. I also didn't mind the thought of being held in Loyd's arms, but he was making no moves in that direction. He was explaining the water system—they evidently had some sort of running water—and how they'd grown squash and corn on the hillside facing the river.

I reached over and ran a finger from his knee to his ankle. He looked up. "I'm talking too much, right?"

I shook my head. "No, keep talking."

"You sure?"

I hesitated. I hadn't expected to have to make the suggestion, and my stomach felt tight. "Yeah. Just, could you move over here and talk?"

His eyes brightened. I'd taken him by surprise. He leaned over and I took his head in my hands and gave him the kiss I'd been thinking about for the last two hours. It lasted a good long while. He twisted his fingers gently through the hair at the base of my skull and held on tight, and my breath stopped while he laid down a track of small kisses from my earlobe to my collarbone. We lay back on the grass and I rolled against him, looking down into his eyes. They were dark brown, a color with depth to it, like stained glass. It was a little surprising to look at brown eyes after all the pale blues of Grace.

Just being held felt unbelievably good, the long drink I'd been dying for. For a second I hugged back as tightly as I could. Something inside his buttoned shirt pocket made a crackling, cellophane sound. I raised up a little and poked it with my finger. "If you've got a condom in your pocket, Loyd Peregrina, this is my lucky day."

He did. It was.


By late afternoon the shade had moved, and we also had rolled over a few times in the grass, I suppose, traveling from our original spot. Anyway we were in the sun. We disconnected and I lay on my back, feeling the forbidden touch of sun on my nipples and eyelids.

Loyd lay with his head propped on his elbow, just looking at me again, the way he had on the day of Emelina's party. With a finger he traced concentric circles around my breasts, and triangles on my abdomen, as if warpainting me for some ceremonial mission. Whatever it might be, I felt up to the job. I knew when reason returned I'd be scared to death of feeling that good with another person, but my body was renewed. I felt like a patch of dry ground that had been rained on.

Jack had come into the courtyard and was sleeping in the shade, a little distance away. "He found his way in here without any trouble," I said. "You boys must come here a lot."

Loyd kissed my cheek and sat up and pulled on his jeans. "Yep, kind of a lot. Not as much as I'd like to."

I thought of the condom in his pocket, the presumption, and felt irritated. "Well it's a good seduction spot. It worked on me." I found the rest of my clothes and concentrated on getting my shirt buttoned up. I'd lost an earring somewhere.

Loyd stared at me for a full half minute, and then lay back down, his hands clasped behind his head, looking straight up. "I don't mean that I *bring* people here. Nobody but me and Jack's ever been here before." He glanced at me, and then away again. "But I guess that's just what you expect me to say." He didn't say anything more for another minute, and then he said, "Shit."

"I'm sorry. I guess I believe you. I do believe you."

He was wounded. I suppose some sharp thing in me wanted to sting him, for making me need him now. After he'd once cut me to the edge of what a soul will bear. But that was senseless. Anybody would say that baby was my own fault, and he didn't even know about it. I looked at this grown-up Loyd and tried to make sense of him, seeing clearly that he was too sweet to survive around me. I would go to my grave expecting the weapon in the empty hand.

"Codi, I couldn't believe it when you said you'd come up here with me. I couldn't even believe I asked."

I sat forward, letting the point of my chin dig into my knee. "I can see what it means to you. I'm sorry for thinking what I did."

He spoke slowly. "I've been looking forward to this ever since Labor Day. Not because I thought we'd . . . Not for any one reason. I just wanted to come here with you."

I looked at him. It was the truth. I could think of nothing at all to say.

"I don't blame you if you're still pissed off at me for when we were in high school."

My heart lost its rhythm for a second. "What for?"

"For being a jerk."

"You remember that?"

I suppose it was an insulting question. He said, "I have a lot of reasons in my mind for the way I was, but they don't make much difference. I hurt a lot of people."

I looked at him carefully. "In what way exactly do you think you hurt me?"

He shrugged. "Well, maybe I didn't. Maybe you didn't care. But still, I could have been a lot nicer. We went out those couple of times, and then so long sucker, that's it. Loyd's a good-time boy, he don't call the same girl twice."

I breathed out. Nobody knew, so Loyd couldn't, but for one minute I'd been afraid. I didn't want him to know how much of a mark his careless love had made on my life. It would oblige him to one of two mean possibilities: compulsory kindness or a vanishing act. I leaned over and kissed him. "You're forgiven," I said. "Plain Jane forgives Mr. High School Honcho for being a red-blooded boy."

"Plain Jane my ass," he said, rolling me over on top of him and grabbing mine. "I like you a lot. A real, whole lot. You buy that?"

"I'll buy it. Just don't try to sell me no knife birds."

He looked straight into my eyes. "I'm serious, Codi."

"Okay," I said. "Sold." I laid my head on his chest and nearly went to sleep while he gently stroked my spine. I felt like a baby being coaxed, reluctantly, into dreamland. A few yards away, Jack was already there. His legs jerked helplessly, making him look vulnerable.

"I've lost an earring. You see it?"

"No. I'll help you look in a minute."

"What's Jack dreaming about?"

"Chasing rabbits," Loyd said.

"That's what everybody says, but I don't think all dogs dream about that. You watch a city dog that's never even heard of a rabbit—it'll do that same thing."

"How do you know they really dream?"

"They do. All mammals that have been tested have REM sleep, except spiny anteaters." I cringed after I said this. I sounded like Codi Noline, brain of the seventh grade, despised by her peers.

"*Spiny anteaters?*"

"Well, I'm sorry, but it's the truth. I read it in the encyclopedia one time."

"You are an amazing person."

He meant it, he wasn't making fun of me. His hand stopped moving and came to rest on the small of my back. He was actually thinking about all this. Carlo wouldn't have paid the slightest attention to a conversation like this; he'd be thinking about whatever men think about, how much gas is left in the tank. Loyd asked, "What do you think animals dream about?"

"I don't know. Animal heaven." I laughed.

"I think they dream about whatever they do when they're awake. Jack chases rabbits, and city dogs chase, I don't know what. Meter readers."

"But that's kind of sad. Couldn't a dog have an imagination, like a person?"

"It's the same with people. There's nothing sad about it. People dream about what they do when they're awake. God, when I used to work for *Tía* sorting the pecans I'd go to bed and dream about pecans, pecans, pecans."

I studied his face. "Didn't you ever dream you could fly?"

"Not when I was sorting pecans all day."

"Really, though. Didn't you ever fly in your dreams?" Even I had done that, though not often.

"Only when I was real close to flying in real life," he said. "Your dreams, what you hope for and all that, it's not separate from your life. It grows right up out of it."

"So you think we all just have animal dreams. We can't think of anything to dream about except our ordinary lives."

He gently moved a lock of hair out of my eyes. "Only if you have an ordinary life. If you want sweet dreams, you've got to live a sweet life."

"Okay," I said, feeling happy. I was sure no other man I'd ever known would have concerned himself with what animals dream about. "I'm going to sleep now, and I'll give you a report." I settled my head back down on his chest. His heartbeat moved faintly against my ear as I looked out across the ground. I saw my silver earring gleaming in the grass.

# HOMERO

# 13

# Crybabies

His name is gone. He understands that this is his own fault. He took a pen to paper and changed it, canceled his ancestors, and now his grandchild—Codi's child—has been erased like something in writing too, rather than flesh and blood. He knows she's no longer carrying it. He's aware of the signs.

The red darkroom light burns like a dying sun, very old: red dwarfs, they call them when they reach that stage. He sometimes reads astronomy now, when he can't sleep. But at this moment, outside this sealed room, it's daytime. He considers carefully the time of day and of year, and his daughters' ages, a ritual he performs a dozen times daily to keep himself rooted in time. That was nearly twenty years ago, when Codi lost the baby. He has photographed the eyes of so many babies. He gets lost among years now, the way he used to lose track when he sat in the dark movie theater for too many hours. He has always loved the dark.

The liquid feels cool on his hands, though it's a chemical bath, not particularly good for the elasticity of human skin. He should use the Piper forceps from the kitchen, but he has misplaced them. He moves the photograph into the fixative and stares at the lines. And frowns. They are a precise copy of what the real world offered his camera, and nothing more: the branched shadow of a cane cholla falling across a square of pale, cracked ground. He found the image while walking in the arroyo, and immediately saw the illusion he could draw out of it: a river in the desert. He'd seen exactly this sight, in aerial view. It was years ago, in wartime—they had taken him in a small plane over the bombing range near Yuma; a soldier lay wounded out there and couldn't be moved. They flew the quickest route, over the Algodones dunes, a dead ocean of undulating sand. The pilot said it was harder to fly over dunes on a hot day than through a tornado; the plane shuddered until its rivets creaked. Then suddenly they were over the Colorado River agricultural plain. He marveled, feeling lucky as a spaceman. Surely no one had ever seen this amazing sight, a complex river fretted with canals cutting an unearthly path through the bone-dry land.

He can't remember the wounded soldier. He closes his eyes and tries, but he can't. Possibly some chest wound, a punctured lung? No, he can't bring the soldier back. But he remembers the vision of that water. He gently agitates the photograph in its stop bath, lost in technical possibilities. He knows there must be a way to transfigure this cactus shadow into that other vision, which no longer exists outside his mind. All his photographs begin in his memory. That is the point. He might be the only man on earth who can photograph the past.

He stops suddenly, feeling a presence outside the door.

"Codi?" He listens. "I'm printing, it will be a few more minutes. Codi, are you there?" He hears nothing. It's a Monday morning, she can't be here. She's teaching school. He drops the print into the fixer, annoyed, and goes back to the enlarger to try again. He should lock that door to guard against accidents. What a shock that would be to the girls, a locked door. They have always had rules about this; a closed door is a sacred thing. Privacy is respected. There is no call for bolted doors in the Noline household. But she still locked him out—she was in the bathroom that night for more than four hours. When he walked by he could see that the upper bolt was turned. She'd gone in right after dinner. There are rules about this.

"Codi?"

He listens again, but there is no sound at all.

He knocks. "I just want to know that you're all right."

"I'm all right."

She is crying softly. "I can hear that you're crying," he says. "Your sister is concerned. You could just tell us what's wrong."

"Nothing's wrong. I'm just a crybaby. You're always telling me I'm a crybaby, so you're right."

That isn't true, he doesn't use that word. He tells them they should try to be grown-up girls. But he hasn't needed to tell them that for years.

In another minute she calls out quietly, "Is Hallie out there? I need to talk to her."

Hallie is in her room, reading. She doesn't seem especially concerned; Codi has been so moody of late that Hallie leaves her alone. They don't argue but there is a new distance between them. A gulf. Codi crossed over into adolescence, leaving Hallie behind for the time being. They both seem lost. All three of them, really: a marooned family, shipwrecked on three separate islands. Before, when the girls were close, he worried about what would happen when they lost each other. Now they have.

"Hallie." He stands in the doorway to their room and repeats her name quietly. "Hallie." She is reading in poor light, ruining her eyes. She looks up, her eyes nearly marble-white under the small, high-intensity lamp above her bed.

"Your sister has asked for you. Can you please find out what she needs?"

She puts her open book face down on the bed and gets up without a word. The two of them confer through the bathroom door. He tries to hear their whispers from the kitchen. He sees that Codi is not letting her in.

"The black one. That old one that was mother's."

Hallie is gone for only a minute, then comes back. "I can't find it. I got your green jacket."

"No!" Codi says something else that he can't hear. He washes the cast-iron skillet and sets it on the stove on low heat, to drive out the moisture. He goes into the living room, where he can't see but can hear better. Hallie glances up as he walks past her in the hall, and she lowers her voice.

"Why do you have to have that exact sweater, Codi? Are you going outside? It's not even cold."

"Just bring me the black sweater. I mean it, Hallie, find it. It's in the bottom of one of my drawers."

After a long while Hallie comes back with it. He hears the bolt slide back, then lock again; the door was not open even for a full second. Hallie returns to her reading.

In another fifteen minutes he hears scrubbing. She is cleaning the floor. The toilet has flushed more than two dozen times. There are rules concerning all of these things.

Much later he watches without lamplight from the living room. The house is dark. Her curtain of hair falls as she leans out, looking down toward the kitchen. She comes out. The small bundle in her arms she carries in the curl of her upper body, her spine hunched like a dowager's, as if this black sweater weighed as much as herself. When he understands what she has, he puts his knuckle to his mouth to keep from making a sound. Quiet as a cat she has slipped out the kitchen door.

He follows her down to the arroyo. She takes the animal path that cuts steeply down the bank. Round volcanic boulders flank her, their surfaces glowing like skin in the moonlight. She is going down to the same dry river where they nearly drowned ten years ago, in the flood. This tributary carved out Tortoise Canyon; it would be the Tortoise River if it had a name, but it never runs. It did years ago when he was a boy, hiking these banks to escape his mother's pot-black kitchen, but now it does not run except during storms. The land around Grace is drying up.

He stands a hundred yards away from Codi, above her, in the shadow of cottonwood trees. She has reached the spot where the rock bank gives over to the gravel and silt of riverbed. Even in the semi-dark there is a clear demarcation where the vegetation changes. She stoops down into the low acacias and he can see nothing but her back to him, her bent spine through the sleeveless cotton blouse. It is a small white square, like a handkerchief. In better light he could photograph it and make it into that, or into a sheet on a clothesline. It's shaking just exactly that way, like a forgotten sheet left out in a windstorm. She stays kneeling there for a long time being whipped like that.

Then her head pushes up through the fringe of acacias and she moves toward him, her face shining beautifully with its own privacy of tears. He sees how deeply it would hurt her if she understood what he knows: that his observations have stolen the secrets she chose not to tell. She is a child with the dignity of an old woman. He moves back up through the cottonwoods and into the house, into his workroom. He can't know who she has buried down there but he can mark the place for her. At least he can do that. To save it from animals. Before he goes to bed he'll cover it with a pile of stones, the heaviest he can move.

He pretends for a long time to be busy in his workroom, period-ically coming out to feign a need in the kitchen. Where has he put the Piper forceps? Codi is emptied out and exhausted and still stays up half the night doing homework. Six volumes of the *Britannica* lie open on the kitchen table; she states that she is doing a report on the marsupial mammals.

So many times he comes close to speaking, but the sentences take absurd forms in his mind: "I notice that you've been pregnant for the last six months. I meant to talk with you about this earlier." He would sell his soul to back up the time, but even if he could do that, could begin where he chose, he can't locate the point where it would have been safe to start. Not ten weeks ago, or ten years. If he has failed his daughters he's failed them uniformly. For their whole lives, since Alice died, they've been too far away to touch. It's as if she pulled them with her through a knothole halfway into the other world, and then at the last minute left them behind, two babies stranded together in this stone cold canyon.

He can't think of anything more to do in the kitchen, and she's still working. There are dark depressions under her eyes, like thumbprints on her white face. She tells him she has a headache, asks for aspirin, and he goes immediately to the closet where he keeps the medications. He stands for a long time staring at the bottles and thinking. Aspirin would increase the bleeding, if she's still hemorrhaging, which is likely from the look of her. But he would know if she were in danger, he tells himself. It was probably uncomplicated as stillbirths go; it would have been extremely small even at six months. She is so malnourished, he could have predicted toxemia, even placenta abruptio. He continues to stare into the closet, tapping a finger against his chin. He can't even give her Percodan— it contains aspirin. Demerol. That, for the pain, and something else for the cramping. What? He wishes he could give her a shot of Pitocin, but doesn't see how he can.

He returns to the kitchen and hands her the pills with a glass of water. Four pills, two yellow and two blue, when she's only asked for aspirin, but she swallows them without comment, one after another, without looking up from her books. This much she'll take from him. This is the full measure of love he is qualified to dispense.

**He bends down again** over the developer bath, his face so near the chemicals that his eyes water. The picture slowly gives up its soul to him as it lies in the pan, like someone drowned at the bottom of a pool. It's still the same: plain shadows on dust. Damn. What he is trying for is the luminous quality that water has, even dark water seen from a distance. There is a surface on it he just can't draw out of these dry shadows.

He straightens up, his eyes still running, and pats his pockets for his handkerchief. He locates it finally in the wrong pocket and blows his nose. He has manipulated this photograph in every possible way, and none of it has yielded what he wants. He sees now that the problem isn't in the development; the initial conception was a mistake. He fails in the darkroom so seldom that it's hard for him to give up, but he does. For once he lets go of the need to work his will. He clicks off the old red dwarf and turns on the bright overhead light, and the unfixed prints lying in the bath all darken to black. It doesn't matter. The truth of that image can't be corrected.

# COSIMA

# 14

# Day of the Dead

On the last Monday of October Rita Cardenal made three announcements to the class: she was quitting school, this was her last day, and if anybody wanted her fetal pig they could have it, it was good as new.

We'd plowed right through the animal kingdom in record time, having had nothing to look at in the way of protozoans. We'd made a couple of trips back to the river and had given due attention to the amphibians and Mr. Bad Fish, whose glass home grew more elaborate with each field trip and was now called the Frog Club Med. There were fern palm trees and a mossy golf green, and the frogs obligingly did high-impact aerobics all over everything. Now we were up to exploring the inner mysteries of an unborn mammal, which had to be purchased mail order.

But Rita hadn't had the stomach to cut into hers, and I couldn't blame her, all things considered. She was expecting twins. She said she was dropping out because she felt too tired to get her homework done; I feared for these children's future.

Rita wore about half a dozen earrings in one ear and had a tough-cookie attitude, and I liked her. She'd been a good student. She seemed sorry to go but also resigned to her fate, in that uniquely teenage way of looking at life, as if the whole production were a thing inflicted on young people by some humorless committee of grownups with bad fashion sense. I was disappointed but unsurprised to lose Rita. I'd been watching her jeans get tight. The pregnancy dropout rate in Grace was way ahead of motor-vehicle accidents, as a teenage hazard. Rita was a statistic. On Tuesday I made my own announcement: we were doing an unscheduled unit on birth control.

The reaction in the ranks was equal parts embarrassment and amazement. You'd think I'd suggested orgies in study hall. There was some hysteria when I got to the visual aids. "Look, there's nothing funny about a condom," I said, pretending to be puzzled by their laughter. "It's a piece of equipment with a practical purpose, like a . . ." Only the most unfortunate analogies came to mind. Shower cap. Tea cozy. "Like a glove," I said, settling for the cliché. I turned from the blackboard and narrowed my eyes. "If you think this thing is funny, you should see the ridiculous-looking piece of equipment it fits over." The guys widened their eyes at each other but shut up. I was getting the hang of this.

"Miss," said Raymo. They'd never learned to call me Codi.

"What is it?"

"You're gonna get busted for this."

I finished my diagram, which looked somewhat more obscene than I would have liked. I brushed my chalk-dusty hands on my jeans and hopped up to sit on the tall lab bench that served as my desk. "I know some of your parents might not be too thrilled about this field of study," I said, thinking it over. "I didn't get permission from the school board. But I think we'd better take a chance. It's important."

"Okay then, tell us something we don't know," said Connie Muñoz, who had even more holes punched in her left ear than Rita. I wondered if this was some kind of secret promiscuity index.

"Shut up, Connie!" said Marta. (Pearl studs, one per earlobe.) "My dad would kill me if he thought I knew this stuff."

"What you *do* is between you and your dad," I said. "Or not. Whatever. But what you *know* is my business. Obviously you don't need to put everything you know into practice, just like you don't have to go spraying the fire extinguisher around because you know how to use it. But if your house is already on fire, kiddos, I don't want you burning down with it just because nobody ever taught you what was what."

Raymo shook his head slowly and said again, "Bus-ted." He drew the laugh he wanted.

"You know what, Raymo?" I asked, tapping a pencil thoughtfully against my teeth.

"What?"

"It doesn't matter a whole lot what the school board thinks." This dawned on me forcefully as I said it. I understood this power: telling off my boss at the 7-Eleven, for example, two days before I left Tucson. The invulnerability of the transient. "There's nobody else to teach this course," I said. "And I only have a one-year contract, which I wasn't planning on renewing anyway. I'm not even a real teacher. I've just got this provisional certification deal. So that's the way it is. We're studying the reproductive system of higher mammals. If I'm offending anybody's religion or moral turpitude here, I apologize, but please take notes anyway because you never know."

They were completely quiet, but toward the end of the day you really can't tell what that means. It could be awe or brain death, the symptoms are identical.

"Miss?" It was Barbara, a tall, thin, shy student (ears unpierced), whose posture tried always to atone for her height. She'd latched onto me early in the semester, as if she'd immediately sniffed out my own high-school persona. "You aren't coming back next year?"

"Nope," I said. "I'm outta here, just like a senior. Only difference between you and me is I don't get a diploma." I gave them an apologetic smile, meant for Barbara especially. "It's nothing personal. That's just my *modus operandi*."

The kids blinked at this, no doubt wondering if it was a Latin name they needed to write down.

"Your *modus operandi* is the way you work," I said. "It's what you leave behind when you split the scene of a crime."

**At Grace High** I taught Biology I, Biology II, two study halls, and I also pinch-hit an algebra class for a fellow teacher who was frequently absent on account of a tricky pregnancy. My favorite class was Biology II, my seniors—Raymo and Marta and Connie Muñoz and Barbara—but on that day I had a mission and didn't discriminate among souls. I gave everybody the lecture on baby prevention. Barbara, who was in my study hall and also in the algebra class, got to hear it three times, poor child, and I imagine she was the least in need.

It surprised me as much as the kids, this crusade, and I suspected my motives; what did I care if the whole class had twins? More likely I wanted to be sure of a terminal contract. After the last bell rang I erased the blackboard and stood for a minute sharing the quiet with the bones of my Illinois compatriot, Mrs. Josephine Nash. Our day was over. She gave me her silent, wide-jawed smile. Here was a resident of Grace who had never hurt me in childhood, didn't make me rack my memory for her name (she wore it on her pelvis), had thrown no spitballs at me nor asked for extra credit, and didn't suggest that I belonged in Paris, France, or a rock 'n' roll band.

From the back of the room I could hear the frogs clicking against the sides of their terrarium, constant as a clock: up and down, up and down, exposing soft white bellies. This time next year there would not even be fish or frogs in the river; these particular representatives of the animal kingdom were headed for extinction. Whoever taught this class would have to write Carolina Biological Supply and order those stiff preserved frogs that smell of formaldehyde, their little feet splayed like hands and their hearts exposed.

I stood over the terrarium and peered down into it from above, like a god. The fish hung motionless in its small lake. Droplets of condensation were forming on the underside of the glass top. Getting ready to rain in there. I'd grown fond of this miniature world, along with the kids, and had added my own touches: a clump of bright red toadstools that popped up in Emelina's courtyard, and a resurrection fern from the cliff behind my house. The terrarium was like a time capsule. I think everybody was trying to save little bits of Grace.

I slid the glass to one side, hating to disrupt the ecosystem but needing to feed the fish. The humid smells of mud and moss came up to meet my nose, and I thought of Hallie in the tropics. What would she do about these troubles if she were here? Well, stay, for one thing, whereas I wouldn't. I had come here with some sense of its being the end of the line, maybe in a positive way, but I found I had no claim on Grace. Seeing it as "home" was a hopeful construction, fake, like the terrarium. I'd deal with Doc Homer insofar as that was possible in one year, and then I'd rejoin Carlo, or think about another research job; I had no specifics in mind. My future was mapped in negatives. Next year I could be anywhere but here.

I'd told Hallie about my bold, ridiculous little deposition on the pH of the river, and a few days later I'd had to follow up with the news of the river's getting dammed—questions of pH being entirely academic. I felt humiliated. Eventually she wrote back to say: "Think of how we grew up. You can't live through something like that, and not take risks now. There's no getting around it." She was admonishing me, I guess. I should have more loyalty to my hometown. I wasn't brave; I was still trying to get around it. A good citizen of the nation in love with forgetting. I pelleted the surface of the water with goldfish flakes. In nature there are animals that fight and those that flee; I was a flighty beast. Hallie seemed to think I'd crossed over—she claimed I was the one who'd once wanted to dig in and fight to save the coyote pups. Emelina thought I'd been ring-leader in campaigns to save stewing hens. In my years of clear recall there was no such picture. When Hallie and I lived in Tucson, in the time of the refugees, she would stay up all night rubbing the backs of people's hands and holding their shell-shocked babies. I couldn't.

I would cross my arms over my chest and go to bed. Later, after my second year of med school, I'd been able to address their external wounds but no more than that.

The people of Grace would soon be refugees too, turned out from here like pennies from a pocket. Their history would dissolve as families made their separate ways to Tucson or Phoenix, where there were jobs. I tried to imagine Emelina's bunch in a tract house, her neighbors all keeping a nervous eye on the color coordination of her flowerbeds. And my wonderfully overconfident high-school kids being swallowed alive by city schools where they'd all learn to walk like Barbara, suffering for their small-town accents and inadequate toughness. It was easy to be tough enough in Grace.

Well, at least they'd know how to use condoms. I could give them that to carry through life. I settled the glass lid back over the terrarium and turned out the lights. I would be long gone before the ruination of Grace; I had a one-year contract. Now I'd made sure of it.


**Rita Cardenal called me** up on the phone. She hesitated for a second before speaking. "I don't think your old man has all his tires on the road."

"It's possible." I sat down in my living-room chair and waited for her to go on.

"Did you tell him about me? About dropping out?"

"Rita, no. I wouldn't do that."

Silence. She didn't believe me. To Rita we were both authority figures—but at least she'd called. "My father and I aren't real close," I said. "I go up to see him every week, but we don't exactly talk." A pregnant teen could surely buy that.

"Well, then, he's got a slightly major problem."

"What did he do?"

"He just sorta went imbalanced. I went in for my five-month checkup? And he said the babies were too little, but he was all kind of normal and everything?" She paused. "And then all of a sudden he just loses it and gets all creeped and makes this major scenario. *Yelling* at me."

"What did he say?"

"Stuff. Like, that I had to eat better and he was going to make sure I did. He said he wasn't going to let me go *out of the house* till I shaped up. It was like he just totally went mental. He was using that tape measure thing to measure my stomach and then he just puts it down and there's tears in his eyes and he puts his hands on my shoulders and kind of pulls me against his chest. He goes, 'We have to talk about this. Do you have any idea what's inside of you?' I got creeped out."

I felt dizzy. There was a long pause.

"Miss? Codi?"

"Rita, I'm really sorry. What can I tell you? He's losing his mind. He's got a disease that makes him confused. I think he was really just trying to do his job, but he got mixed up about what was the appropriate way to talk to you."

"I heard that. That he had that disease where you go cuckoo and turn back into a baby."

"Well, that's not quite the way I'd put it, but it's true. Occasionally rumors are true."

"Is it true you're really a doctor?"

I looked out my east window at the wall of red rock that rose steeply behind the house. "No," I said. "That isn't true. Did he tell you that?"

"No." She paused. "Well, yeah. He said something a real long time ago, that you were in medical school or something. But not this last time. I heard it from somebody else, that you're a doctor and Doc Homer's dying and you're going to take over."

"Take over?"

"Take over being the doctor for Grace. They said you already saved that baby down at Doña Althea's restaurant."

"Oh, Jesus Christ."

"Look, people say stuff, okay?" Rita said. "This town is full of major mouths. It's just what I heard."

"I'm only here till the end of the school year, so you can tell whoever's spreading that gossip they're full of shit."

"Okay. Sor-ry."

I regretted snapping at Rita. "It's okay," I said. "It's not your fault.
I'm not used to living in a place where everybody's into everybody
else's business."

"It's the bottom level, isn't it? My mom found out I was pregnant
from a lady that works at the bank. Mom goes, 'What is the date
today?' and the lady goes, 'The fourteenth. Your daughter will be due
around Valentine's Day, won't she? I had a baby on Valentine's Day.' "
Rita paused for my opinion.

"Yeah," I said. "It's the bottom level."

"Uh-huh. Mom told me after that she had to tear up three
checks in a row before she could make one out right. Like that was
*my* fault."


**I set out to find** Doc Homer the minute I hung up the
phone, but it took me a long time to track him down, and my
energy for drama kind of petered out. First I went to his office in
the basement of the old hospital, up on the plateau—it was four
o'clock on a Wednesday and he should have been there. But Mrs.
Quintana said he'd gone downtown to check on old Mr. Moreno's
oxygen machine because it was making a noise, and then he was
going to stop at the grocery to pick up some pork chops. It had
been half an hour so I figured I'd catch him if I skipped Mr.
Moreno and went straight to the grocery, but I got there too late.
The grocer, Mrs. Campbell, said he had come there *first,* having
forgotten he needed to go to Mr. Moreno's. He'd stood for six or
eight minutes in canned goods, as if lost, and then it came to him.
Mrs. Campbell told me this with a sort of indulgent wink, as if he
were Einstein or something and you could forgive it. He'd left for
the Morenos' house, but first was going next door to the pharmacy
to pick up Mr. Moreno's emphysema medication. I skipped the
pharmacy and headed for the bright pink Moreno house, thinking

I'd catch him as he came out and we could walk together back up the long hill, past the hospital, to his house. So the war on germs in Grace was being waged by a man who got lost in fruit cocktail. There was a clinic in Morse, just across the state line, and according to Mrs. Quintana a lot of people now drove over there. Disloyally, she had implied; she adored my father. She noted primly that they'd have problems with their state insurance forms.

On my way to the Morenos' I stopped at the P.O. There was a letter from Hallie, which I would save for later. I liked reading them alone, with time for filling in whatever she might leave out.

It turned out the Moreno visit had been unexpectedly brief, and he'd left already. The oxygen machine had stopped making noises all on its own. I walked back up the hill alone. By the time I finally did get to Doc Homer's kitchen his pork chops were cooked and he was just sitting down.

He looked surprised, almost pleased, his face turning up from the table, and he offered to put something on the stove for me but I told him I wasn't hungry. I sat down at my old place at the table where I'd passively refused food a thousand times before. But tonight it made me sad to watch him eat his solitary supper—he'd cooked one serving of an entire balanced meal, vegetables and everything. This amazed me. When Carlo went on his work binges at the hospital, I skipped meals notoriously; I was lucky if I hit all the food groups in four consecutive days. But I supposed Doc Homer had gotten the knack of solitude. For him it wasn't a waiting period, it was life.

"I hear you were kind of hard on Rita Cardenal," I said.

He flushed slightly. "Do you know her? She's expecting twins. She needs to take better care of herself."

"I know. She was one of my students till day before yesterday. She's a good kid."

"I'm sure she is," he said. "But she is rather hard to talk to. I wrote down a prescribed diet for her, which she wadded up and threw in the wastepaper basket before she left my office. She said she would eat what she pleased, since her life was already a totally creeped scenario. That is a quote."

I smiled. "Kids here have their own minds, I'm finding out. I hadn't really expected that."

"They do."

"My students talk like a cross between Huck Finn and a television set."

He seemed slightly amused. I knew I was avoiding the issue. I took a deep breath. "I think I've let things go too long. I should have talked to you a long time before now. I don't think you're doing too well, and I feel like I should be taking care of you, but I don't know how. We're the blind leading the blind here. All I know is it's up to me to do it."

"There is no problem, Codi. I'm taking an acridine derivative. Tacrine. It keeps the decline of mental functions in check."

"Tacrine *slows* the decline of mental functions, if you're lucky. And it's experimental. I'm not stupid, I did a lot of reading in the medical library after you told me about this."

"No, you are not stupid. And I am fine."

"You always say you're fine."

"Because I always am."

"Look, I'm only here till next summer. We need to get things squared away. What are you going to do when you can't keep up your practice anymore? Do you think you're being fair?"

He cut up his cauliflower, running the knife between the tines of his fork. He dissected it into neat, identical-sized cubes, and did not answer me until he was completely finished. "I'll do what I've always planned to do. I'll retire."

"You're sixty-six," I said. "When do you plan to retire?"

"When I can no longer work carefully and capably."

"And who's going to be the judge of that?"

"I am."

I stared at him. "Well, I think there's some evidence that you're slipping in the careful and capable department." My heart was beating hard—I'd never come even close to saying something like that to him. I didn't wait for an answer. I got up and walked into the living room. It was the same, piles of junk everywhere. I was startled by something new: a dozen women's shoes from somewhere, arranged in a neat circle, toes pointed in. Superficial order imposed on chaos. It's exactly how I would have expected Doc Homer to lose his marbles. I felt dizzy and unsupported by my legs or Doc Homer's floor, and I sat down. I couldn't even tell Hallie this. She would come home.

The old red-and-black wool afghan, Hallie's and my comfort blanket in old times, was still folded tidily on the sofa. In the months I'd been here it hadn't been unfolded once, I was sure. I took the thick bundle of it into my arms and walked back into the kitchen and sat down, this time in Hallie's chair, the afghan pressed against my chest like a shield.

"I'm taking this, if you don't mind. I'll need it when it gets cooler."

"That's fine," he said.

I stared at him for another minute. "Do you know what people in Grace are saying?"

"That the moon is made of green cheese, I imagine." He got up and began to wash the dishes from his small meal. A large and a small skillet, a vegetable steamer, a saucepan, plate and glass, spoons and knives of various sizes, and the Piper forceps. Including the pot lids, around twenty separate utensils to cook and consume maybe eight ounces of food. I felt obsessive myself for counting it all up, but it seemed to be a symbol of something. The way he'd lived his life, doing everything in the manner he thought proper, whether it made sense or not.

"They're saying I'm a doctor," I said to his back. "That I've come here to save Grace." Hallie and I had already used up all the possible jokes on our town and Doc Homer: Saving Grace, Amazing Grace. Every one left a bitter taste in the mouth.

"And how do they propose that you're going to do that?"

"I don't know. However doctors usually perform their miracles."

"You know very well what doctors do. You finished four years of medical school and you nearly finished your internship. You were only two or three months away from being licensed to practice."

I touched my fingertip to some vagrant bread crumbs scattered across the table. Because his back was turned I had the courage to ask the question point blank. "How *severely* do you hold that against me? That I didn't make doctor?"

"Who is saying you didn't make it?"

"I'm saying it, right now. I don't have it in me, now or ever. Just the idea of me being a doctor is ridiculous. People depending on *me* in a life-or-death situation? Remember when I took Red Cross swimming lessons? I tried out the elbow-hold rescue on Ginny Galvez and we had a near-death experience."

He spoke without turning around. "How did you arrive at the conclusion that you could not be a doctor?"

For a minute I buried my face in the afghan, which smelled like a familiar animal. When I looked up again he was facing me, drying his hands on a dish towel, one finger at a time. "I would just like to know," he said.

"I couldn't make it through my rotation on OB-GYN. I was delivering a premature baby, which turned out also to be breach, and there was fetal distress, and the mother's pressure started to shoot up. I just walked away from it. I don't even remember exactly what I did, but I know I left her there. She could have died." I corrected myself. "They both could have died."

"You were only a first-year resident and it was a high-risk delivery. I'm sure there was someone on hand to back you up. Malpractice laws being what they are."

"That's not the point."

"You don't have to deliver babies to be a physician. I no longer deliver babies myself. There are a hundred specialties you could choose that have nothing to do with obstetrics."

"That *isn't* the point. People were looking to me for a decision, and I lost my nerve. You can't lose your nerve. You're the one that taught me that."

He looked me straight in the eye and said, "I lose my nerve a dozen times a day."

It was the last thing on earth I expected to hear. I felt as if I'd been robbed. I put my face back in the afghan and suddenly I started to cry. I have no idea where the tears came from, they just came from my eyes. I didn't want either one of us to admit helplessness here. I kept my face down for a long time, soaking the wool. When I finally glanced up he was putting something away in the refrigerator. In the dark kitchen, the brightly lit interior of the refrigerator was a whole, bright little foreign land of cheerful white boxes, stacked like condominiums. There must have been fifty tupperware containers in there: pies, cakes, casseroles. I thought of Uda's squash pie, and understood with surprise that all the women of Grace were taking care of Doc Homer. As a caretaker, I was superfluous.

He saw me looking at him. He stood with the refrigerator door half open, illuminating his face. "Codi, you could be a doctor if you wanted to do that. You learned the skills. Don't try to put the blame on something abstract like your nerve—you have to take responsibility. Is it something you want, or not?"

"I don't know."

He didn't move. I kept thinking he ought to close the refrigerator door. He'd always had a million rules about everything. Wasting electricity, for example.

"It's not," I finally said, for the first time.

"No?"

"No. I thought it would be an impressive thing to do. But I don't think it was a plan that really grew out of my life. I can't remember ever thinking it would be all that delightful to look down people's throats and into their nasty infected ears and their gall bladders."

"You're entitled to that opinion," he said. "That the human body is a temple of nastiness."

I held him steady in the eye and he smiled, ever so slightly. "You bet," I said. "People are a totally creeped scenario."

**The news from Hallie** was brief and moderately alarming. There had been contra activity in her district, nobody hurt but four John Deere tractors burnt down to scorched metal hulls. She sounded sick about that. "A Deere is like a hunk of gold here. Because of the U.S. embargo we can't get parts, and the ones still running are Nicaragua's patron saints." She sounded completely, happily settled in, though, much more so than I was in Grace. She talked about waking up in the mornings: Roosters hopping up onto the windowsill. An army of little girls in polyester dresses out in the street with huge baskets on their heads, forging out on a hundred urgent missions. She was making good progress with some new cultivation methods; wished she knew more about diesel mechanics. A man named Julio, a literacy teacher from Matagalpa, had asked her out on a date. (She drew stars all around the word "date," making fun of herself.) They had busy schedules, so finally they met after work and rode together to a meeting in a church where Hallie delivered a lecture on pesticide safety. The church was full of gnats and kerosene smoke and little kids crawling around on a big piece of plastic, crying, impatient for their parents to take them home to bed. She and Julio had ridden over together on her horse, *Sopa del Dia*, and had a nice time going home.

Sunday night was Halloween and Emelina's children took to the streets. Grace was at an interesting sociological moment: the teenagers inhaled MTV and all wanted to look like convicted felons, but at the same time, nobody here was worried yet about razor blades in apples.

Emelina volunteered me to go trick-or-treating with the four older boys while she stayed home to dispense bribes to the rest of the town's marauders; she felt a pagan holiday would do me good. I was only chaperone and crossing guard, not expected to go in costume. There was a state law against anyone over twelve wearing a mask or making direct requests at people's doors. The city fathers of Grace were independent to an extent: they ignored state law when they closed school on November 2 for the town's biggest holiday, the Day of All Souls. But to be on the safe side they were going along with the Halloween mask law. John Tucker was disappointed but tried not to show it. Emelina encouraged him to go with us anyway, more or less as a second chaperone. She was wonderful to watch. I guess I'd never really seen good mothering up close.

He agreed to go, dressed in J.T.'s black raincoat, with a quarter-inch of talcum powder on his face. Emelina ran deep eyeliner shadows under his eyes. It was convincing—he looked either sick or dead, depending on his position. Mason went as a bug, with grocery-bag wings and radio antennae strapped to his head with a yellow sweatband. He instructed Emelina to draw on bug fangs with her eyebrow pencil. I don't think Emelina ever actually wore makeup, she just kept it on hand for emergencies. The twins both were going as teenagers (i.e., convicted felons), but decided they needed fangs also.

We made a pretty good haul; in this fruit basket of a valley, I'd never seen such an orgy of sucrose. Jawbreakers and Gummi Bears multiplied in the kids' bags like the loaves and fishes. The twins pulled me along by both hands, and Mason gripped my leg when we crossed the street. We hit every house on the road that circled the canyon to the south—the longest possible route to the courthouse. John Tucker hung back in the shadows at the edges of yards, but I escorted the boys right up to the doorsteps, secretly enjoying these little peeks into people's bright living rooms. Our last stop was at the lemon-yellow home of Mrs. Nuñez, whom I knew to be an important figure in the Stitch and Bitch Club. I was beginning to learn my way around the matriarchy of Grace, a force unknown to me in childhood.

Old Mrs. Nuñez recognized the kids immediately, but for some reason mistook me for Emelina. I think she just didn't really look. She chattered at the boys as she dropped Hershey's kisses and bubble gum into their heavy grocery bags: "Oh, what an awful-looking bug you are. You get away from my house, you old *cucaracha*. And you ugly old twins, too. You're too scary." She kissed them all on the tops of their heads.

She stopped suddenly, holding her glasses and peering out at the pale apparition of John Tucker, who was hanging back around her shrubs as required by law. *"Cielo santo!"* she said, with real concern. "What's the matter with your brother?"

"He's thirteen," said Glen.

**All Souls' Day** dawned cool, and the people of Grace put on their sweatshirts and gave thanks. The heat wave was broken. By half past eight the sun was well up and sweatshirts peeled off again, but it was still a perfect day. Every able-bodied person in Grace climbed the canyon roads to converge on the cemetery.

It was the bittersweet Mexican holiday, the Day of the Dead, democratic follow-up to the Catholic celebration of All Hallows. Some people had business with the saints on November 1, and so went to mass, but on November 2 *everybody* had business at the graveyard. The families traipsing slowly uphill resembled harvester ants, carrying every imaginable species of real and artificial flower: bulging grocery sacks of chrysanthemums and gladioli; tulips made from blue and pink Styrofoam egg cartons; long-stemmed silk roses bouncing in children's hands like magic wands; and unclassifiable creations out of fabric and colored paper and even the plastic rings from six-packs. The Stitch and Bitch Club had had four special meetings in a row.

When Hallie and I were very small we used to be allowed to participate in this celebration, with J.T.'s family. I wondered if Viola remembered having us in tow. In my own mind it was all vague; what I remembered best was the marigolds. *Cempazuchiles,* the flowers of the dead. I asked Viola about them.

"They come on the truck," she answered cryptically.

"Do you remember when Hallie and I used to come up here with you?"

"Sure I do. You always ran all over the graves and messed up everything." Viola didn't pull her punches.

"Well, we were little," I said defensively. "Doc Homer made us quit coming after a while. I remember that. I remember him saying, 'Those great-grandmothers aren't any of your business.' "

"Well, he was the boss."

"Right. He was the boss."

Emelina and the four older boys were marching ahead, but I was pushing the stroller over gravel and Viola was over sixty, so we both had an excuse to lag. We were a harvester-ant clan ourselves, burdened not only with flowers but with food and beer and soft drinks and sundry paraphernalia. John Tucker was carrying a new, largish St. Joseph for Viola's husband's grave. J.T. was still in El Paso, and Loyd was on a switch engine in Yuma, but we didn't seem to need them all that much. It looked like a female holiday, what with the egg-carton flowers. A festival of women and children and old people and dead ancestors.

Viola stopped for breath, holding the bosom of her shiny black dress and looking down at the canyon. I waited with her, adjusting the red handkerchief Emelina had tied over Nicholas's bald head to shield it from sun. As he vibrated over the corduroy road the kerchief kept slipping down over his eyes, and he looked like a drunken pirate. I bent over and looked into his face, upside-down. He enlightened me with a wicked pirate smile.

It was a spectacular day. The roadside was lined with bright yellow plumes of rabbitbrush, apparently too common a flower for anyone to take to a grave, but I liked them. I would try to remember to pick some on my way back down, to stick into the clay ollas around my house; I was determined to prove to Emelina that I wasn't completely bereft of domestic instincts.

From where we stood we could look down on the whole of Grace plus the many small settlements that lay a little apart from the town, strung out along the length of Gracela Canyon and its tributaries, often inhabited by just a few families, some with their own tiny graveyards. These settlements were mostly abandoned now. A lot of them had been torn right up when Black Mountain chased a vein of copper under their floors; others had been buried; the company had an old habit of digging and dumping where it pleased. Grace's huge main cemetery was located on the opposite side of the canyon, as far as possible from the mine, for exactly that reason. Not even the graveyards were sacred.

At the upstream end of the canyon we could also see the beginnings of the dam that would divert the river out Tortoise Canyon. There had been a ridiculous photo in the local paper: the company president and a couple of managers at a ground-breaking ceremony, wearing ties, stepping delicately on shovels with their wing-tip shoes. These men had driven down from Phoenix for the morning, and would drive right back. They all had broad salesmen's smiles. They pretended the dam was some kind of community-improvement project, but from where Viola and I stood it looked like exactly what it was—a huge grave. Marigold-orange earth movers hunched guiltily on one corner of the scarred plot of ground.

"So what's going to happen?" I asked Viola.

"The Lord in heaven knows," she said.

I prodded. "Well, there was a meeting last night. Have you talked to anybody?"

"Oh, sure. The men on the council had another one of their big meetings about it and decided to have a lawsuit. A lawyer came up from Tucson to meet with Jimmy Soltovedas."

Jimmy was the mayor. The town council had nothing to do with Black Mountain anymore; Grace wasn't a company town in the classical sense, except for the fact that the company owned everything we walked on.

"What did the lawyer say?" In a moment of vanity I wondered if anyone had mentioned my affidavit. My line about "the approximate pH of battery acid" seemed like something a lawyer could gleefully quote.

"The lawyer said we might have grandfather rights to the water, and so we could have a class-action lawsuit to make the company give us back our river."

"How long will that take?"

She shrugged. "Maybe ten years."

"Ten *years?*"

"Right. In ten years we can all come back and water our dead trees."

"Did anybody go to the newspapers to get some publicity about this? It's ridiculous."

"Jimmy called the newspapers half a dozen times. I talked to Jimmy's wife. Nobody's interested in a dipshit little town like Grace. They could drop an atom bomb down on us here and it wouldn't make no news in the city. Unless it stirred up the weather over there and rained out a ball game or something."

"So it's a ten-year lawsuit." I didn't want to believe she was right, though her sources were always irreproachable. "Is that the only thing those guys can come up with against the Mountain?"

"Don't call that company the Mountain," she said curtly. "It makes it sound like something natural you can't ever move."

"I've heard the men call it that," I said.

Viola snorted like an old horse and started up the hill.

When we arrived, half a dozen elderly men were putting a fresh coat of white paint on the wrought-iron fence around the huge cemetery. Wrought iron was a theme here; there were iron crosses and wreaths, and over some of the graves there were actual little iron houses, with roofs. Through the ups and downs of Black Mountain's smelting plant, Grace had been home to a lot of out-of-work metal-workers.

Most families divided their time between the maternal and paternal lines, spending mornings on one set of graves and after-noons on the other. Emelina and the boys staked out the Domingos plot and set to work sweeping and straightening. One of the graves, a great-uncle of J.T.'s named Vigilancio Domingos, was completely bordered with ancient-looking tequila bottles, buried nose down. Mason and I spent half the morning gathering up the strays and resetting them all in the dirt, as straight as teeth. It was a remarkable aesthetic—I don't mean just Uncle Vigilancio, but the whole. Some graves had shrines with niches peopled by saints; some looked like botanical gardens of paper and silk; others had the initials of loved

ones spelled out on the mound in white stones. The unifying principle was that the simplest thing was done with the greatest care. It
was a comfort to see this attention lavished on the dead. In these
families you would never stop being loved.

The marigold truck arrived at ten o'clock. Women swarmed
down on it like bees, coming away with armloads of floral gold.
There were many theories on the best way to put them to use, or to
make them go farthest. Viola, who directed the Domingos family
operations, was of the deconstructionist school. She had the boys
tear the flowers up and lay the petals down over a grave, blanketing
it like a monochrome mosaic.

John Tucker stayed at his work but the twins wandered and
Mason disappeared altogether. Emelina, wasn't worried. "He's refining his begging skills he learned on Halloween," she said, and was
probably right. Grandmothers everywhere, who at lunch had set out
extra plates for the dead, were now indiscriminately passing out the
sweet remains of their picnics.

By mid-afternoon Emelina felt we should send out a search
party, "before he eats so many cookies he busts." Viola volunteered,
and I went with her, more or less as a tourist. I wanted to see what
else there was in the line of beautified graves. We skirted Gonzalez
and Castiliano and Jones, each family with its own style. Some were
devotees of color or form, while others went for bulk. One grave, a
boy who'd died young, was decorated with the better part of a
Chevrolet. There were hundreds of holes drilled into the fishtail
fenders, to hold flowers. It was beautiful, like a float in a parade.

The cemetery covered acres. To the west of us were collections
of small neglected mounds whose stones bore the names of families
that had died out. "Trubee," I read aloud, wandering toward the
desert of the forgotten. "Alice, Anna, Marcus. Lomas: Hector,
Esperanza, José, Angel, Carmela."

"Honey, we better get back to where people are," Viola cau-
tioned, but I wandered on, as distracted in my way as Mason must
have been, wherever he was.

"Nolina," I shouted. "Look, here's my long-lost relatives."

Viola looked at me oddly from her distance across the graves.

"I'm kidding," I said. We came from Illinois, as she well knew. "Here's my Aunt Raquel, my aunt . . . something Maria." Most of the graves were illegible, or so crudely marked there was nothing to read. Then I found one that stopped me dead.

"Viola. Here's a *Homero* Nolina."

"So it is," she said, not really looking. "Son of a gun."

I eyed her. "Do you know something about this?"

"What do you want me to tell you?"

"Who were the Nolinas?"

"Come on back away from there and I'll tell you."

I stood my ground.

"Honey, come on, let's leave these dead folks alone. Nobody put any plates of food out for them for a long, long time. They're not feeling so happy today."

"Okay, but you have to tell me."

She told me the Nolinas used to live up around Tortoise River, in the northern end of Gracela Canyon. There was a little settlement there that dispersed when the area was covered by mine tailings. The Nolinas had dug up what they could of the family graveyard and carried the bones a few miles to bury them up here. It wasn't all that long ago, she said. Around 1950.

"I don't know any Nolinas in Grace now," I said.

"No, they're about gone. They never did settle too good into Grace. The most of them went to Texas or somewhere, after their houses got tore up. They weren't . . ." She stopped and took off her shoe, cocking her stockinged foot against her plump ankle while she examined the inside of it, then put it back on. "The Nolinas weren't real accepted. They were kind of different all the way back. There was one of the Gracela sisters had auburn hair and a bad temper, and she married Conrado Nolina. They say that family went downhill."

"They were trash, is what you're telling me."

"No. Just different."

I followed behind her as she plodded along, dodging headstones.

She was as intransigent, in her way, as Doc Homer. "So how come one of them has practically the same name as my father?"

"You better ask him that," she said. "It's his name."

At that moment something hit me from behind like a torpedo, tackling me around the knees. It was Mason.

"Where have you been, *pachuco?* Your mama was worried to death about you," Viola said. Mason had an enormous sucker ballooning under one cheek. He laughed, recognizing Viola's scoldings as a bald-faced lie.

"I was at a birthday party," he lied back.

It took a while to coax him back to the fold. There were an infinity of distractions: *Calaveras,* little skull-shaped candies for children to crack between their teeth. The promise of a chicken leg for a kiss. Little girls and boys played "makeup," standing on tiptoe with their eyes closed and their arms at their sides, fingers splayed in anticipation, while a grownup used a marigold as a powder puff, patting cheeks and eyelids with gold pollen. Golden children ran wild over a field of dead great-grandmothers and great-grandfathers, and the bones must have wanted to rise up and knock together and rattle with joy. I have never seen a town that gave so much—so much of what *counts*—to its children.

More than anything else I wished I belonged to one of these living, celebrated families, lush as plants, with bones in the ground for roots. I wanted pollen on my cheeks and one of those calcium ancestors to decorate as my own. Before we left at sunset I borrowed a marigold from Emelina's great-aunt Pocha, who wouldn't miss it. I ran back to lay it on Homero Nolina, just in case.

# HOMERO

# 15

# Mistakes

He has to look at her for a long time before he trusts himself to speak. Who is this girl? His daughter Codi, but which Codi? He thinks.

"You look surprised."

"You startled me. I wasn't expecting anyone." He was doing Mr. Garrison's lab work, waiting for the centrifuge to spin down Mr. Garrison's blood cells, and when he looked up she was standing in the doorway. He detests surprises.

"Pop, I called five minutes ago, to see if you were here. I told you I was coming. I came straight here. I spent the day up at the graveyard."

She is leaning against the doorsill holding a bouquet of rabbit-brush and roadside weeds, showering the air with pollen like an old feather duster. She has on purple cowboy boots, which even now are damaging her arches.

"And now you are here," he says carefully.

"I found a surprise in the graveyard, a headstone with a name on it you might recognize. Yours. Almost yours."

"Perhaps I am dead."

She stares. "Do we have relatives from here?"

Uda Dell gave those to her, to both girls, for Christmas: the boots and straw cowboy hats and holsters with cap guns, so that they could run like banshees around the house pretending to fill each other with imaginary bullet holes. He took the guns away, for the preservation of their souls, and the boots on account of their arches. He let them keep the hats.

The minute hand on the wall clock jumps and the centrifuge slows to a stop, clicking suggestively, like the wheel of fortune. Without its mechanical whine the lab is very quiet. He looks up again and she is still there in her stocking feet and red straw cowboy hat, its dark cord knotted under her chin. She understands about the guns, but she wants the boots back. She has come on behalf of herself and her sister, she says. Her left foot in its white sock curls under. Why is it that only girls stand on the sides of their feet? As if they're afraid to plant themselves? Tears stream from her eyes.

He can't relinquish either the guns or the boots. He wishes he could do all these things differently, but he can't. He says, "I don't think we need to discuss this any further."

"Oh, come on, just tell me. Would it kill you to tell me?"

Startled, he looks again: she isn't in stockinged feet, she has boots on. She is much too tall. He is confused and becomes angry. He has a glass vial of blood in his hands. This is his office. She didn't need to sneak down here and startle him in his own doorway.

"I'm doing Mr. Garrison's hematocrit," he says. "I have a good bit more work to do."

She sighs loudly. She must be fourteen. In a year she will be sullen and furtively pregnant. Or has that passed too? He doesn't even look at her because there is too much there, and he's afraid. She is his first child, his favorite, every mistake he ever made.

# COSIMA

# 16

# Bleeding Hearts

At the first sign of winter the trees began to die. Leaves and aborted fruits fell in thick, brittle handfuls like the hair of a cancer patient. The abundance of sun and warmth, which we thought would never end, had led the trees on too, promising the impossible. But now the daylight grew thin and they showed no will to live. A dead sea of leaves drifted deep and undisturbed on the orchard floors. No children played there.

I spent a lot of time considering the mystery of my family tree. I didn't push the subject of the Nolinas, but I did ask people about my mother, whose leavings were scant. I'd grown up with only one sentence, repeated like a mantra: "It wasn't childbirth she died of, it was organ failure." I know this was meant to protect Hallie and me from guilt, but "organ failure," in its way, was equally unhelpful: a pronouncement that reminded me of those doubtfully groomed children in school whose report cards bore failing marks through every season, perennial as grass. "Organ failure" sounded like something our mother ought to be ashamed of, and us after her, *for* her, in death.

Viola dispensed with the organ-failure myth as easily as snapping a wishbone: "No, it was childbirth," she told me.

"But Hallie was born in June," I said. "She didn't die till later in the summer."

"It was a few weeks," Viola conceded. "Hallie gave her a real good round. She lost a lot of blood and after the birth she never got up again."

I was stunned by this news, and we walked in silence for a while. We were on our way to a special meeting of the Stitch and Bitch Club. To my surprise, I'd been invited as a guest scientist to talk about the pH of the river; needlework was not on the agenda.

Viola had on a brown cloth coat and what must have been her dead husband's hunting cap, earflaps down, the whole thing cocked forward to accommodate her thick, coiled bun. She stopped to pick up two stray peacock feathers, which she tucked into her coat pocket. One was perfect, with an iridescent blue eye bobbing at its tip. The other one had no eye.

"What did she look like?" I asked.

"Like you. Exactly like you, only smaller. She had real little hands and feet."

I looked down at my size 9's, defensively. "Not like Hallie?"

"Hallie always favored Doc more," Viola said.

I pondered this but couldn't see it—Hallie was so vital and Doc Homer looked drawn. But then what I saw really was their interiors, not their façades. Your own family resemblances are a frustrating code, most easily read by those who know you least.

"Well, I know she was pretty," I said. "Everybody says that. With a name like Alice how could you not be pretty?"

Viola made an odd sound, like unconsummated laughter.

"What?"

"He was the only one that ever called her Alice. Everybody else called her Althea. It means 'the truth.'"

"*Althea?* What, she was an honorary member of the Doña Althea family?"

Viola said nothing. I never knew what to make of her dark hints, but this one was wildly improbable. My impression was that she'd stayed an outsider, like the rest of us. Doc Homer had married my mother and come out here from Illinois after World War II, after he'd served in the army and finished his internship. Her maiden name was something like Carlisle. We never pressed him for more; when it came to our mother, Doc Homer seemed to be in an extended mourning period that lasted for our whole lives to date.

It made me curious, though. I had visions of trying again, of pinning his fragile shoulder blades against the wall of his basement office and forcing him to tell the whole truth about our family. As if Doc Homer's tongue could be forced.

Abruptly, Viola and I reached the American Legion hall. We walked into a noisy room bright with artificial light and I felt disoriented as to the decade. Women wearing cable-knit cardigans over thin housedresses crowded the hall with their talk, their large purses and imposing bosoms. When they saw Viola and me they began to come to some kind of order. Chairs were dragged, with much metallic howling, from conversational circles back into crooked rows. Many faces were familiar to me now from some encounter, such as old Mrs. Nuñez, who'd been so chatty when I took the boys to her house trick-or-treating, and others like Uda Dell I knew specifically. Doña Althea presided from an overstuffed chair at the front of the hall, but did not speak. Her face was as finely lined as the grain in maple wood, and about the same color. Her pale blue eyes blazed in the direction of the air over our heads. You could have taken her for a blind woman if you didn't know the truth, which was that Doña Althea's vision was sharp as a hawk's.

Norma Galvez, whose shellacked white hair was crowned with a navy bow that coordinated with her Steelworkers T-shirt, brought the meeting to order. It was a packed house. It took a while to achieve perfect quiet. Viola ushered me to a chair at the front table, hurried over to say hello to Doña Althea, and deposited the two feathers in a grocery bag of kindred feathers at the Doña's feet. Then she scurried back and took her seat by me.

"Viola brought a guest," announced Mrs. Galvez, accompanied

by vigorous nodding from Viola. She'd removed her hunter's cap. "You all know Doc Homer's daughter Cosima. She's going to tell us about the contamination."

That was my introduction. I was expecting to hear all about myself and the situation, as is always done at meetings that go on too long. But she was through, and I was on. I stood a little shakily, thinking of Hallie, who felt at home giving a lecture in a church full of mosquitoes and kerosene smoke and squalling babies.

"I'm not an expert," I began. "Here's the chemistry of it. Black Mountain Mining has been running sulfuric acid, which is a clear, corrosive, water-miscible acid, through their tailing piles to recover extra copper. It combines to make copper sulfate, which is also known as 'blue vitriol.' People used to use it to kill rats and pond algae and about everything else you can name. There's a ton of it in your river. And there's straight sulfuric acid in there too. The EPA finally sent a report saying that kind of pollution is very dangerous, and they can't put it near people and orchards, so Black Mountain is building a dam to run the river out Tortoise Canyon. You know that part of the story. And the men on the town council are pushing for a lawsuit that will get some action in the twenty-first century." There was some snickering. I remembered my talk with Viola on the hill overlooking the dam construction site—her disgust. The Stitch and Bitch Club wasn't banking on the good old boys.

"I really don't know any way of helping out with your problem. All I can tell you is that you have a problem, and why, which I guess is what scientists are mainly good for." I paused to swallow. The room was a silent garden of blinking faces, expecting something from me.

"My students and I looked at the river water under microscopes, and the usual things that live in a river aren't there. Then we tested the pH of the river and found out it's very acidic. The EPA has tested it too, and they agree. But your trees knew all this way before we did. Watering them from the river is just like acid rain falling on them, if you've heard of that. The acid-rain problem here in the West comes mostly from mine smelters. It's the same acid, one way or the other. Sulfuric acid." I feared I was losing my grasp of the subject, but they were still listening.

"I don't think I can tell you anything helpful. But Viola said I should come anyway. If you have questions I'll try to answer them." I sat down.

A thin woman in cat's-eye glasses and a red dress stood up and demanded, "You mean the fish and stuff is all killed? My husband claims they was catching croppies out of there a month or two ago."

"Well, no, the fish . . ."

"Stand up, honey, we can't hear you," said Miss Lorraine Colder, my fourth-grade teacher. She and Miss Elva Dann, who sat next to her, had lived together forever and resembled each other although they were no relation.

"Not the fish," I said. "They're still alive, but the smaller things that live in the water . . ." I considered how to phrase this, and started again. "Usually there's a whole world of microscopic things living in a river, and in the dirt, and the air. If you were in an airplane and flew over a city and looked down and saw *nothing* was moving, you'd know something was up. That's how you can tell if a river is healthy or not. You can't see them, but they're supposed to be there."

The woman in the red dress hugged her sweater around her. "Like bugs?"

"Kind of," I said.

Another woman said in Spanish that if the river water killed bugs, she'd better take some and sprinkle it around her son's house. There was a good bit of laughter.

"It won't kill cockroaches," I said. "Too bad. You could sell it for a fundraiser." They laughed again, though there were some surprised looks, and I was secretly satisfied. All my life here, people had spoken Spanish around me the way grownups spell around children.

The woman in the red dress was still standing. "What we want to know is, *is* the river poisoned for good? Would we be better off to let them run it out Tortoise Canyon?"

Every person in the room was looking at me. It dawned on me that they weren't conceiving of their situation as hopeless. What they wanted was not sympathy or advice, but information. "Well, no," I said. "The river could recover. It doesn't *start* here, it starts up on the Apache reservation, in the mountains where the snow melts. As long as that's pure, the water coming down here will be okay."

"So if you could stop Black Mountain from running the acid through the tailing piles, then after a while the junk would get washed out?" inquired Mrs. Galvez. "Like flushing the john?"

"Exactly like that," I said.

Fifty women started talking at once. You'd think I'd commuted a death sentence. After a minute Doña Althea carefully pushed herself up from the arms of her chair and stood, waiting for quiet. In her black dress she rustled like an old crow. She gave a short speech in Spanish, the gist of which was that I'd told them what they needed to know, and now they had to figure out how to get the company to stop building the dam and stop polluting the river and go to hell.

I sat down, a bit stunned. My Spanish was passably good, thanks to the years of Hallie's refugees sleeping on my couch, but some of Doña Althea's more idiomatic swear words were new ones on me. Also, she referred to me as *la huérfana*, the orphan. They always called Hallie and me that. It seemed unkind.

"My husband used to be a crane operator when the mine was running," shouted a woman in the back row. "He would know how to fix up them bulldozers from hell to breakfast."

"My husband was a dynamite man," volunteered another woman. "That would be quicker."

"Excuse me, but your husbands won't put Chinese arithmetic past no bulldozers," said Viola. Mrs. Crane Operator and Mrs. Dynamite seemed unperturbed, but Viola added thoughtfully, "No offense. Mine would be just as lazy, except he's dead."

Mrs. Galvez nodded. "Well, that's the truth. My husband says the same thing, 'The *lawyers* will fix it up, honey.' If the men were any use they'd be here tonight instead of home watching the football game."

"What are you talking about, *football?*" asked Mrs. Dynamite.

"*Muchacha,* didn't you hear? The *Miss America Pageant* is on tonight." She stood up. "Whose husbands was watching the Broncos game when you walked out of the house?"

There was a show of hands.

"Okay, ten seconds and . . ." she leaned forward, dropped her jaw, and bugged her eyes wide like a pair of fried eggs . . . "if you got remote control, *three* seconds."

"Sure, why do you think they hurried us all out of the house tonight?" a woman added from the front row. " 'Why, yes, honey, go on to your club. I'll be okay. I'll just eat me a TV dinner here and watch football.' Like hell. Football in a bathing suit."

"Okay, girls," said Mrs. Galvez, adjusting her hair and rapping the table with her high-heeled pump. "Like Doña Althea says, we got some darn good thinking to do tonight."

"I say we were on the right track with the dynamite," said Viola. There was general nodding.

The woman in the red dress stood again. "We don't know how to use the dynamite, though. And the men, they might be good men but they wouldn't do it. They'd be scared to, I think. Or they don't see no need. These men don't see how we got to do something *right now.* They think the trees can die and we can just go somewhere else, and as long as we fry up the bacon for them in the same old pan, they think it would be . . ." she faltered, hugging her elbows in earnest . . . "that it would be *home.*"


**On the way back** Viola was quiet. She walked quickly, stopping only to pick up the feathers that littered the leafy orchard floor. The sudden cold snap that heralded the certainty of winter had caused the male peacocks to molt in unison. There being no hope of mating for months to come, they had shed their burdensome tails.

The meeting had ended in compromise: the Stitch and Bitch Club would officially sanction mass demonstrations against Black Mountain's leaching operation, to be held daily on the dam construction site, starting at 6 A.M. the following morning. Unofficially, the Stitch and Bitch Club would have no objection if a bulldozer met with premature demise.

Hallie wrote:

*This morning I saw three children die. Pretty thirteen-year-old girls wearing dresses over their jeans. They were out in a woods near here, picking fruit, and a helicopter came over the trees and strafed them. We heard the shots. Fifteen minutes later an alert defense patrol shot the helicopter down, twenty miles north, and the pilot and another man in the helicopter were killed but one is alive. Codi, they're American citizens, active-duty National Guards. It's a helicopter from the U.S., guns, everything from Washington. Please watch the newspapers and tell me what they say about this. The girls were picking fruit. When they brought them into town, oh God. Do you know what it does to a human body to be cut apart from above, from the sky? We're defenseless from that direction, we aren't meant to have enemies attack us from above. The girls were alive, barely, and one of the mothers came running out and then turned away saying, "Thank you, Holy Mother, it's not my Alba." But it was Alba. Later when the families took the bodies into the church to wash them, I stayed with Alba's two younger sisters. They kept saying, "Alba braided our hair this morning. She can't be dead. See, she fixed our hair."*

*Codi, please tell me what you hear about this. I can't stand to think it could be the same amnesiac thing, big news for one day and then forgotten. Nobody here can eat or talk. There are dark stains all over the cement floor of the church. It's not a thing you forget.*

She signed it, perversely, "The luckiest person alive."

I heard nothing. I listened to the radio, but there wasn't a word. Two days, nothing. Then, finally, there was one brief report about the American in the helicopter who was taken prisoner by the Nicaraguan government. He was an ex-mercenary running drugs, the radio said, no connection to us. He was shot down and taken prisoner, and that is all. No children had died in an orchard, no sisters, no mothers, no split skulls. And I'm sorry to say this, I knew it was a lie, but I was comforted.

"Who came up with the idea that Indians are red?" I asked Loyd one morning. If I wasn't careful I could lose myself in this man. His color was like some wholesome form of bread, perfectly done. His forearm, which my head rested on, was sparsely covered with silky black hair.

He turned his head. His hair was perfectly straight, and touched his shoulders. "Old movies," he said. "Westerns."

We were in my bed very late on a Sunday morning. Loyd was a wonderful insomnia cure, good enough to bottle. That's what I'd written Hallie, whom I told everything now, even if my daily letters were comparatively trivial. "He's a cockfighter," I'd confessed, "but he's better than Sominex." When Loyd lay next to me I slept deep as a lake, untroubled by dreams. First I'd felt funny about his being here—exposing Emelina's children, and all that. But he didn't invite me to his place, saying mine was better. He liked to pull books down off my slim shelf and read parts aloud in bed, equally pleased with poetry or descriptions of dark-phase photosynthesis. It occurred to me that Emelina would have a good laugh over my delicacy concerning her children. She probably was daring them to look in the windows and bring back reports.

But the shades were drawn. "Old westerns were in black and white," I reminded him. "No red men."

"Well, there you go. If John Wayne had lived in the time of color TV, everybody would know what Indians look like."

"Right," I said, gently picking up Loyd's forearm and taking a taste. "Like that white guy in pancake makeup that played Tonto."

"Tonto who?"

"Tonto Schwarzenegger. Who do you think? Tonto. The Lone Ranger's secretary."

"I didn't grow up with a TV in the house." He withdrew his arm and rolled over on his stomach, forearms crossed under his chin. It looked like a defensive posture. "After we got plumbing in Santa Rosalia we all sat around and watched the toilet flush. Sounds like a joke, right? How many Indians does it take to flush a toilet."

"It's no big deal. Sorry. Forget it."

"No, it is a big deal." He stared at the painted headboard of my bed, rather than at me. "You think I'm a TV Indian. Tonto Schwarzenegger, dumb but cute."

I pulled up the covers. For a bedspread I'd been using the black-and-red crocheted afghan, Hallie's and my old comfort blanket. "And what is that supposed to mean?" I asked.

"Nothing. Forget it."

"If you said it, Loyd, you meant it."

"Okay, I did." He got up and began to put his clothes on. I reached over and caught his T-shirt when it was halfway over his head, and pulled him to me like a spider's breakfast. I kissed him through the T-shirt. He didn't kiss back. He pulled his head free of the shirt and looked at me, waiting.

"I don't know what you want from me," I said.

"I want more than I'm getting. More than sex."

"Well, maybe that's all I have to offer."

He still waited.

"Loyd, I'm just here till next June. You know that. I've never led you on."

"And where do you go after next June?"

"I don't know." I poked my fingers through the holes in the black-and-red afghan, a decades-old nervous habit. He held eye contact until I was uncomfortable.

"Who do you see yourself marrying, Codi?"

I could feel my pulse in my neck. It was a very odd question. "I don't."

"Yes, you do. But he'd have to be taller than you, smarter than you, more everything. A better job and more damn college degrees. You're like every other woman alive."

"Thanks very much," I said.

"Your height alone kind of limits the field."

"If that's supposed to be an insult, you're way off. I always wanted to be even taller than I am, taller than Hallie."

We sat not looking at each other for a minute. I took his hand and laid it, limp, against mine. It felt like a pancake or something. "This isn't about your deficiencies, Loyd. It's just me. I can't stay here. There's a poem by Robert Frost about this pitiful old hired hand who comes back home when he's run out of luck because he knows they won't kick him out. The poem says, 'Home is the place where, when you have to go there, They have to take you in.' " I stroked the tendons on the back of Loyd's hand. "I don't want to be seen as pitiful. I came here with a job to do, but I have places to go after this. I wish . . ." I turned my face toward the window so he wouldn't see tears. "I'd like to find a place that feels like it *wants* to take me in. But this isn't it. At the end of the school year my time's up. If we get attached, you and me, then it's hard."

"That's your game, not mine, Codi." He got up and walked into the living room to make his hourly call to the depot; he was expecting to be sent to El Paso soon. I was stunned that he would walk away from me when I needed to be taken in. Though I guess that's just what I'd asked him to do, walk away. His T-shirt was inside out, and he took it off and switched it around, still managing to keep the receiver cradled against his ear. He'd been put on hold. I watched him through the doorway and realized that the muscles in his back were taut with anger. I'd never seen Loyd mad, and was surprised he was capable of it.

I felt lost. I got up, throwing back the afghan and draping the flannel sheet around me like a sari, and went into the living room. The floor was cold. I shifted from one foot to the other, feeling vaguely like the Statue of Liberty. Jack on the front doorstep was scratching his neck vigorously, jingling his tags. That dog had the patience of Job.

"What's going on?" I asked, when Loyd hung up the phone.

"I'm five times out. Plenty of time for a fuck."

"That's not what I meant. Loyd, I don't think you're dumb."

"Just not anything worth changing your plans for."

I laughed. "As if I had plans."

He looked at me, his eyes searching back and forth between my two pupils as if he were trying to decide which door concealed the prize. "What would happen if you stayed here, Codi?"

"I would have the wrong haircut. Everybody would remind me that I don't quite belong. 'Oh, honey,' they'd say, 'you're still here? I heard you were on your way to Rio de Janeiro to have tea with Princess Grace.' And I'd say, 'No, I've grown up to be the new Doc Homer. I've moved into his house and I'm taking over his practice so I can save the town.' "

"Save us from what, Great White Mother?"

"Oh, shit, you guys can all just go to hell." I laughed, since the other choice was to cry. He took me in his arms and I crumpled against his chest like an armful of laundry. "This town was never kind to me," I said into his shirt. "I never even got asked out on dates. Except by you, and you were so drunk you didn't know better."

"You know what we used to call you in high school? Empress of the Universe."

"That's just what I mean! And you didn't care that the Empress of the Universe had to go home every night to a cold castle where the king stomped around saying hugs are for puppy dogs and we are housebroken."

Loyd seemed interested in this. "And then what?"

"Oh, nothing much. I'd hide in my room and cry because I had to wear orthopedic shoes and was unfit to live."

He turned my chin to face him. I hadn't noticed before that without shoes we were the same height. Proportioned differently— my legs were longer—but our chins punched in at the same altitude. "So, where you headed now, Empress?"

"God, Loyd, I don't know. I get lost a lot. I keep hoping some guy with 'Ron' or 'Andy' stitched on his pocket and a gas pump in his hand will step up and tell me where I'm headed."

His face developed slowly toward a grin. "I'll tell you. You're going with me to do something I'm real good at. The best."

I tried to figure this out. Behind his smile there was a look in his eyes that was profoundly earnest. It dawned on me. "Cockfights?"

There was no way I could say no.

**A fighting cock** is an animal bred for strength and streamlined for combat. His wings are small, his legs strong, and when he's affronted his neck feathers puff into a fierce mane like a lion's. Individuality has been lost in the breeding lines; function is everything. To me each bird looked like any other. I couldn't tell them apart until they began dying differently.

The deaths are protracted. That was one thing I learned when I went to see Loyd excel in the profession to which he was born.

I'd had in mind that a cockfight would be an after-dark, furtive thing: men betting and drinking and sweating out the animal suspense under cover of night. But it was broad daylight. Loyd cut the wheel sharply, taking us off the road and up a gravel arroyo. He seemed to navigate the reservation by the same mysterious instincts that lead birds to Costa Rica and back home again unfailingly each year. We reached a thicket where a motley herd of pickup trucks were parked at odd angles, close together, like nervous horses ready to bolt. Loyd pulled his red truck into the herd. Beyond the trees was a dirt arena where roosters strutted around clearing their throats, barnyard-innocent.

Loyd steered me through the arena, his arm around my shoulders, greeting everybody. I saw no other women, but Loyd would have been welcome here if he'd shown up with a shewolf. "Lot of people going to lose their shirts today," a man told him. "You got some damn good-looking birds." The man was handsome and thin, with a long ponytail tied up Navajo style. His name was Collie Bluestone. Loyd introduced us, seeming proud of me.

"Glad to meet you," I said. Collie's hand felt taut with energy. A chunk of turquoise on a leather thong rested on his collarbone, below the scar of an old tracheotomy.

"Collie's a cock mechanic," Loyd said. "We go back a ways."

I laughed. "You give them tune-ups before the fight?"

"No, after," Collie said. "I sew them up. So they live to fight another day."

"Oh. I thought it was to the death." I dragged a finger across my throat.

Collie smiled. "Out of every fight, one of them dies and one lives." He turned to Loyd. "How come the girls always forget about the one that lives?"

"Everybody loves a hero, I guess." Loyd winked at me.

"Nothing heroic about a dead bird," I pointed out.

The arena centered on a raked floor of reddish-brown dirt. Loyd maneuvered me through the men squatting and arguing at its perimeter to a dilapidated flank of wooden chairs where he deposited me. I felt nervous about being left alone, though the atmosphere was as innocuous as a picnic, minus women and food.

"I'll be back," he said, and vanished.

The place was thick with roosters but didn't smell like poultry, only of clean, sharp dust. I suppose the birds didn't stay around long enough to establish that kind of presence. Some men took seats near me, jarring me slightly; the chairs were all nailed together in long rows, the type used for parades. I spotted Loyd through the crowd. Everybody wanted to talk to him, cutting in like suitors at a dance. He was quite at home here, and relaxed: an important man who's beyond self-importance.

He returned to me just as a short, dark man in deeply worn plaid pants was marking out a chalk square in the dirt of the center pit. Betting flared around the fringes. An old man stabbed the stump of a missing forefinger at the crowd and shouted, angrily, "Seventy! Somebody call seventy!"

Loyd took my hand. "This is a gaff tournament," he explained quietly. "That means the birds have a little steel spur on the back of each leg. In the knife fights they get blades."

"So you have gaff birds and knife birds," I said. I'd been turning over this question since our trip to Kinishba.

"Right. They fight different. A knife fight is a cutting fight and it goes a lot faster. You never really get to see what a bird could do. The really game birds are gaff birds."

"I'll take your word for it," I said.

The first two fighters, men named Gustavo and Scratch, spoke to the man in plaid pants, who seemed in charge. Scratch appeared to have only one functional eye. Loyd said they were two of the best cockfighters on the reservation. The first position was an honor.

"The roosters don't look honored," I said. Actually they looked neither pleased nor displeased, but stalked in circles, accustomed to life on one square yard of turf. Their tail feathers ticked like weeds and one of them crowed nonstop, as if impatient. But impatience implies consciousness of time and a chicken is existential. I know that much about birds.

"How come you're not down there playing with your friends?" I asked Loyd.

"I've got people to train the birds, bring the birds, weigh in, all that. I handle. You'll see."

"*Train* the birds? How do you teach a bird to fight?"

"You don't, it's all instinct and breeding. You just train them not to freak out when they get in a crowd."

"I see. So you don't train, you handle," I said. "A handling man."

He pinched my thigh gently along the inside seam of my jeans. I'd been handled by Loyd quite a few times since Kinishba. The crowd quieted. Scratch and Gustavo squared off in the center of the pit, their charges cradled at thigh level, and they thrust their birds toward each other three times in a rhythm that was frankly sexual. Each time the men's hips rocked forward, the cocks dutifully bit each other's faces. Apparently the point was to contrive a fighting mood. Two minutes ago these birds were strutting around their own closed circuits, and if they looked away from each other even now they'd probably lose their train of thought and start scratching the dust for cracked corn.

But now they were primed, like cocked pistols. Their handlers set them down on opposite chalk lines and they shook themselves and inflated their pale ruffs. When the plaid-pants referee gave the word, the men let go. The birds ran at each other and jumped up, spurs aimed for the other bird's breast. They hopped over one another, fluttering their short wings, pecking each other's heads and drawing blood. After about thirty seconds the birds' spurs tangled and they lay helpless, literally locked in combat.

"Handle that!" the referee shouted.

The handlers moved in to pull them apart. They faced the birds off, waited for the count, and let them go at each other once more. Within another minute Scratch and Gustavo had to intervene again, this time because one bird had his spurs irretrievably embedded in the breast meat of his opponent. The handlers gently pulled them apart and started them again.

It takes a very long time for one bird or the other to die. Presumably they were dying of internal wounds and hemorrhage. Punctured lungs, for example, and literally bleeding hearts. Eventually they began to bleed from the mouths. At that point I could finally tell Scratch's bird from Gustavo's because it lay down in the dirt and wouldn't get up. Scratch had to place it on its feet and push it back in the direction of combat.

"Why don't they just declare the winner?" I whispered.

"There's rules."

It was a ridiculous answer, but correct. A death was required. It took thirty or forty minutes, and I guess the birds were showing their mettle, but it was hard to watch. The cocks were both exhausted and near death, no longer even faintly beautiful. Their blond breasts and ruffs were spotted with blood, stringy as unwashed hair. Collie Bluestone would have his work cut out for him here.

There seemed to be elaborate rules about how to keep things going after this point, when both birds really just wanted to sit with their beaks in the dirt. If one lay still, the other had no incentive to fight. I've studied a lot of biology; I quickly figured out that this industry was built around a bird's natural impulse for territorial defense, and that's where it broke down. No animal has reason to fight its own kind to the death. A rooster will defend his ground, but once that's established, he's done. After that he tends to walk around ignoring the bizarre surroundings and all the people who have next month's rent riding on him and he'll just act like a chicken—the animal that he is. The handlers had to keep taking the birds firmly in hand, squaring them off and trying to force the fight.

"This is making me sick," I told Loyd.

He looked at me with such surprise it angered me. Nobody could look at this picture and fail to see cruelty.

"I've seen little boys do this same exact thing," I said. "Take some pitiful animal and tease it and drag it back by the legs over and over again, trying to make it fight."

"The knife fights go a lot faster," he said.

"But you don't like knife fights. You like this. That's what you said."

He didn't answer. To avoid the birds I looked at the crowd, whose faces betrayed neither pain nor blood thirst but passive interest. It could have been any show at all, not two animals obliged to kill each other; it could have been TV. They were mostly old men in feed caps, or black felt cowboy hats if they were Apaches. I spotted a few families now, but knew if you asked these women about cockfighting they'd use the word *we*. "Oh, we love it," they'd say in cigarette-husky voices, meaning *he* does. A teenager in a black tank top, a greenish tattoo flowering across her broad back, hoisted a toddler onto her shoulder. She lit a cigarette and paid scant attention to the action in the pit, but her child took it in like a sponge.

Several people yelled loudly for Gustavo's bird. Then finally, without much warning, its opponent passed over from barely alive to dead. Without ceremony Scratch carried his limp loser out by its feet and tossed it into the back of a truck. Loyd Peregrina was called up next. A rooster was delivered into his arms, smooth as a loaf of bread, as he made his way down to the pit. This time I watched. I owed him that.

In the first fight I'd watched birds, but this time I watched Loyd, and soon understood that in this unapologetically brutal sport there was a vast tenderness between the handler and his bird. Loyd cradled his rooster in his arms, stroking and talking to it in a low, steady voice. At each handling call he caressed the bird's wings back into place, stroked its back, and licked the blood from its eyes. At the end, he blew his own breath into its mouth to inflate a punctured lung. He did this when the bird was nigh unto death and clearly unable to win. The physical relationship between Loyd and his rooster transcended winning or losing.

It lasted up to the moment of death, and not one second longer. I shivered as he tossed the feathered corpse, limp as cloth, into the back of the truck. The thought of Loyd's hands on me made the skin of my forearms recoil from my own touch.

"What do they do with the dead birds?" I wanted to know.

"*What?*"

"What do they do with them? Does somebody eat them? *Arroz con pollo?*"

He laughed. "Not here. In Mexico I've heard they do."

I thought of Hallie and wondered if they had cockfights in Nicaragua. In the new, humane society that had already abolished capital punishment, I'd bet money they still had cockfights.

Loyd watched the road and executed a tricky turn. He was driving a little fast for gravel road and dusk, but driving well. I tried to picture Loyd driving a train, and came up with nothing. No picture. No more than I could picture Fenton Lee in his head-on wreck.

"What do they do with them here?"

"Why, you hungry?"

"I'm asking a question."

"There's a dump, down that arroyo a ways. A big pit. They bury them in a mass grave. Tomb of the unknown chicken."

I ignored his joke. "I think I'd feel better about the whole thing if the chickens were getting eaten."

"The meat'd be tough," Loyd said, amused. He was in a good mood. He'd lost his first fight but had won four more after that—more than anyone else that day.

"It just seems like such a pathetic waste. All the time and effort that go into those chicken lives, from the hatched egg to the grave of the unknown chicken. Pretty pointless." I needed to make myself clear. "No, it's not pointless. It's pointed in a direction that makes me uncomfortable."

"Those roosters don't know what's happening to them. You think a fighting cock understands its life is pointless?"

"No, I think a fighting cock is stupider than a head of lettuce." I glanced at Loyd, hoping he'd be hurt by my assessment, but apparently he agreed. I wanted him to defend his roosters. It frightened me that he could connect so intensely with a bird and then, in a breath, disengage.

"It's a clean sport," he said. "It might be hard to understand, for an outsider, but it's something I grew up with. You don't see drunks, and the betting is just a very small part of it. The crowd is nicer than at a football game."

"I don't disagree with any of that."

"It's a skill you have in your hands. You can go anywhere, pick up any bird, even one that's not your own, a bird you've never seen before, and you can do this thing with it."

"Like playing the piano," I said.

"Like that," he said, without irony.

"I could see that you're good at it. Very good." I struggled to find my point, but could come up only with disturbing, disjointed images: A woman in the emergency room on my first night of residency, stabbed eighteen times by her lover. Curty and Glen sitting in the driveway dappled with rooster blood. Hallie in a jeep, hitting a land mine. Those three girls.

"Everything dies, Codi."

"Oh, great. Tell me something I don't know. My mother died

when I was a three-year-old baby!" I had no idea where that came from. I looked out the window and wiped my eyes carefully with my sleeve. But the tears kept coming. For a long time I cried for those three teenage girls who were split apart from above while they picked fruit. For the first time I really believed in my heart it had happened. That someone could look down, aim a sight, pull a trigger. Feel nothing. Forget.

Loyd seemed at a loss. Finally he said gently, "I mean, animals die. They suffer in nature and they suffer in the barnyard. It's not like people. They weren't meant to live a good life and then go to heaven, or wherever we go."

As plainly as anything then, I remembered trying to save the coyotes from the flood. My ears filled with the roar of the flooded river and my nose with the strong stench of mud. I gripped the armrest of Loyd's truck to keep the memory from drowning my senses. I heard my own high voice commanding Hallie to stay with me. And then, later, asking Doc Homer, "Will they go to heaven?" I couldn't hear his answer, probably because he didn't have one. I hadn't wanted facts, I'd wanted salvation.

Carefully, so as not to lose anything, I brought myself back to the present and sat still, paying attention. "I'm not talking about chicken souls. I don't believe roosters have souls," I said slowly. "What I believe is that humans should have more heart than that. I can't feel good about people making a spectator sport out of puncture wounds and internal hemorrhage."

Loyd kept his eyes on the dark air above the road. Bugs swirled in the headlights like planets cut loose from their orbits, doomed to chaos. After a full half hour he said, "My brother Leander got killed by a drunk, about fifteen miles from here."

In another half hour he said, "I'll quit, Codi. I'm quitting right now."

# 17

# Peacock Ladies at the Café Gertrude Stein

"He's giving up cockfighting for you?" Emelina's eyes were so wide I could only think of Mrs. Dynamite's husband watching Miss America.

"I guess. We'll see if he stays on the wagon."

"Codi, that's so romantic. I don't think J.T. ever gave up a thing for me except cracking his knuckles."

"Well, that's something," I said.

"No, it doesn't even count, because I terrorized him out of it. I told him it would give him arthritis or something."

Emelina and I were eating chili dogs at a roadside diner on I-10. Loyd's pickup, which we'd borrowed for the trip, was parked where we could keep an eye on it. Piled high in the back, individually wrapped in dry-cleaner bags, were fifty peacock piñatas with genuine peacock tail feathers. We were headed for Tucson, prepared to hit the streets with the biggest fund-raising enterprise in the history of the Stitch and Bitch Club.

The project was Viola's brainchild, although she shared credit with Doña Althea, who had opened up her storehouse of feathers. They'd held two all-night assembly lines to turn out these master-pieces, and really outdid themselves. These were not the likes of the ordinary piñata, destined to meet its maker at the end of a blind-folded ten-year-old's baseball bat. They had glass-button eyes and feather crests and carefully curled indigo crepe-paper wings. These birds were headed for the city, and so was the Stitch and Bitch Club, *en masse,* by Greyhound. Our plan was to meet at the bus sta-tion and take it from there.

I was surprised when Viola asked if I'd come. She said they needed me, I knew the city; you'd think it was a jail break. But Loyd was doing switch-engine time in Lordsburg and it was Christmas break, so I had time on my hands. I begged Emelina to come too, and spend a few days in Tucson. I needed to walk on flat sidewalks, risk my neck in traffic, go see a movie, that kind of thing. J.T. could stay with the kids. He was home on thirty days' probation from the railroad, for the derailment that was officially not his fault. The rail-road moves in mysterious ways.

Emelina hadn't gone anywhere without a child in thirteen years. Out of habit she packed a roll of paper towels in her purse. As we drove out of Grace she gasped for air, wide-eyed, like a hooked fish. "I can't believe I'm doing this," she kept saying. "Turn the truck around. I can't go."

I drove westward, ignoring my hostage. "What, you think J.T. doesn't know how to take care of his own sons?"

"No," she said, staring at the center line. "I'm afraid I'll come back and find him dead on the kitchen floor with a Conquerers of the Castle arrow stuck on his head and a fistful of Hostess Ding Dongs."

By the time we hit the interstate she'd decided it would work out. The boys could go to college on J.T.'s life insurance.

"Oh, they won't pay if it's murder," I said gravely.

She brightened a little. "I always forget. He's the one that wanted so many kids."

It was mid-December, fourteen shopping days till Christmas, and by afternoon it was clear and cold. Twenty-two women in winter coats and support hose took the streets of downtown Tucson by storm, in pairs, each cradling a papier-mâché piñata in her arms. No one who witnessed the event would soon forget it.

Emelina and I and the truck were more or less set up as headquarters. We parked in front of a chichi restaurant called the Café Gertrude Stein, for the sole reason that it sported an enormous green plastic torso out front and the women felt they could find their way back to this landmark. As soon as they sold their birds, they were to head back for more. Emelina and I held the fort, perched carefully in the midst of our pyramid of paper birds.

A man in a black fedora and glen plaid scarf came out of the café and gave us a startled look. We'd not been there when he went in. "How much?" he asked.

This had been a much-debated question; apparently the Greyhound driver had threatened to stop the bus if the Stitch-and-Bitchers didn't quit yelling about it. Ultimately we'd been instructed to try and get what we could.

"How bad do you want it?" asked Emelina, saucily crossing her legs. Monogamous as a goose, and a natural-born flirt.

A small crowd of homeless people had gathered on the other side of the street from where our truck was parked. It seems we were by a good margin the best entertainment of their day.

"Fifty dollars?" the man in the scarf asked.

Emelina and I looked at each other, cool as cukes. "They're made by hand," I said.

"Sixty?"

"Okay."

He handed us three twenties and Emelina forked over a plastic-wrapped bird. Its tail bobbed gently behind him as he made his way down the street. I mouthed the words, "Sixty dollars!" and we collapsed against each other.

"They're made by hand," Emelina said, eyebrows arched, in perfect imitation of an Empress of the Universe.

Miss Lorraine Colder and Miss Elva Dann came back to the truck almost immediately. They'd enlisted a bag lady named Jessie, who owned her own shopping cart. When Miss Lorraine explained the threat to the homes of Grace, Jessie cried for a little while and then rallied her wits. They were able to pack half a dozen piñatas into her cart, and the trio of women set out to sell them all in a single foray.

Norma Galvez, in the meantime, lost her partner at a crosswalk and had to be escorted back to the big green naked lady by a bicycle policeman named Officer Metz. In a conversation that lasted only five blocks she'd acquired an amazing number of facts about this man: for example, he had twin daughters born on Christmas Day, and wore a hernia belt. She told Emelina and me these things when she introduced him. Officer Metz was sympathetic, but did ask if the ladies had a vendor's permit. Mrs. Galvez, a quick thinker, explained that we weren't selling anything. We were soliciting donations to save our town. Each and every donor got a free peacock piñata. In the interest of public relations she gave him one to take home to his twins.

By five o'clock we were out of birds. As it turned out, Emelina and I didn't make the best sale of the day. While too many peacocks went for only ten or fifteen, Doña Althea haggled one elderly gentleman up to seventy-five dollars. When the transaction was completed, the Doña allowed him to kiss her hand.

By the time they were back in Grace on the last evening bus, I was later informed, the Stitch and Bitch Club had already laid plans to come back in ten days with five hundred peacock piñatas. There would be only two deviations from the original plan. First, each piñata would be accompanied by a written history of Grace and its heroic struggle against the Black Mountain Mining Company. To my shock I was elected, in absentia, to write this epic broadside and get it mimeographed at the school. (Miss Lorraine and Miss Elva had retired.) Second, the price would be fixed at sixty dollars. Some argued for seventy-five but the Doña overruled, pointing out that she couldn't be expected to kiss every damn cowboy in Tucson.

---

**Emelina and** I let ourselves into my old house. Carlo was expecting us and had left the key under the usual brick. The neighborhood seemed even seedier than when I left. There was some demolition going on, with cheerfully nasty graffiti decorating the plywood construction barriers. Our old house with its bolted-down flowerpots stood eerily untouched, inside and out. Carlo had let all the plants finish dying, as expected, but beyond that he'd made no effort to make the place his own. He seemed to be living like a man in mourning, not wishing to disturb the traces of a deceased wife. Or wives.

"This is creepy, Carlo," I told him when he got home late that night from his ER shift. "Why haven't you moved things around? It looks like Hallie and I just walked out yesterday."

He shrugged. "What's to move around?"

Emelina had gone to bed, trying, I believe, to stay out of our way. She'd kept asking me if it wouldn't be awkward for us to stay with my "ex." It was hard for her to understand that Carlo and I were really "exes" right from the start. Having no claim on each other was the basis of our relationship.

I'd stayed up watching the news so I could see him when he got home. He slumped down next to me on the couch with a bag of potato chips.

"That your dinner?"

"You my mother?"

"I should hope not." On the news they were talking about an ordinance that banned charity Santas from collecting donations in shopping malls. The owner of a sporting-goods store was explaining that it took away business. Rows of hunting bows were lined up behind him like the delicately curved bones of a ribcage.

"You look exhausted," I told Carlo. He really did.

"I sewed a nose back on tonight. Cartilage and all."

"That'll take it out of you."

"So what's creepy about the way I'm living?" In his light-green hospital scrubs, Carlo looked paler and smaller than I remembered him. No visible muscles.

"It looks like you're living in limbo," I said. "Waiting for somebody else to move in here and cook a real meal for you and hang up pictures."

"You never did either of those things."

"I know. But it's different when there's *two* people living in a house with no pictures. It looks like you're just too busy having fun with each other to pay attention to the walls."

"I miss you. We did have fun."

"Not that much. You miss Hallie." Being here made me miss her too, more tangibly than in Grace. On these scarred wooden floors, Hallie had rolled up the rugs and attempted to teach us to moonwalk.

"How is she? Does she ever write you? I got one postcard, from Nogales."

"Yeah, we write. She's real busy." I didn't tell him we wrote a *lot*. We'd revived an intensity of correspondence we hadn't had since 1972, the year I escaped from Grace and Hallie came into a late puberty, both of us entirely on our own. This time she was over her head with joy and I with something like love or dread, but we still needed each other to make sure it was real. We had to live with an odd, two-week lag to our conversations. I'd be writing her about some small, thrilling victory at school, and she'd be addressing the blue funk I was in two weeks ago when I was getting my period. It didn't matter; we kept writing, knowing it would someday even out.

"How's your father?"

"Oh," I said, "deteriorating. Forgetting who I am. Maybe it's a blessing."

"Are you sleeping these days?"

"Yeah, I am, as a matter of fact," I said, evasively.

"You haven't had that eyeball dream?"

I'd never been able to explain this to Carlo's satisfaction. "It's not really an eyeball dream."

"What is it, then?"

"Just a sound, like popping glass, and then I'm blind. It's a very short dream. I'd rather not talk about it if you don't mind. I'm afraid I'll jinx myself."

"So you haven't been having it?"

"No, not for a while."

It was kind of him to be interested. He gently squeezed my shoulder in the palm of his hand, releasing the tightness in my deltoid muscle. Not that it applied to us anymore, but people who know a lot about anatomy make great lovers. "So you're getting along okay there?"

"As well as I get along anywhere," I said, and he laughed, probably believing I meant "As poorly as I get along anywhere."

"I've been giving some thought to Denver," he said. "Or Aspen."

"That would be a challenge. You could sew the faces back onto people who ski into trees."

"You want to come? We could ski into trees together."

"I don't know. I'm not really thinking too far ahead right now."

He took my feet into his lap and massaged my arches. He had the famous hands of a surgeon, there was no denying it, but I had no sexual interest in Carlo. I still had a slight hope he'd come up with the perfect plan for the two of us that would make me happy and fulfilled, but even that was fading.

"What else could a modern couple like ourselves do in Aspen?" I asked him. "Besides ski into trees, and try to spot movie stars snorting coke in hotel lounges? Aspen sounds kind of fast-lane."

"After Grace, it would be, yes."

"Don't make fun of my country of origin."

Carlo looked surprised. "I've never heard you defend it before."

"It was a joke."

"Well, what about Denver, then. Not so fast-lane."

"Denver's nice." I felt the familiar tug of a brand-new place that might, this time, turn out to be wonderful. And the familiar tug of Carlo wanting me to go with him. I'd seen Denver once. It had endless neighborhoods of sweet old brick houses with peaked roofs and lawns shaded by huge maples. It would be a heavenly place to walk a dog.

"Would you ever consider getting a dog, Carlo?"

"A dog?"

"They have four legs and say 'woof woof.'"

"Oh, right."

"I've met this wonderful dog, in Grace. He's half coyote and he'll sit for five hours in the back of a pickup truck waiting for you, just because he trusts you to come back."

"This sounds serious."

"He's a good dog." I realized I hadn't thought about Loyd all day, which I viewed as an accomplishment. This must be how it is to be alcoholic: setting little goals for yourself, proving you can live without it. When really, giving it all that thought only proves that you can't. My mood suddenly began to plummet; I'd felt elated all afternoon, but now I recognized the signs of a depression coming. If I timed it right, Hallie's letter addressing my *last* depression would arrive on target.

"Shoot, look at that!" Carlo dropped my feet and jumped to turn up the volume on the TV. "That's you!"

It was. I yelled for Emelina but the spot was over by the time she showed up in the doorway wearing one of J.T.'s shirts, looking stunned.

"You were on the news," Carlo explained excitedly. "They said something about the Peacock Ladies and then they said something about Southwestern folk art, and they showed you two standing up in the truck, and this old lady in a black dress . . ."

"Doña Althea," I said.

". . . holding up the piñata, and another lady and a cop . . ."

"Officer Metz."

". . . and I didn't hear anything else because we were yelling." He stopped suddenly, looking embarrassed by his enthusiasm. He and Emelina hadn't officially met.

"Oh. Carlo, Emelina. Emelina, Carlo. An old friend from a previous life."

I didn't say which one was the previous life, and which was the present. I didn't know.

*Hallie, what I can never put a finger on is the why of you and me. Why did you turn out the way you did? You're my sister. We were baked in the same oven, with the same ingredients. Why does one cake rise and the other fall? I think about you on your horse, riding out to the fields in your gray wool socks and boots and your hair looking like the Breck Girl gone wild, setting off to make a new world. Life must be so easy when you have dreams.*

*I read in the paper that we'll be sending another 40 or 50 million to the contras, so they can strafe little girls and blow you up with your cotton crop. It hurts to know this; I could be a happier American if I didn't have a loved one sending me truth from the trenches. You're right, we're a nation of amnesiacs. I'm embarrassed. It's an inappropriately weak emotion. You risk everything, while I pay my taxes like everybody else and try not to recall the unpleasant odor of death.*

*My life is a pitiful, mechanical thing without a past, like a little wind-up car, ready to run in any direction somebody points me. Today I thought I was a hero. We sold fifty peacock piñatas to raise money for the Stitch and Bitch Club, which will somehow save the town of Grace. But it's not my cause, I'm leaving. I have no idea how to save a town. I only came along today because it looked like a party and I was invited. Remember how we used to pray to get invited to birthday parties? And they only asked us because we were so grateful we'd do anything, stay late and help the mothers wash the cake pans. I'm still that girl, flattered to death if somebody wants me around.*

*Carlo asked me to go with him to Denver or possibly Aspen. Carlo's still Carlo. He wants to know why you haven't written. (I told him you're busy saving the world.) I*

*almost think I could go to Denver. Carlo is safe because I
don't really love him that much. If he stopped wanting me
around one day, it wouldn't be so terrible. I wouldn't die.*

*Hallie, I realize how that sounds. I feel small and ridicu-
lous and hemmed in on every side by the need to be safe. All
I want is to be like you, to be brave, to walk into a country
of chickens and land mines and call that home, and have it
be home. How do you just charge ahead, always doing the
right thing, even if you have to do it alone with people staring? I would have so many doubts—what if you lose that
war? What then? If I had an ounce of your bravery I'd be set
for life. You get up and look the world in the eye, shoo the
livestock away from the windowsill, and decide what portion
of the world needs to be saved today. You are like God. I get
tired. Carlo says "Let's go to Denver," and what the heck,
I'm ready to throw down the banner of the Stitch and Bitch
Club and the republic for which it stands. Ready to go live
in Denver and walk my dog.*

I went out at dawn, alone, to mail my letter and prowl my old
neighborhood. I kept trying to believe I felt good in this familiar
haunt. I'd brought my city clothes: a short skirt and black tights and
stiletto-heeled boots (the sight would have laid Doc Homer flat),
and I walked downtown among strangers, smiling, anonymous as a
goldfish. There was a newsstand four blocks down where I used to
go for the *Times* or the Washington *Post,* which Hallie and Carlo
would spread all over the living-room floor on Sunday mornings.
Hallie would constantly ask us if she could interrupt for a second.
"Listen to this," she'd say. She needed to read it all aloud, both the
tragedies and the funnies.

I ducked into a coffee shop that had decent coffee and wonderful
croissants. As I sat blowing into my cup I realized I was looking
around to see who was there—a habit I must have picked up in
Grace, where you looked at people because they were all identifiable.

A man at a table very close to my elbow kept looking at my legs.

That's another thing you put up with when you're tall—men act like you've ordered those legs out of a catalogue. I crossed them finally and said, "See, look, I've got another one just like it."

He laughed. Amazingly, he wasn't embarrassed at all. I'd forgotten how the downtown scene could be—people cultivating weirdness like it was a disease or a career. He had a neatly trimmed beard and was extremely handsome. "How Emma Bovary," he said.

I smiled. "You seem to have lost your syntax. Perhaps you're in the wrong place. The Café Gertrude Stein is down the street."

"Well," he said. "Well well well. Perhaps you could provide me with some context. Do you have a name?"

"Cosima. It means Order in the Cosmos."

"Cosima, my love, I'm in desperate need of order. If you have the *New York Times* in your bag there, I'd be willing to marry you." I had the *New York Times*.

"I'm not in the habit of marrying strangers," I said. I was suddenly disgusted with what I was doing. I'd go anywhere Carlo wanted, I'd be a sport for my students in Grace, I'd even tried to be a doctor for Doc Homer, just as I'd humiliated myself in the old days to get invited to birthday parties. If I kept trying to be what everybody wanted, I'd soon be insipid enough to fit in everywhere. I grabbed my bag and stood up to go. I told the man, "You don't have the slightest idea who I am."


**The second night** in Tucson I slept like a child, so drenched in sleep that when I woke up I didn't know where I was. For a minute I lay lost in the bed, trying slowly to attach the physical fact of myself to a name, a life, a room in a house within a larger place. It was a frightening moment, but nothing new to me, either. So rarely in my life did I truly surrender to sleep that it took an extra effort for me to pull myself out. It felt like slogging on my elbows up a riverbank.

Carlo wasn't in bed with me, of course; he'd skirted the awkward issue by saying he had a weird shift and might as well sleep on the sofa and not disturb anybody. But he'd had plenty of opportunities in the past to see me wake up confused. He always claimed there was something wrong with the electrical current in the temporal lobes of my brain. He said that explained why I couldn't remember parts of what I'd lived through, and remembered other parts that I hadn't. I was attracted to easy answers but mistrusted them too. Carlo's specialty was the nervous system; he tended to think all human difficulties were traceable to neural synapses gone haywire. And I feared—no, I knew—what was wrong with me was more complicated than what's wrong with a badly wired house.

Carlo was already gone but left a note, saying to think very seriously about Aspen. It sounded like a joke, put that way, but I folded the note and stuck it in my suitcase. Emelina was cheerful at breakfast. She'd sensed the previous day that my mood had turned black and blue, but she was intent on our having a vacation even if neither of our hearts was really in it. We'd gone to the movies and eaten at McDonald's, which by Grace standards is the high life. We ordered Happy Meals; she was collecting small plastic replicas of impossible-looking vehicles for her boys. We had enough now to go home.

On our way out of town she insisted that we stop at an obvious tourist trap called Colossal Cave. It was colossal by no means, but a cave. We stood a long time in the dim entry while the guide in a Smokey Bear hat made small talk, hoping for a bigger crowd. There were only seven or eight of us. It must be hard to give your whole spiel to a group that wouldn't even make a baseball team or a jury.

"So when's Loyd get home?"

"Friday," I said.

"That switch-engine deal gets long, doesn't it?"

"It never seems to bother you," I said, although I had an acute memory of the night I'd glimpsed them making love in the courtyard.

"Mm," she said.

"Then again, Loyd might be making the whole thing up. He's probably got a sweetie in Lordsburg." Emelina looked startled. "I'm kidding," I said.

"Don't say stuff like that. Knock on wood." She thumped the side of her head.

"Well, it's occurred to me to wonder why Loyd wasn't married or anything when I came along. If he's such a hot item."

"He was."

"Married?"

"*No.* Seeing somebody, but not that serious. Definitely not married. He was once, awhile back, for a year or two, I think. No kids. He didn't tell you?"

"I never asked."

"Her name was Cissie. She didn't deserve him." Emelina peeled off her Dallas Cowboys sweatshirt (actually John Tucker's). It was cave temperature down there, only 55 degrees but much warmer than outside, where it was predicted to drop below freezing that night. A woman near us was wearing a mink coat.

"I wasn't about to leave it in the car," she said to us, without provocation.

Loyd had never mentioned even a large personal fact like a previous marriage, whereas this woman in mink felt compelled to explain herself to strangers. That's how it is: some people are content to wait till you ask, while others jump right in with the whole story. It must have to do with discomfort. Once while I was waiting to file off an airplane, a grandmother came down the aisle carrying a doll in one arm and a little boy in the other, and she actually took the time to explain to us all as she passed, "The doll is his sister's, she's up ahead." I could relate to the urge. I remembered all my tall tales to strangers on buses. I was explaining in my own way; making things up so there would be no discussion of what I was *really*.

At last our guide spoke some encouraging words and the little crowd followed him down into the cave. As he walked he told us about an outlaw who'd ducked in here to hide his loot, back in the days of Jesse James, and apparently had never come out. This was meant to give us a thrill of fear, but it seemed more likely that there was a back door somewhere and the bad guy got away with the money. That's how things go. I still believe Adolf Hitler is living in the South Pacific somewhere with sanded-off fingerprints and a new face, lying on a beach drinking mai-tais.

Emelina hadn't seen a cave before and was very impressed. There were delicate stalactites shaped like soda straws, and heavy, hooded stalagmites looming up from the cave floor. She kept pointing out formations that reminded her of a penis.

"You've only been away from home three days," I whispered.

"I didn't say it looked like *J.T.'s*," she whispered back.

The sound of trickling water was everywhere, even over our heads. I shivered to think how many tons of rock and dirt were up there above us. I'd forgotten that caves were not my favorite thing.

The highlight of the tour was the Drapery Room, which was admittedly impressive in size. The guide pointed with his flashlight to various formations, which had names like Chief Cochise and The Drapes. The walls and ceiling glittered with crystallized moisture.

Then, for just a minute—they always have to do this—he turned off the lights. The darkness was absolute. I grabbed for Emelina's arm as the ceilings and walls came rushing up to my face. I felt choked by my own tongue. As I held on to Emelina and waited for the lights to come back on, I breathed slowly and tried to visualize the size of the room, the distance between myself and the roof that I knew was there. Instead I saw random images that didn't help: Emelina collecting the little fast-food cars for her boys; the man in the café who'd suggested I marry him. And then while we all still waited I understood that the terror of my recurring dream was not about losing just vision, but the whole of myself, whatever that was. What you lose in blindness is the space around you, the place where you are, and without that you might not exist. You could be nowhere at all.

# 18

# Ground Orientation

Loyd and I were going to spend Christmas at Santa Rosalia Pueblo. Snow fell steadily as we drove north through the Apache reservation. It enclosed translucent desert trees in spherical white envelopes, giving them form and substance. It was surprising to look out over a landscape that normally seemed empty, and see a forest.

When I closed my eyes I saw papier-mâché peacocks. I'd been helping out on the piñata assembly lines. I'd had nightmares again and wasn't sleeping well; I figured I could be useful. We didn't turn out five hundred piñatas in ten days—that was a little ambitious—but we passed the halfway mark. The last fifty or so were the best by folk-art standards. By then we'd already used up every scrap of blue crepe paper from the attics and bureau drawers of Grace, and so had to be enterprising. Some women cut up denim jeans. Mrs. Nuñez made peacock wings out of the indigo-colored flyleaves of all twelve volumes of the *Compton's Children's Encyclopedia*. To be sure, there were no two alike.

I also sweat blood over my mimeographed broadside. I wasn't a writer except by default. Viola refused to help, saying I was the one that went to college so quit whining. I tried to include all the things that made Grace what it was: the sisters coming over with their peacocks; their blue-eyed descendants planting an Eden of orchards in the idyllic days before Black Mountain; the confetti-colored houses and stairstep streets—everything that would be lost to a poisoned river. All in one page. Viola wouldn't let me go longer, claiming nobody would read it. There was some argument over whether to put the note *inside* the piñata, like a message in a bottle. I said city people didn't buy art just to crack it open; I was respected as an expert on city people. So my modest History of Grace was rolled, bound in ribbon like a diploma, and inserted into each peacock's beak.

The second Tucson excursion filled two chartered buses. Some husbands and kids got into the act, and also my students. I declared it a class project. I told Raymo if he sold ten peacocks I'd give him a C +. But I didn't go. Loyd had asked for a week's layoff and we set out on the trip he'd been planning forever.

"Don't you have to stop somewhere and check on your roosters?" I asked. We were near Whiteriver.

"I don't have any roosters."

"You don't?" I was incredulous. I thought he'd just stop going to fights himself. "What, you sold them?"

"Collie Bluestone kind of took over the business."

"So you could get back into it if you wanted to."

"Nope. He's moved over to the Colorado River reservation. He's fighting them over at Ehrenberg."

This was a good bit more frightening than if Loyd had presented me with a diamond ring. "But I'm not . . . What if you and I don't work out, Loyd?"

He downshifted for a rutted stretch in the road. "No offense, Codi, but I didn't give up cockfighting to impress you. I did it because you were right."

"I was *right?*"

"About what you said."

"What did I say?"

He didn't answer. I vaguely remembered saying something about puncture wounds and internal hemorrhage. Making that a spectator sport. "I can't believe you'd do this thing all your life and then just quit one day after something I said. Maybe you were ready to give it up anyway."

"Maybe I was." We were both quiet for a while, passing through winter-killed fields of grass and sage. Two black horses grazed on bristly shrubs in a field with no apparent fences.

"You and your brother were twins, right?" I asked, apropos of nothing.

He nodded. "Identical. Twins are bad luck."

I laughed. "For the mother."

"No, in the pueblo. When twins are born people say there'll be a poor rainy season or grasshoppers or some darn thing. In the old days you had to let twins die."

"Both? You couldn't pick one and let the other one go?"

"Nope."

"I can't imagine the mother who'd do it," I said, though of course I could. I had probably starved my own child to death *in utero*, rather than risk known disaster.

"There's a Tewa story about a mother sneaking her twins out of the pueblo and leaving them with Spider Grandmother to raise."

"Yeah? See, if there was a story like that, people knew it was wrong to let them die."

"Knew it was hard. Not wrong, necessarily. When Leander and I were bad, our mother said she was like poor old Spider Grandmother, got stuck with the War Twins."

"Were you bad a lot?"

"Just twice as bad as a regular boy." He laughed. "People called us 'Twice as Bad.' Our sisters talked about us like we were just one boy. They'd say 'he went out riding,' or whatever. I think *we* thought we were one person. One boy in two skins."

"Hallie and I feel that way sometimes."

I could see clear crescents of water collecting on Loyd's lower eyelids. "You don't have to talk about this," I said.

"I don't ever talk about him. Sometimes I'll go a day or two without even thinking about him, and then I get scared I might forget he ever was."

I laid a hand on his gearshift arm. "You want me to drive?"

He stopped and turned off the engine. We sat watching snowflakes hit the windshield and turn into identical dots of water. Then he got out. I pulled on my mittens and followed him.

Outside the cab it was impossibly quiet. We'd climbed a little now, and were in forest. Snowflakes hissed against pine needles. Jack sat in the truckbed watching Loyd carefully, exhaling voiceless clouds of steam.

"I ever tell you how I came to keep Jack?" Loyd asked.

I thought about it. "No. You told me how you took in his mother and she had pups. You didn't say how you picked Jack."

"He picked us." Loyd was leaning against the truck with his arms crossed over his chest. He looked cold. "Dad meant to drown the whole litter. He put them in an empty cement bag and tied the top real good and drove down to the river and pitched them in. He didn't know what he was doing; he was drunk as seven thousand dollars, I imagine. On the way back he picked me up from work and I said, 'Dad, here's one of the pups in the back of the truck.' He was hiding down in a box of pipe T-joints. Dad's old truck was a junkyard on wheels; you could find anything in the world back there. So I says to Dad, 'Where's the rest of them?'" Loyd's voice caught, and he waited a second, wiping his eyes. "I don't know what I'm getting all broke up for. God knows what I would have done with seven mongrel coyote pups."

God knows what I'd have done with a baby at sixteen, I thought. It's not the practical side of things that breaks us up. I leaned on the truck beside him and took his left hand between my mittened palms. It felt like a cold bottle. "So what happened? Why did you lose Leander?"

"Why?" He looked up at the sky. "Because we left the Pueblo. We were like the War Twins, I guess. A lot for our mother to handle. Our sisters were all older and having their own babies by that time. And people thought boys should go out in the world some. Be with our dad. He'd been down at Whiteriver more or less as long as we could remember. If we'd stayed up there in Santa Rosalia it would have worked out, but we came down here and Leander just ran into trouble. We didn't have anybody looking after us. Dad couldn't look after himself."

"Doesn't sound like it," I said.

"Everybody always talked like Leander died of drinking, but he wasn't but fifteen. Not old enough to sit down and order a beer. Everybody forgets that, that he was just a kid. We drank some, but I don't think he was drinking the night he died. There was a fight in a bar."

"What did he die of, then?"

"Puncture wounds. Internal hemorrhage."

**I drove through** the pine forest, thinking off and on of Hallie, mindful of the slick road. Loyd was quiet, but took the wheel again when we descended into the Navajo reservation. He pointed out areas that were overgrazed. "It seems as big as the whole world, but it's still a reservation," he said. "There's fences, and a sheep can't cross them."

As dusk took us the landscape changed to an eerie, flat desert overseen by godheads of red sandstone. We were out of the snow now. The hills were striped with pinks and reds that deepened as we drove north and the sun drove west. It was dark when we left the highway and made our way down a bumpy road into the mouth of Canyon de Chelly. We passed several signs proclaiming the canyon bottom to be Navajo tribal land, where only authorized persons were admitted. The third sign, sternly luminous in the headlights, said, "Third and Final Warning."

"Are we *allowed* in here?" I asked.

"Stick with me. I can get you into all the best places."

Down in the canyon we bumped over rough road for an hour, following the course of a shallow river. There was no moon that I could see, and I lost any sense of direction I might have had while we still had sun. I was exhausted but also for the first time in weeks I felt sleepiness, that rare, delicious liqueur, soaking into my body like blotter paper. I almost fell asleep sitting up. My head bobbed as we crossed and recrossed the frozen river and climbed its uneven banks. Finally we stopped, and slept in the truckbed, cuddled like twin mummies inside a thick wrapping of blankets. We turned our bodies carefully and held each other to keep warm. Outside the blankets, our lips and noses were like chipped flint striking sparks in the frozen air.

"No fair, you've got Jack on your side," I murmured.

"Jack, other side, boy," Loyd commanded. Jack stood up and walked over the cocoon that contained us, stepping carefully on our chests. He turned around a few times in the wedge of space behind me, then dropped down with a groan and snuggled against my back. Within minutes I could feel the extra heat and I fell into heaven-sent unconsciousness.

In the morning, a sugar coating of snow had fallen, lightly covering the rocks. Ahead of us the canyon forked into two; from the riverbed a red rock spire rose a thousand feet into the air. Low clouds, or high fog, brushed its top. I held my breath. Looking up at a rock like that gave me the heady sensation of heights. He'd parked so this would be the first thing I saw: Spider Rock.

The canyon walls rose straight up on either side of us, ranging from sunset orange to deep rust, mottled with purple. The sandstone had been carved by ice ages and polished by desert eons of sandpaper winds. The place did not so much inspire religion as it seemed to be religion itself.

I was dressed in an instant and walking around awestruck like a kid, my head bent all the way back. "It doesn't look like a spider," I said, of the rock. "It looks like a steeple."

"It's named for Spider Woman. She lived up there a long time ago. One day she lassoed two Navajo ladies with her web and pulled them up there and taught them how to weave rugs."

The thought of standing on top of that rock, let alone trying to learn anything up there, made me shiver. "Is that the same Spider Grandmother who raised the twins?"

I expected Loyd to be impressed by my memory, but he just nodded. "That's a Pueblo story and this is a Navajo story, but it's the same Spider Woman. Everybody kind of agrees on the important stuff."

I shaded my eyes and looked up the canyon. Its narrows gave window views into its wider places. Giant buttresses of rock extended from the canyon walls, like ships, complete with knobbly figureheads standing on their prows. Some of the figureheads had been stranded, eroded away from the mother rock, and stood alone as sculptured spires. Where the canyon grew narrower the rock buttresses alternated like baffles, so the river had to run a slalom course around them. So did we. The truck crunched over icy shoals and passed through crystal tunnels of icy cottonwood branches. We passed a round hogan with a shingled roof and a line of smoke rising from its chimney pipe. A horse wandered nearby, nosing among the frozen leaves.

Several times Loyd stopped to point out ancient pictures cut in the rock. They tended to be in clusters, as if seeking refuge from loneliness in that great mineral expanse. There were antelope, snakes, and ducks in a line like a carnival shooting gallery. And humans: oddly turtle-shaped, with their arms out and fingers splayed as if in surrender or utter surprise. The petroglyphs added in recent centuries showed more svelte, self-assured men riding horses. The march of human progress seemed mainly a matter of getting over that initial shock of being here.

Eventually we stopped in a protected alcove of rock, where no snow had fallen. The walls sloped inward over our heads, and long dark marks like rust stains ran parallel down the cliff face at crazy angles. When I looked straight up I lost my sense of gravity. The ground under my boots was dry red sand, soft and fine, weathered down from the stone. If the river rose to here, the mud would be red. Loyd held my shoulders and directed my eyes to the opposite wall, a third of the way up. Facing the morning sun was a village built into the cliff. It was like Kinishba, the same multistory apartments and unbelievably careful masonry. The walls were shaped to fit the curved hole in the cliff, and the building blocks were cut from the same red rock that served as their foundation. I thought of what Loyd had told me about Pueblo architecture, whose object was to build a structure the earth could embrace. This looked more than embraced. It reminded me of cliff-swallow nests, or mud-dauber nests, or crystal gardens sprung from their own matrix: the perfect constructions of nature.

"Prehistoric condos," I said.

Loyd nodded. "Same people, but a lot older. They were here when Columbus's folks were still rubbing two sticks together."

"How in the world did they get *up* there?"

Loyd pointed out a crack that zigzagged up from the talus slope to the ledge where the village perched. In places the crevice wasn't more than two inches deep. "They were pretty good rock climbers," he said. Loyd's forte was understatement.

There wasn't a sound except for the occasional, echoing pop of a small falling rock. "What were they scared of?" I asked quietly.

"I don't know. Maybe they weren't scared. Maybe they liked the view."

The doors were built so you'd have to step high to get out. Obviously, for the sake of the children. "Gives you the willies, doesn't it? The thought of raising kids in a place where the front yard ends in a two-hundred-foot drop?"

"No worse than raising up kids where the frontyard ends in a freeway."

"You're right," I said. "No worse than that. And quieter. Less carbon monoxide."

"So you do think about that sometimes," Loyd said.

"About what?"

"Being a mother."

I glanced at him and considered several possible answers. "All the time," and "never" seemed equally true. Sometimes I wanted to say, "You had your chance, Loyd, we had our baby and it's dead." But I didn't. That was my past, not his.

"Sure, I think about it," I said, needing to relieve the pressure in my chest. "I think about hotwiring a Porsche and driving to Mexico, too."

He laughed. "Only one of the two is legal, I'm told."

I wanted to try and climb up into the cliff village, but Loyd explained that we'd crack our skulls, plus you weren't supposed to mess with the antiquities.

"I thought you broke all the rules," I said, as we climbed back into the truck and headed farther up the canyon.

He looked surprised. "What rules have I broken?"

"Authorized Navajo personnel only, for starters. We're not even supposed to be down here."

"We're authorized guests of Maxine Shorty of the Streams Come Together clan."

"Does she live here?"

"Not now. Almost everybody drives their sheep out and spends the winter up top, but the farms are down here. Leander and I spent almost every summer here till we were thirteen."

"You did? Doing what?"

"Working. I'll show you."

"Who's Maxine Shorty?"

"My aunt. I'd like you to meet her but she's down visiting at Window Rock for the holiday."

Loyd was full of surprises. "I'll never get your family straight. How'd you get a Navajo aunt? Are Navajos and Pueblos all one big tribe or something?"

Loyd laughed rather hysterically. It occurred to me that this redneck Apache former cockfighter must find me, at times, an outstanding bonehead. "The Pueblo people were always here," he explained patiently. "They're still building houses just like this—the Rio Grande Pueblos, Zuñi, Hopi Mesa. Not in the cliffs anymore, but otherwise just the same. They're about the only Indians that haven't been moved off their own place into somebody else's."

"And the Navajo?"

"Navajos and Apaches are a bunch that came down from Canada, not that long ago. A few hundred years, maybe. Looking for someplace warmer."

"And this is now Navajo tribal land, because?"

"Because the U.S. Government officially gave it to them. Wasn't that nice? Too bad they didn't give them the Golden Gate Bridge, too."

The truck crunched over frozen sand. "So the Pueblo are homebodies, and the Navajo and Apache are wanderers."

"You could look at it that way, I guess."

"What are you?"

"Pueblo." There was no hesitation. "What are you?"

"I have no idea. My mother came from someplace in Illinois, and Doc Homer won't own up to being from anywhere. I can't remember half of what happened to me before I was fifteen. I guess I'm nothing. The Nothing Tribe."

"Homebody tribe or wanderer tribe?"

I laughed. "Emelina called me a 'homewrecker' one time. Or no, what did she say? A 'home ignorer.' "

He didn't respond to that.

"So how'd you get a Navajo aunt?" I asked again.

"The usual way. My mother's brother married her. Pueblo men have to marry out of the clan, and sometimes they go off the pueblo. The land down here stays with the women. So my uncle came here."

Maxine Shorty's farm, which she inherited from her mother and would pass on to her daughters, was a triangle bordered by the river and the walls of a short side canyon. We parked by the line of cottonwoods near the river and walked over the icy stubble of a cornfield. A sad scarecrow stood guard. It occurred to me that the barrenness of a winter farm was deceptive; everything was there, it was still fertile, just as surely as trees held their identity in the shape and swell of their bare winter twigs.

"Has it changed much?"

I meant it as a joke, I saw nothing that *could* have changed, but Loyd looked around carefully. "Those little weedy cottonwoods have grown up along the stream. And there's a big boulder on that slope, you see the one with dark stripes? That used to be up there." He pointed to a place in the canyon wall, visible only to himself, from which the boulder had fallen. Most men, I thought, aren't this familiar with the furniture in their homes.

"So what did you do here?"

"Worked our butts off. Weeded, picked corn, grew beans and watermelons. And had to carry a lot of water in the bad years."

"Were those peach trees here?" I asked. A weathered orchard occupied the steep upper section of land.

"They're older than my aunt. The peach trees go way back. They were planting orchards down here three hundred years ago."

"A canyon of fruit. Like Grace."

He inspected the trees carefully, one at a time: the bases of the branches, the trunks, the ends of twigs. I didn't know what he was looking for, and didn't ask. It seemed like family business. On this land Loyd seemed like a family man.

"And did the people that lived up in the cliffs grow corn and beans too?"

"That's right."

"So how come this canyon's stayed productive for a thousand and some-odd years, and we can't even live in Grace for one century without screwing it up?"

It was mostly a rhetorical question but Loyd considered it for a long time as he led me along a path up the talus slope to the back of the box canyon.

"I know the answer to that," he said finally. "But I can't put it in words. I'll have to show you. Not here. Later on."

I felt sadly let down, though it was closer to an actual promise of revelation than I'd gotten in nine years of watching Carlo's eyebrows. I could wait for "later on."

At the top of the slope was another ancient dwelling, this one mainly just ruined walls. The floor plan was clear. It interested me that the doors all lined up, I suppose to admit light to the interior.

"I found a whole clay pot in here one time," Loyd said. "It's in my mother's house." He lowered his voice. "Don't tell any Navajos, they'll throw Mama in jail."

"You brought it back to her at the end of one summer, right? As a present. And she still treasures it."

He smiled a little shyly. The image of a ten-year-old Loyd brought the threat of tears to my eyes. I'd spent my life watching mother-child rituals from outside the window.

"So you played in here when you were little?"

"Oh, yeah. This used to be me and Leander's fort."

"Cowboys and Indians?"

He laughed. "Good Indians and bad Indians."

"Which were you?"

"Nobody can be good all the time. Or bad all the time. We took turns."

He led me over a couple of tumbledown walls to the base of the cliff, and knelt down. I looked where he pointed. Set carefully among an assortment of old petroglyphs were two modern ones: the outlined left hands of two small boys, just touching, perfectly matched.

**We crossed the** high desert from Chinle to Ship Rock, New Mexico, and on to the Jemez Mountains. Wind battered the windows and we warmed our hands at the heater vents and talked about everything under the sun. Loyd talked about his marriage to Cissie Ramon, which he said was noisy and short. Cissie was crazy about rooster fighting, men, and unusual colors of nail polish, like green. He'd thought she was exotic, but she was just wild; there was a difference. She ran out on him.

He was a good deal more interested in talking about working in his aunt's pecan orchards, in Grace. This aunt was his mother's sister, Sonia. She married a Pueblo man from her village but moved with him to Grace when Black Mountain drafted Native American men into the mines during World War II. Sonia and her husband planted fruit trees there, thinking the war would last at least twenty years, and when it didn't they felt they ought to stay on in Grace anyway, for the sake of the orchards.

It was a different story from farming in Canyon de Chelly, Loyd said. Sonia had started out as a tenant picker, before buying her own pecan orchard, and she learned harvesting the modern way. Usually the harvest started in October and ran till Thanksgiving. To get the nuts off the trees, they used a machine called a tree shaker.

"I remember guys hitting the branches with sticks, when I was a kid," I said.

"Nah, we were high-tech. After the tree shaker comes the harvester, which is this big thing with a vacuum-scooper that you drive along between the rows. It scoops up everything and blows the sticks and leaves out the back, and the pecans and rocks fall down into this cage at the bottom. More junk falls out the slots as it rolls around, and the hulls fall off, and the idea is you end up with mostly pecans. But really you end up with pecans and pecan-sized dirt clods and pecan-sized rocks."

"So did you get to drive the big machines?"

"Nope. Mostly I got to pick rocks and dirt clods off the conveyor. I think that was the best job I ever had. The hardest, but the best, because I grew up on it. Stopped thinking about myself all the time and started thinking about something else, even if it was just damn pecans."

I took it from Loyd's use of the singular pronoun that Leander was dead by this time. Slowly I was patching together Loyd's life, and it was not the poor little gypsy story I'd imagined. I suppose I'd wanted to see him as a fellow orphan. But everywhere he'd been, he'd been with family.

"How long will Grace last without the river?" I asked.

"Two or three years, maybe. The old orchards will go longer because their roots are deeper." He glanced at me. "You know I have an orchard?"

"No. In Grace?"

"Yep. Not the pecans, those belong to my cousins, but Tía Sonia's leaving me the peach orchard. The fruit trees were always my job, keeping the birds and squirrels off the fruit."

"How do you do that?"

"Well, the main way is by killing them."

I laughed.

"What's funny?"

"I don't know." I stared out the windshield. In the distance, Ship Rock floated like a ghost vessel on the snowy plain. "So you now have a dying orchard to call your own. Your Aunt Sonia's moved back to Santa Rosalia, right?"

"Right. But the orchard's not mine till I have kids."

"That doesn't seem fair."

"No, it makes sense. When you have a family, you need trees." He paused, carefully, it seemed to me, and redirected the conversation. "What job did you grow up on?"

I thought this over. "Maybe I haven't had it yet."

He smiled. "You went to medical school, right? And almost finished. That can't be too easy."

"When it stopped being easy, I quit."

"What were you doing in Tucson, then, before you came to Grace?"

"You don't want to know. Cashier in a 7-Eleven."

"Shoot. And I thought you were too good to go out with a locomotive engineer. What about before that?"

"You don't want to know."

"Yes, I do."

"Well, I did medical research at the Mayo Clinic in Minnesota."

"Damn! Really?"

"Yep. I was living up there two years ago when I first found out Doc Homer was sick."

"And before that?"

I rolled my head back and looked at the roof of the car. "You *really* don't want to know."

"You were President of the United States."

"Guess again."

"You hotwired Porsches."

I laughed. "The biggest thing I ever stole was a frozen lobster, for my boyfriend's birthday. I was working in frozen foods and I think I actually wanted to get fired. Doesn't that sound stupid?"

"Yes, it sounds stupid. So that came before Mayo Clinic?"

"That, and a bunch of different odd little things. A few piddly research jobs in between. Believe me, I never put everything on the same résumé."

"And what's the one you never mention? The one you're trying not to tell me about."

"For a few years in there I lived overseas."

"No kidding. Did you fly? Shoot, I'd love to go someplace in an airplane."

"Flying's okay," I said. In truth, flying terrified me. It's the one thing I knew I had in common with my mother, who'd flat-out refused, there at the end. In my own life I handled it by means of steadfast denial. I'd flown over the Atlantic Ocean twice without even checking to see if there really was a flotation device under my seat; flotation seemed beside the point. Oh, I flew like a bird.

"So, okay, what were you doing overseas?"

I glanced at him. "I was my boyfriend Carlo's girlfriend. On the island of Crete."

He seemed amused. "What, you mean you cleaned house and made cookies?"

"Kind of. Sometimes I'd help out in the clinic. One time I set the broken leg of a sheep. But mostly I was a housewife."

"So you'd, what, go shopping in a bikini?"

I laughed. "It really was not that kind of island. You know where it is, right? In between Greece and Egypt. The women wear black wool dresses and crucifixes the size of a hood ornament. Getting the picture?"

He nodded.

"The main baby present for a boy is a silver knife, which they present in this ceremony where the godparents list all the enemies of the family going back to around Adam and Eve."

"You liked it that much, huh?"

I took my coat off. It was finally warming up. "Well, it was interesting. It was someplace to go. It was like going to another century, actually. But I felt like a complete outsider." I closed my eyes, fighting an old ache.

"How do you mean?"

"I'm pretty good at languages but I never could get the hang of fitting in. Not anywhere, but especially not there."

"Why do you think you don't fit in? Give me an example."

It was plain that I'd always been an oddity in Grace, so he must have meant how was I an oddity in Crete. "Well, my first day there I marched into the bakery and asked for a *psoli*. The word for a loaf of bread is *psomi*. A *psoli* is a penis."

Loyd laughed. "Anybody could make a mistake like that."

"Not more than once, I promise you."

"Well, you were foreign. People expect you to say a few dumb things."

"Oh, every day I did something wrong. They had complicated rules about who could talk to who and what you could say and who said it first. Like, there were all these things you were supposed to do to avoid the Evil Eye."

"How do you do that?" he asked. Loyd was full of curiosity.

"You wear this little amulet that looks like a blue eyeball. But the main thing is, you never *ever* mention anything you're proud of. It's this horrible social error to give somebody a compliment, because you're attracting the attention of the Evil Eye. So you say everything backward. When two mothers pass each other on the road carrying their babies, one says to the other, 'Ugly baby!' And the other one says, 'Yours also!' "

Loyd laughed a wonderful, loud laugh that made me think of Fenton Lee, in high school. Who'd died in the train wreck.

"I swear to God it's true."

"I believe you. It's just funny how people are. People in Grace do that too, in a way. You give them a compliment and they'll say, 'Oh, no, that's just something I've had a long time.' We're all scared to be too happy about what we've got, for fear somebody'll notice and take it away." He reached over and stroked the underside of my arm, from the elbow up. "Like you, Codi. You're exactly like that. Scared to claim anything you love."

"Am I?" I was willing to believe whatever he said. Talking with Loyd was like talking to myself, only more honest. Emelina was always asking me what it was like to live overseas, and I knew she would love the penis story, but I'd never told her much about Crete. I was afraid of her seeing me as more of an outsider in Grace than I already was. But Loyd didn't make those judgments. I could have told Loyd I'd lived on Neptune, and he'd say, "Uh-huh? What was it like, was it cold?"

**In the Jemez Mountains** we drove up the slope of what looked like a huge old volcano. A fluted core of granite jutted from its mouth, and twisted black ridges of old lava flows ran like varicose veins down its sides. The snow was deep and the road icy. We crept along, then stopped. Loyd got out of the truck and started down the bank toward a frozen creek that cut between the road and the steep mountainside.

"Are you nuts?" I inquired.

"Come on." He waved energetically.

"Why should I follow you down there?" I demanded, following as fast as I could.

"It's a surprise."

It was near sunset, near or below freezing, and Loyd wasn't even wearing his jacket. I slipped several times behind him and then we both slid flat-out down the hill on our backs. We were sledding, not on snow but on an exposed hillside of bizarre, rounded gravel. I picked up a handful in my mitten and tossed it in the air. It was

porous and weightless like Styrofoam popcorn. "What is this stuff?"
I asked, but Loyd was already crossing a log over the frozen creek. I
scrambled behind him up the forested slope on the other side. I
picked my way between rocks, grabbing roots and tree trunks to pull
myself up. Halfway up I had to stop, hugging a pine trunk and panting. The cold air cut my lungs, and I blinked hard against the sensation that the water in my eyes might freeze over.

"It's the altitude," I whined. Loyd grabbed my hand and pulled
me gently uphill. Suddenly we were following the course of an odd
unfrozen stream with lush plants thriving alongside it, their leaves
glossy green against the snow. I'd never seen anything like this in
nature, only in the sort of paintings that show improbable and
dreamlike things. Loyd, who had gotten ahead of me again, was now
taking off his shirt. I wondered if perhaps I was, after all, in one of
my strange dreams, and whether I would soon be looking under the
foliage beside the stream for my lost baby.

I climbed over the top of a boulder and there stood Loyd, naked,
smiling, an apparition bathed in steam. He slid into the blue pool at
the base of the boulder. I touched the steaming water and it bless-
edly scalded my fingertips. I undressed more quickly than I probably have in my life, before or since, and immersed myself up to my
eyes.

The sun set. Venus opened her eye on the horizon. From where
we sat we could see the Jemez range and the valley floor fifty miles
to the south, its buttes and mesas still lit by a distant sun. When our
bodies turned red we stood up briefly among the snow-covered boulders, shouting, and the steam rose off our uplifted arms like smoke-
stacks.

Loyd asked, "So, am I nuts?"

I stretched my legs along the sandy bottom of the pool until my
toes found his. The heat relaxed every muscle and sinew and reflex
in my body, and most of the ones in my head. This kind of happiness
was sure to attract the attention of the Evil Eye. "Have you got any
more surprises?" I asked. "Or is this the last one?"

"I've got some more."

He scooted over and lifted me off the sand, supporting my floating body with both hands under the small of my back. "I don't give them away all at once, though," he said. "Only a half dozen a year."

I counted on my fingers: Kinishba. Spider Rock, the Cliff house, and Maxine Shorty's farm. And this, volcanic hot springs. I didn't know whether to count the cockfights or not. That he could give up cockfights, I'd have to count that. "So I've used up my half-dozen already," I said.

He lifted me slightly out of the water and kissed my ribs, one at a time. "If you're only staying around for a year. That's the rules."

"That's bribery."

"Whatever it takes." He kissed my navel and the damp hill over my pubic bone.

The front of my body was very cold and the back was very hot. Somewhere in the middle, near my heart, I was just right. I opened my eyes and saw constellations whose names were their own business. "Were you ever in love with my sister?" I asked.

He looked at me oddly.

"It's just a joke. Every man I've ever been with, it seems like, was really in love with Hallie."

"I can't picture your sister. She's shorter than you, right?"

I ducked my chin a little, immersing my smile. Right then I could have signed on for life.


**The day we left Grace,** there had been four airmail letters in the P.O. box. Lately Hallie's letters sometimes came in bunches, owing to the accumulated pauses in postal service between Chinandega and Grace. But I saved them and read only one per day. It supported the pleasant, false notion that she was available to me all the time and would always be there tomorrow.

The fourth day of our trip was Christmas Eve. In the morning as we drove down from Jemez, before we arrived in Santa Rosalia, I laid out all four letters on the dash in order of postmark and spent one last hour with my sister.

I reread the old ones before opening the fourth one. Hallie's week had gone wildly up and down. On Tuesday she was nigh unto manic because the government had had a successful national meeting on the pesticide problem. Central America was becoming a toilet bowl of agricultural chemicals, she said, because of war-strained farming economies and dumping from the First World. In the seventies, when Nicaragua was run by the U.S. Marines and Somoza, it was the world's number-one consumer of DDT. But it seemed the new Nicaragua (*our* government, she called it) planned to take responsibility for its poisons. She also mentioned that her friend Julio was back in Chinandega after a stint of literacy work near the Atlantic coast. I couldn't read anything between the lines.

On Wednesday, a child was rushed in from the village of San Manuel to the Chinandega clinic in critical condition because someone had stored paraquat in a Coke bottle.

On Thursday she was grimly happy. Five contras were making a secret sabotage raid on a hydroelectric plant, somewhere to the east, and were surprised by some armed farmers who took them captive. The culprits had passed through town in the back of an open Jeep, slit-eyed with dishonor, on their way to trial in Managua. Wouldn't it be something, she mused, if that Jeep hit one of the contra road mines? But there was the driver to consider, and even if there hadn't been, it wasn't something she could wish for. She said, "You can't let your heart go bad like that, like sour milk. There's always the chance you'll want to use it later."

I wondered at what point I'd given up on later and let mine go sour. I didn't know, although Hallie might. I reread each of the three letters with fascination but also the same dissatisfaction I'd had on the morning I'd opened it. It was all just *things happening,* and selfishly, I wanted Hallie. Even if she didn't speak to me directly, I wanted her to speak.

I tore open the last envelope and was hit full in the face with what I wanted. It was four pages long, in a cursive enlarged by rage. When God wants to punish you, as Isak Dinesen declared, He answers your prayers.

*I am like God, Codi? Like GOD? Give me a break. If I get another letter that mentions SAVING THE WORLD, I am sending you, by return mail, a letter bomb. Codi, please. I've got things to do.*

*You say you're not a moral person. What a copout. Sometime, when I wasn't looking, something happened to make you think you were bad. What, did Miss Colder give you a bad mark on your report card? You think you're no good, so you can't do good things. Jesus, Codi, how long are you going to keep limping around on that crutch? It's the other way around, it's what you do that makes you who you are.*

*I'm sorry to be blunt. I've had a bad week. I am trying to explain, and I wish you were here so I could tell you this right now, I am trying to explain to you that I'm not here to save anybody or any thing. It's not some perfect ideal we're working toward that keeps us going. You ask, what if we lose this war? Well, we could. By invasion, or even in the next election. People are very tired. I don't expect to see perfection before I die. Lord, if I did I would have stuck my head in the oven back in Tucson, after hearing the stories of some of those refugees. What keeps you going isn't some fine destination but just the road you're on, and the fact that you know how to drive. You keep your eyes open, you see this damned-to-hell world you got born into, and you ask yourself, "What life can I live that will let me breathe in & out and love somebody or something and not run off screaming into the woods?" I didn't look down from some high rock and choose cotton fields in Nicaragua. These cotton fields chose me.*

*The contras that were through here yesterday got sent*

*to a prison farm where they'll plant vegetables, learn to read and write if they don't know how, learn to repair CB radios, and get a week-long vacation with their families every year. They'll probably get amnesty in five. There's hardly ever a repeat offender.*

*That kid from San Manuel died.*

*Your sister, Hallie*

"What's new with Hallie?" Loyd asked.

"Nothing."

I folded the pages back into the envelope as neatly as I could, trying to leave its creases undisturbed, but my fingers had gone numb and blind. With tears in my eyes I watched whatever lay to the south of us, the land we were driving down into, but I have no memory of it. I was getting a dim comprehension of the difference between Hallie and me. It wasn't a matter of courage or dreams, but something a whole lot simpler. A pilot would call it ground orientation. I'd spent a long time circling above the clouds, looking for life, while Hallie was living it.

# 19

# The Bread Girl

Five miles outside of Santa Rosalia Pueblo, Loyd stopped the truck, pulled off his cowboy boots, and put on moccasins. Shortly we were going to have to get out and walk through snow.

"Saving your boots?" I asked.

He ignored me. Those particular boots looked as though they'd hitchhiked to hell and back without getting a single ride.

"Me and Leander used to come home at the end of the summer wearing cowboy boots and Mama would have a fit. And cowboy hats. She'd grab off our hats and swat us with them and say, 'Ahh! You look like Navajos!'"

I'd never seen Loyd wear a hat of any kind, now that I thought about it. His story brought back a memory, vague and incomplete, of cowboy boots and a hat I'd had myself, as a child. I could just recall the sheen of lacquered straw, and a terrible sadness.

"You see it yet?"

I squinted toward the south, but saw only snow-covered hills dotted with dark, spherical juniper bushes. The horizon was punctuated with bleak mesas whose rock shoulders stood exposed to the cold. "See what?"

"Where we're going to sleep tonight."

"I hope not."

A few minutes later he asked again. I saw mesas and scalped hills with rocky outcroppings on their tops. I saw juniper trees, and snow. "Is this an eye test?" I asked.

We were practically inside Santa Rosalia Pueblo before I saw it. The village was built on a mesa and blended perfectly with the landscape, constructed of the same stones as the outcroppings that topped all the other, empty mesas. Horses and broadfaced cattle looked up at us from their pens as Loyd's red truck, the newest-looking thing within a hundred miles, rolled up the dirt track into town.

It was a village of weathered rectangles, some stacked stepwise in twos and threes, the houses all blending into one another around a central plaza. The stone walls were covered with adobe plaster, smooth and appealing as mud pies: a beautiful brown town. The color brown, I realized, is anything but nondescript. It comes in as many hues as there are colors of earth, which is commonly presumed infinite.

We left the truck in the company of other pickups and station wagons at the edge of town, and walked up into the narrow streets. In his moccasins Loyd walked with a softer, less aggressive gait. Jack stayed close to his left knee. There wasn't a soul out, but lines of smoke drifted from chimneys and the big adobe beehive ovens that squatted in every third or fourth backyard. A black dog pawed at the edge of a frozen puddle. The ladders that connected one rooftop to the next were drifted lightly with snow. One house had a basketball hoop nailed to the end beams. Front curtains everywhere glowed with warm interior light, though it was still early afternoon, and strings of bright red chilies hung by the front doors.

Loyd's mother's house had a green door. The front window was crowded with artificial flowers and ceramic animals. Loyd's oldest sister, Birdie, met us at the door. The two of them spoke rapidly in a language that sounded like song, as if the pitch might be as important as the syllable. Birdie had a perm, and wore a large turquoise necklace over her flowered blouse. She stopped talking to Loyd just long enough to touch my arm and say, "He still has that dog, don't he?" and "Come get warm." We followed her into the kitchen, where Loyd's mother enveloped him with a hug, then tugged his ponytail and lightly boxed his ears.

"What's she saying?" I asked Birdie.

"She's saying he looks like a Navajo."

The kitchen smelled of cedar smoke. Inez Peregrina was cooking a goose, among other things. She wore a large dress composed of about six different cotton fabrics, florals and plaids, somehow colorfully harmonic. The frames of her glasses were large and owlish. Her gray hair was trimmed in bangs and a pageboy over her ears, but long in back, twisted into a heavy, complicated coil and tied with red cloth. Her hands were noticeably large. I wanted her to hug me too, but she only smiled and touched my cheek when Loyd introduced us. She continued talking to him in a steady, musical downpour, to which he was attentive.

Birdie disappeared and soon returned at the head of a flock of women, and I was introduced, but the conversation between Inez and Loyd went on, uninterrupted. One at a time, each of the other women held out both hands to me, which I took, trying to appear gracious while I struggled to get their positions straight. They were Loyd's sisters; a niece; his Aunt Sonia, who had lived in Grace during the war and after; and someone Loyd called his "navel mother." I couldn't discern the generations. Aunt Sonia spoke to me in Spanish and poured cups of coffee for Loyd and me from a huge tin pot on the wood-fired stove. There were also a propane stove and the adobe oven in the backyard, and all three were in use.

I felt spectacularly out of place. For one thing, I stood a foot taller than any other woman in the room; we don't even have to get into matters of wardrobe. But I was also fascinated to watch Loyd being his mother's son, his sisters' brother, the apple of the family eye. The only remaining boy. The sisters asked him in calm, uninflected English about the drive and the length of our stay and whether he'd seen Aunt Maxine, who evidently had a heart condition. Aunt Sonia asked several specific questions about people in Grace, some of whom I knew better than Loyd because of my Stitch and Bitch association, but I was reluctant to speak. She and the sisters drifted away to other tasks, and Inez still hadn't stopped talking.

"Is it okay if I look around?" I asked Loyd.

"You can dance on the table if you want to, you're the guest," he said, grabbing me around the waist.

"I don't want to dance on the table."

He held on to me for just a minute, asking Inez in English what she thought of me. I passed a hand through my hair, thankful that it had had time to grow out from Billy Idol to a more or less regulation Mary Martin.

Inez smiled and said something, running the ladle in her right hand up and down an imaginary line. I looked at Loyd for translation.

"She says I'm lucky to have gotten such a big, strong girl. She thinks I'm lazy."

"Tell her I don't put up with lazy men. I make them pull their weight."

He told her and she laughed, giving me the hug I'd coveted.

The frosted windowpanes looked out onto the cold plain and dish-shaped, empty cornfields that lay to the south, but the kitchen was smoky and warm. The open pantry behind Inez was stocked with jars of dry yellow corn, cans of Spam, and fruit cocktail. (No orchards here, evidently.) And hominy. In Grace it was golden jars of home-canned peach halves that sat smug on kitchen shelves. Here it was puffy white hominy, jar after jar of it, hominy enough for an army.

The kitchen was at the end of a big room that contained a long wooden table, a sofa, numerous small chests, and many, many photos. A radio in another room played Hank Williams. I moved around the living room, idly looking out the windows and examining photographs. There was one of Inez and a man I presumed to be Loyd's father standing together in formal dress: he in silver-buttoned moccasins and a royal blue velvet shirt, Inez in turquoise bracelets and a silver squash-blossom necklace over her dark ceremonial dress. Her legs looked like white birch stumps in their buckskin leggings, and the woven blanket folded across her shoulders seemed to weigh her down. She looked much older than she must have actually been.

Most of the available tabletops were populated by little ceramic animals of the pastel, cute variety. Loyd had told me Inez made the best pottery in the Pueblo, but evidently it was made for Anglo collectors, not for home use. I did find in a china cabinet a display of extraordinary black-and-white pots, their glazed surfaces covered with microscopically fine geometric designs. Some of the pots were slightly less well made, maybe some of the proud early efforts of Inez's daughters. A crude, dark bowl with a chipped rim sat in the cabinet's central place of honor, and I stared at it, puzzled, until I realized this was Loyd's pot, the one he'd found in the ruins. Loyd's offering from Canyon de Chelly.

I peeked into the next room. Charlie Rich was singing from the radio now, and Birdie hummed "Behind Closed Doors" while she bent over an electric sewing machine. Its small light glowed on her face. A baby slept on a flat, fur-lined cradle board that hung like a swing on ropes from the ceiling. On every fifth arc of the swing, Birdie reached up without looking and gave it a push. She noticed me standing in the doorway and inclined her head toward the end of the room, where an iron bed stood behind a drawn-open curtain of blankets. "You can put things there. That's for you and Loyd."

"Thanks," I said. "Who's the little one?"

"My daughter's girl. Hester."

"How old?"

"Three weeks."

"Does your daughter live here too?"

Birdie pulled her cloth from the machine and shook her head slightly while she broke the thread with her teeth. "She goes to boarding school in Albuquerque."

I returned to exploring the living room. I was stunned to run across a small framed photo of two little Loyds, identical, sitting astride very different horses. Behind them was a backdrop of dry hills and a brown water tank. Loyd and Leander, nine years old, looking as if they owned the world. Until I saw that picture I hadn't really heard a word he'd told me about losing his brother. You can't know somebody, I thought, till you've followed him home.

**That evening Inez's house** filled with relatives for the feast. Cousins and uncles and aunts showed up, stamping the snow off their moccasins, bringing covered dishes and their own chairs. All the older women had their hair cut in the same style as Inez's, with short flaps over the ears and the heavy chignon in the back, and they wore silver necklaces and elaborate turquoise rings that shielded their knuckles. The teenage girls wore jeans and about everything else you'd expect on a teenage girl, except makeup. One of them nursed a baby at the table, under her T-shirt.

Loyd and I shared one chair; apparently we were the official lovebirds of this fiesta. He spent a lot of time telling me what I was eating. There were, just to begin with, five different kinds of *posole,* a hominy soup with duck or pork and chilies and coriander. Of the twenty or so different dishes I recognized only lime Jell-O, cut into cubes. I gave up trying to classify things by species and just ate. To everyone's polite amusement, my favorite was the bread, which was cooked in enormous, nearly spherical loaves, two dozen at a time, in the adobe ovens outside. It had a hard brown crust and a heavenly, steaming interior, and tasted like love. I ate half a loaf by myself, believing no one would notice. Later, in bed, Loyd told me they were all calling me the Bread Girl.

Our bed was small, but after three nights in the truck it felt deliciously soft. I cuddled against Loyd. "What's a navel mother?" I asked, drowsy with warmth and a half loaf of bread.

"She's like a special aunt. She's the one that cuts the cord when you're born, and helps your mother get up out of bed when she's ready. They count that as your birthday—the day your mother gets up."

"Not the day you were born?"

"Not the day you came out. They count the mother getting better as all part of the birth."

"Hallie doesn't have a birthday, then," I said. "After she was born, our mother never got up. She got real sick, and then a helicopter tried to come get her and she died. All without ever putting her slippers on."

"Then Hallie never finished getting born," Loyd said. He kissed the top of my head.

I was aware of the sleeping sounds of Inez and Hester on the other side of the makeshift curtain. I asked, "Is it okay that we're sleeping together?"

Loyd quietly laughed at me. "It's okay with me. Is it okay with you?"

"I mean with your family."

"They're not hung up about it. Mama wanted to know if you're my woman."

"Meaning what?"

"As opposed to woman of the week, I guess."

"Woman of the year," I said.

In the morning snow had fallen, as deep as five or six quilts. The windows were round blue tunnels to the light, like the mouths of caves. Loyd got up and went outside, where, at dawn, Inez and Birdie were already involved with the day's industry. He was sent back to bed with a whole fresh loaf of bread.


**"How did your dad** meet her?" I asked. Loyd and I were sitting on the roof of Inez's house now, facing south, waiting for ceremonies to begin in the plaza.

"At a dance over in Laguna. In the summertime. It was a corn dance. Everybody says she was a knockout when she was young. A real good dancer."

"I think she's a knockout now."

"He grew up over at Jicarilla."

"Where's that?"

"Not too far from here. It's another Apache reservation. Everybody goes to everybody's dances. We used to go over to the Navajo powwows in the fall."

Today, on Christmas Day in Santa Rosalia, there were supposed to be dances from morning till night. Half the town seemed to be preparing to dance, while the other half were busy getting good seats. I had no idea what to expect. Anxious-looking little boys clutching feather crowns and fox pelts ran across the corners of the plaza bent low, as if this would make them invisible. Earlier in the day these same little boys had run in boisterous gangs from house to house banging on doors and begging for warm crusts torn from the morning loaves. A wholesome version of trick-or-treat. Give these kids one Halloween in Grace, I thought, and they'd never be content with complex carbohydrates.

"So he married your mother," I said. "And came here."

"The women are kind of the center of things up here. The man goes to the wife's place."

"But he didn't stay."

"I never really knew Dad that well. He was already gone when he was still here, if you know what I mean. I don't know what it was that hurt him. I know he grew up at a boarding school and never had much family and he couldn't keep to the old ways. Or didn't know them. I don't know. It was real hard for him here."

I let the subject go. As the twig is bent, so grows the tree, Doc Homer used to say, referring mostly to the bone structure of the feet but it applied to moral life as well. And who knew how the kinks happened; they just did. I ought to know. As Hallie had bluntly pointed out in her letter, I'd marked myself early on as a bad risk, undeserving of love and incapable of benevolence. It wasn't because of a bad grade on a report card, as she'd supposed. It ran deeper than that. I'd lost what there was to lose: first my mother and then my baby. Nothing you love will stay. Hallie could call that attitude a crutch, but she didn't know, she hadn't loved and lost so deeply. As Loyd said, she'd never been born—not into life as I knew it. Hallie could still risk everything.

Loyd and I dangled our feet over the side of the roof, looking out over the plaza and beyond, to where the plaza ended suddenly, perforce, by the drop of a sheer cliff. I could only see this precipice as a threat, and wonder how toddlers lived to the age of reason without toddling over it, but many little feather-bedecked children were running along its edge as if it were nothing more than the end of a yard.

I heard a drum and a brief burst of what sounded like sleigh bells. Then nothing. If anything ever did happen, we'd have a good view. We'd climbed a ladder to get where we were. Jack had given a long, dejected look up the rungs as if he might consider the climb, if he weren't so dignified. Now he lay curled at the bottom keeping watch. Old wooden ladders and aluminum extension ladders were propped everywhere; second- and third-story roofs served as patios. All around the plaza, legs hung like fringe over the sides of buildings. I spotted Inez and some other relatives across the way. Inez's owlish glasses were the type that turn dark outdoors; two huge black disks hid her round face as she sat, hands folded, inscrutable as a lifeguard.

Not far from us in a sheltered corner of the roof was a wire pen full of geese and turkeys muttering the subdued prayers of the doomed. "Does your mama know you were a cockfighter?" I asked Loyd.

"No." He hesitated. "She knew Dad did it, and that he took Leander and me to the fights when we were little, but she didn't care for him doing that. She never knew I went on with it. And you better not tell her."

"I'm gonna tell," I said, poking him in the ribs. "I'm going to look up in my *Keres*–English dictionary, 'Your son is a dirty low-down rooster fighter.'"

Loyd looked pained. Pleasing his mother was nothing to joke about. He'd given up cockfighting for Inez, not for me, I now understood. I'd just been the cricket in his ear. But that wasn't insignificant, I decided. I could settle for that. I looked down at the plaza, whose quilt of fresh snow remained a virginal white, unmarred by tracks. This seemed miraculous, considering the huge number of people crowded around its edges—a good two hundred or more. People must have come from outside the Pueblo. Jicarilla Apaches looking for knockout wives.

"How come those houses over there near the edge of the cliff are falling down?" I asked. Their adobe plaster had cracked off, revealing the same artful masonry as Kinishba, in a state of collapse.

"Because they're old," Loyd said.

"Thank you. I mean, why doesn't somebody fix them up? You guys are the experts, you've been building houses for nine hundred years."

"Not necessarily in the same place. This village was in seven other places before they built it up here."

"So when something gets old they just let it fall down?"

"Sometimes. Someday you'll get old and fall down."

"Thanks for reminding me." I shaded my eyes, looking to the east. Something was happening near the kiva, which was a building with a ladder poking out through a hatch in its roof. Loyd had suggested I shouldn't show too much interest in it.

"The greatest honor you can give a house is to let it fall back down into the ground," he said. "That's where everything comes from in the first place."

I looked at him, surprised. "But then you've lost your house."

"Not if you know how to build another one. All those great pueblos like at Kinishba—people lived in them awhile, and then they'd move on. Just leave them standing. Maybe go to a place with better water, or something."

"I thought they were homebodies."

Loyd rubbed his hand thoughtfully over my palm. Finally he said, "The important thing isn't the house. It's the ability to make it. You carry that in your brain and in your hands, wherever you go. Anglos are like turtles, if they go someplace they have to carry the whole house along in their damn Winnesotas."

I smiled. "Winnebagos. They're named after an Indian tribe." It occurred to me too late that Loyd already knew both these things.

For months, I think, I'd been missing his jokes. Empress of the Universe, instructing the heathen.

"We're like coyotes," he said. "Get to a good place, turn around three times in the grass, and you're home. Once you know how, you can always do that, no matter what. You won't forget."

I thought of Inez's copious knickknacks and suspected Loyd was idealizing a bit. But I liked the ideal. The thought of Hallie's last letter still stung me but I tried to think abstractly about what she wanted to tell me: about keeping on the road because you know how to drive. That morality is not a large, constructed *thing* you have or have not, but simply a capacity. Something you carry with you in your brain and in your hands.

I'd come on this trip knowing I still had to leave Loyd in June, that Grace wouldn't keep me, but maybe I was just keeping to the road. I felt guilt slip out of me like a stone. "It's a nice thought," I told him. "I guess I'll probably carry something away with me when I leave Grace."

He looked at me carefully, started to speak, then stopped. And then did speak. "It's one thing to carry your life wherever you go. Another thing to always go looking for it somewhere else."

I didn't respond to that. I blinked hard and tried to look unconcerned, but the guilt nudged back along with the sharp glass edge of my own rationalization, recognized for what it was. I wasn't keeping to any road, I was running, forgetting what lay behind and always looking ahead for the perfect home, where trains never wrecked and hearts never broke, where no one you loved ever died. Loyd was a trap I could still walk out of.

I listened to the sad geese in their pen, and realized the crowd was quiet. The snowy plaza was marked with a single line of tracks: in the center of the white square stood a tall young woman in a black dress that hung from one shoulder. Her other shoulder was bare. Her waist, her upper arms and wrists, and her buckskin moccasins were all decorated with garlands of colored yarn, fur, and sleigh bells; at the crest of her head was a tuft of white eagle down. The sun shone purposefully on her hair. It was cut like Inez's, but hung loose to her waist, swaying as she moved slightly from one leg to the other, her feet barely leaving the ground. She looked graceful and cold.

The sound of drums and then the drummers themselves emerged from the kiva. The four old men took their position at the edge of the plaza and propped their huge drums on their knees without missing a beat. They began a soft chant. A second line of men with blankets draped over their shoulders climbed down from the kiva, also singing, and took their places behind the old drummers.

Then deer arrived, from everywhere. They were men and boys with black shirts and leggings, white kilts, and deer antlers. Their human features disappeared behind a horizontal band of black paint across the eyes. They moved like deer. They held long sticks in front of them, imitating the deer's cautious, long-legged grace, and they moved their heads anxiously to the side: listening, listening. Sniffing the wind. The woman in black stepped forward shaking her gourd rattle, and they followed her. They *became* deer. They looked exactly as deer would look if you surprised them in a secret rite in the forest, moving in unison, following the irresistible hiss of a maiden's gourd rattle.

I was entranced. More people climbed down out of the kiva. Some were dressed and armed as bow hunters who stalked the deer with patience. One man, who didn't seem to have any realistic function in the drama, was nearly naked and bizarrely painted. His body was ringed with black and white horizontal stripes, he had black rings painted around his eyes and mouth, and his hair was pulled up into a pair of corn-tassel horns. He bounced around like a hysteric, possibly in the interest of keeping warm.

"Who's the striped guy?" I asked Loyd.

"Koshari," he said. "A kachina. He has to do with fertility. His home's in the East."

This struck me as humorous. "The East, as in New York? Area Code 212?"

"The East as in where the sun rises."

"That's all part of his job description?"

"All the kachinas have whole histories and families and live in one of the important places."

"I thought a kachina was a little doll."

"That's right."

"And also a person dressed up?"

"Yep. And a spirit."

"A spirit with a family and a mailing address."

"That's right. When the person dresses up a certain way, the spirit comes into him. And into the doll, if it's made right."

"Okay," I said.

"What?"

"Nothing, just okay. I understand."

He smiled at me sideways. "You think it sounds voodoo?"

"All right, I'm narrow-minded. It sounds kind of voodoo."

We both paid attention to the dancers for a while. I needed to keep a little distance from Loyd.

"Anglos put little dolls of Santa Claus around their houses at Christmas," Loyd said without looking at me.

"Yeah, but it's just a little doll."

"And does it have a wife?"

"Yes," I conceded. "A wife and elves. And they live at the North Pole."

"And sometimes one guy will dress up like Santa Claus. And everybody acts a certain way when he comes around. All happy and generous."

I'd never been put in a position to defend Santa Claus. I'd never even *believed* in Santa Claus. "That's just because he stands for the spirit of Christmas," I said.

"Exactly." Loyd seemed very pleased with himself.

One of the hunters had drawn his bow and shot an invisible arrow into a deer. It gave an anguished shiver, and then the other hunters lifted its limp carcass onto their shoulders.

"I've seen Jesus kachinas too," Loyd said. "I've seen them hanging all over people's houses in Grace."

Now there was a thought to ponder.

Koshari must also have been the spirit of nuisance, or a good belly laugh. The other deer dancers still followed the maiden, ignoring the hunters and their own fallen brother, but Koshari clowned and cut between them, getting in their way and generally interfering with their solemnity. But when one of the youngest dancers lost his antlers, Koshari picked up the headdress and carefully reattached it by its buckskin laces. The boy kept dancing, eyes front, paying no attention to the hobgoblin who was putting his costume back together.

At some later point, I noticed, Koshari had acquired a new-looking straw cowboy hat, which he cocked ridiculously on one of his horns. I had a feeling it wasn't the Navajo he was aping here. He walked duck-footed with a John Wayne swagger and was using a length of two-by-four as a gun. He knelt and fired repeatedly at the dancing deer, grandly falling over backward each time. Later he stalked them, trailing his gun in the snow and tripping over it with admirably practiced body comedy.

The deer eventually retreated to the cliff, and the plaza filled with two lines of new dancers—a row of black-clad women and a row of men in white kilts—whose bodies beat a loud rhythm as they walked. Their chests were crisscrossed with lines of seashell bells. The two rows of dancers faced one another and stamped their feet, shaking the bells, crowding the air above the plaza with a loud, hollow clicking like summer insects. The men wore crowns of eagle feathers and the women wore spectacular wooden headdresses painted with stylized clouds and slanting blue lines of rain and green blades of corn. This was the corn dance, officially a summer prayer but danced at every important occasion, Loyd said, because you couldn't pray it often enough.

"Most of the dances have to do with rain," he said. "Here, that's what everything hangs on."

Santa Claus kachinas and the beauty of the spectacle notwithstanding, I still felt outside of it. "So you make this deal with the gods. You do these dances and they'll send rain and good crops and the whole works? And nothing bad will ever happen. Right." Prayer had always struck me as more or less a glorified attempt at a business transaction. A rain dance even more so.

I thought I might finally have offended Loyd past the point of no return, like stealing the lobster from frozen foods that time, to get myself fired. But Loyd was just thinking. After a minute he said, "No, it's not like that. It's not making a deal, bad things can still happen, but you want to try not to *cause* them to happen. It has to do with keeping things in balance."

"In balance."

"Really, it's like the spirits have made a deal with *us*."

"And what is the deal?" I asked.

"We're on our own. The spirits have been good enough to let us live here and use the utilities, and we're saying: We know how nice you're being. We appreciate the rain, we appreciate the sun, we appreciate the deer we took. Sorry if we messed up anything. You've gone to a lot of trouble, and we'll try to be good guests."

"Like a note you'd send somebody after you stayed in their house?"

"Exactly like that. 'Thanks for letting me sleep on your couch. I took some beer out of the refrigerator, and I broke a coffee cup. Sorry, I hope it wasn't your favorite one.' "

I laughed because I understood "in balance." I would have called it "keeping the peace," or maybe "remembering your place," but I liked it. "It's a good idea," I said. "Especially since we're still here sleeping on God's couch. We're permanent houseguests."

"Yep, we are. Better remember how to put everything back how we found it."

It was a new angle on religion, for me. I felt a little embarrassed for my blunt interrogation. And the more I thought about it, even more embarrassed for my bluntly utilitarian culture. "The way they tell it to us Anglos, God put the earth here for us to use, westward-ho. Like a special little playground."

Loyd said, "Well, that explains a lot."

It explained a hell of a lot. I said quietly, because the dancers' bells were quieting down, "But where do you go when you've pissed in every corner of your playground?" I looked down at Koshari, who had ditched his cowboy hat and gun and seemed to be negotiating with Jack.

I remembered Loyd one time saying he'd die for the land. And I'd thought he meant patriotism. I'd had no idea. I wondered what he saw when he looked at the Black Mountain mine: the pile of dead tailings, a mountain cannibalizing its own guts and soon to destroy the living trees and home lives of Grace. It was such an American story, it was hardly even interesting. After showing me his secret hot springs, Loyd had told me the Jemez Mountains were being mined savagely for pumice, the odd Styrofoam-like gravel I'd thrown into the air in handfuls. Pumice was required for the manufacture of so-called distressed denim jeans.

To people who think of themselves as God's houseguests, American enterprise must seem arrogant beyond belief. Or stupid. A nation of amnesiacs, proceeding as if there were no other day but today. Assuming the land could also forget what had been done to it.

**Our Koshari friend** had somehow bought off Jack and taken away the ladder that was Loyd's and my only way down. He was standing down there clowning now, pantomiming a smooching couple and talking at great length, playing to the crowd, which was laughing. At one point they all applauded. Loyd was plainly embarrassed.

"What's he saying?" I asked.

"I'll tell you in a minute."

When Koshari had gone to another part of the plaza and people had stopped staring, I pressed Loyd again.

"He said now we'll have to stay up here together a long time."

"He talked for five minutes, Loyd. I know he said more than that."

"Yeah. He said by the time the snow melts, we'll . . . Basically he said in the spring there'd have to be a wedding."

I made a face. "And people *liked* that idea? Of you marrying me? They were clapping."

"You're not . . ."

He stopped, because a kind man in the crowd had come over to replace our ladder.

"You're not the Ugly Duck, you know," Loyd said, once the man had gone.

"They don't even know me. I'm an outsider."

"I'm an outsider too," he said. "They probably know my mother likes you."

"How would they know that?"

"Word gets around."

"I mean, how does *she* know that? I can't even talk to her."

"Do you like her?"

"Yeah. I do."

"How do you know?"

"I like her hugs. She makes good bread."

"Well, maybe that's why she likes you. You like her bread."

It was hard to stay mad at Loyd.

**The corn dancers** had remarkable stamina. Sometimes they danced in two facing lines, their whole axis rotating around the plaza like a wheel. At other times the women's line moved into and through the men's and then they broke into pairs, the men leading, practically prancing, while the women held their eyes on the ground with such concentration as to render it fertile. I would have believed a thunderclap just then, and a summer rainstorm. They danced on and on. The women's moccasined feet and thickly wrapped legs moved only a fraction of an inch with each step, but the restrained action of that step must have cost more effort than jumping jacks. They did it, and did it, and did it until early afternoon.

The corn dance was followed by an eagle dance, which seemed to involve all the young children in the village and a few older, more skillful dancers. Each one was dressed in a dark shirt and leggings, a white embroidered kilt, and a hood of white eagle down, complete with eyes and a hooked beak. Running from fingertip to fingertip across their backs, they had eagle-feather wings. The youngsters trembled with concentration as they crouched low, then rose in unison, raising their wings and soaring in convincing eaglelike fashion.

It seemed slightly less reverent than the previous dances, more akin to the childhood phenomenon of the dance recital, but Loyd said this was also a prayer. Every dance is a prayer. The eagle carries people's thoughts to the spirits in the sky. Animal messengers for the small, human hope. As they danced, the children's lips moved constantly in silent recitation.

"Watch," Loyd said. "One will go toward the east." One did. It was one of the older, more reliable dancers. He glided with outstretched wings to the edge of the plaza and past it, down the central street toward the eastern end of the village. Loyd explained that he was carrying the mothers' concerns for all the boys in the armed service.

Koshari was now solemnly busy among the children, who needed a good deal of prompting and putting-together of costume parts. At several points he left the dancers and made his way around the crowd taking requests for special blessings, special worries. I asked Loyd to get his attention.

"For my sister," I said, and Loyd translated. "She's in the south. A long way to the south."

Near the end of the dance, one small eagle arched his wings and ran all the way to the southern end of the plaza. The wind lifted his feathers as he paused on the edge of the precipice and for just a second I was sure he would have to fall, or fly.

# HOMERO

# 20

# The Scream

The kettle is about to boil, and the telephone rings. He dries his hands slowly and goes to answer it, expecting Mandy Navarrete's fourth child. Christmas Day, a long silent day, will end now with a long unpleasant night. There was a time when deliveries excited him; during the gene-pool study he looked forward to those infant eyes, and setting up his camera and lights. But there is nothing to study now. Mandy Navarrete is all muscles and resistance, a woman who delivers in her own time. Her grandmother Concepcion Navarrete was his first-grade teacher. She was similarly muscular, and disapproved of his family.

He lifts the receiver slowly on the fourth or fifth ring. The voice speaks in hurried Spanish but he answers in English because he knows they can understand. He hasn't spoken Spanish since the day he married Alice. "There is plenty of time," he says. "I know this process. We don't need to be in a panic."

He hears silence, static, several different voices and questions and then the same voice again, emphatically repeating its word: *Secuestrada*. Kidnapped.

"Who is this?"

He listens. The voice is very distant and often breaks. It is a woman, a friend of his daughter. He tries to understand which daughter they mean. *Secuestrada*. Codi has been away for several days but this voice is saying "Hollie." Someone is keeping her. She was in the field alone, with her horse, when they came to blow up the building where she has chemicals for the crop. He understands none of this and lets it sift past him like pollen, like his life. There are many more words in his life than he would like, most of the time.

*Hollie,* the woman insists, as if she is trying to wake him from sleep. Are you the father? *El padre de Hollie Nolina?* We are very much afraid.

We are very much afraid.

In the first grade she hit a boy and they kept her after school. The boy's name was Simon Bolivar Jones. He was angry at her and had called her vicious names because she climbed to the top of the tall slide the wrong way, up the slide and not the steps, and stood up there and danced, shouting, her hands outstretched. No boy could do it.

"You should let her come home. She hasn't done anything wrong. She's being punished for an act of bravery." He isn't sure whether he has just spoken in Spanish or English.

*Sí,* the voice answers after a moment. *Claro que sí.*

"Where is she?"

*No estamos seguros.* We think they must have taken her into Honduras, where they're camped. A large patrol has gone to look for her. Thirty people, more than half of them from the village where she lives. There were more who wanted to go. Even an eight-year-old boy. Hallie has many friends.

Even an eight-year-old boy. Thirty people.

The words are so much fine dust suspended in the air before him, in the long, trapezoidal block of sunlight from the window. He examines the dust. He sees the word "Hallie." It was Codi who stood up and danced on the slide.

"You should let her come home," he says again. He can remember precisely the muscular line of Mrs. Navarrete's disapproving jaw. "Let my daughter come home now."

The voice rejects this statement, says nothing.

He touches the corner of his eye and is surprised to find moisture on his fingertips. He stares at an iron coal bucket beside the fireplace, trying to recall its history, how it came to him. He thinks, for no reason, that this iron coal bucket could save his life, if only he could remember. He remembers instead that he no longer delivers babies, the telephone call could not possibly be Mandy Navarrete. It is a woman from another country, who knows his daughter. He is trying hard not to look at the dust in the air but the sun has illuminated each particle so that it glows. Each word burns.

"Is there something I can do?" he asks finally. "I know she has friends in the Ministry of Agriculture. Do they know?"

"Everyone knows. Our Ministry of Agriculture, your Ministry of Agriculture." There is a pause. "You understand that this occurs every day. We're a nation of bereaved families. The only difference this time is that it happens to be an American. It happens to be Hallie." The voice weakens again, and he waits, and it goes on. "We sent a telegram to your President and the NBC. We think if they are embarrassed enough by their contras, they could do something."

If they are embarrassed enough.

"Wait. Let me take down the number where you are. So I can call you tomorrow."

"I'm in the office of a church in Managua. Nobody here knows anything. You can call the Ministry of Agriculture if you want. Or your President. He is the responsible party."

He understands that she is being as helpful as she can. She is a kind, tired voice. He doesn't want her to hang up, because then his life will begin. There is a pause while she talks to someone else who is there with her, and then she returns to him and says, "I'm sorry."

"Is there anything more? Besides waiting?"

"I'm sorry. There is nothing."

Carefully he puts down the receiver and looks at the air in front of the window in this empty room. The dust. He listens inside himself for a long time before he understands that it's the teakettle that is screaming.

# COSIMA

# 21

# The Tissue
# of Hearts

Hallie was somebody's prisoner. Whether my eyes were open or closed, I saw her with a white cloth tied tightly over her mouth. That's the only image that would ever come.

If she couldn't scream, I did. I was in every way unreasonable, especially with the kids at school. Even at the time, I was lucid enough to be thankful that Rita had dropped out. One member of my family had already yelled at her; she didn't have to know that neither one of us had all our tires on the road.

The students had tried to be cooperative. They went to Tucson to assist the Stitch and Bitch Club, as I'd requested, and found the city to be a superb adventure. They discovered a video arcade; Raymo sweet-talked more than ten young women into buying piñatas; there were rumors that Connie Muñoz gave Hector Jones a hand job in the back seat of the bus on the way home. What did I expect? They were teenagers. I knew that, but still I screamed at them because Black Mountain was poisoning their mother's milk and all they cared about was sex and a passing grade.

I had rational intentions. I talked about evapotranspiration and rain forests and oxygen in the biosphere, how everything was connected. The last virgin timber cleared and milled to make way for a continent of landfills choking on old newspapers. It was a poetic lecture. Marta made the mistake of asking me how much of this poetry was going to be on the test.

I glowered. "Your life is the test. If you flunk this one, you die."

The whole front row looked stunned. Their pens stopped moving.

"What you people learn for a test you forget the next day. That's bullshit. That's a waste of your brains and my time. If I can't teach you something you'll remember, then I haven't even been here this year." I crossed my arms and glared at them. "You kids think this pollution shit is not your problem, right? Somebody will clean up the mess. It's not your fault. Well, your attitude stinks. You're as guilty as anybody. Do you, or do you not, think the world was put here for you to use?"

Nobody was fool enough to answer. I observed during the long silence that half the kids in the room were wearing stone-washed jeans. I yanked up Hector Jones by the arm and made an example of him. I have to admit I disliked Hector partially for unfair reasons: his father was a former hoodlum named Simon Bolivar Jones who'd been noticeably unkind to me in school.

"Stand up here," I said. "Show everybody your jeans. Nice, right? Turn around. Nice ass, Hector. Wonderful jeans. They were half worn out before you bought them, right?" I smacked Hector lightly on the butt and let him sit down.

"You know how they make those? They wash them in a big machine with this special kind of gravel they get out of volcanic mountains. The prettiest mountains you ever saw in your life. But they're fragile, like a big pile of sugar. Levi Strauss or whoever goes in there with bulldozers and chainsaws and cuts down the trees and rips the mountainside to hell, so that all us lucky Americans can wear jeans that look like somebody threw them in the garbage before we got them."

"Trees grow back," Raymo said. Raymo was a brave young man.

"Excuse me?"

He cupped his hands around his mouth and spoke as if I were his deaf grandmother: "Trees . . . grow . . . back."

I cupped my hands around my mouth and said, just as loudly, "Not if the whole . . . damn . . . mountain is gone, they don't."

"Well, there's other mountains."

"Sure, there's some other mountains," I said, feeling that I might explode if I weren't careful. "If you got hit by a truck, Raymo, I guess your ma would say, 'Well, I have some other kids.' "

About half the class thought that was funny. The other half was probably trying to figure out how to get out of my classroom alive.

I stared them down, ticking like a bomb. "Sure. Trees grow back. Even a whole rain forest could grow back, in a couple hundred years, maybe. But who's going to make it happen? If you had to pay the real price for those jeans—the cost and the time and the work of bringing that mountain back to life instead of leaving it dead—those pretty jeans would have cost you a hundred dollars."

I felt strangely high. Furious and articulate. "Think about the gas you put in a car," I said. "The real cost. Not just pumping it out of the ground and refining it and shipping it, but also cleaning up the oil spills and all the junk that goes into the air when it gets burned. That's part of what it costs, but you're not paying it. Gas ought to be twenty dollars a gallon so you're getting a real good deal. But soon the bill comes due, and we pay it, or we eat dirt. The ultimate MasterCharge."

I can't swear they were listening, but they were watching me carefully. Thirty-six blue eyes ticked back and forth as I paced the floor in front of my desk.

"If Grace gets poisoned, if all these trees die and this land goes to hell, you'll just go somewhere else, right? Like the great pioneers, Lewis and Clark. Well, guess what, kiddos, the wilderness is used up." I walked around my little square of floor like a trapped cat. "People can forget, and forget, and forget, but the land has a memory. The lakes and the rivers are still hanging on to the DDT and every other insult we ever gave them. Lake Superior is a superior cesspool. The fish have cancer. The ocean is getting used up. The damn *air* is getting used up." I pointed at the ceiling, meaning to indicate the sky. "You know what's up there? Ozone. It's this stuff in the atmosphere that acts like an umbrella."

I stopped and reconsidered this effete analogy. Teenagers who won't use condoms aren't impressed by the need for an umbrella. I surveyed the class thoughtfully and demanded, "Whose Dad or Mom ever worked in the smelter?"

About half the hands went up, reluctantly.

"You know what they did up there, right? One way or another they were around thousand-degree hot metal. You ever see them dressed for work? They wore coveralls like Mr. Neil Armstrong walking on the moon, and a big shield over their faces, right?"

They nodded, relieved, I suppose, that I wasn't going to single them out for humiliation. I sat on the desk and crossed my arms. "Imagine that's you, working up there with that hot metal in your face. Now, somebody rips that mask off you while you're working. Goodbye face. Goodbye nose and eyelids, beauty queens. You're dead."

They might well have been dead, for all the sound they made.

"That's what the ozone layer does for us, boys and girls, it's a big face shield in the sky." I was skipping a few steps here, but not really exaggerating the consequences. Not at all. I attempted to lower my voice and sound faintly reasonable. "And it's slipping away from us. There's a big hole in it over the South Pole. When you use a spray can you make that hole bigger. There's something in most aerosol cans and refrigerators and air conditioners, called chlorofluorocarbons, that neutralizes the ozone. Factories are still making tons of it, right now."

I suspect "chlorofluorocarbons" was the largest word ever spoken within the walls of Grace High, and I'm fairly sure also that nobody forgot it for at least the rest of the day.

After the bell rang, Connie Muñoz eyed me and said, "Miss, I seen you wear stone-washed jeans to school sometimes." The other kids were already out of there like bats out of hell.

"You're right," I said. "I didn't know about the mountains when I bought them. Just like Hector didn't, and you didn't."

"Yeah?" She chewed her gum and held me under a neutral, military sort of gaze. I'd publicly humiliated her new boyfriend; this would require some diplomacy.

"I've been learning a lot of this stuff just lately," I told her. "I'm not saying I'm not part of the problem."

"So how come you're so mad at us, Miss?"

I felt conscious of my height, and embarrassed. "Connie, I don't really know. Because I'm guilty too, I guess. And now I'm trying to fix it all at once."

A hint of life came into her eyes. "Don't sweat it," she said. "I think it's cool that you cuss and stuff when you're mad. Everybody was paying attention. What you said was right, these guys just think when they use something up there's always going to be more."

"I shouldn't have cussed," I said. "I'm supposed to be setting an example. And I shouldn't have picked on Hector the way I did."

She laughed and cracked her gum. "Hector Jones is a dickhead."

**I had dinner at** Doc Homer's house. I'd done so every night since I got back from Santa Rosalia and found out Hallie had been kidnapped. If I badgered him enough, I kept thinking, he would have something more to tell me. But he couldn't remember anything. If I'd ever doubted Hallie was his favorite, there was no question about it now—I'd never seen him so affected by any event in our lives. He still functioned, cooked for himself and went to work, but it was only an obstinate ritual; he was a mess. I'd found some of his medication bottles in a cache in the living room, inside an old iron coal bucket. There was no way to know whether he was taking them. Half the time he talked to me as if I were six years old.

"Who was the person you spoke with on the phone?" I asked again. "Was she somebody in the government? There's got to be somebody we can call." I cautiously eyed the plate he set down in front of me. Doc Homer had prepared liver with steamed apples and yellow squash. In certain restaurants things like this passed for *haute cuisine,* I knew, but here it passed for weird. It was getting to where he'd combine anything he found in his refrigerator. I'd started shopping for him, lest he get down to refried beans and ice cream.

"She suggested that we call the President of the United States," he said.

I set my fork down on the table. He'd said this quite a number of times before. "I think I *will* call the President." I moved my chair back from the table. It was an idle threat; I'd probably just get a polite recording. But I knew Doc Homer wouldn't want what he would consider an absurd long-distance call on his bill.

"I understand you have a boyfriend," he said, cutting his liver and apples into small pieces.

"What do they think will happen? Did this person you talked to sound real worried? Or did she say this was a routine kind of thing? Sometimes they'll just take a foreign hostage to get attention and then they'll let them go the next day. She's probably back at her house already." I knew this was unlikely. The contras, as I understood it, didn't need attention. They were fully supported by the richest sugar daddy in the modern world.

"He drinks, Codi. He will take advantage of you."

I stared at Doc Homer for a long time. "Not anymore," I said. "He doesn't drink anymore. And he couldn't take advantage of me if he wanted to. I'm as sweet and innocent as the Berlin Wall. Your concern is approximately two decades too late."

"My concern is for your welfare."

"Your concern." I picked up slices of apple and ate them with my fingers, to annoy him. "I'm going to have to go down there. I can get a bus to Tucson tonight and a plane to Managua and be there tomorrow." I doubted it was this easy.

The teakettle boiled and he jumped up. He seemed edgy. He got out the filter paper and slowly set up the drip machine for coffee, carefully positioning each part of the apparatus as if it were some important experiment in organic chemistry.

"I told you it wasn't a good idea," he said, pouring boiling water into the funnel. I waited for some further clue. He could be evaluating any mistake I'd made since age three.

"What idea is that?" I prompted, since he didn't go on.

"Loyd Peregrina."

We both watched the water pass through the dark grounds, absorbing their color and substance. He'd never mentioned Loyd's name before; I was surprised he knew it. I wondered whether Doc Homer had a whole other life in his head, in which he dispensed kind, fatherly advice. This gulf—between what Doc Homer believed himself to be and what he was—brought out the worst in me, or the most blunt. "Don't worry about Loyd Peregrina," I said. "I can't get hurt now. I'm leaving him this time. It's just a short-term thing."

"He won't elevate your life."

"Damn it, you don't know the first thing about my life. What's to elevate? I'm a medical-school dropout who works graveyard shifts in quick-marts."

"You left the profession by choice. We've established that."

"Okay, so I walked out the door with my eyes open. What did I choose instead? What am I good at? Name one thing."

He balked. I knew he would. Doc Homer wasn't fluent in the language of compliments.

"I have no career, no kids, not even a place I consider home. Basically I'm a bag lady with an education."

"That's a preposterous assessment."

"How would you know? You don't really see me, you just see what you want. You take pictures of people and turn them into rock walls."

"That is not what I do. I begin with a picture in my head, from the past. I try to duplicate it from the images I have at hand."

This was a new one. "I don't believe I give a damn about the images you have at hand." I lowered my voice. The quickest way to lose points with Doc Homer was to lose control. I said, "You always just wanted Hallie and me to be above everybody in Grace."

"You *were* above your peers."

I snorted at that. "I was as trashy as Connie Muñoz and Rita Cardenal, without half their guts or one-tenth of their sex appeal. I was ugly and embarrassed to be alive."

Doc Homer had a strange way of actually getting quieter when he raised his voice. "My daughters were not trash," he said.

I looked him square in the eye. "I got pregnant when I was fifteen."

"I know. I watched you bury the baby in the riverbed."

I felt an odd flush in my neck and face. For about a minute we both listened to the dripping of the coffeepot. Then I said, "Why do you lie about everything?"

"I've never told you anything but the truth."

"You've never told me anything, period. You said you and mother came from Illinois. But you came from here. You've got a whole family lying up there in the damn graveyard."

"We did come here from Illinois. I was stationed there, and went to medical school there. We moved back here after the war."

"What kind of war had people stationed in Illinois?" I asked absurdly, close to tears. "I'm sorry, but in history class they never told us about the Midwestern Front."

"Alice's family despised me."

I stopped, remembering how Viola had averted her eyes and said, "that family went downhill," the day I discovered Homero Nolina up in the cemetery. The red-haired Gracela sister with the temper, who married Conrado Nolina and produced a legacy of trash—that was my father's family. What he believed he came from, and what we still were. Auburn-haired and angry, living in exile in our own town. There wasn't enough air in the kitchen for me to breathe, and get all this in.

"So you, what, ran off to the army. Got yourself educated on the G.I. Bill, and then came back here as the mighty prodigal doctor with his beautiful new wife, and acted like nobody could touch you."

I watched him closely, but could read nothing. I couldn't even *see* him, really; I had no idea how he'd look to a stranger. Old? Sick?

Mean-spirited? He poured coffee into two mugs and gave the larger one to me.

"Thank you," I said.

"You're welcome."

"Why did you come back here? If it was so important to you to start over, you could have gone anywhere. You could have stayed back there in Illinois."

Doc Homer sat down opposite me. He clenched and unclenched his left hand, then spread it flat on the table and examined it abstractly, as if it were a patient. I looked at the framed photograph on the wall over his head: his portrait of a hand that wasn't a hand, but five cacti with invisible spines.

"Why do you suppose the poets talk about hearts?" he asked me suddenly. "When they discuss emotional damage? The tissue of hearts is tough as a shoe. Did you ever sew up a heart?"

I shook my head. "No, but I've watched. I know what you mean." The walls of a heart are thick and strong, and the surgeons use heavy needles. It takes a good bit of strength, but it pulls together neatly. As much as anything it's like binding a book.

"The seat of human emotion should be the liver," Doc Homer said. "That would be an appropriate metaphor: we don't hold love in our hearts, we hold it in our livers."

I understand exactly. Once in ER I saw a woman who'd been stabbed everywhere, most severely in the liver. It's an organ with the consistency of layer upon layer of wet Kleenex. Every attempt at repair just opens new holes that tear and bleed. You try to close the wound with fresh wounds, and you try and you try and you don't give up until there's nothing left.


**For Christmas,** Loyd had given me an Apache burden basket. It was exquisitely woven, striped with the colors of dried grass, and around its open mouth hung tin bells on leather thongs that made whispery, tinkling sounds. It wasn't much bigger than a teacup.

The night he gave it to me in Santa Rosalia I felt it would easily hold all my burdens, forever. Now it hung on the wall over my bed, and at night I looked at it and wept for my own stupidity in trusting that life could be kind.

I apologized to my classes. I couldn't see trying to maintain the recommended authoritative distance; I told them my sister had been kidnapped and that I was scared to death. I told them everything seemed very serious to me now, including things like the ozone layer. The kids were extremely quiet. I don't think any adult had ever apologized to them before. From the storeroom we got down a pre–World War II map that showed all the world's climatic zones, and we found Nicaragua, Honduras, Costa Rica, El Salvador. The shapes and names of many nations had changed during the lifetime of that map, but not the climatic zones. We talked more calmly about the rain forest and the manner in which fast-food chains were cutting it down to make hamburger farms. We talked about poor countries and rich countries and DDT in the food chain, and the various ways our garbage comes home to us. The memory of the land. My students understood these things perfectly well. There is nothing boring about the prospect of extinction.

On Friday I took the day off to make phone calls. Hallie had left me a list of emergency telephone numbers, mostly speculative, and I called them all. It took the whole morning. I got nowhere with the State Department and the U.S. Department of Agriculture, and ended up with the Nicaraguan Ministry of Agriculture. Viola helped me contend with the impenetrable Spanish of international operators. Emelina sat on my other side holding my hand, wringing the fingers, apparently forgetting that it wasn't hers. Mason and the baby sat on the floor in front of us, silent, wondering as children always must wonder in a crisis what terrible thing they had done to wreck the world.

We learned nothing useful. They were sure now that Hallie had been taken across the border into Honduras, probably to a camp where many other prisoners were held. It was a well-outfitted camp; they had Sony radios and high-quality C-rations. It made me smile, a little, to think Hallie might be eating C-rations I'd dutifully paid for with my taxes. Dinner was on me. So were the land mines.

I spoke with a dozen secretaries of this and that and finally with the Minister of Agriculture himself. He knew Hallie. He talked for a long time about what an extraordinary person she was; it made me suspicious that she was dead, and I started crying. Viola took the phone and translated until I was fit to talk again. The Minister promised me she wasn't dead. He would call me the minute they knew anything at all. He was fairly sure the contras took her by mistake, not knowing she was an American citizen, and now were probably confused as to how to release her without generating too much bad publicity. He asked, had I called the President of the United States?

In the meantime, Hallie's letters still came to the Post Office box. I knew she had mailed them before she was kidnapped, but their appearance frightened me. They looked postmarked and cheerful and real, but they were ghosts, mocking what I'd believed was a solid connection between us. I'd staked my heart on that connection. If I could still get letters like this when Hallie was gone or in trouble, what had I ever really had?

I didn't read them. I saved them. I would open them all once I'd heard her voice on the phone. I wouldn't be fooled again.


**At some point** between Christmas and mid-January, Grace became famous. The several hundred piñatas planted in Tucson had grown into great, branching trees of human interest, which bore fruit in the form of articles with names like "This Art's Not for Breaking" and "What Piñatas!" in slick magazines all over the Southwest. The Stitch and Bitch Club's efforts in papier-mâché became a hot decorator item in gentrified adobe neighborhoods like the one in Tucson that Hallie used to call Barrio Volvo.

It was the birds that caused the stir, but because it was there, people were also reading my urgent one-page plea for the life of Grace. Where Mayor Jimmy Soltovedas's repeated calls to the press had failed, Stitch and Bitch succeeded: our story became known. Hardly a day passed without some earnest reporter calling up to get a statement from Norma Galvez. The club designated her the media spokeswoman; Doña Althea was more colorful, but given to unprintable remarks. Ditto for Viola, who was even more unprintable because she spoke English.

But when a scout crew from CBS News came to town, they wanted the Doña. They sat in on a meeting at the American Legion hall and zeroed in on the Stitch and Bitch figurehead with her authority and charm and all she represented in the way of local color. They got some of the meeting on tape, but made an appointment to come back on Saturday with a crew to interview the Doña in her home. Norma Galvez would be (for safety's sake) her interpreter. By the time Saturday morning came, when CBS rolled into town in their equipment Jeeps like Jesus into Jerusalem on Palm Sunday, the whole town was anticipating the visit of what Viola had been calling "the B.S. News."

There were about fifty of us packed into Doña Althea's living room, just there to watch. The Doña looked as she always looked: tiny, imperious, dressed in black, with her long white braid pinned around her head like a crown. As a concession to the cameras she clutched an embroidered shawl around her shoulders.

She refused to close the restaurant, though, and it was lunchtime, so there were still comings and goings and much banging of pots. Cecil, the sound man, had to run his equipment off the outlet in the kitchen, since it was the only part of the house that had been wired in the twentieth century. "Ladies, we're just going to have to be cozy in here," he said, turning sideways and scooting between two Althea sisters to reach the plug.

"Son of a," he said, when one of the sisters tripped over his cord and unplugged it for the third or fourth time. The Althea in question stopped in her tracks and looked for a minute as if she might deck him, but decided to serve her customers instead. She was so burdened with plates it's lucky Cecil didn't get *menudo* in his amps.

The director of the crew had the Doña sit in a carved chair that normally stood in her bedroom and held the TV. Two men carried it out, sat her down in it, and arranged vases of peacock feathers at her feet. "Just cross your ankles," the director told her. Norma translated, and the Doña complied, scowling fiercely. She looked like a Frida Kahlo painting. "Okay," he said, wiping sweat off his forehead. He was a heavy man, dressed in Italian shoes and a Mexican wedding shirt, though his mood was not remotely festive. "Okay," he repeated. "Let's go."

There was a camera on the interviewer and two cameras were on Doña Althea: bright, hot lights everywhere. A crew member dabbed the interviewer's nose and forehead with a powder puff, eyed the Doña once, and backed off. The interviewer introduced himself as Malcolm Hunt. He seemed young and wore an outfit that suggested designer-label big-game hunting or possibly Central American revolutions. He probably meant well. He carefully explained to Doña Althea that they would edit the tape later, using only the best parts. If she wanted to go back and repeat anything, she could do that. He suggested that she ignore the cameras and just speak naturally to him. Norma Galvez translated all this. The Doña squinted at the lights, fixed her scornful gaze on a point just above the kitchen door, and shouted all her answers in that direction. Cecil took it personally and slinked around behind the steam table.

Mr. Hunt began. "Doña Althea, how long have you lived in this canyon?"

*"Desde antes que tú cagabas en tus pañales!"*

Norma Galvez shifted a little in her chair and said, "Ah, since before your mother was changing your diapers." The Doña scowled at Norma briefly, and one of the Altheas laughed from the kitchen.

Mr. Hunt smiled and looked concerned. "When did your family come to this country?"

The Doña said something to the effect that her family had been on this land before the Gringos took over and started calling it America. The prospectors came and mined out the damn gold, and the Black Mountain company mined out the damn copper, and then they fired all the men and sent them home to plant trees, and now, naturally, they were pissing in the river and poisoning the orchards.

Mrs. Galvez paused. "A long time ago," she said.

Mr. Hunt lost his composure for the first time. He made an odd, guttural noise and looked at Mrs. Galvez, who spread her hands.

"You want an exact translation?"

"Please."

She gave it to him.

It wasn't the afternoon anybody had expected. Malcolm Hunt kept adjusting his posture and his eyebrows and appearing to start the whole interview over, framing new questions that sounded like opening lines.

"The Black Mountain Mining Company is polluting—and now actually diverting—the river that has been the lifeblood of this town for centuries. Why is this happening?"

"Because they're a greedy bunch of goat fuckers" (Mrs. Galvez said "so-and-sos") "and they got what they wanted from this canyon and now they have to squeeze it by the balls before they let go."

"They're actually damming the river to avoid paying fines to the Environmental Protection Agency, isn't that right? Because the river is so polluted with acid?"

The Doña waited for Norma's translation, then nodded sharply.

"What do you think could stop the dam from being built, at this point?"

"*Dinamita.*"

Mr. Hunt appeared reluctant to follow this line of questioning to its conclusion. "In a desperate attempt to save your town," he said, trying another new tack, "you and the other ladies of Grace have made hundreds of piñatas. Do you really think a piñata can stop a multinational corporation?"

"Probably not."

"Then why go to all the trouble?"

"What do you think we should do?"

She had him there; Malcolm Hunt looked stumped. He looked

from Norma to the Doña and back to Norma. "Well," he said, "most people write their congressmen."

"*No sé.* We don't write such good letters. I don't think we have any congressman out here anyway, do we? We have a mayor, Jimmy Soltovedas. But I don't think we have any *congressman.*" She pronounced the word in English, making it stand out from the rest of her speech like a curse or a totally new concept. "*Si hay,*" she went on, "If we do, I haven't seen him. Probably he doesn't give a shit. And also we don't know how to use dynamite. What we know how to do is make nice things out of paper. Flowers, piñatas, *cascarones.* And we sew things. That's what we ladies here do."

I smiled, thinking of Jack following old habits, turning around three times on the kitchen floor and lying down to dream of a nest in the grass.

"But why peacocks, what's the history?" Malcolm persisted, after hearing the fully translated explanation. "Tell me about the peacocks."

"What do you want to know about peacocks?" the Doña asked, giving him a blank look. The full Spanish name for peacock is *pavo real,* "royal turkey," but Mrs. Galvez let that one slip by.

"How did they get here?"

Doña Althea lifted her head, adjusted her shawl, leaned back and put her hands on her knees, which were spread wide apart under her black skirt. "*Hace cien años,*" she began. "More than one hundred years ago, my mother and her eight sisters came to this valley from Spain to bring light and happiness to the poor miners, who had no wives. They were the nine Gracela sisters: Althea, Renata, Hilaria, Carina, Julietta, Ursolina, Violetta, Camila, and Estrella."

She pronounced the names musically and slowly, drawing out the syllables and rolling the r's. They were the names of fairy princesses, but the story, in her high, sustained voice, was Biblical. It was the Genesis of Grace. And of Hallie and me. Our father's own grandmother—mother of Homero Nolina up in the graveyard—was one of those princesses: the red-haired, feisty one. I could picture her barefoot, her hair curly like Hallie's and coming loose from its knot. I saw her standing in the open front door of her house, shaking a soup spoon at her sisters' arrogant children who came to tease her own. Perhaps she was Ursolina, the little bear.

When Hallie and I were little I used to make up endless stories of where we came from, to lull her to sleep. She would steal into my bed after Doc Homer was asleep, and I would hold her, trying to protect her from the wind that blows on the heads of orphans and isolates them from the living, shouting children who have inherited the earth. "We came from Zanzibar," I would whisper with my mouth against her hair. "We came from Ireland. Our mother was a queen. The Queen of Potatoes."

I could never know the truth of my mother, but there was another story now. Another side. I closed my eyes and listened to Doña Althea with the joy of a child. I don't know what they heard on the CBS news. I heard a bedtime story thirty years late.

# 22

# Endangered Places

It rained and rained in Gracela Canyon. February passed behind a mask of clouds. It seemed like either the end of the world or the beginning.

The orchards, whose black branch tips had been inspected throughout the winter for latent signs of life, suddenly bloomed, all at once: pears, plums, apples, quince, their normal staggered cycle compressed by the odd weather into a single nuptial burst. Through my classroom window I watched drenched blossoms falling like wet snow.

Water, in Grace, is an all-or-nothing proposition, like happiness. When you have rain you have more than enough, just as when you're happy and in love and content with your life you can't remember how you ever could have felt cheated by fate. And vice versa. I knew, abstractly, that I'd been happy, but now that I was in pain again, that happiness was untouchable. It was a garish color picture of a place I had not been. Memory runs along deep, fixed channels in the brain, like electricity along its conduits; only a cataclysm can make the electrons rear up in shock and slide over into another channel.

The human mind seems doomed to believe, as simply as a rooster believes, that where we are *now* is the only possibility.

But it isn't. In spite of the promise of plenty that dripped from the rooftops and gushed down Gracela Canyon's ravines throughout February, the winter rains would soon dry up. Then there would not be another drop until July. During those brittle months the taste and smell of rain would be lost to us, beyond the recollection even of children and the deepest root tips of trees. That is the way of the seasons in a desert place. Only the river ran continuously. The river was Grace's memory of water.

**We heard nothing** from Hallie. First I tried to tell myself she was already out of danger. In the past, the two-week delay of her letters had caused me to keep a distrustful eye on Hallie, like a star so many light years away it could have exploded long ago while we still watched its false shine. Now I tried the reverse psychology: we would hear, soon, that she'd been safe while we worried.

But we didn't, and I gave over to panic. I began to call Managua every week. The Minister of Agriculture, whose secretary now knew me by voice, said there wasn't any reason for me to fly down to Nicaragua; there was nothing I could do there but wait, which—he implied—I was doing badly enough where I was. He really was not unkind, just frustrated, like any of us. He pointed out that Hallie was an exceptional person, to those of us who loved her, but not an exceptional case—the contras made daily forays across the border to attack workers in their fields, sometimes even schoolchildren. Thousands of civilians had died. "If you came here," he said, "you would see." Every home had a framed photograph on a table that stood for a fresh empty space in the family, he said. Teachers and community workers were particularly at risk.

He said I might try making Hallie's status known to the general public in the United States. It could pressure her captors to show restraint; or, he warned me frankly, it could do the opposite.

I knew nothing else to do, so I wrote letters. Emelina helped.

We papered her kitchen table with letters in progress. I drafted mine on stationery from the Grace High School principal's office, but the letterhead intimidated Emelina, who preferred lined paper from her kids' loose-leaf notebooks. Viola put a request to the Stitch and Bitch Club, and after that we had volunteers in Emelina's kitchen for nightly letter-writing sessions. I dictated the main ideas and then they all got the hang of it. I looked up who had voted for sending the guns, and who had voted against, and either way we tried to work it in. I expect we sent out more than a thousand letters. When we lost track of which congressmen we'd written, we wrote them again. We wrote radio stations and any other public entity we believed might be reading its mail. Sometimes I stopped and laid my head on my arms. Emelina would massage the back of my neck and say nothing, because we both suspected words were beside the point.

There may have been publicity we never knew about. We didn't get the *New York Times* in Grace. I do know there was a short piece in the Tucson morning paper, in the "Money" section, of all things, right next to an article about how to reduce your mortgage with twice-monthly payments. There was a small, smiling photo of Hallie, who was identified as a former employee of the University Extension Service. The reporter had called up the Minister of Agriculture as I'd suggested, and said that he "alleged" she had been kidnapped by agitators based in Honduras. This was followed by a much longer quote from a state senator who said the Nicaraguan civil war was a tragedy, and that the United States was doing its best to bring democracy to the region, and that no U.S. citizen could go there without expecting to be caught in crossfire.

The reporter, believing I would be pleased, sent me the clipping along with a note wishing my family all the best. The breadth of his ignorance made me feel hopeless, as I've sometimes felt in dreams, when the muscles dissolve and escape is impossible. I wept uncontrollably all day. At school I asked my students to read *Silent Spring* for an hour while I put my head down on my desk and cried. They were subdued. I suspected people in Grace of walking around me on tiptoe now, the way a town might avert its eyes when its resident crazy lady hikes up her skirt and scratches an itch and swears at the blackbirds watching from a telephone wire.

I stopped going to Doc Homer's for dinner. We were in the worst position to comfort one another. I guessed he could go on about his routine—that had always been the core of his resilience—but I don't think I'd slept a single night since she'd been taken, and I was reaching an abnormal state of exhaustion. I fought off hallucinations. Late one night Hallie appeared in my bedroom doorway, very small, looking up at me. With those same eyes she used to ask without words to crawl into my bed.

"Hallie, I'm trying so hard. But I don't know how to save you."

She turned on stocking feet and walked back into the dark.

I got up and rifled my desk drawers till I found the newspaper clipping with her picture. I looked at it hard, trying to convince myself that Hallie wasn't a child. I had the black-and-red afghan bundled around me but I felt chilled and hard as a frozen branch. My hands shook. I tucked the clipping into an envelope and wrote a note to the President of the United States, begging him please just to look at her. "This is my only sister," I told him. "I'm coming to understand responsibility. You gave those men a righteous flag to wave and you gave them guns. If she dies, what will you tell me?" I licked the envelope and sealed it. I knew the address by heart.

We began to get letters back, to the effect that the matter would certainly bear investigation. They weren't form letters, each one was typed by a different secretary, but they all said the same thing. It surprised me to see how a meaningless phrase repeated again and again begins to resemble truth.

**In the middle** of that gray month Emelina's youngest son learned to walk. I was alone with him when it happened. The sun had come out briefly as I walked home from school, and the baby and I were both anxious to be outdoors. Emelina asked if I could just not let him eat any real big bugs, and I promised to keep an eye out. I settled with a book in the courtyard, which was radiant with sudden sunlight. The flowers were beaten down, their bent-over heads bejeweled with diamond droplets like earrings on sad, rich widows.

For quite a while now Nicholas had been cruising the perimeters of his world, walking confidently from house to tree to lawn chair to wall, so long as he had something to hold on to. Sometimes what he touched was nothing more than apparent security. Today I watched the back of his red overalls with interest as he cruised along a patch of damp, tall four-o'clocks, lightly touching their leaves. He had no idea how little support they offered.

He spotted a hummingbird. It buzzed around the red tubes of a potted penstemon that stood by itself in the center of the courtyard. His eyes followed the bird as it darted up and down, a high-strung gem; Nicholas wanted it. For a long time he frowned at the brick path that lay between himself and the bird, and then he let go of the wall. He took one step and then more, buoyed up by some impossible anti-gravity. After two steps the hummingbird was gone, but Nicholas still headed for the air it had occupied, his hands grasping at vapor. It was as if an invisible balloon floated above him, tied to his overall strap, dragging him along from above. He swayed and swaggered, stabbing one toe at a time down at the ground, pivoting on the ball of one foot, and then suddenly the string was cut and down he bumped on his well-padded bottom. He looked at me and screamed.

"You're walking," I told Nicholas. "I promise you it gets easier. The rest of life doesn't, but this really does."

I stayed out there with my book for the rest of the afternoon, surreptitiously watching as he tried it over and over. He was completely undeterred by failure. The motivation packed in that small body was a miracle to see. I wished I could bottle that passion for accomplishment and squeeze out some of the elixir, a drop at a time, on my high-school students. They would move mountains.

**The Stitch and Bitch Club** was now wealthy beyond historic measure. On the heels of the blockbuster piñata sale came a steady flow of donations from the outside. Loulou Campbell, the treasurer, had always kept the club's funds in a coffee can in the back of the Baptist Grocery where she worked. But when the volume of cash filled twelve baby-formula cans she grew nervous. Loulou opened an account at the bank and turned the passbook over to Doña Althea, whose years as a top-notch restaurateur had made her somewhat more comfortable with affluence.

The cash languished in its vault while the women pondered its meaning. Having sent their peacocks out into the world like Noah's dove over the flood, they waited for the world to inspire their next move.

Inspiration came in the guise of an art dealer from Tucson. His name was Sean Rideheart, and he was a funny, charming little man who understood people as well as he understood beauty. The spectacular popularity of the Grace piñatas (some had been resold for as much as five hundred dollars) moved him to make a pilgrimage to the source. Mr. Rideheart was already an expert and he became a connoisseur; before he ever set foot in Grace he could already recognize the works of several individual piñata makers. Of particular value were those made by Mrs. Nuñez, who had been so resourceful with her *Compton's Children's Encyclopedia*. He wanted to know this town better.

I met him on his third visit, when he came to meet Viola. There was no school that day—I believe it was the birthday of a President—and I was staring at clouds. Emelina didn't bother me on my bad days; I was allowed to do nothing, not even pretend to feel better, which I recognized as a rare act of human kindness and I appreciated. I spent the morning sitting on Emelina's front porch, watching our neighbor, whose roof was on the same level with our floorboards. We were having another brief break in the rain, as if the clouds had called a time-out to muster their resources. Our neighbor Mr. Pye was taking advantage of the moment to climb up and inspect his roof.

"Got a few leaks," he called out in a friendly way. I waved back, unsure of how to answer. I watched the top of his engineer's cap bob down the ladder out of sight, and shortly thereafter, appear again.

Mr. Pye negotiated the ladder with one hand while balancing a small, old-looking cardboard box against his hip. It made me think of the surprises coming out of the kiva at Santa Rosalia Pueblo. Mr. Pye knelt near his chimney pipe and opened the box like a birthday present, carefully lifting out some shingles. They were green, and shaped like the ace of spades—an exact match to the ones on his roof, only a little brighter. Grass-green rather than the green of old bronze. I remembered once, months ago, looking at that roof of antique shingles and assuming them to be irreplaceable.

Curiosity overcame my lassitude. "How'd you match those shingles?" I called out.

He looked at me, puzzled.

"Where'd you get the new shingles? They're a perfect match."

He examined the shingles in his hands, as if noticing this for the first time, and then called back, "Well, they ought to be, they're all from the same lot. I bought two hundred extras when I put this roof on."

"When was that?" I asked.

He looked up at the clouds. I don't know whether he was divining the weather or the past. "Right after the war," he said. "That would have been forty-six."

Just then Mr. Rideheart came walking up the road under a navy blue umbrella. Maybe it was still raining down the way, where he'd just come from. He walked directly to the front porch where I sat, jauntily hopped up the steps, stomped his feet delicately a few times as if to knock off mud (though his shoes were immaculate), and extended his hand to me. I'd expected to spend the day in numb, depressed solitude, and now I felt uncomfortably honored to sit at the end of Mr. Rideheart's long line of effort—like a princess in a tale of impossible tasks. Although I was fairly sure he hadn't come all this way looking for me.

"Sean Rideheart," he said. He had white eyebrows and bright green eyes; an appealing face.

"Codi Noline." I shook his hand. "I've heard about you. You're the piñata collector."

He laughed. "I've been called many things in my time, but that's a first. I'm looking for Viola Domingos." At my invitation he sat down in the only other chair on the porch, wicker, of doubtful character.

"She's not here," I said. "Nobody's home today. Viola and the kids have gone down to the church. They're having some kind of a big party down there today, painting the saints."

"Painting the saints?" Mr. Rideheart extracted a largish blue handkerchief from the pocket of his tweed jacket and cleaned his wire-rimmed glasses with extraordinary care. I watched for a long time, mesmerized, until he glanced up at me.

"The statues of saints, in the church," I explained. "I guess they have to get freshened up every so often, like anybody else. The women paint the saints and the kids paint each other."

He replaced his glasses and observed the rooftops and treetops that led stepwise down the hill. Mr. Pye had his back to us now. He was industriously tacking down shingles he'd secured for this purpose ten years before Hallie was born.

"Quite a place," Mr. Rideheart said, finally. "How long have you lived here?"

It wasn't an easy question to answer. "I was born here," I said slowly. "But right now I'm just on an extended visit. My time's up soon."

He sighed, looking out over the white path of blossoming treetops that led up toward the dam. "Ah, well, yes," he said, "isn't everybody's. More's the pity."


At first the Stitch and Bitch was divided in its opinion of Mr. Rideheart. While he was graciously received into the kitchens of half the club members, where he drank tea and stroked his white mustache and listened in earnest while the piñata artists discussed their methodologies, the other half (led by Doña Althea) suspected him of being the southwestern equivalent of a carpetbagger.

But for once the Doña judged wrong. His intentions were noble, and ultimately providential. When the club assembled in March for its monthly meeting in the American Legion hall, Mr. Rideheart was the guest speaker. He was supposed to lecture on folk art, which he did, but mostly he talked about Grace. He told these women what they had always known: that their town had a spirit and disposition completely apart from its economic identity as an outpost of the Black Mountain Mining Company. During the last century while men labored underground to rob the canyon of its wealth, the women up above had been paying it back in kind. They'd paid with embroidery and peacocks and fruit trees and piñatas and children. Mr. Rideheart suggested that he had never known of a place quite like Gracela Canyon, and that it could, and *should,* be declared a historic preserve. There existed a thing called the National Register of Historic Places. The landmarks on this list, he said, were protected from the onslaught of industry, as if they were endangered species. He allowed that it wasn't perfect; listing on the register would provide "a measure of protection from demolition or other negative impact," he said. "In other words, a man can still shoot an elephant, even though it has been declared endangered, and the elephant will still be dead. But the man will come out looking like a very nasty guy."

"But really it's not our houses that are going to get endangered by the poison and the dam," Norma Galvez pointed out. "It's the trees."

Mr. Rideheart replied, "Your trees are also historic."

He knew all the ins and outs of becoming a historic place. He explained where to begin, and where to go after that, to see that the river would run clean and unobstructed. There was a fair amount of bureaucracy involved, but the process was reasonably speedy. "Considering the amount of publicity that has already been brought to bear," he said, gesturing toward the window, or possibly the invisible airwaves of CBS, "I think it could be done in less than two years."

He said we would need to document everything, to prove the age and architectural character of the community. "All the photocopying, photography, and so forth can be expensive. Sometimes communities apply for block grants."

After a brief silence Viola said, succinctly, "We don't need any block grants. We're rich." And that was that.

**At some point** during the spring I got a letter from Carlo. He'd finally made plans: he was going to Telluride. The clutch had gone out on our old Renault and he'd junked it—he hoped I wasn't attached. He was thinking of getting a motorcycle, unless I was coming to Telluride, in which case we'd get another car.

I was in such a state, running on so little sleep and such dead nerve endings, I didn't know what to think. I knew I'd have to make plans soon. And I was touched that he still took me into account when he made his move, as if we were family. But I felt nothing when I read his words; maybe it was just the same nothing there had always been between us. The words seemed to be coming from a very great distance, with the same strange, compressed tone as a satellite phone call. I looked carefully at each sentence and then waited for it to register. All I could really get clearly was the name of the town, with its resonant syllables: Telluride. It sounded like a command.

**I'd become estranged** from Loyd after our trip. Of course, because of Hallie. I felt guilty for being away when the call came. Loyd and I had been laughing and making love for all those days while the news was laid out like a corpse in Doc Homer's house. I didn't even call him the night we got back into town. We hadn't wanted the vacation to end, so we just went straight to Loyd's house and spent the night. Surprisingly, I'd never slept in his bed. Loyd's house was entirely his own: a mobile home set up against the cliff of upper Gracela Canyon on a masonry foundation he'd built slowly himself, over the years. Through his efforts the stonework had gradually grown up over the metal shell, so that now it was pretty much a rectangular stone house, overgrown with honeysuckle vines.

Leafless for winter, the honeysuckles made a lace curtain over the bedroom window. Their shadows left faint tracings on the walls, which I watched all through the bright, moonlit hours of that first night home. Loyd held on to me tightly in his sleep. I couldn't find sleep myself, but I was happy.

The next morning he left at dawn for a seven-day stand in Yuma, and I walked down to have breakfast at Emelina's. But of course as things turned out I didn't eat—not that day or the next. By the time Loyd got back from Yuma I was too far gone to be touched.


**It was Uda Dell** on the phone, telling me Doc Homer had gone to Tucson for a CAT scan. She called it a "skin the cat."

I sat up in bed, cradling the phone and pulling the red-and-black afghan around me; school was out for the spring break, so my life had lost what little sense of order daily work could still impose. "When did he go?" I asked. "Just this morning?" What I wanted to ask her was "Why did he tell you, and not me?" But I guess I knew the answer to that.

"No, honey, he went yesterday. He took the bus." Uda seemed industrious on her end of the phone, even as she spoke. Every few seconds she paused and I could hear a high ascending sound like cloth ripping.

"Did he tell you how long he'd be gone?"

There was another rip, then Uda's voice. "Honey, he didn't tell me a thing about it. I don't think he wanted anybody to know. You know Doc. He don't want anybody to make a fuss. [Rip . . .] But he come over and asked me to look after the house. If you or anybody was to come looking for him, he said just tell them he'd gone to Tucson for the weekend to get some medical supplies. [Rip . . .] Now, I knew that didn't sound right. I never heard of him doing that before, and you'd think whatever we all got along without for forty years we could get along without till the Judgment, don't you think? [Rip . . .] So I said, 'Doc, are you pulling my sleeve, there's something up, ain't it,' and he said there was more to it, he was going to get tested for his Alsizer's and get a Cat Skin Test done on him."

"Oh, well, that's good," I said. It was a challenge to follow this trail of reason. I could perfectly picture Uda: her large face, the cheeks tightly packed and shiny like a plum. I rubbed the top of my head and looked at the clock, with astonishment. I'd fallen asleep around 4 A.M. and slept an unprecedented seven hours.

"So, honey, what I'm calling you for is [Rip . . .] I've been itching to get into that house and clean. I know he hasn't been up to it, and I don't mean any offense, Lord knows I think the world of Doc, but I expect he needs somebody to get up there and clean. And I was thinking now'd be a good time but I didn't feel right about just going in. I've had the key all this time, ever since I used to keep you girls. He never did want the key back." She paused. "But I thought I better call and see what you said."

The key was more or less a symbolic matter. He didn't lock his front door. Nobody in Grace did. "I think the cleaning's a good idea. But I also think he'd be mad." I hesitated, uncertain of my loyalties. Outside my window I could see John Tucker in the courtyard with a tape measure. He appeared to be measuring the hundred-year-old beams that supported the roof of the back porch. I knew what it was about—the Historic Register. I had a brainstorm.

"Uda, let me go up there with you. I've got to go through the attic and dig up some old documents on the house and the land for the historic preserve thing. I've been meaning to do it, and you could help me. We could tell him you were helping me look through stuff, and that we just got carried away and beat the rugs and mopped the bathroom while we were at it. If he even notices."

Uda undertook the conspiracy with the relish of a criminal. I agreed to meet her at Doc Homer's in half an hour.


**The attic was** pleasantly chilly and smelled of pine. Decades of summer heat had forced droplets of resin out of the rough floorboards, which in cooler weather hardened to little amber marbles that scattered in all directions as we shifted trunks and cardboard boxes. The afternoon is fixed in my memory with the sharp smell of resin and that particular amber rattle, like the sound of ball bearings rolling around in a box. It's surprising how much of memory is built around things unnoticed at the time.

I was amazed by what we found. Doc Homer's disease had manifested itself mostly downstairs; up here, our past was untouched by chaos. Stacked boxes of Hallie's and my old clothes, school papers, photo albums, and all kinds of other detritus stood in neat rows, labeled chronologically and by content. I felt overwhelmed by so much material evidence of our family's past. I couldn't think why he'd kept it. He was so practical. What conceivable use did he foresee for a box marked "ALICE, MATERNITY," for example? But you don't ask questions of an attic. Museums are their own justification.

"Look," I said to Uda, tipping up a cardboard box so she could see inside: some thirty pairs of black orthopedic shoes stacked from small to large, toes up, neat as eggs in a crate. There was a little more variety than I'd remembered. Two pairs were rather dapper little saddle oxfords, black and maroon. Another year—I vaguely did remember this—we'd been allowed to order them in charcoal suède.

Uda had a full-front apron over her old trousers and a print blouse, and she looked prepared for anything. Her lavender hoop earrings matched her wedgies, and she'd tied a red handkerchief over her hair. I was tempted to ask what she'd been ripping up this morning. She bent over beside me and picked out one of the smallest shoes, cradling it like an orphaned bird. "Law, he was so careful about you girls and your feet. I remember thinking, Oh, mercy, when those girls get big enough to want heels there's going to be the Devil to pay."

I laughed. "He wasn't just careful. He was obsessed."

Uda looked down at me. "He just wanted awful bad for you kids to be good girls," she said. "It's hard for a man by himself, honey. You don't know how hard. He worried himself to death. A lot of people, you know, would just let their kids run ever which way."

She stopped, cocking her head a little, staring at the shoe in her hand. "One year for Christmas I gave the two of you little cowboy outfits, with guns, and you just loved them, but he had to take away the guns. He didn't want you killing, even pretend. I felt awful that I'd done that, once I thought about it. He was right."

As she talked, I remembered the whole story: the cowboy outfits and the guns. Hallie and I had tried to claim moral high ground, saying he was taking away what belonged to us. He stood in front of the window, his thin face turned to the light, speaking to the world outside: "I will not have the neighbors arming my children like mercenaries." I'd looked up "mercenaries" in the dictionary, later, and felt ashamed. I explained the ethics of armament to Hallie.

"How long did you take care of us?" I asked Uda.

"Oh, I expect close to ten years all in all. Till you was about fourteen and Hallie was eleven. You remember that. You'd come up after school and we'd play Old Maid or you'd play swinging statues out in the yard. We had us a time. And I'd come up here at night when he had to go tend a baby or something. Sometimes of an evening you'd run off with the Domingos kids without telling me where you'd gone to." She laughed. "I liked to skinned you alive a couple of times. You girls was a couple of live potatoes. She was bad and you was worse."

I remembered her arms when they were thinner; a younger Uda. And I remembered standing at a kitchen counter, on a stool, patting out my own handprints in floured dough while she wove strips of piecrust, pale and thin as flayed skin, over and under to make a perfect pie top. I was experiencing a flash flood of memories. I feared I might drown in them. My skull was so crowded with images it hurt.

"He raised you to be good girls," she said again. She reached over and squeezed my upper arm before returning the shoe to its box.

I didn't know what to tell her we were looking for, for the historical project—anything documenting the age of the house would be helpful, and more generally, old photographs of any kind. Uda seemed content to poke into boxes at random, but I tried to ground myself by reading labels: "CROCKERY AND FLATWARE." "GARDEN RECORDS." One bore the mystic title "ELECTRICITY." I looked inside: socket hardware, lamp cord, the reflector from a heat lamp, a pair of rubber gloves.

I couldn't resist getting sidetracked by one marked, "ARTWORK, H.,

AGE 3–6." The subjects of Hallie's crayon drawings were mainly the two of us, stick sisters holding hands, or else just me, my orangeish hair radiating from my head like a storm of solar flares. There was not one figure anywhere representing Doc Homer. I wondered if he'd noticed. But he must have. He was the one who'd picked up each drawing, rescued it from destruction, and finally labeled the box. The invisible archivist of our lives.

Out of curiosity I tracked down the corresponding box called "ARTWORK, C." As I'd expected, it was full of family portraits. Big sister, little sister, father, mother, a cockeyed roof over our heads and above that an omnipresent yellow sun. It didn't resemble anyone's reality but mine, but there it was. Or maybe it wasn't so much a matter of reality as of expectation—what I felt the world owed me. I held two of our drawings side by side and concluded that there was no puzzle as to why we were different. Hallie and I had grown up in different families.

"Here's pictures," Uda reported suddenly. There was a whole aisle of boxes marked "PHOTOGRAPHS," with inscrutable suffixes. I picked up one marked "PHOTOGRAPHS, AM JOUR GEN" and found it surprisingly light, so I carried it over to the east window and sat down on a steamer trunk, settling the box on my lap before opening it. Inside were stacks of ancient eight-by-tens, their brown edges curled like autumn leaves. Each one was a photograph of a newborn baby with a startled-looking face and marble-white eyes. I leafed through them, one after another, awestruck by the oddity of these children. Of course I knew about the eyes, an anomaly of pigmentation that was genetic proof of Gracela heritage on both sides. But I'd never seen them. They tended to darken just hours after birth, and in modern times a person can easily go through life, in Grace or anywhere, without seeing a newborn.

On top of the stack of photos was a handwritten page with the heading: "Notes on Methodology." The ink had faded to brown. This would all be for his genetics paper: Doc Homer's careful notations on how he'd set up the camera, the distance, the amount of light. Apparently he'd rigged some set-up that used powerful flashbulbs, the old-fashioned kind that popped once and then were used up. It was before the days of modern electronics.

All those babies. How they must have screamed, one second after he shot them in the name of science. Or in the name of his own desire to set himself apart. What could be more arrogant than to come back and do a scientific study of your own townspeople, like so many natives in Borneo? I looked through the photos again and kept coming back to one that had an arresting familiarity. The eyes looked back as if they knew me. I stared at the baby for a long time.

It was *me*.

"You were a doll baby," Uda said. She was looking down over my shoulder.

"That's me? Are you sure?"

She took the stack and shuffled through it like a card trick. She produced another photo. "There's Hallie. You didn't look a thing alike when you were born." To her the eyes were commonplace, not a feature to connect us, but they were the only feature I could see. To me, we looked identical.

I held the two photographs up to the light, mystified. The eyes were unearthly. We were two babies not of this world. Just like every other one in the stack of photos; two more babies of Grace. He was doing exactly the opposite of setting himself apart. He was proving we belonged here, were as pure as anybody in Grace. Both sides. *Our mother's name was Althea. Her family despised him.*

"We're *puro*," I said out loud. And then I dropped the photographs because I heard the broken-glass pop of the flash and went blind. I heard myself make an odd little whimper.

Then Uda appeared in my field of vision, moving away. "Codi, hon, I'm going on downstairs and beat the rugs or something. I'll try not to scare up too much dust."

# 23

# The Souls
# of Beasts

"Hallie, I'm going to die."

"I'm Codi."

"I'm dying."

"Well, I know. We all are, more or less." After a lifetime on the emotional austerity plan, my father and I were caving in to melodrama. When I put my hand on his hand it lay dead on the sheet. It was the diagnosis that killed him. Sometimes that's how it happens.

"Where is Hallie?"

"Please don't ask me that again. We don't know where she is. Don't worry about her right now, okay? We can't do anything."

He looked at me accusingly. "You shouldn't have stood on the slide. I defended you on principle, but it was dangerous."

How do people live with loved ones after their minds have fallen into anarchy? I rejected his ruined monologues every day, still expecting order to emerge victorious in Doc Homer's universe. I can remember once seeing a monument somewhere in the desert north of

Tucson, commemorating a dedicated but ill-informed platoon of men who died in a Civil War battle six months after Lee had surrendered at Appomattox. That's exactly who I was—a soldier of the lost cause, still rooting for my father's recovery. Pain reaches the heart with electrical speed, but *truth* moves to the heart as slowly as a glacier.

He'd gone off the Tacrine, his experimental drug; the doctors in Tucson found his liver was wrecked from it. Now his mind scuttled around like a crab, heading always for the dark corners. People with this disease can linger on for six or seven years, I'd read, and on average they do. But Doc Homer wouldn't.

"Do you want something to eat? Uda brought over this thing made out of crackers and walnuts and apples. It looks like one of your concoctions."

"No, thank you."

His bedroom was the largest upstairs room, with dark green walls and a high white ceiling and dormer windows across the west side. As children, Hallie and I rarely came into this room; it held an aura of importance and secrecy, the two things that most attract and frighten children. But for two days now I'd been taking care of Doc Homer here, and when I stopped to notice, I found myself the most commanding presence in the room. I felt long-legged and entitled, and strode around in my boots, adjusting curtains and moving furniture to suit myself. I'd tried to close the blinds, but he wanted them open. He insisted on the light, so I let it be.

I'd been keeping a restless vigil by his bed throughout the late afternoon, watching for signs of a lucid moment. I'd about decided it wasn't coming. I pulled my chair closer and squeezed his hand hard in an effort to make him pay attention. "Pop, I want to talk to you about Mother."

"Her kidneys were weak, and we knew it was a possibility. She had already had one episode of renal failure with the first pregnancy. She knew the risk."

I didn't really try to absorb this information. "Her name was Althea. How was she related to Doña Althea?"

"No relation." The answer, quick and firm.

"*What* relation? I know she came from here. I found some things in the attic. What was she, a great-niece?"

"What things in the attic?"

"Cousin?" I crossed my arms like the obstinate child I was.

No answer.

"Granddaughter?"

His face changed. "*Malcriado.*"

"Doña Althea's family didn't want you to marry her, right?"

He let out a short, bitter little laugh unlike any sound I'd ever heard him make. "We were *Nolinas.*" Just the way he said it told me plenty.

"And you married her anyway. You eloped." I leaned forward and touched his forehead, something I'd never done. It felt cool and thin-skinned, like a vegetable. "That's so romantic. Don't you know that's what all of us would like to think our parents did? You didn't have to hide something like that from us."

"You understand nothing." He seemed very lucid. At times I suspected him of feigning his confusion, or at least using it to his advantage.

"That's probably true," I said, withdrawing my hand.

"We were a bad family. Try to understand. We learned it in school along with the multiplication tables and the fact that beasts have no souls. I could accept the verdict, or I could prove it wrong."

"You did that. You proved it wrong."

In the slanted afternoon light his eyes were a cloudy blue and his skin was translucent. He looked up at the ceiling and I had a disturbing view of his eyes in profile. "I proved nothing," he said. "I became a man with no history. No guardian angels. I turned out to be a brute beast after all. I didn't redeem my family, I buried it and then I built my grand house on top of the grave. I changed my name."

"You still have plenty of guardian angels."

"I don't think anybody in this town remembers that I'm a Nolina."

"No, you're wrong about that, they do remember. I think people are sorry. And they love you. Look at your refrigerator."

He gave me an odd, embittered look. How could he not know this was true? "Refrigerators don't preserve love," he said.

"The hell they don't. Yours does. The women in this town bake you casseroles and pies like the world was going to end."

He made a slight sound by breathing out of his nose. He seemed strangely like a child.

"They probably can't forgive themselves for the past," I said. "Mother died before they could get everything straightened out. And then you kind of took your phone off the hook, emotionwise."

He looked away from me again. "We aren't from here, we came from the outside. That is our myth and every person in Grace believes it, because they want to. They don't want to see a Nolina when they look at me. They want a man they can trust with their children's ear infections. And I am that man. If you change the present enough, history will bend to accommodate it."

"No. I'm pretty sure you're wrong about that. What's true is true, no matter how many ways you deny it."

He closed his eyes for a while. I'd never seen him frail or impaired. All the time I'd been his daughter, he'd never been sick.

"How long are you going to stay in bed?" I asked softly, in case he was falling asleep.

"I'm exhausted."

"I know. But after you rest, you might want to get up for a while. I can warm up some soup."

He didn't open his eyes. "Do you think Hallie is coming back?"

"I don't know what to think. We have to think yes, don't we?"

"You're the advocate of ordained truth. Are you telling me now that we can *will* Hallie back to safety?"

"No. I don't guess we can. We just have to wait."

It was the first honest conversation we'd had about Hallie. It took us both by surprise. We were quiet for a long time then, but I knew he wasn't sleeping. I could see his eyes working back and forth under his eyelids, as if he were reading his own thoughts. I wondered what his thoughts looked like, in his clear moments and in his confusion. I very much wished to know him.

"Pop?"

He slowly opened his eyes and looked at the ceiling.

"Did you really see me bury the baby?"

He looked at me.

"Why didn't we ever talk?"

He sighed. "You get beyond a point."

"You could have just given me a hug or something."

He turned away from me. His short, gray hair stood up in whorls on the back of his head. He said, "It's Friday, isn't it? Mrs. Nuñez's lab work is due back today. Can you pull her chart?"

"Okay, sleep now," I said, reaching over to pat his shoulder. "But after a while I want you to get up and get dressed. Today or tomorrow, whenever you're feeling up to it."

"I feel fine."

"Okay. When you're feeling better, I want you to take me to the place where I buried it. I can remember a lot of that night. Cleaning up the bathroom, and that old black sweater of Mother's, some things like that. But I can't remember the place."

He didn't promise. I think he'd forgotten again who I was. We were comically out of synchrony—a family vaudeville routine. Whatever one of us found, the other lost.


**I received a letter** from the school board. It was early April, a long time after I'd stopped my hopeful excursions to the Post Office box and had given the key back to Emelina, so this letter appeared on my table among the breakfast dishes while I was at school. I saw it the minute I walked in, but tried to ignore it for the longest time. I carefully went around to the other side of the table and dropped a heavy pile of tests and began to grade them, trying not to see it. "A predator is a big guy that eats little guys," wrote Raymo. "A herbivore is your wussy vegetarian. In other words, lunch meat." She'd wedged it between the coffee cup and a bottle of aspirin. Did she think it would be bad news? I gave in and tore it open.

I can't really say what sort of news it was. Surprising news. It was notification that my contract was going to be renewed for the next year. The term wasn't over, but the school board recognized my circumstances as unusual and wanted to give me ample notice; they were eager for me to return in the fall. My temporary teaching certificate could easily be extended, especially if I had intentions of working toward certification. It was a personal letter written on behalf of the entire board and signed by someone I knew of but had never met, a Mr. Leacock. His letter cited my popularity with the students and commended me for my "innovative presentation" and "spirited development of a relevant curriculum." It didn't mention contraception or Mrs. Josephine Nash or the ozone layer. I wondered how much they really knew; it made me nervous. I kept looking sideways at that word "spirited." After knocking myself out to be accepted, I'd finally flown off the handle in a seditious direction, and won a gold star. "We are all aware of the difficulties of engaging teenagers in a vital course of academic instruction," wrote Mr. Leacock. Someone apparently felt I'd succeeded in this endeavor. I was going to be named something like teacher of the year. Teachers and kids all voted, secret ballot.

I was stunned. I stuck the letter into the pocket of my corduroy jumper and went out for a walk. I tramped quickly down the hill past Mr. Pye's green roof and Mrs. Nuñez, who sat in a rocker on her front porch, leaning precariously forward out of her chair, trying to nail a fast-moving spider with the rubber tip of her cane. She lifted the cane and stabbed the air sociably as I passed by; I waved back. I wondered about the lab work Doc Homer had mentioned in his delirium. Was she really waiting for someone far away to examine her cells or her blood and pronounce a verdict? Or was this history, a sentence she was already serving?

In town, the 4-H Club had set up a display of rabbits and fancy chickens in cages in front of the courthouse. A little county fair was planned for Easter weekend. The rabbits were of an odd-looking breed but all exactly alike, fancily marked with black-tipped ears and paws and a gorget under the throat, and it occurred to me how much simpler life would be if people were like that, all identically marked. If I were not the wrong breed. I corrected an old habit of thought: both my parents were born in Grace, and their parents before them. Possibly Doc Homer was right—I'd believed otherwise for so long it had become true; I was an outsider not only by belief but by flesh and bone.

Children knelt by the cages and talked to the rabbits in high voices, poking in sprigs of new grass from the courthouse lawn. Some shoppers had strayed over from their errands across the street. Mary Lopez, a middle-aged woman I knew from Stitch and Bitch, waved at me. She was there with her mother, a very short, broad woman with a long black braid down her back. The old woman leaned over the rabbit cages like a child. Mary rested a hand on the back of her mother's neck, a slight gesture that twisted my heart. I turned up the road toward Loyd's house. I knew he was home, or would be shortly. He was on a fairly regular schedule these days, running the Amtrak to Tucson and back. We stayed in touch.

The air had a fresh muddy edge, the smell of spring. I had several choices of route, and on a whim I took a less familiar road. I found myself walking through a neighborhood that wanted to pull me into it: the dirt shade of salt cedars, the dogs that barked without getting up. A woman and her husband argued congenially while they picked grapefruits off the tree in their backyard. The fruits rustled solidly into grocery bags while the woman talked in a low, steady voice and the man answered, on and on, a cycle of gentle irritation and love that would never be finished.

"Gee, you're pretty. Are you the new schoolteacher?"

I turned around, startled by a man on a moped. I'd never laid eyes on him before, but I was completely charmed by his line. I felt like Miss Kitty in *Gunsmoke*.

"Well, yes," I said.

"You want a ride? There's a wicked pair of brindle bulldogs up at the corner."

"Okay." I gathered my skirt and straddled the back of his bike. We buzzed smoothly uphill past the putative wicked bulldogs, who lay with their manifold chins on their paws.

"My son Ricky's in one of your classes. He says you give them a pretty good round."

"They give me one, too," I said.

He laughed. "You're Doc Homer's girl, aren't you?"

"That's right. Homer Nolina of the white trash Nolinas. He married his second cousin for mad love." I'd been lying to strangers all my life, and no wonder. Here was the truth and it sounded like a B-grade fairy tale. But I wanted to know if Doc Homer was right—if everyone had forgotten.

"I never heard that," my driver said. "I just heard she was dead."

"She's dead all right. But she was born and grew up right here. You're around the same age I am, you wouldn't remember her, but it's the truth. Her family thought unkindly of my daddy, so they ran off for a while and he put on an attitude."

He laughed at that, but said, "You oughtn't to talk bad about a man like him."

"Oh, I know. Doc Homer's inclined to be useful. But I swear it looks to me like he's been running his whole life on vengeful spite."

"I got me an old Ford that runs on something like that."

Ten seconds later he let me off at the base of the path up to Loyd's house. Loyd was sitting outside, drinking coffee under the huge mesquite that shaded his front yard. He was just out of the shower, wearing only a pair of soft gray sweatpants. His damp hair lay loose on his shoulders. He looked very happy to see me but also unsurprised; typical, maddening Loyd. Jack betrayed excitement in his thumping tail, but Loyd made no sudden movements. He let me come to him, bend over to kiss him, sit down in the chair beside him. I was oddly conscious of his skill with animals.

"You want coffee?"

"No thanks."

He sat looking at me, smiling, waiting.

"Guess what," I said finally, handing him the letter. He read it, grinning broadly.

"It doesn't mean anything," I said. "I still can't stay."

"It does mean something. It means they want you, whether you stay or not. It means you're real good at what you do."

I took the letter back and looked at it, not at the words but the object itself. "I guess you're right," I said. "I don't think anybody ever told me that before. Not in a letter. I guess that's something."

"Sure it is."

"I was thinking of it as just one more choice I'd have to make. A complication."

"Life's a complication."

"Sure," I said. "Death is probably a piece of cake by comparison."

We looked at each other for a while. "So tell me about your day, honey," I finally said. We both laughed at that.

"Another buck in the bank, doll."

"Is that it? Do you like driving trains? You never talk about it."

"You really want to hear about it?"

"I think so."

"Okay. Yeah, I like driving trains. Today I went out on a dog catch."

"Not the Amtrak?"

"No. A special mission."

"You had to catch a dog?"

"A dog catch is when you go out to bring in a train after the crew's died on the main line."

"The whole crew died?" I was visited by the unwelcome thought of Fenton Lee in his sheared-off engine, after the head-on collision. I knew this couldn't be what Loyd meant.

He smiled. "Died on the hours-of-service law. They'd worked a full twelve hours but there were holdups somewhere and they still hadn't gotten to a tie-up point. You can't work more than twelve hours straight because you'd be tired and it would be dangerous; it's federal law. So you just stop where you are, and wait for a relief crew."

"Good thing airline pilots don't do that," I said.

"I bet they go to sleep at the wheel more than we do, too." Loyd said.

"So you went out and caught the dog."

"Me and another engineer and a conductor and a brakeman all deadheaded out to Dragoon to pick up the train. The dead crew came back to Grace in a car."

"And you, what, took the train on into Tucson?"

"Yep."

"So what does that mean, what do you do exactly? Is there a steering wheel?"

He laughed. "No. You adjust throttles, you set brakes, you watch signals. You use your head. Today I had to use my head. I was the lead engineer and it was a real heavy train, over ten thousand tons. There were two helper engines coupled at the rear of the train."

"Ten thousand tons?"

He nodded. "A little better than a mile and a half long."

"And you're in the front engine, and there's two engines pushing on the back?"

"Yep. The hard part was topping over Dragoon. That's a real long hill, a long descending grade from Dragoon to the Benson bridge, and there's a siding you sometimes have to pull into there, at twenty-five miles an hour. But the train is so damn heavy it wants to take off on you down that hill. I've messed up on that hill a bunch of times before. Just between you and me, one time I went flying through there at sixty, hoping to God there was nobody coming on the main line. I never could have gotten into the siding track."

"I guess there was nobody coming."

"No. But today there was, and I got us in safe and sound. Today I did it exactly right." He smiled at me over his coffee cup.

"So tell me about it."

"Well, we topped over the hill way below the speed limit, and when I got about half the train over the hill I set a minimum amount of air brakes. Then I waited for it to take hold. The brakes take hold all along the train, in every car, front to back. And then I just watched the speedometer keep coming up."

"You're still speeding up? Even after you've set the brake?"

"You've got six thousand tons and a mile of train coming down the hill behind you. What do you think it's going to do?"

Doc Homer used to pose puzzles like this to Hallie and me, to develop our cognitive skills. "But you've also got some-odd thousand tons still coming *up* the hill behind you."

"That's right. A little less coming up, and a little more coming down, every minute. That's the tricky part. That's the Zen of Southern Pacific."

I was extremely impressed.

"On a normal train you'd be real leery of setting the brake while half your train's still coming up the hill. The rear would start pulling backward and you'd break in two."

"Oh," I said. "So then you'd have two trains."

"Then you'd have a nice long vacation without a paycheck."

"Oh."

"But I had helper engines that could push on me from the back, so I was pretty sure we wouldn't break in two. I radioed my helper engineer back there to keep pushing up the hill at full throttle, that's throttle eight, and then cut it back to throttle one when he topped over."

"So he was pushing and you were braking at the same time."

"Yep. Setting the brake early enough, that was the part I never got before. It kind of goes against what you think's right."

"Nobody can just tell you how to do that hill?"

"No, because every train's different on every hill. Every single run is a brand-new job. You have to learn the feel of it."

"So you can't necessarily do the same thing next time?"

"Not exactly the same thing, no. But on this train the minimum set worked perfect. And then I worked the throttle to maintain forty miles an hour. I came down the hill through Sybil and Fenner, the last siding before the Benson bridge. I got a flashing yellow after Sybil so I knew we'd probably have to go into Fenner. Then we went by a yellow, and the next signal was a diverging approach, a red over yellow, and I had to be down to twenty-five at that signal so we could get into the siding. Sure enough, there was a train on the main line headed east."

"What if you'd been going sixty, like last time?"

He winked. "I wouldn't be getting any nice letters telling me how good I am at my job."

"Seriously. What if you saw a headlight coming at you in the dark?"

"You heard about Fenton Lee, then, did you?"

"What would you do?"

Loyd looked at me. "Jump off."

"Yeah?"

"Oh, yeah. I did it one time already, when I was a fireman. The engineer hit a siding too fast and that sucker looked like it was going off the track. I was out of there like buckshot. I got a big old bruise on my butt, and the guys laughed at me because they didn't derail. I don't care. There's things worth risking your life for, but a hunk of metal's not one of them."

I watched him drink his coffee. In the hot sun his hair had dried to its normal glossy, animal black. The mesquite leaves cast feathery shadows all over his face and the muscular slope of his chest. The sight of his bare feet stirred me oddly. I badly wanted to take him inside to bed.

"Well. But you *are* real good at your job," I said.

"I'm getting there."

"I guess I never knew there was so much to it."

He set down his cup and crossed his arms. "Pretty good for an Injun boy, huh?"

"You could have told me more about it."

He smiled. "Codi, did anybody ever tell you a damn thing you didn't want to know?"

I stalled, avoiding the question. "If I told you I wanted to go to bed with you right now, would you think I only loved you for your mind?"

His eyes sparkled. "I think I could overlook it."


**That night** I lay in Loyd's arms and cried. Since the day I spent with Uda in the attic, wishes and anger had backed up in me, and now they rushed out, rocketing my mind around on a wild track toward emptiness. I told Loyd about the photographs and unrelated things, old things, like making pies with Uda Dell. "I have all these memories I couldn't get hold of before, but it doesn't make me feel any better," I said.

"What kind of memories?"

"Everything. Really, my whole childhood. Most of it I had no idea was there. And most of it's happy. But Loyd, it's like the tape broke when I was fifteen, and my life started over then. The life I'd been living before that was so different—I don't know how to say this, but I just couldn't touch that happiness anymore, I'd changed so much. That was some other little bright-eyed, righteous girl parading around trying to rescue drowning coyotes and save chickens from the stewpot. A dumb little kid who thought the sun had a smiley face on it."

"And what happened when she was fifteen?"

I withdrew from Loyd's arms. Had I set him up to ask? I lay looking at the wall, considering whether I could tell him. If I only had two more months in Grace, it wasn't long enough. "I can't explain it," I said. "I guess it finally hit me that nobody was going to take care of me."

"In high school you were doing a pretty good job of taking care of yourself."

"That's what it looked like. It probably looks like that now, too."

Loyd took me back onto his shoulder, which felt hard like a cradleboard under my head. He stroked my cheek. "You still have all the family you grew up with. Hallie's somewhere out there. She'll come back. And Doc's still here."

"Neither one of them is *here*."

"Codi, for everybody that's gone away, there's somebody that's come to you. Emelina thinks you're her long-lost sister. You know what she told me? She wants you there in that little house forever. She said if I let you leave Grace she'll bust my butt. She loves you to death."

"So this is all a conspiracy, I said."

"Yeah. Emelina bribed me to fall in love with you." He laughed and kissed my hair. "Honey, there's not that much money in the world."

I didn't wish to be comforted. "You can't replace people you love with other people," I said. "They're not like old shoes or something."

"No. But you can trust that you're not going to run out of people to love."

"I don't think I can trust life that far. I lost my mother. You don't know what that's like."

"No, I don't."

"You don't have any idea what the whole story is, Loyd. You don't know everybody I've lost."

He gathered me into his arms and we didn't talk anymore, but in my chest I could still feel a small, hard knot of anger and I held on to it. It was my wings. My exit to safety.

**Finally I read** all of Hallie's letters. There were half a dozen I'd never opened, the ones that came after. I knew she'd mailed them before she was kidnapped—I could read the postmarks—but I still held the hope that there might be some clue in there that would help bring her back. Once I opened the letters that hope would be gone.

But I was past a certain point now, like Loyd's train going over the hill. The momentum of wanting to hear Hallie, even for a few minutes, was growing heavier than anything I might have had to lose. More than ever in my life I needed to ask her what to do, how to live without guarantees, without safety.

So I read the letters, and there were no clues. Only the ordinary, heartbreaking details of war and rural life and the slow progress of hope.

I'd forgotten that her last letter, which I'd read on the trip to Santa Rosalia, was a tirade. I had to get it out and read it again to remember, and the sting was gone. "If I get another letter that mentions SAVING THE WORLD, I am sending you, by return mail, a letter bomb." (Had I really used those words? But I knew I had, more than once.) "I don't expect to see perfection before I die. What keeps you going isn't some fine destination but just the road you're on, and the fact that you know how to drive." Two hours after she'd mailed that, she had written a pained apology that reached me now, a lifetime later. Any one moment could be like this, I thought. A continental divide.

*Codi [she wrote], I'm sorry, I didn't say it right. I'm touchy about being worshiped. I'm afraid of becoming Doc Homer Junior, standing on a monument of charity and handing down my blessings, making sure everybody knows where we all stand. I don't feel like I'm doing that, but it's the thing you fear most that walks beside you all the time. I don't want you of all people to see me that way. I'm not Saving Nicaragua, I'm doing the only thing I can live with under the circumstances. The circumstances being that in Tucson I was dying among the garden pests. Working with refugees, and also subsidizing the war that was killing them. I had to get out.*

*By virtue of our citizenship we're on one side of this war or the other. I chose sides. And I know that we could lose. I've never seen people suffer so much for an ideal. They're sick to death of the embargo and the war. They could say Uncle, vote for something else, just to stop this bludgeoning. And you know what? I don't even consider that, it's not the point.*

*You're thinking of revolution as a great all-or-nothing. I think of it as one more morning in a muggy cotton field, checking the undersides of leaves to see what's been there, figuring out what to do that won't clear a path for worse problems next week. Right now that's what I do. You ask why I'm not afraid of loving and losing, and that's my answer. Wars and elections are both too big and too small to matter in the long run. The daily work—that goes on, it adds up. It goes into the ground, into crops, into children's bellies and their bright eyes. Good things don't get lost.*

*Codi, here's what I've decided: the very least you can do in your life is to figure out what you hope for. And the most you can do is live inside that hope. Not admire it from a dis-*

*tance but live right in it, under its roof. What I want is so*
*simple I almost can't say it: elementary kindness. Enough to*
*eat, enough to go around. The possibility that kids might one*
*day grow up to be neither the destroyers nor the destroyed.*
*That's about it. Right now I'm living in that hope, running*
*down its hallway and touching the walls on both sides.*

*I can't tell you how good it feels. I wish you knew. I wish*
*you'd stop beating yourself up for being selfish, and really be*
*selfish, Codi. You're like a mother or something. I wish you*
*knew how to squander yourself.*

I sat with this letter for a long time trying to understand what
peace she was asking me to make.

The others were impersonal, full of description and the usual
manic-depressive mélange of experience. The weather had been too
dry. A shipment of Yugoslav tractors had come in and they were
working out well. "The Deeres were better," she lamented, "but you
have to run them like glass hammers, they can be drydocked for lack
of a bolt. The U.S. refuses to trade with us and then makes secret,
niggling lists of what we get from the Eastern bloc. The embargo
having slipped their minds, apparently."

In another letter she said they heard gunfire almost every night.
"People talk about the second reconstruction. They mean after the
U.S. invades. We get up every day and scan the horizon for holocaust." In this same letter she talked about her young trainees and
the joy of seeing a new idea take root in a mind; I knew the moment.
When Raymo grasped DNA, his countenance was touched with
light. We'd shared something.

I stayed up most of the night rereading letters, all the way back
to the first one from the Guatemalan border, where she saw women
running from the army carrying babies and backstrap looms. And
earlier, on the beach, where she'd watched a man sell shrimp from a
bucket that was counterweighted with a plastic jug of drinking
water. He drank as he went along, to keep the load balanced. The
purity of direct necessity.

But the letters ended, finite as a book or a life, and I had no choice but to keep coming back to the last one, scrutinizing it for a sign of goodbye. It wasn't there. It was a description of the children's Christmas Eve pageant, three or four words about Julio, and a self-effacing story of how she'd broken her plate that morning at break-fast. Of course it was a disaster; there was only one anything per person in the house. She was mad at herself for being careless, but the neighbor women rounded up a new plate. They made a joke of its being tin, unbreakable.

Nothing else. The closest thing to prescience had come a few days earlier, in a pensive pared-down note that said: "Sometimes I still have American dreams. I mean literally. I see microwave ovens and exercise machines and grocery-store shelves with thirty brands of shampoo, and I look at these things oddly, in my dream. I stand and I think, 'What is all this for? What is the hunger that drives this need?' I think it's fear. Codi, I hope you won't be hurt by this but I don't think I'll ever be going back. I don't think I can."

**I had my own** nightmare again, but this time I understood that it wasn't blindness. It was a flashbulb in my father's camera. Even from inside the dream I knew that, and I didn't wake myself when I heard the glass pop. I took the risk of staying where I was, and went on dreaming. What I saw next was an infant face that wasn't my own but my child's, lit in the flash. Then I saw her whole body in moonlight. She was a seventeen-year-old girl, naked and long-limbed, walking up the path toward our house. I stood in the kitchen and watched her through the screen door as she came up the path from the river. For a second she disappeared in the inky shadows under the cottonwoods and I felt completely afraid, but then she emerged again in the light. Her skin glowed white.

I thought: "If she tries to walk through this screen door into Doc Homer's kitchen, she'll evaporate. She can't come in here." So I ran outside and gathered her up, a ridiculous bundle of long arms and legs. I carried her back through the cottonwood grove and down the path, away from the house. Over our heads was a chalky full moon with cloud rubbed across it, like something incompletely erased. I was hunched over and stumbling and I started to run along the dry riverbed, absurdly burdened with this long-legged child as big as myself. I didn't talk or look at her, I just carried her along.

Hallie followed me down the path. I didn't see her come, but I heard her voice right behind me.

"Codi, stop. She's too heavy. You can put her down now."

I clamped her weight against my chest. "No I can't, she'll fall."

"Let her go. She won't fall."

"I can't."

Hallie urged gently, "Let her go. Let go. She'll rise."

And then I woke up with empty arms.

# 24

# The Luckiest
# Person Alive

The call came sometime before dawn.

While I brushed my teeth I watched the mirror closely and became aware of my skull: of the fact that my teeth were rooted in bone, and that my jawbones and all the other bones lay just under the surface of what I could see. I wondered how I could have missed noticing, before, all those bones. I was a skeleton with flesh and clothes and thoughts. We believe there is such a safe distance between the living and the dead. I recalled how I'd used Mrs. Josephine Nash to shock my students into paying attention, on the first day of school. I'd thought I understood something they didn't, about death. That it was understandable.

I was still at the mirror when Loyd came. I saw him appear behind me. First he wasn't there, and then he was. He was going to drive me to Tucson. I had to go to the Mexican consulate to get a registered letter and some papers, and then I would sign some other papers from the Nicaraguan government. Of course, there was no

Nicaraguan consulate. It was the Minister of Agriculture who called. We had become something like friends, though we would probably not speak again now. Or perhaps we would. I'd heard of people united by disaster keeping track for years afterward, holding reunions. I thought of boat people. Business executives stranded overnight in elevators. How would they celebrate? What specific moments would they recall for each other? My thoughts kept straying onto random paths like these, hoping to get lost in a thicket.

The Minister said there would be a package coming later. Not her body, but a parcel of personal things, some books and journals. Her plate and cup, her clothes, those items were distributed to neighbors. The body would stay there. She had requested of somebody, at some point, that she be buried in Nicaragua if that ever had to happen. She said Nicaragua could use the fertilizer.

*What was the last thing she said to me in person? How did she look? Why can't I remember?*

"Loyd," the face in the mirror said. "What do I do now?"

"Put on your shoes."

"Okay."

The sun was just coming up as we drove away from Grace. The world looked inhospitable.

"I should have gone down there," I said.

"And done what?"

We drove past an old junkyard outside of town. I'd never noticed it before, though it must have been there since before I was born. A man stood on the bonnet of a rusted car, shading his eyes, looking down into the ravine.

"On the phone they said her hands were tied," I told Loyd. "He said they found her that way. But I can't believe that. It doesn't sound right to me that she would let anybody just tie her up and then shoot her in the head."

"Maybe they made a mistake," he said. "Maybe it didn't happen exactly that way."

"I know my sister. I think she would get away somehow," I said.

"Wait for the letter. That'll tell everything."

"Maybe they made a mistake," I repeated. "Maybe so."

Within an hour the daylight had overcome its early bleakness. Now it looked like any normal, slightly overcast day. The normalcy made me angry, but it was a weak kind of anger that held no pleasure.

"If I'd told her about Doc Homer back in December, how bad he was, she would have come home."

"You can't make this your fault."

"But she would have come home."

"Codi," Loyd said, looking at me and not finishing. His face held such pain I didn't want to see it. Finally he said, "You could probably think of a hundred little things that would have made this turn out different. But you'd be wrong. A life like your sister's isn't some little pony you can turn around any way you want. It's a train. Once it gets going it's heavier than heaven and hell put together and it runs on its own track."

I didn't say anything to that. Loyd barely even remembered meeting my sister. How could he know what her life meant?

On the interstate we passed the site of a bad accident. You could see it coming: the cop cars and ambulances all huddled around, lights flashing importantly, making their scene. As we came closer we had to slow down; one lane was blocked by a trailer rig with a smashed front end. Out in the median, at an angle that bore no relation to the direction of traffic, sat a white convertible with its frame bent violently into a V-shape.

When we passed it I saw that it wasn't a convertible after all; the top had been sheared off, and lay on the other side of the road. An arc of glass and chrome crossed the highway like a glittering river littered with flotsam and jetsam: a pair of sunglasses, a bright vinyl bag, a paperback book. At the trail's end was the pile of steel. I'd never seen such a badly wrecked car.

"Doesn't look like anybody walked away from that one," Loyd said.

I thought of Hallie walking out of the library that time, years ago, then remembering her sunglasses and turning back just before the marble façade fell down. She could just as well have died then. It made no difference now.

*The luckiest person alive.*

The ambulance pulled out right behind us, its warning lights alternating like crazy winking eyes. We quickly left it behind, though, and we weren't speeding by any means. Loyd saw me watching the ambulance and glanced up at the rear-view mirror. "They're not in much of a rush, are they?"

Just then, while we watched, the lights stopped flashing. I understood that I had just seen someone die. No reason to hurry anymore. My limbs flooded with despair and I didn't see how I was going to survive. I kept imagining what that little white car must have looked like half an hour ago, and the driver, some young woman listening to the radio, checking her hair in the mirror, preoccupied with this afternoon or tonight or whatever small errand had taken her out.

"Why does a person even get up in the morning?" I asked Loyd. "You have breakfast, you floss your teeth so you'll have healthy gums in your old age, and then you get in your car and drive down I-10 and die. Life is so stupid I can't stand it."

"Hallie knew exactly what she was doing. There wasn't anything stupid about her life."

I practically shouted at Loyd, "I'm not crying about Hallie right now. I'm crying about that person that just died in the ambulance."

He was quiet.

"Loyd, I don't know what I'm going to do." I was afraid the muscles in my chest might tear themselves apart. I thought senselessly of Doc Homer's discussion of liver tissue and heart tissue. As if it mattered what part of your body was the seat of emotion, all of it could be torn up, it was just flesh. Doc Homer didn't even know about this yet. I'd called, and we talked, and it was clear he didn't know what I was telling him. He talked about Hallie being kept after school. Maybe he never would understand, maybe his mind would just keep wandering down other happy trails. Loyd handed me his handkerchief and I tried to blow my nose.

"What would she want you to do?"

"*She* would be crying for a person in a damn ambulance that she didn't even know. Not *me*."

I saw lightning erupt in the dark clouds behind the Catalina Mountains. It was an impossible time of year for a lightning storm. I'd seen photographs of lightning frozen in its terrible splendor, ripping like a knife down the curtains of the sky. They say that to take those pictures you just open your camera on a dark night, in a storm, and if you're lucky you get a wonderful picture. You have no control.

"Hallie isn't dead," I said. "This is a dream." I laid my head back against the headrest and cried with my knucklebones against my mouth. Tears ran down to my collarbone and soaked my shirt and still I didn't wake up.

# 25

# Flight

Getting on the bus was the easiest thing in the world. I only took what I could carry. Emelina would send my trunk to Telluride.

I noticed the junkyard again on the way out of town. They should have had a sign there: Welcome to Grace. Farewell to Grace. Dead grass poked up through the rusted husks of big old cars that hunched on the ground like elephants, the great dying beasts of the African plain. It was early June, soon after the end of school. The land was matchstick-dry and I felt the same way, just that brittle, as if no amount of rain could saturate my outer layers and touch my core. I was a hard seed beyond germination. I would do fine in Telluride. Carlo had lined up a job for me as a model in a summer fine-arts school. I would sit still for solid hours while people tried for my skin tones.

Uda Dell and Mrs. Quintana, Doc's assistant for twenty-one years, were going to take shifts with Doc Homer. His office was closed for good, and everybody now drove over to New Mexico to be healed. There were no thunderclaps when it happened; all this time we'd thought he was indispensable. Uda and Mrs. Quintana revered him. I couldn't picture them feeding him, buttoning up his shirt, but I knew they would do those things. Somehow reverence can fashion itself into kindness, in a way that love sometimes can't. When I went up there to tell him goodbye, he was eating a soft-boiled egg and said he couldn't tarry, he was in a hurry to get to the hospital.

I bobbed along with the motion of the Greyhound bus, leaning with the curves. When I relaxed enough I could feel like a small chunk of rock in outer space, perceiving no gravitational pull from any direction: not from where I was going, nor where I had been. Not Carlo, not Loyd, not Doc Homer. Not Hallie, who did not exist.

"Where do you think people go when they die?" Loyd asked, the day before I left. He was on his way out to take a westbound into Tucson; the next day he would fetch home the Amtrak. We stood in my front door, unwilling to go in or out, like awkward beginners trying to end a date. Except it wasn't a beginners' conversation.

"Nowhere," I said. "I think when people die they're just dead."

"Not heaven?"

I looked up at the sky. It looked quite empty. "No."

"The Pueblo story is that everybody started out underground. People and animals, everything. And then the badger dug a hole and let everybody out. They climbed out the hole and from then on they lived on top of the ground. When they die they go back under."

I thought of the kivas, the ladders, and the thousand mud walls of Santa Rosalia. I could hear the dry rattle of the corn dancers' shell bells: the exact sound of locusts rising up from the grass. I understood that Loyd was one of the most blessed people I knew.

"I always try to think of it that way," he said, after a minute. "He had a big adventure up here, and then went home."

Leander, he would mean. My spleen started to ache when I thought of Hallie fertilizing the tropics. Thinking about how much she loved stupid banana trees and orchids. I said, "I have this idea that if I don't stay here and cry for Hallie, then there's no family to absorb the loss. Nobody that remembers."

"And that's what you want? For Hallie to be forgotten?"

I couldn't have said what I meant. "No. I just don't want to be the one that's left behind to hurt this much. I want to be gone already. If you're dead when somebody stabs you, you don't feel it."

"Leaving won't make you dead. You'll just be alive in a different place."

"This place has Hallie in it. When I lived here, I was half her and half me."

"Going away won't change how you feel."

"I won't know that till I'm gone, will I?"

He picked up my hand and examined it as if it were a foreign object, which was just how it looked to me. He was wearing a green corduroy shirt with the sleeves rolled to the elbows, and I felt I could look at that shirt for as long as Loyd might choose to stand in my door. There were all those small ridges, the greenness, the nap of the cloth. If I kept my focus minute enough I could remain in the world, knowledgeable and serene.

"Anyway you're wrong," he said. "There's family here to absorb the loss."

"Doc Homer, Loyd, he's . . . I don't think he understands she's gone."

"I wasn't talking about Doc Homer."

I shifted my field of vision to include the lower part of Loyd's face and the blunt dark ends of his hair. A whole person seemed an impossible thing to take in all at once. How had I lived so long and presumed so much?

"I'm sorry about everything, Loyd."

"Listen, I know how this is. You don't think you'll live past it. And you don't, really. The person you were is gone. But the half of you that's still alive wakes up one day and takes over again."

"Why should I look forward to that?"

He turned my hand over. "I can't answer that."

"Well, I'm sorry, Loyd."

"I'm sorry too."

"Well. You've got to go to work." I avoided his eyes.

Loyd took my face in one hand and put the other hand on the small of my back and he kissed me for a long time. His mouth felt cool as green corduroy, a simple thing I could understand. We began the kiss standing up, and when we finished we were sitting on the step.

"You have to go," I said again. That was the last thing, my last words for Loyd.

When he and Jack were gone I stood for a long time looking out at the rambling jungle of the courtyard. A hummingbird, possibly the same one that had inspired Nicholas to learn to walk, was hovering at the red funnels of the trumpet vine climbing my wall. I watched the bird move stiffly up and down over an invisible path, pausing, then moving left, then up again and back, covering the vertical plane with such purpose it might have been following a map.

I felt Emelina's presence. She stood in her kitchen door, shading her eyes, watching me. I waved, but she didn't wave back. Her face was drawn tight with mute, unarmed rage; it must have been the worst thing she was capable of aiming at a friend. She didn't know my tricks, that you could just buckle up your tough old heart and hit the road. My course must have been as indecipherable to her as the hummingbird's. We are all just here, Emelina, I wanted to say. Following our maps, surviving as we know how.

The kitchen door closed quietly and I understood that it was her kindest goodbye. The sun was strangely bright on the whitewashed wall and the hummingbird hung in the air, frozen inside its moment. A photograph of the present tense.

**All morning** on my last day people came pecking softly at my door like mice. A legion of mice bearing gifts. It was mostly women from the Stitch and Bitch. No one else was as succinct as Emelina. They wanted to know what I would be doing, where I would live. I mentioned the art school, but wasn't specific.

"We sure do love you, hon," said Uda Dell. "I packed you a

lunch. There's yellow banana peppers in there from the garden. They're not as big as some years but they've got a right smart bite. Stay another year," she added.

"Do you have a good winter coat?" Norma Galvez asked me. "It snows up there. You'd just as well stay here."

In their eyes my life should have been simple, purely a matter of love and the right wardrobe. It was as if I had fifty mothers.

In the last hour before I left I had to go through Emelina's kitchen to retrieve a pair of jeans from the laundry room. John Tucker was folding laundry. He told me Emelina was lying down upstairs with a bad headache.

"You got a baseball game today?" I asked.

"Yeah."

"Sorry I won't be around to see you win."

He smiled. In a year I'd watched him grow into his elbows and lose the better part of his shyness. His voice was beginning to crack. "Mom's really going to miss you. She'll be a witch for the next month. She'll make us clean out the chicken pens and stuff."

"It's all my fault," I said, grabbing a runaway corner of a sheet and helping him fold it. "You guys can send me hate mail in Telluride."

He laughed. "Okay."

"If it gets too bad you can run away from home. Come up and see me. We'll go skiing."

He hoisted his laundry basket and headed for the stairs.

When I came back out through the kitchen Viola was there at the table, lying in wait like a predator.

"Sit down," she said. "Save your shoes."

I was lunch meat. I sat down.

"Boy oh boy, kiddo," she said.

"What does that mean? That I should stay here?"

"Sure you should."

"Well," I said.

"But nobody ever could tell you a darn thing."

"That's what I hear."

"I been wanting to tell you something."

"I know Emelina's pissed off at me."

She snorted. "If you don't know that already you're not going to hear it from me."

"Oh." I thought about what else she might have to reveal to me. "I know about my mother," I said. "I know she came from here, that she was a cousin or something to Doña Althea. And that she and Doc Homer ran off."

Viola smiled a little. "Son of a gun. He told you?"

"More or less."

She adjusted the coil of hair on the back of her head, reclaiming its territory with the planting of a few long bobby pins. "Well, that's not what I was wanting to tell you."

We sat looking at each other for a good while. Her T-shirt said I WAS DEEP DISHED AT MAMA LENARDA'S. I had no idea where it might have come from.

"I'm not supposed to tell you," she added.

"Says who?"

"Says me. Doc Homer would shoot me if he found out."

"I don't think there's much danger, Viola."

"Well, but it's the principles."

Now I was curious. "So, did you sit me down here to tell me something or not?"

She hesitated, shifting her weight forward onto her elbows on the table. "I was looking after you girls the day your mama died."

"You kept us at home?"

She nodded. "I was supposed to."

"But you didn't."

"I thought you had the right to say bye to your mama, like anybody else. To tell her, '*Vaya con Dios.*' Anybody else had no business up there, they just went to watch the show, but you had business and you was not allowed to go. Hallie was just born, she didn't know anything anyway so I left her with Uda Dell."

"And you took me up to the field to see the helicopter come down."

Viola leaned back in her chair. "I'm not saying I did, and I'm not saying I didn't."

"What are you saying?"

"Just that you had a right. That's all. Now, skedaddle. *Que le vaya bien.*"

**The Greyhound was** mostly empty, a dry gourd rolling across the desert, occasionally spilling out a seed or two in an inhospitable outpost: Bowie, Willcox, Benson. It was 110 degrees down there, not something people would travel through unless they were desperate to be elsewhere.

As things had turned out, Grace was not going to dry up. The women of the Stitch and Bitch had won back the river. A vice-president of the Black Mountain Mining Company called a press conference in Phoenix to announce that after seventy years of productive and congenial relations with the people of Gracela Canyon, the mine operation there was closing up shop. It was a matter of the leaching operation's being no longer profitable, he said. The dam would be deconstructed. Naturally, if any harm had been incurred, all necessary reparations would be made to the people of Grace. He made no mention of the historic registry petition that had been filed one week earlier. So mountains could be moved. Now I knew.

When my bus paused in Willcox a woman climbed aboard and chose to sit by me, rather than take her chances on something worse that might come along, I guess. She wore an ample white jogging suit and had an odd, metallic hair color. I spent the next fifty miles in fear of a conversation I wasn't in the mood for, but she just kept scowling at a gardening magazine.

Then suddenly she held out her magazine as if it had offended her. "That kills me, how people can grow four o'clocks like that," she said, whacking the page with the back of her plump hand.

I glanced over at the unbelievable floral displays in her magazine. I could relate to her frustration. You just knew they trucked in those flowers from a climate-controlled greenhouse somewhere and arranged them on the lawn, right before snapping the photo.

"I'm Alice Kimball," the woman explained. "I get the worst slugs."

Alice. Would my mother be wearing tepid jogging suits now, if her organs had not failed her? I tried to smile. "Where do you get them?"

"In my four o'clocks. That's what I'm trying to tell you, I can't grow a four o'clock to save my life. The leaves get so full of holes they just look pitiful. And they get in the lawn, too. My husband says he hears them out there eating up his grass. What can you do?"

"I'm not the right person to ask," I said. "My sister could sure tell you, though. She got a degree in Integrated Pest Management. She used to answer the Garden Hotline in Tucson, 626-BUGS."

Mrs. Kimball brightened as if I'd offered her a peppermint. "I've called that before. They have the nicest little girl on that line, she'll tell you anything you want to know."

"That was my sister you talked to. Hallie Noline." I was amazed by the coincidence, but then again probably half of Tucson had turned to Hallie for advice. And half of Nicaragua. "That was part of her job," I said. "She did that for six years."

Mrs. Kimball looked around at the neighboring seats as if Hallie might turn up for consultation. "Well, do you mean she's quit? I just thought the world of her."

"Yep, she quit. She left the country."

"Left the *country*?"

"She went to Nicaragua." Everybody in this country should know her name, I thought. During the Iran hostage crisis they had a special symbol on the newscasts: a blindfolded man, and the number of days. A schoolchild glancing up from a comic book would know that this story was about *them*. But a nation gloats on the hostility of its enemies, whereas Hallie had proved the malevolence of some men we supplied with machine guns. Hallie was a skeleton in the civic closet.

Some people knew. I'd gotten a card from a nun in Minneapolis who had known Hallie. She was one of several thousand people who had gone down to Nicaragua for just a week or two, she said. They helped pick coffee, or if they had training they did other helpful things. The idea was just to be there in the danger zone, so that if the U.S. should attack, it would have to attack some of its own citizens. This nun, Sister Sabina Martin, had helped give vaccinations. She met Hallie at the clinic in Chinandega the day Hallie brought in a child who'd drunk paraquat from a Coke bottle. Sister Martin and Hallie sat with the child the whole day, and she said that although I might not think it possible, she felt she'd come to know Hallie well during that time. In some circumstances, she said, an afternoon can be a whole life.

"Oh, well," Mrs. Kimball said, after quite a while. "You must miss her."

"I will, when it really sinks in. She hasn't been gone that long."

"I know what you're going through," said Mrs. Kimball. "I lost my sister in 1965."

I hadn't told her Hallie was dead. Mrs. Kimball had seized the subject of death all on her own. "I'm sorry," I said, not really wanting to be encouraging, but you couldn't just ignore it, either.

"She's been dead all this time of an aneurysm and there are still days when I think, 'Oh, wait till I tell Phoebe about that!' Before I realize. I always think it's harder to believe they're gone when it's sudden."

"My sister," I said, and then stopped, afraid of the lie I was about to tell. I was going to say, "isn't dead." I heard an old voice in my head, the teller of tales: I am a cello player running away from home. We are from Zanzibar, we're from Ireland, our mother is the Queen of Potatoes. I was through constructing myself for other people. I didn't say anything.

Several seats ahead of us, a teenage couple had begun necking enthusiastically. You couldn't blame these kids, the scenery was boring and would drive you to anything, but they made me feel hopelessly alone.

"Well," Alice said, apparently remembering it was garden pests we'd agreed to talk about. "What would *you* do for the slugs?"

"I really don't know, I'm not that good with plants." I considered the problem for a while. "I think what Hallie used to do was put out beer for them, in little tin cans. The slugs are attracted to it and they fall in, or something. I know that sounds crazy but I'm pretty sure it's right."

"Well." She stared at me thoughtfully. "My husband and I aren't drinkers, but I guess I could go out and get some beer for the slugs. Do you know what brand?"

"I don't think it matters. I'd get whatever's on sale."

"All right, I'll do that," said Mrs. Kimball. She opened her magazine again to the incendiary four o'clocks, but then closed it right back up, holding the place with her finger. "You ought to try to keep in touch with your sister," she told me. "Young people think nothing will ever happen. You should treasure your family while you have it."

"Well, really I don't have it," I said, resentful of her assumptions. "It's gone. My mother died when I was little and my father will probably be dead before the year's out, and my baby died, and now my sister is dead too. Maybe I'm not as young as you think."

Mrs. Kimball looked stunned. "Your sister? The one on the phone?"

"She got killed by the contras. The ones down there that we send all the money to. I think you probably heard about it."

She looked uneasy. "I don't know. I might have."

"It made the news in Tucson, at least for a day. You just forgot. That's the great American disease, we forget. We watch the disasters parade by on TV, and every time we say: 'Forget it. This is somebody else's problem.'"

I suppose I was going, as Rita Cardenal would say, mental. I didn't look at Mrs. Kimball but I could see her magazine drift slowly to her lap. I looked at the bright garden on the magazine cover and felt strangely calm. "They kidnapped her one morning in a cotton field," I said. "They kept her as a prisoner for weeks and weeks, and we kept hoping, but then they moved everybody to another camp and some of the prisoners they shot. Eight of them. Hallie and seven men. All of the men were teachers. They tied their hands behind them and shot them in the head and left their bodies all sitting in a line at the side of a road, in a forest, right near the border. All facing south."

I felt a hard knot in my chest because this was the one image I saw most clearly. I still do. My voice sounded like a voice that would come from some other person's throat, someone who had a dead sister and could speak of such things. "The man that found them was driving up from Estelí, coming along the road, and at first when he saw them all sitting there he thought, 'Oh, that's too many. I can't give them all a ride, they won't fit in my truck.' "

Mrs. Kimball and I didn't speak again after that. I looked out the window. Far to the south, low cone shapes pushed up against the flat, bright sky. Those distant mountains were probably in Mexico, I knew, though borders in this barren land seemed beside the point. I heard Mrs. Kimball turn a page of her magazine. We'd been silent for over an hour before she first spoke up about the four o'clocks, but the silence was much more noticeable now, after we'd broken it with our little conversation. Awareness is everything. Hallie once pointed out to me that people worry a lot more about the eternity *after* their deaths than the eternity that happened before they were born. But it's the same amount of infinity, rolling out in all directions from where we stand.


**My airplane was** said to be bound for Denver, but it sat on the runway for a very long time. I had a window seat and could watch other planes lift their noses one after another and plow their way up an invisible road into the sky. I wasn't impatient. Normally at this point in a flight my heart would pound and my mouth would go to cotton, but today my viscera were still. It didn't matter especially if we burned in a fiery crash.

I thought maybe the air traffic controllers were trying to decide whether we were worth the trouble; we were only a small, twin-engine plane, incompletely filled. A few seats ahead of me a mother coached her preschooler, who was already crying because he knew his ears would hurt when we went up. This was not the first leg of their trip.

"You swallow, honey. Just remember to swallow, that makes your ears feel better. And yawn."

"I can't yawn."

"Sure you can." She demonstrated, her voice stretching wide over the yawn: "Think about being real, real sleepy." People yawned all the way back to the smoking section, so strong was the power of motherly suggestion. I felt overcome with sadness.

The aisle seat of my row was occupied by a teenager, and the empty seat between us was filling up with her overflow paraphernalia. She threw down a hairbrush and a curling iron—whack! whack!—and pulled a substantial mirror out of a makeup case the size of my carry-on luggage. She began applying careful stripes of pastel eye shadow. When she blinked, her eyelids waved like a pair of foreign flags.

"Give it a rest, Brenda," said the man sitting across the aisle. "You're not going to see your boyfriend for ten whole days. Why not take this wonderful opportunity to let your face get some fresh air?"

Brenda ignored this advice, staring with deep absorption into her makeup mirror while her parents in B and C beamed her the Evil Eye. The mother was wearing a polka-dot jumpsuit with coordinated polka-dot earrings, all a little too eager-looking even for the first day of vacation. The man had on sunny golf pants that clashed with his disposition. It was hard to ignore them, but Brenda was practiced. She glanced serenely at her left wrist, which bore three separate watches with plastic bands in the same three shades as her eye shadow. Her hair looked as if each strand had been individually lacquered and tortured into position. No matter how you might feel about the aesthetic, you had to admire the effort. Most people put less into their jobs.

"Brenda, honey, please pay attention when your father is talking to you," said the woman in the polka dots. "Could you please just try? Listening to you and your father bicker for a week and a half is not my idea of a vacation."

"You should have left me at home," Brenda said quietly, staring directly ahead. " 'Honey, I think we forgot something. Did I leave the iron on? No, we forgot Brenda.' " She shot me a glance, and I think I smiled a little. I couldn't help being on Brenda's side here. In my term as a schoolteacher I'd gained sympathy for adolescence. If I had to take a trip with those two I'd probably paint my face blue for spite.

The plane jerked a little and then began to roll creakily down the runway, gathering speed. We were taking off without a warning announcement of any kind. "Flight attendants prepare for takeoff" came out in a single scrambled burst over the intercom, and the women in pumps and dark suits ran as if from an air-raid siren. I closed my eyes and laid my head back, trying to hold on to my visceral indifference, but it fell right away. My heart had caught up with me. I heard the little boy chattering to his mother and I yawned nervously. So much of life is animal instinct: desire and yawning and fear and the will to live. We left the earth and climbed steeply into the void.

My habit was to count seconds during the lift-off, with my mind on news stories that ran along the lines of "crashed into a meadow only seconds after takeoff . . ." Somewhere I'd gotten the idea it took seven minutes to get past imminent peril. I counted to sixty, and started over. We'd been airborne for maybe three or four minutes when our pilot's deep Texan voice came over the intercom. "Folks, I apologize for the delay in taking off today. We had trouble getting one of these cantankerous old engines started up."

The announcement startled my eyes open. I looked at Brenda, who widened her eyes comically. "Great," she said.

"It's nice to know you're riding the friendly skies in a bucket of bolts."

Brenda laughed. "Like my boyfriend's car."

"I think we'd be safer in your boyfriend's car."

"Not in their opinion," she said, inclining her head across the aisle.

I closed my eyes again. I tried to relax, but couldn't help listening to every change of pitch in the engine noise. They sounded wrong. Suddenly I confided in Brenda, "I hate to fly. You know? It scares me to death."

I hadn't admitted this aloud before, and was surprised to hear it come out so naturally. The truth needs so little rehearsal. Brenda reached over and patted my hand.

"Folks, this is Captain Sampson. I'm sorry to report that we've lost that engine again."

Against my will I glanced out at the wing to see if anything had actually fallen off. My heart beat hard and out of synch with itself and I felt I might die of fright. I let the fingertips of my right hand lie across my left wrist, tracking the off-rhythm of my aimless heart. If I were really dying, I wanted to be the first to know.

After another minute, during which I imagined Captain Sampson and his copilot trying everything, his paternal drawl crackled on again. "We could probably make it to Stapleton on one engine," he said, "but we'll play it safe. We're going to turn around and head back into Tucson to see if they'll let us have some new equipment."

I hated the sound of the word "equipment." I had visions of men in coveralls running out to strap a spare engine onto the wing. If we made it back to the airport at all. Suddenly we banked so steeply my stomach turned. I must have looked pale, because Brenda reached over and squeezed my hand again.

"Try to think about something relaxing," she said. "Think about kissing your boyfriend."

"That's *relaxing?*"

She smiled. "No. But it takes your mind off."

She was right; it did, for a second or two. I thought of Loyd's last kiss on my doorstep in Grace. But it also made my chest ache, further distracting my heart from the task at hand. Nausea pressed on the back of my throat. I closed my eyes, but vertigo is an internal distress; shutting out the world does nothing to help. The plane took another steep bank.

We were in an unnatural position, vertical in the air and slipping down, with nothing to support us.

When we finally leveled out again I opened my eyes. We were skimming low over Tucson and I was comforted—irrationally I know—by the nearness of things. Clusters of houses huddled together as if for reassurance, and in between them lay broad spans of flesh-colored desert. The freckled ground was threaded with thin, branched lines of creeks, like veins in the back of a hand. It looked as if there were water in the creeks, although I knew better. At this time of year they were bone-dry rivers of sand.

The rush of adrenalin had rinsed me clean. I looked hard out the window and understood suddenly that what I saw was full of color. A watercolor wash of summer light lay on the Catalina Mountains. The end of a depression is that clear: it's as if you have been living underwater, but never realized it until you came up for air. I hadn't seen color since I lost Hallie. I thought hard, trying to remember; it seemed unbelievable, but there was none. Almost none. Loyd's green corduroy shirt, and the red flowers and the hummingbird against the brightly lit wall, the moment Emelina said goodbye. And that was all. Before that, the last thing I clearly remembered in color was Santa Rosalia in its infinite shades of brown.

I laughed at myself for carrying my mother's phobic blood in my veins. And for telling Alice Kimball how to cure slugs. Practicing all this family business without a license. It seemed extraordinary and accidental that I was alive. I felt crowded with all the sensory messages that make up life, as opposed to survival, and I recognized this as something close to joy. As we slipped down over the city every building and back lot was beautifully distinct. I forgot about my heart, left it to look after itself. We passed south of downtown, over the railyard, where the boxcars stood in line looking sweet and mismatched like a child's toy put together with no eye for color coordination. Just past the railyard was a school where a double row of corn-colored school buses were parked in a ring, exactly like one of those cheap Indian necklaces made for tourists. Bright backyard swimming pools gleamed like turquoise nuggets. The land stretched out under me the way a lover would, hiding nothing, offering up every endearing southwestern cliché, and I wanted to get down there and kiss the dirt.

I made a bargain with my mother. If I got to the ground in one piece, I wasn't leaving it again.

**The Amtrak didn't** depart until three-thirty; I made it with time to spare. The station clerk wouldn't sell me a ticket to my destination, saying it wasn't a passenger stop. I argued. I knew the train stopped there for a crew change. Finally I realized he could sell me a ticket for anywhere at all on the eastbound line, it didn't matter. I knew where I was getting off.

We pulled out of the station and I hugged myself, cradled in the wide reclining seat, letting the rails rock me like a baby. The car smelled like smoke and old leather. I lay sideways in the seat, facing the window, my legs curled under me. Tucson, Arizona, passed slowly enough to nod at, take notice of, and then let go. At a steady, measured pace these things were revealed to me: the backs of brickyards, the backs of barrios, a large outdoor factory where Mexican women painted tiles. We passed buildings whose high walls, empty of windows, were spray-painted with huge secrets seen by no one but the travelers of the Southern Pacific. And then came the broad, open desert—mile after mile of it. I understood the appeal of train travel. You couldn't help knowing where you'd been.

At some point I fell asleep, and at some point I woke up again. I felt I'd been on that train for the whole of my life. We approached Grace from a direction that was new to me. We didn't go by the junkyard. There was a tunnel through the granite cliffs and we entered it fast—the dark rock wall magnifying the rocketing clamor of tons of forward motion—and then, quiet and sudden, out into the bright light again. I blinked against the overexposed world. By the time my eyes adjusted we were right downtown behind the old jailhouse, pulling the sighing brakes, slowing down. We came gliding under the long wooden porch of the depot. The sun glinted on its pleated tin roof, and I noticed a carob tree there with a trunk the size of a rain barrel. It must be the male—the mate to the one up by the liquor store. The one I'd been looking for.

The conductor looked a little surprised when I pulled my bag off the rack and hopped down onto the concrete apron of the depot.

"This isn't anywhere, sweetheart," he said, looking down at me from the doorway. He was a very old, very dark-skinned man whose uniform looked as if it could hold up its shoulders without him.

"I know," I said.

"You can't get back on," he warned. "Ten minutes for a crew change, and then we're headed out for El Paso."

"I know. I don't want to get back on. I live here."

"Well, how do you do," he said. He stepped back into the car and waved at me through the window. His gloved hand fluttered like a dove.

A hundred yards up the line I saw the fireman climb down the ladder from the engine. It was someone I'd gone to school with—Roger Bristol. Loyd tossed down Roger's grip and his own, one at a time, and then swung himself easily down the ladder as if he were born for this work. He talked briefly with two other men—the oncoming crew, I guessed. They would speak in their magical language of dog catchers and sun kinks and the ones that had died on the line, picking up trains from the dead and moving on. They parted ways and the new crew climbed into the engine. The other two men walked toward the depot carrying their grips and lunch buckets: one short and stocky, the other taller, broad-shouldered, with his hair in a ponytail. The people you love always look perfectly proportioned from a distance.

Shortly the train began to move again, very slowly, the speed of a living creature. You could still run and catch it. Loyd and Roger kept walking toward me without seeing me. Standing there watching him, knowing what he didn't, I had so much power and none at all. I was on the outside, in a different dimension. I'd lived there always.

Then he stopped dead, just for a second. I'll remember that. The train moved and Roger moved but Loyd stood still.

He caught up to me in an instant, with a twinkle in his eye and his bag slung over his shoulder like a ready traveler.

"Thanks for the ride," I said.

He put one arm around my neck and gave me the kind of kiss no fool would walk away from twice.

# 26

# The Fifty Mothers

For several days I kept coming back to this: we had no body. I wanted to have a funeral for Hallie, but I was at a loss. I knew the remains should not have been important, but in a funeral the body gives the grieving a place to focus their eyes. We sit facing it, bear it on our shoulders, follow it down the road in procession and finally long to follow it into the ground. The body would have provided an agenda and told me what to do, in lieu of Hallie, who was gone.

I went to look for something else that in my mind stood for her: the *semilla besada,* one of the supernaturally blessed trees that in the old days were festooned like Christmas trees with the symbols of people's hopes. We could hold a funeral there, outside, under the leaves. I wanted to find the exact plum tree where we'd hidden a lock of our intertwined hair. I knew the orchard but couldn't find the tree. Either it was gone, or it was no longer exceptional. Maybe the trees all around it had stretched their taproots and found the same nurturing vein.

It was June, a week before Hallie's thirtieth birthday. The canopies were in full green, each one as brilliant as a halo. The blossoms had dropped and left behind incipient fruits swelling three and four to a cluster, not yet pruned by nature or by hand. Every tree in every orchard looked blessed. So we had the funeral there, in the old Domingos plum orchard.

I'd asked people to bring something that reminded them of Hallie. I spread the black-and-red afghan on the ground and we stood around that. Instead of decorating a tree with our hopes for the future, we decorated a blanket with icons from the past. All the women from Stitch and Bitch were there. And J.T. and Emelina, of course, and Loyd. All of my students, as well. Doc Homer didn't make it. He didn't go very far out of his house these days, or very far out of his head.

It was awkward getting started. I remembered the last time I'd hugged her, thinking I could hold on and stop our lives right there. I took some breaths. "Hallie asked to be buried in Nicaragua," I said. "She wanted that. To enrich the soil of a jungle. But I wanted something here too." I stopped, because it sounded to me like small talk. Words only cover the experience of living. I looked around at the unpretentious faces like slices of bread, all the black dresses, the dark shoes, and I looked up at the bright leaves lit from above. It was a brilliant, hot day and I didn't feel at all like crying. The black dresses made me think of Greece. Nothing seemed quite real.

Several peacocks had gathered in the trees behind our heads, keeping their distance, but curious, probably hoping for food. A peacock wouldn't know the difference between a picnic and a funeral. The outward signs were similar.

"Do you think we should sing?" I asked.

"Yes," said Emelina. "We ought to sing."

"What?" I couldn't think of any particular song that Hallie liked, except some silly things from our teenage years. "Mother and Child Reunion" and "Maggie May." I thought of Hallie moonwalking to "Thriller," and then I thought abstractly about never seeing her again, what that really meant. In the back of my mind I was still wondering when she would come home. I couldn't concentrate. Someone suggested "Let the Circle Be Unbroken," so we sang that, and then we sang "De Colores" because everybody knew it. Norma Galvez's husband Cassandro played the guitar.

Then it was quiet again. People shifted slightly on their feet, the same motion repeated many times throughout the crowd, like the dancers at Santa Rosalia. Except unconscious, and unrehearsed. I pulled some letters out of my pocket and read parts of them that Emelina had helped me pick out. I read what Hallie said about not wanting to save the world, that you didn't choose your road for the reward at the end, but for the way it felt as you went along. And I read some things she'd said about nations forgetting. Refusing to sell tractor parts, then wondering why people would turn to Yugoslavia for tractors. I was aware that my reading might seem a little rambling, but I felt there was some logic to it, and people were tolerant. Truly, I think they would have listened to me all day. It occurred to me that such patience might be the better part of love.

I read a quote she'd written me that seemed important, a thing said by Father Fernando Cardenal, who was in charge of the literacy crusade: "You learn to read so you can identify the reality in which you live, so that you can become a protagonist of history rather than a spectator." I waited a minute, while a peacock screamed. Then I read some words of Hallie's: "The very least you can do in your life is to figure out what you hope for. And the most . . ."

Another peacock suddenly howled nearby. I saw Emelina's twins craning their necks, trying to spot it. I went on:

"And the most you can do is live inside that hope. What I want is so simple I almost can't say it: elementary kindness. Enough to eat, enough to go around. The possibility that kids might one day grow up to be neither the destroyers nor the destroyed."

I finished by reading the letter from Sister Sabina Martin. She said thousands of people joined us in mourning Hallie. "I know that doesn't make your grief any smaller," she wrote. "But I believe it makes Hallie's presence larger. Certainly, she won't be forgotten."

Several peafowl had hopped to the ground and were making insistent, guttural noises, impatient for food. I saw Glen and Curtis sneak off into the trees in pursuit of a peacock they'd never catch.

"This is what I brought." I knelt by the afghan and set down a pair of Hallie's small black shoes, about second-grade size. They could have been mine, it was impossible to tell, but I said they were Hallie's. I put them in the center of the red-and-black crocheted blanket. "I brought these because they just reminded me of growing up with Hallie. We had to wear these ugly shoes. It was just one of the important things we did together. I don't know. We felt kind of alone sometimes." I stood up and looked at the trees through the curtain of water in my eyes.

Viola laid down some marigolds. She had on her polyester, the funeral dress for all seasons, and she was perspiring; broad damp spots underlined her bosom. "Whenever I think of you kids I think of the *cempazuchiles* and being up at the graveyard for All Souls'. You were always a very big help."

I looked at Viola. She stared back, rubbing the bridge of her nose. There was the faintest light of a smile.

Several women had things they claimed we'd left in their houses when we played there as children: a doll with unpleasant glass eyes and a gruesomely pockmarked head where its hair had come out; a largish plastic horse; a metal hen that, when you pushed her down on her feet, made a metallic cluck and laid a small marble egg. Also a pink sweater, size 6X. Mrs. Nuñez swore it was Hallie's. "It was behind the refrigerator. I didn't find it till last year when the refrigerator give out and we had to call the man to move it out and get us a new one in there. The dust, I hate to tell you! And there was this little sweater of Halimeda Noline's. She used to set up there on top of the refrigerator, because I told her she couldn't drink beer till she was as tall as her daddy."

This was the truth, dead center. I remembered her up there huddled among the Mason jars and bright cracker boxes. I stared at the freshly laundered pink sweater lying with outstretched arms and thought about how small Hallie had been at one time. Miss Colder and Miss Dann were just then displaying an ancient-looking picture book, but there was a roaring in my ears and I lost track of what they were saying. I believe it was the physical manifestation of unbearable grief. But you learn in these situations that all griefs are bearable. Loyd was standing on one side of me, and Emelina on the other, and whenever I thought I might fall or just cease to exist, the pressure of their shoulders held me there.

I could hear people's words, but my vision was jarred by showers of blue sparks. Or the world went out of focus. And at other times I could see but couldn't hear. Doña Althea clumped forward with her cane and set down a miniature, perfectly made peacock piñata. It perched there on the pile of childhood things, its small eyes glittering and its tail feathers perfectly trimmed. It was an exquisite piece of art that could have made it into Mr. Rideheart's gallery, but it was for Hallie. I tried to listen to what she was saying. She said, "I made one like this for both of you girls, for your *cumpleaños* when you were ten."

To my surprise, this was also true. I remembered every toy, every birthday party, each one of these fifty mothers who'd been standing at the edges of my childhood, ready to make whatever contribution was needed at the time.

"*Gracias, Abuelita,*" I said softly to Doña Althea as she clumped away.

She didn't look at me, but she heard me say it and she didn't deny that she was my relative. Her small head crowned with its great white braid nodded a little. No hugs or confessions of love. We were all a little stiff, I understood that. Family constellations are fixed things. They don't change just because you've learned the names of the stars.

Uda Dell went last. "I brought this bouquet of zinnias because every spring Hallie helped me dig my zinnia bed." She laid down the homely, particolored bouquet, and added, "I crocheted that afghan, too."

"You did?"

She looked at me, surprised. "Right after your mommy died. Well, I don't guess you'd remember."

"This blanket got us through a lot of tough times," I said. I was feeling a little more steady on my feet. I folded in the corners and drew it all up into a bundle against my chest. About everything Hallie and I had ever done was with us there in the Domingos orchard. Everything we'd been I was now.

"Thank you," I said, to everybody.

I turned my back and headed alone with my bundle up the Old Pony Road to Doc Homer's house.

# HOMERO

# 27

# Human Remains

There are women in every room of this house, he thinks: Mrs. Quintana upstairs, and now there is Codi, standing in the kitchen with her baby. Her arms and chest clutch the black wool bundle and it weighs her down like something old, made of stone. The weight makes him want to turn away. He thinks, This is the fossil record of our lives.

"I'm going to bury this. Do you want to help me?" She looks up at him and tears stream down. The grief on her face is fresh as pollen.

"You already buried it."

"No, no, no!" she screams, and slams the screen door behind her. He follows her down the path but she doesn't go down to the riverbed this time, she turns and goes right around the house into the backyard. When he catches up, a little breathless, she is standing with her boots on the ground like rooted stalks. Standing beside the old plot where Hallie used to grow a garden. A few old artichoke bushes have gone thistly and wild around its perimeter. Codi drops the knotted bundle and goes to the tool shed to retrieve a shovel. She comes back and digs hard into the ground. It hasn't been disturbed for many years.

"Are you sure this is a good place?" he asks.

Without speaking, she steps on the shovel and its tip bites into the sandy soil again and again, lifting, digging, and lifting out a deep, square hole.

"You might want to have a garden here again someday. When this house is yours."

The shovel stops suddenly. "Did you know I'm staying?" She looks at him.

He looks back, waiting.

"I told Loyd about the baby. Yesterday I took him down there to the riverbed where you showed me. I can remember every minute of that night. You gave me some pills, didn't you? You really did want to help." She looks up at the sky, using gravity and the small, twin dams of her eyelids to hold in tears. "So Loyd knows about that now. He's sad. I didn't think about that part—that he would be sad. I was thinking the baby was just mine."

"It wasn't just yours."

"I know." She wipes her cheeks with the back of her hand, leaving a faint dark smudge under each eye. She looks at him very oddly. "We might have another one. Loyd and I. I don't know. There's time to see."

"Yes."

"Did you know I'm a good science teacher? The kids and the teachers all voted. They say I'm spirited. How do you like that?"

"It's what I would expect."

"I'm teaching them how to have a cultural memory." She looks at her hands, and laughs, but looks sad. "I want them to be custodians of the earth," she says.

He also looks at her hands. They remind him of something. Whose hands?

"You really can't approve of me staying, can you?" she demands, suddenly angry. "You raised me to turn my back on this place. That worked for you, but the difference is you *knew* it was really your home. You knew you had one. So you had a choice."

"That's all very well and good," he says, "but you still might want a garden. These artichoke bushes still produce. Every summer they bloom as if their hearts depended on it. Never mind that there was nobody taking in the harvest." He takes the tip of a silvery leaf between his fingers. It looks knifelike, but is yielding and soft.

She looks at him for quite a long time, smiling, and then she looks down at the bundle. "It's all right to bury this here," she says. "There are no human remains."

No human remains. No. Human. Remains. The three words chime in his head like large, old bells, three descending notes that ring and ring, speeding up in tempo until they clang against one another.

"How true," he says finally.

She shaves out the edges of the hole so it is neat and square, and then drops the bundle in. She throws a handful of dirt on top of it and stands there looking down.

"We're a pair of scarred old souls, aren't we, Codi?"

"I don't know what we are. I'm trying to figure out what I hope for."

"It's a most dangerous thing, hope."

Her eyes flash with something bright. Love or anger. But she doesn't speak.

"Hope involves giving a great deal of yourself away," he tells her.

"That's a pitiful excuse."

"Oh, it's pitiful all right, but there you have it. It's hard to give much away when you're the subject of widespread disapproval and your heart is leaking from puncture wounds."

"That's true. We got punctured pretty bad. But we still gave the world a lot, Pop. We gave it Hallie."

"We did. We surely did."

She begins shoveling dirt back into the grave. He thinks about the fact that all these particles of dirt have now been rearranged. No fixed strata. Alice was the gardener. When she has finished she moves to his side and he takes her elbow. They stand side by side in their small garden of sand and buried children. The bones in his wife's arm are as thin as whistles. "Do you have any idea how much I love you?" he asks her.

She stares at him, then squeezes his hand. "Hallie was a protagonist of history," she says.

"She wanted to save the world."

"No, Pop, that's not true. She wanted to save herself. Just like we all do."

He looks at the tall, living daughter his wife has suddenly become. He is no longer angry about these changes. "Save herself from what?"

"From despair. From the feeling of being useless. I've about decided that's the main thing that separates happy people from the other people: the feeling that you're a practical item, with a use, like a sweater or a socket wrench."

He asks, "Are we the other people?" He is curious.

"You're not useless. You gave yourself to this town for forty years. Scarred soul or not."

"Yes. But I gave for the wrong reasons. As you have pointed out."

She laughs. "I did, didn't I? Damn!" She pulls at the end of a silver artichoke leaf. "I was scared to death I was going to grow up to be just like you." She looks at him, and laughs again. She says: "God, I could never be just like you."

They are standing in the garden, in a dwarf forest of artichokes. She has just dug a hole and buried God knows what and now has made a confession of either contempt or admiration. He waits to see what will happen next.

"Maybe the reason you gave yourself to this town doesn't matter that much. Maybe what matters is just that you did it. Maybe that makes you a good man. You know what Loyd told me one time?"

"No."

"He thinks people's dreams are made out of what they do all day. The same way a dog that runs after rabbits will dream of rabbits. It's what you do that makes your soul, not the other way around."

It's what you do that makes your soul. Standing opposite him, staring down into the grave, he sees two sad little girls in cowboy hats. Is this what he has done? "I don't think you should be here," he says to them.

The elder daughter looks up, her pale eyes steady. "But we are here, Papa."

"Yes, you are."

"Why don't you want us?"

"Oh, God, I do." He kneels down and takes them both in his arms and pulls them against his chest. He understands for the first time in his life that love weighs nothing. Oh God, his girls are as light as birds.

# COSIMA

# 28

# Day of
# All Souls

Gracela Canyon, if you strip it down to the enduring things, is a great, granite bowl of air. It's a wonderful echo chamber. Voices of women and children in the cemetery reached Viola and me from all the way across the canyon, rising on invisible air currents with the ravens and the spirits of all those old bones being tended by their children. It was getting on toward late afternoon, and we walked slowly. Viola had spent the morning supervising family operations, and said she was tired. But she'd promised that any day I asked her she would take me to the place where we watched my mother go. I chose that particular day in 1989, the end of a decade, the Day of All Souls, when we were all up decorating the graves. I don't know why.

I'd finished sweeping off my father and the other Nolinas and had decked them out with little bunches of marigolds at their heads and feet. It was something like tucking children into bed. I was their historian and their guardian angel. I never found Ursolina, the little bear. I imagine she's somewhere closer to the mine, where the earth has been shifted too many times to bear witness to what it has buried in it. The rest of the family, for all the times they'd had to be exhumed, had stayed together surprisingly well.

I knelt all morning in the dirt, laying out a border of creek rocks around Doc Homer. He'd been gone more than two years, but it took me awhile to decide on this. Emelina's boys had hauled the rocks up there for me. When we took them out of the water and piled them into the wheelbarrow they lost their luster, all drying to the same whitish color of dust, and I was afraid after all that work they would be the wrong thing, but they were fine. Uniform and shipshape, washed smooth by the abrasion of natural forces. I laid them end to end around the dirt mound, knocking them together and working them back and forth a little to find a natural fit. As I worked I thought of the masonry walls of Kinishba, with the bones of children inside.

When I stood back finally and dusted my chapped hands against my jeans, I saw I'd achieved nothing so fine as Kinishba, but had marked out a clear boundary, anyway. He would like it. I'd brought some order to his cosmos finally.

I squinted into the sun. Across the tops of about a hundred gravestones and many people I saw Viola in her black dress, standing on a little rise, her gray hair wandering from its knot. She pressed one hand to the small of her back while Mason and Nicholas danced in front of her with their hands full of candy, begging for something, wearing her out. Nicholas was three and a half; John Tucker was talking about quitting school to be a hoghead for Southern Pacific. I thought: "I can't wait forever." So I went and asked her right then and she said fine, after lunch we would go. "I'm about done here," she'd said, cracking the sugar skull of a *calavera* between her molars. "They can figure out which end of the flowers to put in water without me."

We took the quickest road down into town, then cut across the hill behind the high school and through the splendid canopies hung with fruit that the Stitch and Bitch Club had won back from Black Mountain Mining. From there we headed up the Old Pony Road toward the abandoned mine. The tops of the flat tailing mounds were dimpled with rain-catching basins and I'd noticed that sprigs of rabbitbrush were starting to grow up there.

The road was steep. No route out of Grace was an easy climb. Twice I had to ask Viola to let me catch my breath. I held a fist to my breastbone, panting hard, a little embarrassed by my infirmity but also a little pleased by the external proof of what was still mostly an internal condition. I was pregnant.

"I feel like I don't have any energy. I come home from school and sleep till Loyd wakes me up for dinner, and then I go back to bed." This new relationship with sleep was a miracle to me.

"Oh, yeah," she said. "All your get-up-and-do-it goes to the baby. Right from the start you know who's gonna be the boss."

Those first few weeks are an unearthly season. From the outside you remain so ordinary, no one can tell from looking that you have experienced an earthquake of the soul. You've been torn asunder, invested with an ancient, incomprehensible magic. It's the one thing we never quite get over: that we contain our own future.

I'd written this to Hallie in the pages of a bound notebook that would never be torn out or mailed. These letters stayed with me. I told her: it feels like somebody's moved in. It's a shock. You find you're not the center of the universe, suddenly it's all flipped over, you have it in you to be a parent. You're not all that concerned any more with being someone's child. It helps you forgive things.

We reached the crest of the canyon where the white salt crust of the old alfalfa fields began. Dead for two decades, the earth was long and white and cracked, like a huge porcelain platter dropped from the heavens. But now the rabbitbrush was beginning to grow here too, topped with brushy gold flowers, growing like a renegade crop in the long, straight troughs of the old irrigation ditches.

A wind was picking up from the south, and Viola and I could smell rain. High storm clouds with full sails and a cargo of hail made their way in a hurry across the sky. Viola's hair blew around her face as she walked. I asked, "Did you know her kidneys had failed her once before, when she was pregnant with me?"

"Sure," Viola said. "She was real sick both times."

"But she went ahead and had Hallie anyway."

"You don't think about it that much. You just go on and have your kids."

I wanted to believe my mother had thought about it. That Hallie was her last considered act of love—an act with unforeseen consequences, some of them just now coming into flower in the soil of another country. I said, "I always knew I was up here that day. I can remember seeing the helicopter."

"You remember that?"

"I thought I did. But people told me I hadn't, so I'd about decided I'd made it up."

Viola took my hand. I could feel the soft flesh and the hard wedding band in her grip. "No, if you remember something, then it's true," she said. "In the long run, that's what you've got."

I knew the place when we came to it. We were right there already.

This is what I remember: Viola is holding my hand. We're at the edge of the field, far from other people. We stand looking out into the middle of that ocean of alfalfa. I can see my mother there, a small white bundle with nothing left, and I can see that it isn't a tragedy we're watching, really. Just a finished life. The helicopter is already in the air and it stays where it is, a clear round bubble with no destination, sending out circular waves of wind that beat down the alfalfa. People duck down, afraid, as if they're being visited by a plague or a god. Their hair is blowing. Then the helicopter tilts a little and the glass body catches the sun. For an instant it hangs above us, empty and bright, and then it rises like a soul.

## About the author

## About the book

Insights,
Interviews
& More . . .

## Read on

# Meet
# Barbara Kingsolver

© David Wood

BARBARA KINGSOLVER was born in 1955 and grew up in rural Kentucky. She earned degrees in biology from DePauw University and the University of Arizona, and she has worked as a freelance writer and author since 1985. At various times in her adult life she has lived in England, France, and the Canary Islands, and she has worked in Europe, Africa, Asia, Mexico, and South America. She spent two decades in Tucson, Arizona, before moving to southwestern Virginia, where she currently resides.

Her books, in order of publication,

are: *The Bean Trees* (1988), *Homeland* (1989), *Holding the Line: Women in the Great Arizona Mine Strike* (1989), *Animal Dreams* (1990), *Another America* (1992), *Pigs in Heaven* (1993), *High Tide in Tucson* (1995), *The Poisonwood Bible* (1998), *Prodigal Summer* (2000), *Small Wonder* (2002), *Last Stand: America's Virgin Lands* (2002; with photographer Annie Griffiths), *Animal, Vegetable, Miracle* (2007), *The Lacuna* (2009), and *Flight Behavior* (2012). In the 2001 edition of the Best American Short Stories series, she served as editor. Her books have been translated into more than two dozen languages and have been adopted into the core literature curriculum in high schools and colleges throughout the nation. Kingsolver has contributed to more than fifty literary anthologies, and her reviews and articles have appeared in most major U.S. newspapers and magazines.

Kingsolver was named one the most important writers of the twentieth century by *Writers Digest*. In 2000 she received the National Humanities Medal, our country's highest honor for service through the arts. Critical acclaim for her books includes multiple awards from the American Booksellers Association and the American Library Association, among many others. *The Poisonwood Bible* was a finalist for the Pulitzer Prize and Britain's prestigious Orange Prize, and it won the national book award of South Africa before being named an Oprah Book Club selection. *Animal, Vegetable, Miracle* won numerous prizes, including the James Beard award. *The Lacuna* won the Orange Prize for Fiction in 2010. In 2011, Kingsolver was awarded the Dayton Literary Peace Prize for the body of her work.

Kingsolver established the Bellwether Prize for Fiction, the nation's largest prize for an unpublished first novel, which since 1998 has helped establish the careers of more than a half dozen new literary voices. Through a recent agreement, the prize has now become the PEN/Bellwether Prize for Socially Engaged Fiction.

She has two daughters, Camille (born in 1987) and Lily (1996). Her husband, Steven Hopp, teaches environmental studies. Since June 2004, Barbara and her family have lived on a farm in southern Appalachia, where they tend an extensive vegetable garden and raise Icelandic sheep. She is grateful for the good will and support of her readers. ᔕ

# Community and Hope:
## A Conversation with Stephen L. Fisher and Barbara Kingsolver

*(Recorded at the Emory & Henry College Literary Festival, September 30, 2011. Published in the* Iron Mountain Review, *Volume XXVIII, Spring 2012.)*

**Stephen L. Fisher:** *Critic Priscilla Leder argues that two basic themes run throughout your impressive array of genres and settings: an appreciation, first, of the natural world, and second, of human diversity. I'm interested in your reaction to this observation and, if it is at least partially on the mark, in your commenting briefly on why that is the case.*

**Barbara Kingsolver:** Certainly an appreciation for nature is an important feature of my work, and it arose in part because I grew up running wild in the woods with little adult supervision, studied biology as a college student, and then went to graduate school in biology. I am one of thousands of species that live in this place, and I don't ever forget the other ones are there. Species diversity is a biological fact. I think a lot about the world out there beyond the artifice that human beings have created. As for human diversity, I'm very interested in the fact that everybody in this room has something different in mind right now. I'm not accusing you of not paying attention, but you're each seeing the world in a different way and all of you are right. Well, a couple of you are not [laughter]. But seriously, as a novelist, one gets to create all kinds of minds and then put them together and look at their intersections, their interactions. Cultural differences are really exciting territory, not just for literature but for learning in general, because sparks fly when there's friction among different viewpoints. People invest themselves differently in the same set of truths. Because of my training as a scientist, I'm always looking at the dialectic between the truth we believe exists outside ourselves and the truth we invent for ourselves. So, yes, I'm very interested in human diversity.

**Fisher:** *I'd like to focus now on what I consider to be two crucial themes in your work: community and hope. First, community. You've said that you always write about individualism vs. community, and that you see independence as stupidity and instead celebrate dependency. As you once put it, "the most remarkable feature of human culture is its capacity to reach beyond the self and encompass the collective good; yet, here in the United States we are blazing a bold downhill path from the high ground of 'human collective' toward the tight little den of 'self.' " Would you elaborate on the importance of seeing ourselves as part of something larger and on the role of fiction in helping people understand and move toward that vision?* ▶

> 66 As a novelist, one gets to create all kinds of minds and then put them together and look at their intersections, their interactions. 99

**Community and Hope** *(continued)*

**Kingsolver:** Well, I do apologize for the "bold downhill path" part. That didn't sound very good, did it? We do have some strong traditions of community in the United States, but it's interesting to me that our traditionally patriotic imagery in this country celebrates the individual, the solo flier, independence. We celebrate Independence Day; we don't celebrate We Desperately Rely on Others Day. Oh, I guess that's Mother's Day [laughter]. It does strike me that our great American mythology tends to celebrate separate achievement and separateness, when in fact nobody does anything alone. Nobody in this auditorium is wearing clothing that you made yourself from sheep that you sheared and wool that you spun. It's ridiculous to imagine that we don't depend on others for the most ordinary parts of our existence, let alone the more traumatic parts when we need a surgeon or someone to put out the fire in our home. In everyday ways we are a part of a network. I guess it's a biological way of seeing the world. And I don't understand the suggestion that interdependence is a weakness. Animals don't pretend to be independent from others of their kind—I mean no other animal but us. It seems like something we should get over [laughter].

**Fisher:** *A key component of building community and leading a meaningful life is hope. Environmentalist John Nolt observes that "everyone needs a place of refuge, but hope withers if we do not carry it out from that place." You echo that notion in the quotation from* Animal Dreams *that you feature on your web page—the passage in which Hallie writes to Codi: "The very least you can do in your life is to figure out what you hope for. The most you can do is live inside that hope, running down its hallways, touching the walls on both sides." Hope, in my mind, is at the core of your political vision and runs throughout your writing. But to be hopeful is not an easy task in these mean-spirited times. In an interview with Elisabeth Beattie in the mid1990s, you described yourself as, along with your dad, one of the most ridiculously optimistic people on the face of the earth. I'm wondering how your optimism is faring these days, and how you today live out Hallie's charge: What is it you hope for, and what are the ways you live inside that hope?*

**Kingsolver:** I would like to revise my earlier words: I think that my dad is still the most optimistic person I know. I've been thinking a lot lately about the difference between being optimistic and being hopeful. I would say that I'm a hopeful person, although not necessarily optimistic. Here's how I would describe it. The pessimist would say, "It's going to be a terrible winter; we're all going to die." The optimist would say, "Oh, it'll be all right; I don't think it'll be that bad." The hopeful person would say, "Maybe someone will still be alive in February, so I'm going to put some potatoes in the root cellar just in case." And that's where I lodge myself on this spectrum. Hope is a mode of survival. I think hope is a mode of resistance. Hope is how parents get through the most difficult parts of their kids' teenaged years. Hope is how a cancer patient endures painful treatments. Hope is how people on a picket line keep showing up. If you look at hope that way, it's not a state of mind but something we actually do with our hearts and our hands, to navigate ourselves through the difficult passages. I think that as a fiction writer—or as any kind of writer—hope is a gift I can try to cultivate. ∾

*Steve Fisher is Professor Emeritus at Emory & Henry College and coeditor of* Transforming Places: Lessons from Appalachia.

# Have You Read?
## More by
## Barbara Kingsolver

### THE LACUNA

In this powerfully imagined, provocative novel, Barbara Kingsolver takes us on an epic journey from the Mexico of artists Diego Rivera and Frida Kahlo to the America of Pearl Harbor, FDR, and J. Edgar Hoover. *The Lacuna* is both the poignant story of a man pulled between two nations and an unforgettable portrait of the artist—and of art itself.

### FLIGHT BEHAVIOR

Set in the present in the rural community of Feathertown, Tennessee, *Flight Behavior* is the story of Dellarobia Turnbow, a petite, razor-sharp young woman who had nurtured worldly ambitions before becoming a mother and wife at seventeen. Now, after more than a decade of tending small children on a failing farm, suffering oppressive poverty, isolation, and her husband's antagonistic family, she mitigates her boredom and frustration through an obsessive flirtation with a handsome younger man.

On her way to his secluded cabin to consummate their relationship, Dellarobia walks into something on the mountainside she can neither explain nor understand: a forested valley filled with silent red fire that appears to Dellarobia to be a miracle. Her discovery, both beautiful and terrible, elicits divergent reactions from all sides. Religious fundamentalists claim it as a manifestation of God; climate scientists scrutinize it as an element of forthcoming disaster; politicians and environmentalists declaim its lessons; charlatans mine its opportunity; international media construct and deconstruct Dellarobia's story; and townspeople cope with intrusion and bizarre alterations of custom.

After years of living entirely within the confines of one small house, Dellarobia finds her path suddenly opening out and leading into blunt and confrontational engagement with her family, church, town, continent, and finally the world at large. Over the course of a single winter, Dellarobia's life will become the property of the planet and, perhaps for the first time, securely her own.

## THE POISONWOOD BIBLE

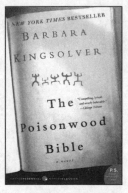

*The Poisonwood Bible* is a story told by the wife and four daughters of Nathan Price, a fierce, evangelical Baptist who takes his family and mission to the Belgian Congo in 1959. They carry with them everything they believe they will need from home, but soon find that all of it—from garden seeds to Scripture—is calamitously transformed on African soil. What follows is a suspenseful epic of one family's tragic undoing and remarkable reconstruction over the course of three decades in postcolonial Africa.

**Have You Read?** *(continued)*

The novel is set against one of the most dramatic political chronicles of the twentieth century: the Congo's fight for independence from Belgium, the murder of its first elected prime minister, the CIA coup to install his replacement, and the insidious progress of a world economic order that robs the fledgling African nation of its autonomy. Against this backdrop, Orleanna Price reconstructs the story of her evangelist husband's part in the Western assault on Africa, a tale indelibly darkened by her own losses and unanswerable questions about her own culpability. Also narrating the story, by turns, are her four daughters—the self-centered, teenaged Rachel; shrewd adolescent twins Leah and Adah; and Ruth May, a prescient five-year-old. These sharply observant girls, who arrive in the Congo with racial preconceptions forged in 1950s Georgia, will be marked in surprisingly different ways by their father's intractable mission, and by Africa itself. Ultimately each must strike her own separate path to salvation. Their passionately intertwined stories become a compelling exploration of moral risk and personal responsibility.

Dancing between the dark comedy of human failings and the breathtaking possibilities of human hope, *The Poisonwood Bible* possesses all that has distinguished Barbara Kingsolver's previous work and extends this beloved writer's vision to an entirely new level. Taking its place alongside the classic works of postcolonial literature, this

ambitious novel establishes Kingsolver
as one of the most thoughtful and daring
of modern writers.

"There are few ambitious, successful,
and beautiful novels. Lucky for us, we
have one now, in Barbara Kingsolver's
*The Poisonwood Bible.*"    —Jane Smiley,
*Washington Post Book World*

"A powerful new epic. . . . [Kingsolver]
has with infinitely steady hands worked
the prickly threads of religion, politics,
race, sin, and redemption into a thing of
terrible beauty."
    —*Los Angeles Times Book Review*

"Haunting. . . . A novel of character, a
narrative shaped by keen-eyed women."
    —Verlyn Klinkenborg,
    *New York Times Book Review*

### ANIMAL, VEGETABLE, MIRACLE

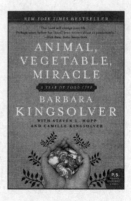

*This is the story of a year in which we
made every attempt to feed ourselves
animals and vegetables whose provenance
we really knew . . . [and] of how our
family was changed by our first year of
deliberately eating food produced from
the same place where we worked, went
to school, loved our neighbors, drank
the water, and breathed the air.*

*As the U.S. population made an
unprecedented mad dash for the Sun Belt,
one carload of us paddled against the tide,
heading for the Promised Land where
water falls from the sky and green stuff
grows all around. We were about to begin*

*the adventure of realigning our lives with our food chain.*

*Naturally, our first stop was to buy junk food and fossil fuel. . . .*

Hang on for the ride: With characteristic poetry and pluck, Barbara Kingsolver and her family sweep readers along on their journey away from the industrial-food pipeline to a rural life in which they vow to only buy food raised in their own neighborhood, grow it themselves, or learn to live without it. Their good-humored search yields surprising discoveries about turkey sex life and overly zealous zucchini plants, en route to a food culture that's better for the neighborhood and also better on the table.

Part memoir, part journalistic investigation, *Animal, Vegetable, Miracle* makes a passionate case for putting the kitchen back at the center of family life, and diversified farms at the center of the American diet.

"Cogent and illuminating. . . . There are many ways for a writer to tell you to eat your vegetables. . . . Barbara Kingsolver's way is both folksy and smart. . . . Without sentimentality, this book captures the pulse of the farm and the deep gratification it provides, as well as the intrinsic humor of the situation."
—Janet Maslin, *New York Times*

## SMALL WONDER: ESSAYS

Kingsolver began work on this astonishing and powerful collection of essays as a response to the immeasurable grief and confusion 9/11 left in its wake. When she finished, she had given us, out of one of history's darker moments, an extended love song to the world we still have. Whether she is contemplating the Grand Canyon, her vegetable garden, motherhood, genetic engineering, or the future of a nation founded on the best of all human impulses, these essays are grounded in the author's belief that our largest problems have grown from the earth's remotest corners as well as our own backyards, and that answers may lie in both these places. *Small Wonder* is a hopeful examination of the people we seem to be, and what we might yet make of ourselves.

"A passionate invitation to readers to be a part of the crowd that cares about the environment, peace, and family."
—*San Francisco Chronicle*

## PRODIGAL SUMMER

Kingsolver's novel is a hymn to wildness that celebrates the prodigal spirit of human nature, and of nature itself. It weaves together three stories of human love within a larger tapestry of lives amid the mountains and farms of southern Appalachia. Over the course of one humid summer, this novel's intriguing protagonists face disparate predicaments but find connections to one another

**Have You Read?** *(continued)*

and to the flora and fauna with which they necessarily share a place.

"As illuminating as it is absorbing. . . . Resonates with the author's overarching wisdom and passion." —*New York Times*

### THE BEAN TREES

A modern classic, Kingsolver's first novel is a memorable exploration of the American Southwest. It is the story of Taylor Greer, a rural Kentucky girl who grew up poor with only two goals: to avoid pregnancy and to get away. She succeeds on both counts, buys a '55 Volkswagen, and heads west. But by the time she pulls up on the outskirts of Tucson, Arizona, at an auto repair shop called Jesus Is Lord Used Tires, she's "inherited" a three-year-old American Indian girl named Turtle. What follows is at the heart of this unforgettable novel about love and friendship, abandonment and belonging, and the discovery of surprising resources in apparently empty places.

"The work of a visionary. . . . It leaves you open-mouthed and smiling."
—*Los Angeles Times*

## PIGS IN HEAVEN

When six-year-old Turtle Greer witnesses a freak accident at the Hoover Dam, her insistence on what she has seen and her mother's belief in her lead to a man's dramatic rescue. But Turtle's moment of celebrity draws her into a conflict of historic proportions. The crisis quickly envelops not only Turtle and her mother, Taylor, but everyone else who touches their lives. *Pigs in Heaven* travels the roads from rural Kentucky and the urban Southwest to Heaven, Oklahoma, and the Cherokee Nation, as it draws the reader into a world of heartbreak and redeeming love, testing the boundaries of family and the many separate truths about the ties that bind.

"There is no one quite like Barbara Kingsolver in contemporary literature. Her dialogue sparkles with sassy wit and the earthy poetry of ordinary folks' talk; her descriptions have a magical lyricism rooted in daily life but also on familiar terms with the eternal."

—*Washington Post Book World*

## ANIMAL DREAMS

Dreamless and at the end of her rope, Codi Noline returns to her hometown of Grace, Arizona, to confront her past and face her ailing, distant father. What she finds is a town threatened by a silent environmental catastrophe, some startling clues to her own identity, and a man whose view of the world could change the course of her life.

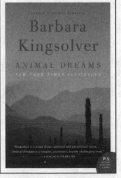

**Have You Read?** *(continued)*

Both a suspenseful love story and an insightful look at the most crucial issues facing America, *Animal Dreams* is another Kingsolver masterpiece.

"An astonishing book. . . . *Animal Dreams* is a novel that feels closer to the truth about modern lives than anything I've read in a long time." —*Cosmopolitan*

### HOMELAND AND OTHER STORIES

A rich and emotionally resonant collection of Kingsolver's distinctive short fiction.

### HIGH TIDE IN TUCSON: ESSAYS FROM NOW OR NEVER

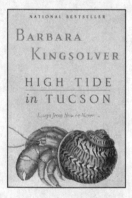

With the eyes of a scientist and the vision of a poet, Kingsolver offers twenty-five essays on the urgent business of being alive in the world today.

Don't miss the next book by your favorite author.

Sign up now for AuthorTracker by visiting www.AuthorTracker.com.